A SPY
AFTER ALL

A SPY
AFTER ALL

John Lewes

First published in 2017 by Serpent & Dove

Copyright © John Lewes 2017

ISBN 978-1-911195-36-8

Also available as an ebook

ISBN 978-1-911195-37-5

Typeset by Jill Sawyer Phypers

Cover design by Stuart Polson

Tangle within tangle, plot and counter-plot, ruse and treachery, cross and double-cross, true agent, gold and steel ...

Winston Churchill

Those who believe absurdities will commit atrocities.

Voltaire

The most dangerous fanatics, despite their conspiracy theories, are calculating and often dangerously effective...

We should be foolish at the beginning of the 21st century not to attempt to learn from our past successes as well as our past failures.

Christopher Andrew

For Esmé Barrett (née Wailes) of MI6
Ann Hadfield MBE
and Anna

PROLOGUE

OXFORD

AUGUST 1939

David Wintour tapped the cameraman on the shoulder. 'Jock, here comes the bride.'

Jock started filming as his sister proceeded along the path in the beautiful reception garden behind Holywell Road. 'Gorgeous, isn't she?' He kept his eye on the filming and didn't look up. 'Look at that beautiful dress flow ... Followed perfectly by Mary and Peggy, the adorable cousins.'

Jock bent down a little to capture the billowing honey and peach silks that caught the early afternoon breeze. Every so often, the beaming smile of a bridesmaid appeared between the folds of the buoyant material; Jock moved in to film them more closely, and Mary and Peggy moved out of the line a little, avoiding the lens and sidestepping Jock, both giggling with embarrassment. The garden was now a hubbub of excitement and chatter. Introductions were made, drinks passed around, canapés hungrily eaten and cigarettes swiftly lit. Jock let the camera run for a minute and hadn't yet noticed the beautiful young woman behind him sipping champagne. He suddenly walked backwards to fit his subjects into the frame and knocked into her.

'Oh, I am terribly sorry. I ...'

Madeleine started speaking at the same time. 'Don't worry.' Their eyes met. 'Carry on. It's Jock, isn't it?'

Jock looked at the dark-haired beauty and smiled. 'Yes, the proud older brother. I believe you already know the bride over there?'

1

'Yes, she kindly invited me.'

'Clever girl, my sister.'

Madeleine blushed a little, looked away at the beautiful bride and turned back to Jock. 'Doesn't it run in the family?'

Jock noticed the delicately arched eyebrows, now denoting a sensitivity and innocence that he had not seen in such a beautiful young woman. 'Let's hope so. That way I might have a chance of renewing our acquaintance.'

'I'm at Somerville.'

'I'm coaching some crews here in the summer, but I work in London. If you'd like, I'll take you to the 100 Club one evening.' Jock wanted her to laugh again; it was when she looked most beautiful. 'Do you like jazz?'

'I do now.' They both laughed. Madeleine blushed again. 'I would love that very much.'

'I look forward to that, Madeleine.'

'Me too. I'd better let you get back to the filming, otherwise I won't be invited to the christening ceremony in a year's time.'

They both laughed again. David Wintour brought over a new roll of film for Jock, and passed Madeleine a fresh glass of champagne. Jock reloaded the camera and filmed the two as they walked off chatting, thinking as he did so that they made a good couple. He also thought they might well become his two best friends.

THE HEART OF ENGLAND

SPRING 1940

I

Jock wore his new Welsh Guards uniform with two pips on each shoulder. Sunshine broke through the clouds after a flash flood of rain. The driver had said nothing as they came out of London along the Great North Road, and the glass screen prevented Jock gaining his attention, even if he had wanted to. He wound down his window as far as vehicle security would allow and breathed in the fresh smell of pine. They were now driving alongside an ancient, tree-filled park and he was admiring the park's very fine, extensive drive between rows of firs and laurels. The woman standing at the gatehouse tipped her face down a little to avoid being blinded by the spring light and drifts of soundless rain. As the car pulled up, she stood still, and Jock was mesmerised by the sunlight that had formed an amber aura about her head. He snapped out of his reverie as the young woman, wearing brown-tinted goggles, he now saw, strode out towards the car at a military clip.

She directed the driver into the park. Jock felt drawn to the soft pink and fleshy face hidden mostly by a peaked cap, and a few blonde wisps that had escaped the constraints of the dress code. Finally, the car stopped before the iron grille of a reinforced door, behind which was a guardroom. Jock could see men in uniform cleaning sub-machine guns, their barrels glistening in the half-light.

A cockney voice hailed, 'Welcome to the country, sir.' A document was passed through the car window.

'Please be so good as to sign this after reading it over.' A hand extended again to take the papers after Jock signed them. 'Mr Gaitskell will see you in the Canaletto Room.'

On the journey out of London, the windscreen wipers had barely kept up with what had been almost horizontal rain and a combination of the lack of visibility and the fact that Jock had not yet travelled extensively in England meant that he was still not sure of exactly where he was. His svelte escort opened the opposite door of the Wolseley and eased herself into the red leather seat next to him. She was to join him for the brief drive towards the east wing of a considerable stately home.

A policeman came up to the car and took a careful look at the young woman to identify her, then opened the grille and let them through. Jock considered that the security must be as good as the meticulous precautions that he had witnessed in Berlin just before the war. A short distance farther on, the car slowed in front of a hermetically sealed, blacked-out building. The blonde angel, breeched and high booted, was beckoning Jock to step out, herself alighting from the motorcar. He noticed now how slender her waist was, tightly strapped into her uniform. Her cheeks were flushed by the clean spring air, her crimson lips slightly parted. She was smiling as she took off her goggles, and her peaked cap couldn't quite hide the dazzling green eyes beneath as she spoke.

'Please kindly telephone when you're ready to return to London.'

The young woman then introduced him to a tweed-skirted young secretary on the porch, who ushered Jock upstairs, saying, 'This way to the Venetian Drawing Room, Lieutenant Steel.'

Both wings of the main house made an enormous square. Jock and the secretary went up the main steps and into the house down a long corridor. He was shown into the room by the secretary, who had indulged in a little small talk by mentioning that the elaborate 'office' had once boasted a ceiling by Cipriani. As he walked across the vast room, over to Hugh Gaitskell's desk, Jock's 220 pounds of body weight sank into the beautiful Savonnerie carpet; his old tutor's desk-lamp lit up the rich gentian-blue floor. The calm was briefly disturbed by some foreign workers – Italian, judging from the snippets of conversation he could hear – who were trying to move a stove in the ante-room nearby. It did make him wonder what was going on in the centre of England.

'Welcome to Woburn.' Gaitskell gave Jock an avuncular smile and a firm hand to shake. 'Don't worry about them – they're turncoats, and very useful too, if a little clumsy.' He was wearing a charcoal-grey suit and white shirt with a college tie.

'Pity about the carpet, sir.'

'Put some wood under that stove, will you?' he barked at the Italians. 'Now what can I do for you, Steel? Sherry?' Jock declined the drink, but was offered a Hepplewhite chair, upon which he balanced carefully. With his back to the fountains beyond the terrace, he took in the sixteen paintings of views of Venice; six other Canalettos had been stacked against one of the walls. Despite the size and grandeur, the room felt claustrophobic; a window had been blocked up and after the last few hectic days, he was glad to have views to look at, albeit painted ones. He noticed how much younger his tutor looked, at home here after Oxford, except that the architecture was staid by comparison with the rooms he had at college, and the pictures more modern. Gaitskell was clearly in charge of this wing of the well-appointed estate, and the war seemed to be the mission that lecturing had not fully provided.

Jock sounded out his former tutor. 'I have been requested by Colonel Hollings in Whitehall to consider a job offer for MI6.'

'Why not, Jock? Plenty of your neighbours at Christ Church now work for men like Hollings.' Gaitskell had an in-tray of unenviable proportions, but he looked at Jock as if this was his only commitment that day.

'Yes, but I'm training to fight abroad. This isn't what I planned.'

Gaitskell was curious. 'Is Hollings's proposal particularly dangerous?'

'It might well be. Since the overture, I've suspected that someone is watching me and taking an unhealthy interest in my life. I have been followed on each of the occasions I've met with Colonel Hollings.'

Gaitskell seemed concerned. 'Let's hope that they haven't come all the way to the heart of England then? Actually, a little research this morning yielded a rather interesting fact. I thought you'd like to know that you have recently been put on the Führer's blacklist of British subjects.'

5

'Only now on Arrest GB?' Jock was privately disappointed at this relegation to the back end of the most hated and wanted.

'I thought you were soldiering?' Gaitskell sipped his sherry and coughed as the foreigners trailed off down the corridor adjoining. 'You are hardly ready to be on a hit-list yet, surely?'

Jock knew that he had incurred the wrath of Oswald Mosley as a student, and Gaitskell's next comment echoed his thoughts.

'The British Union of Fascists has helped Herr Hitler compile his little but ever-growing hate-list.' He looked serious. 'You must have made some enemies as well as friends in Oxford, Jock?' He leant back in his chair. 'No, I remember now: didn't you remove Mosley's flag from his Oxford base one night?'

'Yes.' Jock grinned. He had achieved a thorough reconnoitre of the fascist grounds as a member of the Oxford University Air Squadron. At Oxford, his flying skills had attracted interest from prize-hunters who wanted to test-fly new plane designs that could win the last Schneider Trophy. Instead, Jock had opted for local surveillance from the air. Flying from Abingdon, he had detoured to survey the pros and cons of an evening raid on Mosley's supposedly impregnable extremist organisation. On the night of his sortie on foot, he had managed to avoid about fifty Blackshirts who were swilling beer in their clubhouse nearby. Crawling under a fleet of two-tone Hillman Minxes, he had elbowed his way to the Party of Action's hideous totem in the centre of the Oxford headquarters. It had been a solo operation to guarantee his escape, as the removal of the fascist cloth was likely to attract attention, and once he had shinned down the pole, there was a high wall to vault over at speed. It was a pleasure to take it, but after pulling the Tiger's tail it wouldn't be much fun hanging around afterwards.

'Well, someone clearly can't have kept quiet about that, can they?' Gaitskell looked out towards the landscaping. 'I think you've been listed for something bigger than the settling of an old student score. Watch your step, keep me informed and come back and see me if you think I can help.' Then with a smile, he added, 'In the meantime, I understand that our very attractive WAAF is waiting to escort you back to London, so I won't delay you. Miss Turner, or Corncurls, as she's also known, was a Land Girl until we plucked her from the relative obscurity of a pig farm. She speaks fluent German, and it wouldn't surprise me if she is asked to volunteer for "Special Duties".'

'If Hollings does want me involved, I'm damned if I'm going to be seconded to MI6 and stay with Military Intelligence forever. What I want to do is fight, not pander my way into enemy organisations for the duration of the war – especially guided by the likes of Hollings.'

Gaitskell empathised. 'I know, Jock, that when you do fight, you'll want to work for leaders you respect. If they aren't good enough, you certainly won't be emulating them. You'll strike out on your own somewhere if you have to.' A brow furrowed. 'Careful with Hollings, though – while we do black propaganda here, the Colonel does a strong line in other black arts. Are you one of his people, Jock?'

'I don't know, sir.'

II

It was time to return to grey, forlorn London, the phoney war, a few decisions and a reality check. Jock didn't have to wait too long. He was waved back past the guard room, monitored at the metal grille and was heading through into the moist and sweet afternoon air when he noticed the presence of someone behind him making his own exit from another building. Jock recognised him, but couldn't place exactly where he had seen him before; he instinctively distrusted the slightly older man, who would have easily disappeared in a crowd. Someone was negotiating a lift to London with the passenger of an official Rolls-Royce that had emerged from huts that Jock thought might also be black propaganda departments; the only distinguishing feature of the man cadging a lift was a pair of cold blue eyes. He wondered if this was the same person who had attempted to follow him the day his life seemed to have changed forever. The new passenger of the Rolls-Royce might not have actually spotted him, since the figure was at that moment so concerned with acquiring a seat. Apart from Corncurls, why were things so *black* at the moment – shirts, lists, propaganda? War was like a hydra that permeated all of life and cast its ugly shadow nearly everywhere.

The man cadging the lift went out of view as Jock was ushered by his efficient guide into a sidecar attached to a standard Army-green BSA motorbike. British Intelligence couldn't stretch to a car for the return journey, but the young officer was not one to complain. There was a war on. He had to sit passively in the bike's cabin while his blonde motorcyclist (he couldn't even see her curls clearly now) took the controls and enjoyed all the action. She turned the ignition and thrust the bike into life. As the machine began to roar, Jock discerned a perceptible wink, and with that brief eclipse of an eye still sparkling beneath the cap, they were off down the drive, lined with trees that were already bursting into leaf. The reality of being tailed over the past months still hadn't sunk in. It was about to.

They returned on the Great North Road. Jock felt claustrophobic in the tiny cabin, but the one consolation was he had time to think about how best to serve his country: to contribute most to victory, with all the physical strength backed by spiritual faith, would likely find him firmly on the front line. He wanted to be spared home service or training, and go at once and take his place among men who were risking their lives for their country's cause. He looked at his driver and thought about the good she might do with her linguistic skills in an era of peace, during which Anglo-German relations could prosper without the pseudo-spirit of the Nazis, who had already crushed the essence of childhood – vivid imagination, unbounded affection and, above all, unassailable truth. He and Corncurls were alone in the countryside, which was flat and ordinary but for the budding hedgerows that broke the monotony of the arable land.

Almost alone. Jock noticed an open-top sports car in the bike's mirror. It looked like an Alvis. It was driving fast, but that was not unusual; he had raced his own version of the car at high speeds to Oxford with his friends at night until they reached Magdalen Bridge. This car, however, seemed to be in a race of its own. It was racing directly towards them now, but not overtaking. Jock's reflections, within the relative comfort of the sidecar, had been brought up short. He glanced sideways at his driver, and his musings of service were broken by the visible consternation in her eyes. Corncurls was opening up the throttle. The roar of a big engine sounded dangerously close, impossible to ignore. Unless he was mistaken, it was evident that he and Corncurls had unexpected company.

It was a powerful machine that was following them, matched by what appeared to be a similarly well-built owner; the driver's head would have touched the roof if it had not been down. Corncurls gave it full throttle, but the BSA was no match for what looked like an earlier version of Jock's own Alvis. Closer up, it appeared to have no front wheel brakes on it, and its beaded tyres scorched the road as the driver attempted to lunge nearer to the bike. Jock had also noted the type of his sidecar, a Watsonian, which he was well aware gave him a lot more protection than his intrepid driver. Corncurls knew the chase had begun. If she kept this up, Jock would definitely request her beatification.

But it was no time for fantastic thoughts of that nature just yet. They had both seen and recognised the threat, and now it was time to avoid it – and, if necessary, neutralise it. Perhaps Jock could also eliminate it too. Yet he had to think of something fast, and he only had seconds rather than minutes. As the powerful engine roared behind him, he recalled that Watsonian sidecars had three or four fittings screwed to their bike. Every standard-issue M20 bike had a small toolkit attached, and if he could just undo some brackets with Lady Luck still on his shoulder, he might completely detach the car after mounting the back of the motorcycle. Yet he could only partly do this while still in the passenger-car. Initially, Jock planned to jettison the cabin and make the BSA more manoeuvrable – there was a chance that the pair could lose the Alvis down an alley. However, narrow, drivable pathways were few and far between along the land parallel to the Great North Road, and Jock saw another opportunity in his scheme. He might be able to use the passenger-berth to block the path of the Alvis and permanently stop its driver if necessary. In that case, Corncurls would have to be as brave as St Joan in order to compensate for the inevitable shock.

But the sidecar wouldn't just disengage by itself; Jock would eventually have to climb out, and he and his rider would have to detach the side-cabin by leaning to and fro until their body weight in tandem loosened it from the bike itself onto the sports car behind.

He caught sight of his pursuer as he bent over the side and undid the first bracket. If he wasn't mistaken, the driver behind had the look of one of the Biff Boys who frequently did Mosley's dirty work. *They really were still upset about their missing flag.* Jock let the second nut go; it hit the Alvis's windscreen, which partly shattered. He looked in the mirror to see the damage before tackling the top two brackets. The sports car's tyres squealed as its bumper rammed the back of the Watsonian. Jock jolted forward and Corncurls accelerated as he worked rapidly with the spanner. The Biff Boy meant business and he was trying to put the pair in the ditch, but the sudden impact had loosened the third bracket Jock was trying to finish … *Thank God there were only four.* If his driver could stand it, Jock needed to complete the last detachment, but he would also have to wait for an oncoming car. He would cut down the chances of his opponent's survival by restricting him to driving in only one lane of the road, but for this piece of improvisation to work his biker had to keep the pursuing Alvis behind them.

Fortune favours the deserving and, as luck would have it, he could just make out the outline of an approaching car in the distance. Quickly, Jock put the finishing touches to the last support as the sports car again screamed and screeched up close behind him. There was no doubt that the driver wanted them dead. Corncurls rose to the occasion, swiftly grasping the significance of Jock's plan with another nod of her head before meandering across the road to bar the path of the Alvis. Yet Jock demanded more than his companion's approval. He unscrewed the final fixing, leaving the passenger-berth hanging off the bike, while he now mounted behind her. He began swaying the pair of them this way and that in order to complete the disengagement of the cabin from the bike as the car travelled towards them from the opposite direction.

The Biff Boy had wanted a hunt, and he'd found it. The advancing motor was still speeding towards them, and Jock prayed that it wouldn't turn off at either of the junctions ahead. He would have to push free of the passenger-car at precisely the right moment or the vehicle ahead would pass them by and the fascist would be free to kill the couple. Jock used his powerful legs to control more of the sideways movement so that the

Watsonian would release. The base of the sidecar was now scraping away at the macadam road. As sparks flew in all directions, Jock reckoned one hundred yards and a few seconds would do it. He gave the cabin door a kick with his heel. There was no escape now, as the Blackshirt couldn't move anywhere. Then the Watsonian started to tip back, spinning round as it did so, bouncing towards the Alvis's bonnet. The Biff Boy screamed. As he peered into the bike's mirror, Jock saw the man's distorted face behind the shattering glass of the Alvis's screen just before the sports car skidded into a tree.

Jock clung more tightly to the young woman, and the two drove on. A rush of cold air froze the sweat down his back, but it was replaced with a wash of warmth bathing his insides, like the first tasting of a really good wine at the end of a long day, as he realised that he was closer now to this particular non-commissioned officer than most men would ever get. The purr of the bike enhanced a relaxation that he had not felt for some time, and an intimacy that he had not enjoyed for months. He would be happy to stay on this vehicle for a while ...

'Thank you,' he shouted above the engine of the now much faster bike. 'You've solved that problem.'

'We both deserve a break,' she chimed.

Jock's motorcyclist slowed down to a gradual stop on the side of the road bordered by hawthorn and hazel hedgerows. They had travelled about a mile since they had collided with the Biff Boy. Her heel flicked out the bike's stand and Jock slid off the bike. Corncurls followed suit, and as she peeled off her leather helmet, her blonde locks fell about her shoulders. Her intake of breath was pleasantly audible as she put her hand out.

'I'm Charlotte ... I mean, Corporal Turner, sir.'

'I'm Jock,' he replied, putting the WAAF at her ease. 'Lieutenant Jock Steel.'

'Don't you think we should go back, Lieutenant?'

Jock couldn't hide his surprise. 'Go back? Go back for what?'

She lost some of her benevolent smile. 'I think we should return, Lieutenant.'

'You don't mean for the sidecar?' Jock chipped in, now becoming less easy-going in his turn.

'No. I'll have a bit of explaining to do about that. No, Lieutenant, for our crash victim.'

'He was trying to kill us, Charlotte. Isn't that all we need to know?'

'You seem to know, but I am required to file a report.' Her green eyes flashed at Jock. 'Who is he?'

'I know what he is, and that is enough.'

'For you, yes, but not for me.'

Jock tried to prevent this first proper exchange going sour. 'I know his origins … The police will be here soon, and I suggest that, unfortunate as the Watsonian's presence on the road might be, they'll probably record it as accidental.'

'He could be alive, Lieutenant,' she implored.

'He tried to kill us … He chose to do what he did, and he has reaped the consequences.'

'He might be injured. Do you MI6 boys have a policy of letting people bleed to death?'

Jock winced at the description. 'I'm not MI6.'

'Who do you work for?'

The question, coming as it did for the second time that afternoon, was anti-climactic. 'I'm a friend of SIS.'

'You could still be in a lot of trouble then.'

Jock enjoyed Charlotte's concern. The tension of the day was too much. Charlotte stood close and very still next to him. He was between her and the hedgerows that walled the Great North Road. Tired, bemused and stirred, he felt a little like Burne-Jones's Merlin, beguiled by the temptress Nimue. As he unbuttoned Charlotte's overcoat and put his arms inside the canvas jacket beneath her warm and seductive heavy thermal, discovering what he had previously only imagined, Jock certainly felt like the painter who had been bewitched by his model; his hands wrapped around her hourglass waist. Whispering 'Thank you' in Charlotte's ear, he kissed her without hesitation.

'Perhaps …' He mounted the bike. 'Anyway … I need to go back for any paperwork … I won't be long.'

Charlotte passed her goggles to him and fixed Jock with her emerald eyes. 'I won't forget you in a hurry.'

'No, you won't … You're coming with me. You're responsible for His Majesty's property; losing a sidecar would be unfortunate, but to lose the bike too would be a tragedy. Typing up your report might just then take up your whole evening – some of which I will have to claim as an apology for vandalising your vehicle.'

Jock swung his leg over the M20 and started to let out the throttle, bellowing over the engine's roar but smiling.

'Let's hope that if this Biff Boy is still alive, he's grown up a bit. Hop on.'

LONDON

EARLY SUMMER

1940

'Hello, Jock Steel speaking.'

'Good afternoon, Lieutenant Steel. Hollings here. Your regiment reckons that you might be able to help us with a new item of security. I can't speak further, except to invite you to a short meeting with me in St James's late afternoon – say 4 p.m. – today?' Hollings was already hanging up as he said, 'I've left some details at your Officers' Mess.' Then the phone went dead. Jock thought it was odd that his CO hadn't mentioned anything.

It was 2.30 p.m. Jock was on leave and needed some exercise, so he decided to walk from his flat in Holland Park. Strolling across Westminster Bridge that blustery day, he crossed the Thames, recalling as he did so the recitation of the Wordsworth sonnet that he had been highly commended for as a boy. Finishing the last lines in his head – 'And all that mighty heart is lying still' – he suddenly became acutely aware of a pedestrian whose face he could never quite catch sight of under his shock of light hair. He was a man of about twenty in a grey raincoat who appeared to be dissembling disinterest. As Jock looked across the Thames, he couldn't help feeling that the words 'lying still' took on a darker meaning now. Jock slowed down and stopped to attend to an already laced shoe. The figure appeared to be lying low, very absorbed with a boat on the Parliament bank. There was nothing particularly unusual about his interest, since boats were not supposed to moor there without a portcullis pennant, and this one bore nothing official.

It was beginning to rain stair rods, so Jock leapt onto a No. 73 bus on its way towards Parliament. He was careful not to give the impression that he had spotted the man shadowing him. If he didn't want another tail to replace the watcher, he'd have to keep up the pretence. A sideways glance told him his assailant had just turned away. For the moment, perhaps, Jock had shaken him off. He briefly basked once more in the memory of the school recitation competition, when Seddon had tried to get the better of him in the preparation room. Jock had won the fight but not the event, and had to be content with second place on that occasion. He remembered that the fight had disturbed his breathing, and respiration was everything in recitation – and in being followed, for that matter. After that, he hadn't let that type of encounter mar his chances again.

There were no shop windows in which to catch a reflection of the stalker. The pace of the 73 allowed Jock to alight as easily as he had boarded. He dived into a pub on the corner of the Embankment, walked right through the foggy lounge until he found a door. Putting a handkerchief to his mouth and mumbling something about 'sick', he pressed on to a kitchen via a back door. No one was there preparing food. He stepped into an alleyway just in time to see an edge of a grey raincoat pass by. Jock waited for him to walk towards Parliament, and then moved out into the street in the opposite direction, hoping to end this particular piece of theatre.

As he walked towards the government building, he paused at the gate, which was marshalled by a bored Lance Corporal. Jock signed in and was pointed down a stone staircase with immaculately painted iron railings. He supposed that these were unlikely to be cut down and turned into armoured vehicles once war fully embroiled the sleepy British Isles. He entered what looked like an underground cinema. As he descended the steps, he glanced past the NCO towards the Embankment to take one last check that he remained unobserved.

Down in the cinema, Jock took in the red seating for about forty people and the royal-blue curtains facing the auditorium. There was a table with a small box, letter opener and newspaper on it, and a lectern: typical military simplicity and style. There was some muffled coughing

15

up in the gallery above, and at this point the Colonel chose to enter the room. Jock wasn't sure what type of soldier he was; he wore no insignia on his epaulettes. He bore the unmistakable mark of the aristocrats who had been almost a foot taller than the lower ranks in previous centuries. That must have been a factor in why so many had been picked off by snipers in the trenches. Clearly, despite his bulk, Hollings had escaped the cull of innocents. The Colonel's six-and-a-half feet had conditioned him to a slightly self-deprecating hunch, so that he always appeared to be craning himself a little towards those below him – not that Jock was much shorter. As an oleaginous hand pressed his flesh, Jock noticed the heavy eyelids, freckled above thick eyelashes. He found it difficult to suppress laughter because the officer's countenance seemed almost like that of a half-made-up pantomime dame, despite its patrician nose and enigmatic mouth.

'Do have a seat, Steel.' Loose, wrinkled skin buttressed the wings of Hollings's collar as he sat down opposite. Jock's name was spoken with a sneer. Hollings gave with one hand and took with the other as he drawled, 'It's very good of you to come over again for a chat.' He paused. 'At long last.'

The Colonel's articulation took on greater precision as he became more enthusiastic.

'I wanted to show you a film taken a few summers ago in Berlin.' Jock quickly thought back to the rowing tour in Germany with a scratch Oxford crew. His thoughts were broken by the officer's monotone. 'A gathering when Goering awarded his personal medal for the race that his supermen were supposed to win.' Hollings smiled with a vanity that Jock had not previously noticed. This seemed to be the real Hollings; it was perceptible in the lazy mouth that seemed now more suited to the rim of a gin and tonic than genial conversation.

Someone else, probably an NCO, was in the cinema, because the lights dimmed and the 16mm tape began to roll.

Hollings perked up. 'Ah, there you are, shaking Goering, the Luftwaffe leader, by the hand no less. Here, now. Stop the tape … Franks … Franks? Are you deaf, man?'

Jock gazed at the still of a German spectator in the foreground. He recalled the unpleasant events that had preceded the filmed meeting. It came back to him again after so long. The man was Marz, the Nazi who had been caught spitting onto the Oxford boat as it passed under the bridge and finishing line at a previous regatta at Bad Ems. And here he was now, smoking as usual, and unctuously oozing compliments to Jock because the heavy-limbed Prussian could do little else in front of the cameras.

'Do you remember Marz, Steel?'

'I met him at a few race meetings, sir. Athletic, heavy build, sadistic and warped humour – if you can call it that. Chain-smokes, which is unusual for Heydrich's favourites. But Marz is very generous with his cigarettes and obsessional about what he smokes: "Atikah Zigaretten" are one of his main poisons. I remember he offered me one. He could be described as handsome in a traditional thick-set, blond and Aryan look that his peer group have been moulded into since their schooldays.'

'He's changed a bit since then. Would you know him again – or at least recognise him from his profile?' The Colonel was suddenly becoming less of the gin-swiller, displaying more of the repentant sobriety of the morning-after-the-night-before kind.

'Probably.' Jock inched his way towards a point of connection with the senior officer.

'It's just that he's had a bit of work done on his face after a motor-racing accident on the Nürburgring, and MI6 have lost track of him.' Hollings leant in a little. 'Jock, we need you to monitor him.' He filled the silence. 'Can you help at all?'

The young officer knew that the Great Game had become an amateurish affair in England, with little backing from government so soon after the Depression. His uncle Herbert, who had monitored Russo-Japanese relations as a Singer salesman, travelling between Singapore and Calcutta in the previous decade, had always warned him that the tight-fisted approach of the Treasury to both MI5 and MI6 was hampering Britain's earlier advances in Intelligence. The monitoring of new totalitarian powers in Germany and the Soviet Union could have been nurtured more carefully.

Hollings broke his own momentary reflections. 'Franks, let's have some more footage, shall we?'

The Colonel relaxed a little as he sank back in his larger, red velvet seat. Jock straightened a little more in his.

Hollings had done some homework. There was the Oxford crew, smiling with relief, arms round shoulders. Jock was shaking hands with municipal officials, while all the time trying to get through the crowd to embrace his beautiful German girlfriend, Senta Mariano. He felt his heart race at the sight of Senta again; she still had some hold over him. His chest swelled. He was also aware of a resentment towards Hollings as the Colonel gloated over the spectacle. Senta was, as usual, immaculately dressed, in black pantaloons and a striped sailor-suit top – a boyish look but for the conspicuous bow in auburn curls of hair. *What else did Hollings possess of his?* The monochrome film could not show her dazzling, dark blue eyes, but had recorded the energy in her nimble movements as she meandered around oarsmen's bodies, waving at her Jock and smiling all the while.

The 16mm film came loose from its connecting spool and flicked helplessly against the wall of the booth above; in the projector light, it flitted like a dying Catherine wheel. What Jock was not sure about was whether the Colonel's seeming civilities and charm were matched with wisdom and knowledge.

'What has the last clip of film to do with Marz?'

'Nothing, Steel, nothing,' Hollings croaked.

'So?'

'So why show it?' tolled the older man in a wearisome tone. Jock couldn't help wrinkling his nose as the Colonel clasped his hands slowly together, self-consciously forming a steeple with his fingers. He seemed more like a bogus churchman about to deliver a sermon than an intelligence officer.

'Yes, sir, why?' Jock was sure that the urbane figure opposite was going to involve Senta in all this.

'I thought you'd jump at the chance to see your old flame again?'

'What has she got to do with all this, Colonel?'

'You were close to Miss Mariano, weren't you?'

'What of it?' Jock said.

'Did you know that she is a fully paid-up member of the Nazi Party?'

'What exactly are you driving at, Colonel?'

'Well, I don't think your old boss at the British Council or your CO would be too keen on a man who keeps a Nazi girlfriend in Berlin.'

'Past tense, Colonel. Kept, sir – kept. Isn't it somewhat easy to be wise about the Nazis after the event?' Jock realised how insular some of the officers of the last war had become. 'When I was in Berlin, Germans joined the Nazi Party as if it were a club, a fad. Significant numbers of Germans were unaware of a trend that then seemed to be where the future of Germany lay, however dangerous it would increasingly become. Let's face it, it was the only 'phoenix' that emerged from the ruins that the previous government left smouldering for its people.'

'Do you think you'll return to the British Council after the war?'

'I am not exactly sure how long this war will be, sir.'

Hollings sat back and lit a cigar. 'Quite so, but helping us locate Marz wouldn't harm your prospects as one of Lord Lloyd's blue-eyed boys.'

Jock diverted the older officer. 'I am aware that MI5 and MI6 don't have many resources at the moment. I thought that you mainly monitored extremists posing as journalists?' Hollings looked as if he had just sucked a lemon rather than his Havana, but Jock couldn't resist raising issues of security himself. 'Was that one of your trainees following me on the bridge?'

The Colonel's jowls, which had been a plethoric pink, began to colour-code with the furnishings. Vexing unreliable people into wrong-footing themselves was a useful tool Jock had learned as captain of the Oxford boat when he had sparred with the Press.

Hollings smiled with pursed lips. 'We like a man who is alert, Steel. We lead the world in almost everything, and that goes for our intelligence services too.'

Jock pressed Hollings. 'There must be others who could properly identify Marz … Why especially me, Colonel?'

'Interestingly, we have found no one in Britain who could do so. Don't forget that Marz has had his face rearranged; he isn't averse to cloak-and-dagger outfits either. That means anyone who has actually seen him in the flesh will have a much better chance of identifying him.' He seemed to be quickly scribbling something on a card. 'You also have plenty of contacts after three consecutive visits to Germany in your capacity as an oarsman, journalist and socialite. Mixing with the great and the good at the Hotel Adlon, and with Countess Solf as your hostess in Berlin, has put you in a privileged position, as far as I am concerned. You won't be short on gossip, will you?'

Even Jock knew that Germany had been way ahead of Britain in intelligence matters just before the war – as in most material things.

He probed further. 'I would have thought Intelligence, Colonel, needed something rather more elevated than gossip or similar tittle-tattle in newspapers? Gossip at the Adlon is somewhat anodyne: staff report to the Gestapo.'

Hollings parried back. 'It is not just that, Steel. You were the best all-round athlete in your year, an amateur pilot, a linguist, one of the best shots in your regiment, and I understand that you are one of the fittest in the new commando programme.' He looked away towards Westminster. 'You are as much a Berliner as you are an Oxford man. You could be nominally on duty with the Welsh Guards, but paid and commanded by MI6?'

Jock thought back to those carefree days with his rowing team, his extended stay with Countess Solf at Villa Delos and his passionate affair with Senta. The Solfs had warned him about Marz even then. The Countess's Wannsee apartment was adjacent to those of both Admiral Canaris, head of the German secret service, and Heydrich, chief of internal security, and Countess Solf was privy to discreet snippets of news from the Admiral's wife, Erika. Jock himself had espied some of the movements between the residences of the two security chiefs with good views from within the Solf's clock tower. Marz was considered a fine specimen of the Master Race, but it was another misleading example of the so-called majesty of the Aryan type. Jock remembered watching Marz's boss, Heydrich, who was tall and aristocratic in his demeanour. Even then he understood that there were few of Heydrich's *Sicherheitsdienst*, or SD, who physically mirrored their leader's physique or bearing, and that the whole organisation was full of animals with human heads – although 'animals' was too good a term for them. Perhaps that was why they called their SD chief the 'blond beast'? Even so, Heydrich more than paid lip service to culture on those evenings while he was a guest of the Admiral. Heydrich would angrily play croquet in summer, but Countess Solf told Jock that on winter nights, she observed how the SD leader would suppress his demons: he would sit down by his music stand ready to play in the quartet of intelligence chiefs and their wives.

Heydrich's violence was reflected in his blazing eyes. What gave them their peculiar aspect was that his upper eyelids seemed too small, creating a hooded effect, so that he appeared to stare ahead like a large predator. Countess Solf recalled that he was too gangly to comfortably sit down without his legs falling akimbo, until he had his violin resting upon his shoulder. She had mentioned then how Erika Canaris had encouraged her spouse to join the soirees because the loyal wife wanted to protect her admiral. The dutiful husband fell in with his wife's requests, as he hoped the combination of Haydn, Schumann and Brahms would still the volcanic anger that he suspected would be unleashed by Heydrich in a torrent, threatening to undermine the very civilisation that had created the music.

Now, Jock was being tasked to monitor one of Heydrich's men.

The phone rang in a back room. The Colonel pushed *The Times* across the table towards Jock, made his excuses and disappeared to take the call. Jock was irked at the suggestion that he put action as a soldier on hold on the merit of having bumped into one of the Nazis' agents during a rowing competition. He'd known fellow students on his staircase at Christ Church who were carving out good careers at MI5 and MI6, but this offer from Hollings sounded cheap and opaque, just like the surveillance on the bridge that afternoon.

Jock discerned a cleared throat as a phone clattered into place.

'You make the post sound so impressive, sir,' Jock said sardonically. 'You are press-ganging me, aren't you, Colonel?'

Was it MI6's service rivalry that made Jock view Hollings as being on the back foot? If Intelligence was currently impaired by Whitehall's internal rivalries, Jock was not about to jump at the Colonel's suggestions.

'Look, Jock – may I call you Jock?' Jock said nothing and listened. 'We both know that appeasement of the Nazis never worked, and that Chamberlain has been fed misinformation. Did you really believe that London would be significantly flattened by aerial destruction?'

'It hasn't happened yet, sir.'

Hollings took a draw on his cigar. 'We are unprepared for war, but people like you and me, Jock, aren't going to sit on the fence and watch Britain subsumed by the New Germany – or continue to be pacified by Halifax, for that matter.'

Unwittingly, the Colonel had made a stronger connection with his visitor, who considered the likes of Halifax to be one of a number of overpaid sheep who until recently had been braying in Parliament at the slightest mention of the need for action against Hitler.

'You know enough about me, sir,' Jock conceded.

'You seem to be a confirmed anti-fascist, but with plenty of German contacts.'

Hollings couldn't drop that subject. Yes, Hollings would be much happier on a bum-warmer at the Athenaeum Club, surrounded by some of the fossils of the last war, in spite of his politics.

Hollings made his recommendation. 'I suggest that you operate in most local theatres of war and in Germany itself. You speak Italian and French too, don't you?'

'Yes, but I need to know a bit more than you've sketched out for me, Colonel.'

Hollings's face hardly changed, and he seemed to be studying his ivory letter opener rather hard while rearranging it in front of a small box of index cards. 'You've told me very little about Marz.' Jock was struggling to avoid insubordination. 'With respect, sir, why is he so vital to monitor?'

Hollings lifted his elephantine bulk out of his chair and looked out across the river. He didn't often maintain eye contact, and the Thames view allowed him to position himself adjacent to Jock.

The older officer continued to stare ahead. 'Marz will be used by the Nazis where he can do most damage to us. He's one of their best; we don't believe that they have many accomplished agents as yet. Some of us don't expect to easily repel the lightning attack on the French; many of us believe that the most serious blow of all will be from an Italo-German front in the Mediterranean. If Marz is not on duty spying on our friends in Germany, he may well be used to undermine our defence of Egypt.'

Jock played for time, dissembling spontaneity as if the thought had just occurred to him. 'I'd like to see my old tutor, if that's all alright with you, sir? I'd certainly talk things over with him. He has been a mentor of mine since my move to England.'

'Dalton or Ryle?'

'Gaitskell.'

Hollings's expression didn't change. 'Yes, by all means.' With mock warmth, he added, 'That's fine, Jock.' He signalled the meeting's end with a cavalier sweep of his cigar. 'The car's waiting.'

Hollings had been holding something back. Part of Jock wanted Hollings to shine as a mentor. 'Have you any standard rules or practical hints?'

Hollings turned away – rather sheepishly, Jock thought. 'I don't think there are any really,' he said. Then, with a cheerless guffaw, he added, 'It's rather like a lifelong initiative exercise.'

'I wonder how long an agent can operate in this war, Colonel?'

Ominously, Hollings turned to face him. 'Longer, hopefully, than your friend Captain Wintour.'

Jock had been expecting something from left field, but not this. David Wintour had been Jock's closest friend, and had recently been posted missing in France before the evacuation.

'Where is he now, sir – a POW camp?'

Hollings gave him the body blow. 'No. Marz killed Captain Wintour forty-eight hours after his capture. The captain was a uniformed intelligence officer, but his treatment had nothing to do with the Geneva Convention.' It was Jock's turn to look across the water now. 'As far as we know, he didn't talk. He gave nothing of any significance away to Marz. You keep good company, Jock.'

'Kept – kept, sir,' was all Jock managed.

Kept – kept up to speed by Hollings with the subtlety of a sledgehammer, even though David's inevitable courage was some consolation. He searched the

Colonel's craggy face for answers: the pain seared deeper when it occurred to him that Hollings might have been David's handler. But he'd have to find that out for himself; now he wasn't certain that he could contain his own incandescent fury.

Hollings couldn't resist a tinge of one-upmanship on Jock's exit, speaking with deceptive dreaminess. 'By the way, Jock, that wasn't one of our men following you this afternoon … Oh, and I'm sure Hugh Gaitskell will organise things for you; help you think things over.' There was another clip-on smile, with the eyes reflecting little.

Jock walked out into the courtyard, surveying the Embankment, which was awash with detritus; a newspaper swirled up with a harsh, northerly wind. A black-and-grey Hillman Minx pulled up yards from the Lance Corporal on duty, who barely noticed as Jock climbed into it.

Jock hadn't wanted to give Hollings the satisfaction of an answer to his recommendations, but Hollings knew.

BERLIN

SUMMER
1940

A broad-shouldered man in his thirties strode passed Berlin's Landwehr Canal and looked up at the contrived grandeur of the pompous-looking buildings and the grey granite structure of the Tirpitzufer, the Abwehr centre for German Military Intelligence. Locally, it was nicknamed *Fuchsbau* – the 'Fox's Earth' – so-called on account of its labyrinthine passages, innumerable doors and gloomy offices. He considered it well named, as its master, Admiral Canaris, was known as 'the wily fox'.

Gallmüller, a veteran Berliner and long-time doorman of the mysterious premises, stiffened to semi-attention as the muscular figure entered the section of the Reichswehr Ministry. The visitor knotted his not inconsiderable forehead; he was visibly surprised by the two small decrepit lifts facing him. One of them took him to the third floor, where he eventually negotiated the folding metal grille that shielded unwanted outsiders. The offices, rather dark and dismal at this hour, lined a corridor leading to twin doors that faced him at the end of the landing. It was exactly six o'clock in the evening.

Constricted by his jacket as he lifted his arm to knock on the door, Marz was irritated. The SD henchman had read the transcripts of a Soviet report to Moscow from London that revealed a British initiative to secure the frontier posts of Egypt. It had mentioned the code name of a British spy capable of passing himself off as a German or Italian officer on the

Italo-German front, or as one operating within Berlin itself. There was little other information about him, except that he was known as MIRAGE. Marz had been briefed by Heydrich himself because no one in the SD knew anything more. It was expected that the Abwehr would co-operate. As his fist touched the door, it was flung open, and he found himself staring down at the azure eyes of Admiral Canaris, the Abwehr Chief.

The spymaster beckoned his visitor into his modest office. As Marz strode into the room, Canaris recognised the long strides and arms that swung in rhythm with his legs, almost as if he were about to mark time on the parade ground; the shoulders were hunched as he moved, and 'the little Admiral', as Canaris was known, observed that there was something Palaeolithic about Marz – the recent scars of the sutures around his forehead exaggerated his heavyset features. He had heard about his disastrous foray into racing on the Nürburgring. It was a pity for everyone at the Abwehr that Marz had survived it.

Canaris reflected that this had undoubtedly helped his rival Heydrich. Hitler was relying on men of brutality, not men of great intelligence, but if you possessed both those qualities, as Heydrich did, you were especially dangerous, particularly to men like the Admiral. Hitler's 'Suspect-hunter in Chief', as Canaris had recently christened Heydrich, was particularly arrogant at the moment too. Signing himself 'C' for internal correspondence was outrageous – didn't his old naval cadet from the training ship *Berlin* realise that he, the Admiral, was actually the opposite number to 'C', Britain's Secret Intelligence Service chief? As the two men stood motionless, the Abwehr chief regarded the pockmarked skin and eyes set slightly too close together. He noticed too the unfortunate ears, which were unnaturally small – that was when he took a complete dislike to the SD's new champion spy. Of course, the 'Ape', as Canaris had christened him, had come to spy on him, but he was used to such visits. That such a specimen should be assigned to monitor the Abwehr's security in Egypt was what infuriated him most. For the moment, he decided to curb his distaste and hear what Marz had to say for himself.

The Admiral had still not spoken. He continued to observe the SD man, who was taking in his surroundings in the utilitarian office while he was being kept waiting. A pair of dachshunds growled at him from beneath a low military camp bed; their master didn't shush them, watching instead Marz's discomfort at the frosty welcome. Canaris saw Marz look around the shack from which the Abwehr led its merry dance around the Nazi security systems. The SD man took in the hazy photograph of Colonel Nicolai, a famous recent ancestor of the Abwehr chief, and then his gaze shifted from the threadbare rug, upon which some of the world's diplomats were supposed to be welcomed by this branch of the Third Reich, to a map of the world fastened to the wall. The Admiral saw Marz's eyes move to the plain wooden desk nearby. There sat a model of Canaris's beloved cruiser of happier days, the *Dresden*, the vessel that had taken the shine off the Royal Navy's unbroken record of naval defence. Not far from it rested three small bronze apes, representing 'see no evil, hear no evil, speak no evil'. Some took this to be the motto of the Abwehr, but in fact it had a wider symbolism, with echoes of Kipling and the world of the Great Game – something that the SD 'Ape' knew little about.

A growl came from Seppel and Sabine, the two wire-haired dachshunds, as Marz shifted a little from foot to foot; he was still standing, not having been offered a seat. The SD officer did his best not to flinch; the hounds had now come into view, noses pushing out from under the bed. The Admiral bent his head down as if he were about to ram his visitor.

'How good of you to drop by,' Canaris purred.

Marz did not seem duped by the 'mild little man', who appeared colourless and impersonal. Canaris sensed the SD agent was not impressed by his lack of military bearing, the tired uniform hanging off his frail physique, the snow-white hair, which the SD regarded as belonging to Father Christmas, or his diminutive height. These were characteristics that appalled Marz, who had risen meteorically from Hitler Youth leader to SA thug in just a few years. 'The cunning old fox', as Canaris was also called, was everything that he had been taught to despise about the old order, who had failed to challenge the liberalism of the Weimar government, and who had allowed the weaker elements of German society to proliferate.

'Admiral, I am here to register the SD's interest in the protection of double agents serving under the auspices of the Abwehr in support of the

Italian campaign in the desert. They are technically under your control, but we will request that they return to the SD, where they were first scouted.' Motionless and silent, Canaris's gaze was fixed on his visitor. Marz went on, as Sabine lifted her head, sensing her master's displeasure, 'I am requesting that I am privy to all counter-espionage data. The SD would appreciate updated information on all foreign agents posing a threat to internal and external security. Does MIRAGE mean anything to you, Herr Admiral?'

'No, nothing.' Canaris's inscrutable reply gave no indication of his awareness of Marz's slip of information. 'Is that all, Captain?'

This had been Heydrich's attempt at a 'courtesy call' between the two security forces. Canaris would feed Marz what he chose; just, he thought, as his type of animal deserved.

'I am acting Major now, and a full Major in Egypt. Heil Hitler.' Marz saluted and swallowed his distaste for the old order.

'Heil Hitler, Major Marz.'

Canaris watched in disbelief as the acting Major turned to leave. He was reminded of a world away from the powerful Nazi order. The older officer's mind flooded with the memory of a rather different German a decade before, during the dark days of 1929. Then, Marz had been jobless and a part-time Stormtrooper. He had been too young to understand the élan of the officer class that had risked so much to avert the threat of communism, and not old enough to have escaped the indoctrination programmes of the Hitler Youth. During the Depression, the Admiral had once seen the raw and green youth wrestling for a few marks in the circus by the Potsdamerstrasse. Canaris had held hands with his little girls, who had clutched onto him tightly as they tried to catch up with their mother. Erika had shown her disapproval of this particular martial display by walking ahead at a pace that the rest of the family couldn't match. Canaris had suspected that it might have been the base sounds emitted by the wrestlers rather than their disappearing mother that had made his daughters anxious. Marz might now be about to represent the SD's counter-espionage desk in Egypt, but the Abwehr would make sure that, as far as possible, he would not get above himself.

Very carefully, the Admiral showed him the door, closed it and went over to stroke Sabine. As he watched the preposterous Nazi through the window, making his exit from the Tirpitzufer, he reckoned that he had surely been everything that Marz had expected. It was far better as chief of the Abwehr to remain a caricature of himself if an enemy – especially this one, it seemed – were to be kept at a safe distance. If the SD satirised him as a decrepit 'Father Christmas' figure, they were deceiving themselves. Canaris knew Marz's past: he was something of a hand-to-hand fighter; 'wrestling' was rather an elaborate term for it. Captain Marz, as he was then, had first climbed up the ranks of the Stormtroopers with a speciality in street fighting, where he was known for tearing the side of an opponent's mouth several inches so that the wound stretched across the victim's face. Canaris looked across at the stagnant waters of the canal opposite and then turned back to watch the swagger of the new Major as he walked towards the Brandenburg Gate.

This was what Germany now prized highly. The Admiral knew that this was the type of security man who interrogated his suspects by tying their hands behind their ankles with barbed wire before horsewhipping them into talking. As Canaris put his arms around Sabine and Seppel, he couldn't help but wish for a return to those dark days of the Depression when life was so much simpler than now. He reflected that Erika no longer raced ahead in disapproval as she had done that summer's day; she put her energy into organising home life rather too much these days. Croquet with Marz's boss had been arranged for the forthcoming weekend because she was now concerned that cordial relations with Heydrich were necessary, as tensions between the two men's departments grew. He knew that she was right. The two security branches were arguing like a couple in a savagely hostile divorce case. That's why he loved his dachshunds so much: they could never betray him.

The Admiral knew too that MIRAGE would have to be the very best that the British could produce.

LONDON

SUMMER 1940

I

Lieutenant-Colonel Dudley Clarke stopped looking pensive, rubbed a pair of prolific black eyebrows, lit his pipe and blew an arabesque of blue smoke rings towards the other end of his MO9 office. Standing by the windows that looked down on Horse Guard's Arch, he thought once more of the telephone call that he had been informed was expected that morning from Lieutenant-General Haining, Vice Chief of the Imperial General Staff. The army grapevine suggested that Clarke was going to be presented with an opportunity that would be difficult to refuse. He brushed down an already immaculate tunic and chewed on the end of his pipe as the phone rang.

'MO9. Clarke speaking.'

'Morning, Colonel. General Haining here. How are things?'

'Good. Good, thank you, sir.'

'Excellent. Now, I have been given a telegram from the Commander-in-Chief, Middle East. General Wavell has asked if you would take up a completely new area of responsibility that he believes only you are fit for.'

Clarke bit his lip and let Haining make the Commander-in-Chief's offer. Clarke was being pulled in two directions. MO9 operated coastal and airborne raids on the enemy, and as MO9 controller, he was conscious that it was still a fledgling organisation that had yet to win over its critics. Britain faced superior numbers of Axis forces in every theatre of war. He had been working on an elite force to revitalise British morale, and was reluctant to relinquish specialised commando units that had taken their name from his native South Africa. The Boer 'Commandos', like the Spanish in the Peninsular War against Wellington, had the mobility, surprise and training that was a blend of the stamina of Rogers' Rangers and the agility of the Palestine Arabs who had challenged the regular British troops a few years before.

At last he spoke. 'MO9 is in the process of proving to the world that the Commandos could emulate a combination of all previous elite soldiers, and it is rather a wrench to leave the job unfinished, sir.'

Haining had an answer for the moment. 'One consolation is that my predecessor, General Dill, has insisted the Middle East will get the highest priority after Dunkirk.'

Clarke remembered Dill's words, which had also sounded ominous, given that the 40,000 British in Egypt were outnumbered by one million troops.

Haining continued. 'It is likely to be our only front for some time to come.' The Lieutenant-General made a harder sell. 'This brief – Project "A" Beam – is the greatest chance that anyone has so far been given to hoodwink fascist forces with fake armies and airborne divisions, and Egypt is now where the most audacious schemes are being dreamt up by both sides.'

Lieutenant-Colonel Clarke didn't want to sound ungrateful. 'What men, and how many will be at my disposal, General?'

Clarke looked fondly above him at the picture that he had bought in the Muski, a bazaar in Cairo's medieval quarter. The photograph was of a scene that had remained unchanged since the September day in 1898 when Kitchener routed the Dervish Army of 'The Khalifa'. It didn't escape his attention that at Omdurman the British had slaughtered the 11,000 Dervish because of their superior technology, the Maxim gun. Now, nearly forty years later, the British again were outnumbered, this time by mechanised divisions of Axis opponents, who were poised to embark on a slaughter that would overshadow battles like Omdurman, threatening Britain's control of the Suez Canal and numerous peoples of the British Empire. Clarke knew his history, and wanted to maintain British supremacy against the Nazis.

Lieutenant-General Haining coughed and swallowed. 'You will be put

in charge of Deception in the Middle East. In that role, you could potentially make more contribution to winning this war than any other soldier,
simply by persuading the enemy that they can't move quickly against us
because we have more armies there than they do – currently your staff will
consist of just a few administrators and officers and two active soldiers, a
bombardier and a trooper, who will front "A" Beam's "A" Force, but it's a
start. It's not without its risks, of course; however, we hope to offer you an
intelligence officer, code name MIRAGE, who will support you in coun-
tering Nazi surveillance in Egypt soon after you arrive.'

The Lieutenant-Colonel wasn't the sort to succumb to impatience, but
he had found the idea of relinquishing a command of thousands for a small
bureaucracy disconcerting. The closest many of the idle type of bureau-
crat got to any action was observing the Provost Marshal being harangued
in the streets of Cairo by Australian troops who were brawling with their
allies. They could safely watch such conflicts from the bum-warmer of a
cane chair on the balcony at Shepheard's Hotel, or on the roof gardens of
the local clubs and bars.

'Where will the office be based, Lieutenant-General?'

'I was just coming to that. Kasr el Nil.'

Clarke knew the area and had some misgivings. 'Oh, yes, sir.'

'The flat has just been converted.' Haining spat it out. 'Your new office
will be based on the third floor, safe from local thieves.'

'The current neighbours, sir?'

'I think you're familiar with the locale … You will be below a whorehouse.' The General cleared his throat. 'There are some plus sides to that,
… I am, of course, not talking about the access to those facilities by the
men.'

'Of course not, sir.'

'I must emphasise, that this is an opportunity of a lifetime. Please trust
that this next move to Egypt would be a promotion of sorts.'

Clarke swallowed hard. 'Quite, sir. Thank you for thinking of me.'

Haining said his goodbyes and hung up. Perhaps someone at HQ
Cairo thought that his outfit was just another bunch of amateurs; they'd
soon find out otherwise. MO9 in Europe would have to wait. Clarke

wondered if he had been prised from the shell of MO9 to maintain his career. The commandos' progress in North Africa was patchy, and he knew their training was geared to fighting in Western Europe. Yet how was he to shorten the war with fake airborne gliders, vehicles, a minor bureaucracy in a spy-infested city, four soldiers and a secret agent called MIRAGE? Only Lisbon rivalled Cairo in its seething mass of agents and would-be spies in the intelligence war, making the secret of Britain's 'numerous armies' almost impossible to keep secure.

As the Lieutenant-Colonel blew out more smoke, he realised that at least his new office, sandwiched between whores and would-be soldiers on their late-night visits, would be the butt of local jokers, and might just be the best cover for operational planning that any intelligence officer could ever hope for. Perhaps the journey out would take his mind off the detail: flying boat from Poole, gambling outside Lisbon, then on to Las Palmas, the Gambia, across Nigeria, with a night in the walled city of Kano, and back to Sudan. On the sixth day of the trip, he would be in the Nile Hotel at Wadi Halfa, before lunch the next day at Luxor, and back in Cairo for the afternoon. Avoiding enemy territory had some advantages.

II

Jock noted the brass plaque indicating 'The Minimax Fire Extinguisher Company' before walking into Broadway Buildings, a dingy warren of wooden partitions. A policeman scrutinised him over a pane of frost-tinted glass while telephoning to arrange an escort for the visit. He cupped the phone. 'Morning, sir. The SIS office is at the top. You will be met by the lift.'

The door of the old-fashioned elevator slid back with a clang. The lift was operated by a shiny brass lever that sent the contraption noisily up four of eight floors. On the fourth, he was met in the corridor by an attractive secretary and shown into a long Whitehall office. It was deliberately created to foil any intruder as Sir Simon Majoribanks, Chief of the Secret Intelligence Service, or 'C', kept his own office in the middle of the far end of the SIS's secretariat. Jock saw a green light flash up as a buzzer sounded, and a welcoming, tweed-suited secretary greeted him mid-carpet, before escorting him across the long room.

Sir Simon Majoribanks finished signing off a thick file, and welcomed him with a firm handshake. 'I've had a very unusual request for a meeting with the enemy in Spain.' 'C' – the Chief – pallid but broad shouldered, with thinning, silvery-blond hair, was looking at his new Venetian blinds. He cleared his throat and turned to Jock. 'It is particularly unusual and highly sensitive.'

'Originally I was asked to operate in Germany, sir.' Jock could not bear the thought of straying off his chosen course of bringing the soldier's fight to the enemy in a theatre of war that would shake the Nazis' confidence to the core. Once he'd located Marz, he would indeed be free to pursue his own ambitions of innovative warfare. Or so he thought.

Two clear, pale-grey eyes shot a swift glance at Jock. 'You must have wondered why you have been called upstairs?'

The young soldier had thought it odd that he, a junior staff member, had been invited up to the top of Broadway Buildings so soon after his attachment there; he took the smaller chair with a due sense of protocol.

'We have gone through your background with a very fine comb and singled you out as a new recruit for Section D. It's one of my projects, a sabotage group, which I understand you would be ideal for. I believe you have been pioneering something very destructive with the new plastic explosive?'

'Yes, sir. Explosives became a small hobby of mine. My younger brother introduced me to it as a boy.'

'Perhaps he would be interested in Section D, Steel?'

'He is spending most of his time putting people back together again.' There was an awkward silence as Jock cleared his throat. 'He is a doctor … I will mention it, sir.'

'Good. Thank you, Steel. You have been selected as a candidate for this singularly important job to make contact with Admiral Canaris in Spain, and then journey to North Africa and protect the interests of an elaborate plan to intimidate the enemy into believing they are faced with hordes of soldiers, of whom are fictitious parachutists, a phantom force: "A" Force, part of Project "A" Beam. However, while these are important missions in themselves, they will conveniently allow you the opportunity to collect any information on suspects here at home who may be passing our secrets on such missions not only to the enemy, but also to foreign powers who undermine our security in the war against the Nazis – I am, of course, particularly concerned about the Russians. You have been headhunted partly because you don't appear on any security records, you are being recruited as a safe pair of hands to find the source of intelligence leaks here in the heart of London, and you alone are in a position to properly identify the work of German Intelligence's current protégé, a Gunther Marz, facing us in the desert.'

Jock noted the tag of 'current'. Were operatives on both sides so expendable?

'C' picked up his pipe and started to light the mound of tobacco. 'People are often born in the wrong century, but it does seem that you have been born in the right one, and at the right time. I've seen your file: you're hard as steel – no pun intended. Your whole demeanour is that of a warrior, with the bearing, intelligence and physique to go with it. I understand that you know Marz from before the war, and the icing on the cake is that you are a linguist and your heritage is in intelligence. I've also invited you here because this intelligence work involves much more than the security of the Middle East.'

Jock sat impassively watching the lean, nervously energised figure before him; the wide frontal lobe of the chief seemed to contain whirring, well-oiled and synchronised motors. His stare was not unlike the searchlights of one end of a gigantic ocean vessel in motion.

'Your quarry, and by that I mean Marz, is also undermining the position of my equal in Germany.'

'Admiral Canaris,' Jock chipped in.

'Quite.'

Majoribanks swiftly moved on, but Jock knew that not asking questions was like trying to walk a thousand miles without legs, and he needed answers.

'Why would that particularly perturb you, if I may ask, sir?'

'The menace posed within Germany to my opposite number?' Majoribanks smiled, eyes bright with zeal. 'We have to track Marz for diverse reasons. This cannot go further than these four walls, and I would not be telling you now if it was not absolutely essential to the success of this mission: Marz is almost certainly in touch with someone in this building who is a sympathiser of the Soviet cause, for instance. Let's remember that the Germans and Russians have been sharing intelligence on and off for the last generation. In fact, our Broadway House traitor might simply be someone who is not sympathetic to Canaris's contacts because they have made an overture of peace to us. We don't entertain ideas of peace with the Hun unless it is an unconditional surrender, but it doesn't mean that we will tolerate any of their messages to us being destroyed, or worse, being duplicated for foreign eyes, particularly those belonging to Hitler or Stalin.'

Jock began to gauge the size of the task facing British Intelligence. He waited for Majoribanks to take a puff of his pipe behind a desk adorned with vivid blue stationery and a large bottle of green ink.

'C' spoke more quietly now. 'I want you to find out who is not passing on information to me about these particular pacifists in Germany. One very reliable, but independent source, known only to myself, has confirmed what we have suspected for some time: that there has to be a member of MI6 who is totally opposed to peace with Germany – at any price.' He sucked in more smoke. 'Peace offers are being binned before I have had a chance to read them.'

Jock's own mind raced ahead. 'That would make the German ploy to assess our "A" Force operation a tempting opportunity for Marz, who might be able to discredit Canaris's lack of knowledge about Britain's fake desert force, gaining credit for it himself rather than the Abwehr. Our danger at home is also the sharing of all this intelligence with the Soviets.'

'Quite. Neither the Nazis nor the Soviets want Canaris to be in cahoots with the British. Yet it's hardly a web of deceivers that I would crawl into if I had the choice. You would be tasked with capturing Marz, who has to be stopped now for many reasons. If he identifies the phantom force in the desert, it will likely lead to Britain's military exposure there; he will then possess all the information that our government does not want him to have. In that case, you will have failed in your task, Jock.' He paused and looked sober. 'With a man like Marz, that will mean death. And I understand a very painful one with his use of barbed wire around ankles and wrists.'

Jock was gripped by the extent of his mission that was being rolled out by the Chief.

'The other reason why you must succeed,' 'C' went on, 'is that if you apprehend Marz, you may have a chance of discovering whose reports he is reading from London to Moscow. This would help any allies we might have in Germany, quite apart from assisting our own security, and target for an early military victory in North Africa, which will protect our continued control of the Suez Canal. We now have reason to believe that Marz will operate unofficially – under Heydrich's command in the Middle East. His move from Germany is imminent.'

'It seems that you already have excellent intelligence in Hitler's backyard?'

'C' sat poker-faced and didn't reply. Hollings hadn't been up to speed with events; he'd said Jock was likely to go to Germany. Yet the MI6 offers were changing. Even the chance of seeing Senta again in Berlin would not compensate for a suicidal mission there. Jock had mixed feelings about that suggestion, and he couldn't help but suspect a man like Hollings. Was this another reason why Hollings might not have been called to any further briefing with him? Jock didn't have a problem with taking responsibility for the protection of Western Europe, but that didn't mean he was about to sacrifice himself, and be a martyr for some charade. He had to know if this increasingly intricate network of espionage was an amateur game, an under-resourced and over-imaginative organisation dedicated to puffing up its own self-importance like Aesop's frog while competing aggressively for funding.

'If Marz does undermine Canaris's position as Head of the Abwehr, surely it would checkmate a highly influential member of the German High Command, sir?' 'C' looked at Jock with great attention. Possibly he treated everyone like this. Jock warmed to the charm that supplemented a regular cavalryman's brain with dextrous polish. However, Jock still felt surprise that he was being recruited as one of a few solutions to a potentially enormous problem for Intelligence. The older man picked up the MO9 machine from his desk. Jock wondered if it were something that Section D had passed on for 'C''s approval, and hoped that his question hadn't perturbed the Intelligence chief.

The mechanism was still being brandished as 'C' replied. 'I'm in no position to assess these so-called "Good Germans" and their intentions. I'm hardly able to advise the PM as to whether Canaris is or is not truly sympathetic to the democracies – not while we have a viper in our nest.'

It appeared that the older man was somewhat rattled by the whole business. There was a long pause while 'C' put the Section D kit down carefully, and then tapped out the spent embers of his briar into the ashtray. Jock had a deep sense of foreboding about the vulnerability of Canaris.

Finally, 'C' spoke. 'He's asked to meet with one of our own agents.'

Jock cleared his throat. 'Who would that be, sir?'

'C' managed a tight-lipped smile. 'You, of course, man. There was talk of the Admiral meeting with someone senior like myself, but our relative positions in this particular case make you the obvious choice. I would need you to facilitate communication between myself and the Admiral by passing over my personal codes to him in person. You are new to this organisation, but not exactly new to Intelligence; I understand that you can pass for a German, Italian or Spaniard, and anyone working against us in England knows precious little about you at present – another good reason for you to pilot this project. Canaris believes that Marz is on to him.'

Jock realised that there was something that might win the confidence of Canaris that even the likes of Hollings would have trouble estimating: Jock had had more friends in Berlin before the war than he sometimes cared to admit.

'C' sucked on his now empty pipe. 'It's not only the question of tapping information from the "Good Germans" before it's been tampered with by the Soviet insider in this building. We want Canaris protected from the extending tentacles of Heydrich.' 'C' reignited his tobacco and blew the smoke for emphasis. 'Canaris might know where all the bodies are buried in the Nazi chamber of horrors; he might be holding back revelations about Heydrich's boss, Himmler, but the SD is on to him. If the Admiral isn't given maximum protection from the zealots on his own side, he'll be one of the latest casualties in the cemetery of political victims.'

'Sir, I am grateful to be considered for such an enterprise, but I do want to lead soldiers in war as soon as it is possible.'

The Intelligence chief was focussing heavily on the 'Good Germans', and Jock still wasn't sure where all this conversation was going. There was a photograph of a much younger Majoribanks in his tennis garb on the wall behind 'C', staring out from the centre of his college squad. There were fewer lines on that forehead below a thatch of wiry hair now long gone.

Jock's glance at the picture caught 'C' unawares for a moment. 'C' followed the young officer's gaze. '1926. That was the year I coached the winning team. Do you play?'

'I'm a River Man.'

'Of course you are. You wouldn't have had much time for tennis with that 1937 victory ending Cambridge's thirteen consecutive wins.'

Jock smiled, and remembered that rowing had first brought him into contact with Senta – but also Marz. Hopefully those two were far apart. 'I found time to coach younger crews and give something back to a new generation.'

'C' breathed in audibly and sighed. 'Of course you did.' Both were comfortable with silence: there was a genuine connection now between the two men – an empathy, a commitment and a shared understanding. 'Look, I am sorry to hear about your own peer group; I had heard about David Wintour. Some of the Oxford Eight have been killed already, haven't they?'

'It rather puts this mission, or missions, into perspective, sir.'

A different secretary opened the door. She was older and more formidable, but she smiled and placed a huge file quietly on 'C''s desk, which the Chief acknowledged with a nod of the head, and an 'Excuse me' to Jock.

David. Where was he now? David … Jock and he were like the biblical David and Jonathan. Jock insisted that the Oxford crew would go faster if he stepped out of the boat; days before the Boat Race, he offered his place to David, who then stroked the crew after replacing Jock. Jock fondly recalled the friendship of a highly intelligent college man, who had been gifted as a poet, writer and trainee medical student. He was the first to die from that daring and skilful team. They were going to pair together at the Tokyo Olympics of 1940. The posthumous DSO would never heal the wounds of David's beloved sisters – Judy and Bridget – and the rest of that wonderful family. The Battle of Boulogne had ended everything for him. Jock visualised how invaluable an intelligence officer his fellow oarsman would have been at the Battle of Boulogne. He remembered reading a Guardsman's letter:

'No one had time to think, no moment to be afraid; it all happened so fast, and was over in thirty hours. The bloody horror of it all, the futile order to move at once, the muddle on embarking, the shambles on disembarking, where amid a quay littered with kits and supplies, derelict cars, standstill trams and cowering refugees, somehow the 20th Guards Brigade made their landing and forced a way through the town, swarming with unarmed and untrained French soldiers, and took up position to stem the mechanised advance of the German force. Just two battalions in a vast town protected solely by a barrage of balloons, the last of which was sinking as we left the port … The activities of spies within our midst seemed incredible … Snipers from the housetops were continually shooting at our troops in the streets.

The worst was to come, for after the order to withdraw was given and the first destroyer was berthed ready to embark, sudden and terrific crossfire swept the harbour from the coastal batteries which the French had failed to spike, and the Germans turned on the harbour they used to protect; the destroyers were firing back, the range under 800 yards, and sheets of flames cut between me and the front of the Company. The first destroyer was ablaze, yet firing from every gun, cliff and forts were collapsing and the coast was ablaze; we cowered under a train. Then the bombers were on us, pouring down their rain of fire and bombs – the train was alight, our ammunition exploded and the petrol dump poured out its bilge of smoke – and then peace for a moment, the batteries were silent and one of the Naval epics was over; indeed Narvik was a picnic for the men who had been there too …'

After his own family, he was closest to David Wintour's, so Jock was determined to serve Britain in order to prevent people like David's parents and sisters becoming just another military or civilian statistic. David had proved to be a compassionate cornerstone of the winning Eights team, and wrote two good novels after being awarded the poetry prize at Oxford; except for his family and the memories, that was all that was left of him.

Was this to be another condoned slaughter of an entire generation? Press barons, bankers, industrialists and politicians had a great deal to answer for. He had better be careful what he said out loud: half of MI6 seemed to be from the City. This was reason enough to meet with Canaris in order to cease the drubbing that the British were experiencing. The governing classes, no better than grunting parliamentarians, were as well ensconced in Intelligence as the military, but their ideas still seemed no match for Hitler's mobile and armoured forces that had swept through most of Europe. Hadn't they read J.F.C. Fuller's writings that pre-dated the Blitzkrieg, or even *The Art of War*?

'C' scribbled a note in a margin of his file and glanced up at Jock. He looked deadly serious. 'What on earth do you make of a country that's produced Luther, Beethoven and Kant, but has plunged the chances of civilisation down to an all-time low?'

'Kant's "Out of the crooked timber of humanity, no straight thing was ever made" seems to mean little to them, and yet I've left a lot of friends in Germany, sir. None of us can quite make it out. There's something deeply divided about the mentality of the Germans – an almost completely … black heart.'

'Didn't one of your relatives write a biography of Goethe?' Jock nodded. 'I thought so. Some of that philosophy's obviously rubbed off onto the Steels.'

'I also believe the situation to be urgent: "A General who is too stingy to spend generously on intelligence is not fit to be called a General."'

'C' gave a knowing look. 'A phrase after my own heart, but one I understand you could have coined yourself, Lieutenant?'

'Sun Tzu, sir.'

'Of course.'

'C' seemed reassured, and he knew that German Intelligence could only be checked by the best that Britain had to offer. If the Germans were bi-polar, wasn't that just what made them dangerous spies? A touch of the schizoid might also seem to be an essential quality. He wanted dedication, determination and raw courage to match the corruption of the Nazi state.

'Italy's activation of its pact with Germany will further threaten the security of the Mediterranean, with more sabre-rattling by Mussolini,' he went on. 'This country is almost alone, but Britain is pivotal to global events in a way that she has never totally been since the last war.' The forehead lines deepened. 'And perhaps never will be again. It would be no exaggeration to suggest that at present you are in a good position to help save the free world.'

'Is that all, sir?' Jock allowed himself some irony now.

'C' pressed on, seeming to ignore Jock's comment. 'If you decide to accept, Delahay will be your case officer. He'll be overall in charge of oper-ations. You'll be briefed about the details tomorrow. I'm giving you the opportunity to sleep on this, but I'm hoping very much that you'll take all three jobs.'

'Three missions, sir?'

'Well, there is a possibility that Canaris might want you to be a link man with the "Good Germans", some of whom are not always as secure as they should be. This would happen only if the first two objectives were achieved: locating the Broadway traitor and protecting the phantom forces in the desert from prying eyes.'

'In that case, I'd rather not be known as a "link man", sir, if that's alright with you? Isn't there a pro-German fifth-column group called "The Link"?'

'C' blinked a little. 'You're quite right, Steel – a tad thoughtless of me.'

Jock saw the photographic memory that had served 'C' so well, yet even so sharp a mind couldn't be expected to be infallible.

'C' quickly recovered from his faux pas. 'I know that you spent a considerable amount of time with Countess Solf at Villa Delos, and that you were for all intents and purposes an adopted member of the "Solf Circle" that was in embryonic form by the time you left Germany in '38. As long as such circles of opponents to Nazi rule show discretion, it is possible that your history with them will endear you to Canaris, and it may help us foster relationships that hitherto seem to have been blocked by our enemy within. It just might help us turn the clock back for Anglo-German relations.'

'I could not compromise Frau Solf's security in any way; she is a dear friend.'

'You might be able to kill two birds with one stone.'

'How, sir?'

'I understand your concerns, but you might be able to help her. She is, as you probably know, a neighbour of the two security chiefs, so she would need to be careful.'

'C' didn't elaborate. Jock had heard some of the rumours about Canaris, both in England and in Germany. Apparently, the Admiral had begun to surround himself with followers who were not especially competent, men who had very senior positions in the Fatherland's foreign intelligence. Opinion was divided about Canaris's loyalties. Some believed him to be a valued advisor of the Führer; others suspected him of working against the interests of Hitler's unfolding plans to dominate the globe. There were others who believed that the Admiral was capable of all these stances towards Hitler, and credited Canaris with purposefully creating some deputies who either appeared to be incompetent or in fact were so. Yet this seemed to be considered by 'C' to be part of Canaris's smoke and mirrors to appear loyal to Hitler, even if his Abwehr were thought of as inefficient by desperate SD men like Marz.

Canaris was complex. What plethora of deadly games was he playing? He certainly seemed to be playing his peers off one another. Perhaps he cared little for how history would remember any of his good deeds? A screen of corruption and incompetence would be a fairly reliable cover in the New Germany, with its Führer personifying the worst excesses of it himself. Jock wondered if Canaris, with his multiple roles and voices, was capable of covering all his diverse tracks, even the ones where he protected some of his men, who not only made peace overtures but, more significantly, were privy to some of the greatest strategic plans and policies of both Germany and its enemies. Jock couldn't resist the opportunity to see if he could verify some of the rumours that surrounded the Admiral. With Hitler's invasion of England pending, he had a duty to find out anything that might advance the cause of Britain.

Jock noticed another glimpse of the enigmatic 'C', half hidden in the background of a photo with a young woman in front of a hut on stilts, reminiscent of South East Asia – Malaya, perhaps? Jock looked around the office. A satinwood drinks cabinet rested majestically in front of the shaded bay windows. Essential equipment adorned the walls, and on either side of the glass were newly polished clocks with time zones from every major location between London and Sydney. Apart from the clocks and the combination safes, it looked more like Bond Street than Whitehall.

'You'll get back to soldiering, Steel – eventually,' 'C' said. 'If you accept, you'll be given a code name.' Then he became more serious again, and turned slowly towards Jock. 'Yet don't have any illusions. If you join this initiative, remember it will be disliked by some people in this building, and even some in Whitehall. The more it succeeds, Steel, the more others will dislike it and what we are trying to do. There are times when you may have to reveal something, but don't tell anyone more than you have to. The first thing to remember about people is that we know almost nothing about them; many of them are simply enigmas. Don't forget that Canaris is also your enemy and, while we don't want him replaced by an SD mandarin, we know that he is trying to subvert British authority in the Middle East. But that's his job.'

Jock saw the Chief of the Secret Intelligence Service's eyes flick in the direction of one of his three phones, and gauged that this was the moment to close the meeting. He stood up, shook hands and walked to the door.

The Whitehall chief delivered his punchline. 'Anyway, it'll be a lot better than guarding a gasworks for the duration.'

'Thank you, sir.' How did 'C' know about his worst fears?

The interview was definitely over. 'C' picked up his pipe, popped it into his mouth and grabbed a telephone.

CAIRO

LATE SUMMER
1940

A civilian aeroplane landed at Cairo airport. The staircase snapped into position soon after the aircraft came to an abrupt stop. The midday sun was warm, but the array of clothing around the first passenger who emerged from the plane didn't initially seem out of place, until it became clear to the welcoming plain-clothes officer that the person he was due to meet appeared to have jaundice. That was until on closer inspection he realised that it was a senior officer with a liberal helping of stage make-up, who was also wearing very loud orange-and-black plus-fours, dark glasses and a check cap over a mop of fair hair. Lieutenant-Colonel Clarke aimed to start as he meant to continue: weaving elaborate disguises, beginning with himself.

Clarke drawled, 'Hi, I'm Wrangel. Bumpy flight in those crates; it even had an outside toilet.'

'Hello, sir. I'm Major Tony Pemberton. I'll take the golf clubs, if you wish, sir?'

The Major from British Military Intelligence quickly shook the hand of his boss, grabbed his luggage and struggled to avoid looking furtive before swiftly whisking the new arrival into a taxi.

'I'm doing a little sketch on the Army of the Nile for the *Washington Post*.'

Pemberton whispered, 'Do you always disguise yourself so fully, sir?'

Clarke, in his screaming check trousers, was smaller in stature than his burly colleague and second-in-command, Pemberton, who couldn't help feeling a little touchy at Clarke's rather unconventional start to leading Deception in the Middle East.

Clarke smiled at Pemberton. 'I couldn't resist the camouflage. It's a bit over the top, but I thought it'll be a bloody miserable war otherwise.'

The cab managed to negotiate its way past wheeled and pedestrian traffic, crowded coffee shops, overburdened donkeys and noisy street sellers. There was a distinct smell of sweat mixed with ordure. Finally, they reached the sedate 'Grey Pillars', which housed HQ Cairo. Lieutenant-Colonel Clarke picked up some post and made a quick wardrobe change in the Officers' Mess, which surprised Pemberton, who was slightly unnerved by the way his boss silently entered the otherwise empty mess lobby in his shorts and said 'Ready when you are' not far away from him.

Pemberton was relieved to drive to the barracks at Kasr el Nil. He dropped Clarke off and wondered exactly what MI9, Escape and Evasion, was going to produce for Allied servicemen.

Lieutenant-Colonel Clarke was more than happy to see his colleague drive off in a state of perplexity. Lord Wavell, Commanding Officer, Middle East, was an enigma to his men and it might not hurt for Clarke to be like that too; MIRAGE would certainly need to be a conundrum to the enemy. In fact, MI9, Escape and Evasion, was just the official cover story for work that was 'Most Secret', although staff members were interchangeable. He soon learned that the key to his job of deception was not just getting the enemy to think the way you would like, but getting them to do what you wanted.

Clarke now knew he was being given a very special desk job to plan for his CO the continual and systematic hoodwinking of the enemy about British aims, intentions and capabilities. Only recently, Major-General Platt, with a territory almost the size of Europe to control, had told the Deception chief that he had little more than one man to each mile of frontier. Clarke fully realised that Platt was doing on a smaller scale what Wavell had to also achieve: attack as the best form of defence, with far fewer numbers. On paper, the British forces in 1940 were little more than a Robin Hood force facing hordes of Italian soldiers supported by increasing numbers of Germans. One man had to appear as a group of ten, being outnumbered by enemy men and machines three to one. Attacking irregularly and with small numbers at any time of day and night, disappearing, and sometimes calling the Italians' bluff by returning again to attack them behind enemy lines, all added to the enemy's uncertainty as to where the raid was going to come next, how and when. Clarke's boss must not be attacked without adequate armour and supplies. That's why he very much hoped that Agent MIRAGE would contact him imminently.

The new MI9 leader walked into one of the dirtiest alleys in the Kasr el Nil. As he went up some stone steps, he noticed that there were no windows looking out onto the street. Neither were there any fittings that could be stripped off the walls for a few piasters. When Clarke entered his new base, he found that he wasn't able to stand up straight. His moustache twitched as he inspected the paintwork and contours of the room with his usual care and efficiency, palms brushing slowly against the newly painted but uneven walls. It was then that he deduced that his office was a converted washroom. He ignored the rank smell that emanated from the floorboards, which a liberal dose of disinfectant barely disguised. Few senior officers would have regarded this move to a slum as a promotion. But it dawned on Dudley Clarke that in one sense he had come home: he really was going to operate from an ideal centre for controlling one of the greatest plans for Deception that the war was now presenting to any of its combatants.

He picked up the phone and asked several of his men to report to his office. Almost immediately, he set to work and started sketching out proposed positions for notional armies that he planned to use in order to convince the Italians that thousands more British soldiers existed and so ensure that the enemy believed the British could match the numbers of the Italians' six divisions.

Clarke also began to create a meticulous filing system, and took out two photographs from his attaché case and a magnifying glass, which he placed next to his pipe. He then returned to his sketches – the left-hand side for British forces, the other side for the enemy. He carefully wrote out each of the units he knew both sides possessed, including their 'order of battle'. With different-coloured crayons, he wrote in the notional brigades and divisions that the enemy might be persuaded to believe that the British kept in the Middle East. The first of these fictitious units was 'A' Force.

His office was made ready for the first active soldiers under his command to pay an initial visit. Nothing was too much of a chore in the intelligence war. The bathroom's conversion into an office below the brothel, and its location, were further manifestations of the resourcefulness of MI9: they showed flexibility, adaptability, imagination, perseverance, theatricality and plain bluff – characteristics he hoped epitomised much of his work. It did seem a perfect cover; no one gave a second glance to the daily or nocturnal visits from various officers and civilians.

There was a knock at the door.

'Come in.' Clarke might have said 'Enter', but he wasn't going to be anything other than supportive to the few men that he had under his command.

Two soldiers entered. The first, Captain Jones, was academic, bald and rather scrawny-looking. The portly Captain Parry followed in his wake, and they both stood to attention.

Clarke asked them to sit down on a couple of stools. 'Good afternoon, Captains Parry and Jones. Please be so kind as to take one of these photographs each and study it.'

Both captains did as they were requested and sat gazing at the prints while Clarke lit his pipe.

Parry spoke while Jones's jaw was dropping. 'But they are of Stonehenge, sir.'

'Precisely, Captain Parry. Agree, Jones?'

'Yes, sir.'

'Good.' Clarke's oval face beamed at them. 'So why are we looking at patterns in the earth around the druid site?'

Jones and Parry looked at each other for inspiration. The senior officer watched them shift uncomfortably on their small seats, but, being generous by nature, he eventually put them out of some of their discomfort.

He raised his thick eyebrows and sighed. 'No, this isn't an image for use by the Home Guard, but it is of great interest to us in Egypt. Look at the bottom right corner of the photographs. The marks on those pictures, taken from two thousand feet, show trails miles away from Stonehenge that the worshippers made before finally erecting their considerable stones. Do you see, gentlemen? This is what we have all got to get used to now.'

The officers stared at each other, still nonplussed. The photographs were hastily studied and turned this way and that. Their boss forced them to think, but eventually enlightened them.

'Every journey leaves a footprint. The tracks of an army, especially, leave conspicuous markings quite different from the activities of non-combatants: flattening the grass by playing rounders on a June day in England will create marks for days, if not weeks; the runs across a field can be photographed from high in the sky. The desert offers almost no natural cover and armies leave their own distinctive patterns in the earth that they mess in. There are even scars from previous battles which can be cover for future battles. Our job will be to hide some evidence of military movement from enemy photo-reconnaissance, but perhaps the most useful role for camouflage in the desert is less concealment and more planting and displaying things that don't actually exist: false but distinctive signs of movement that we want the Hun to look at, hear, and act upon.' Clarke puffed merrily away at his pipe. 'All Intelligence essentially requires is the hiding from the enemy's eyes and ears of what we don't want them to know, and suggesting to them what we want the Hun to think about and listen to.' Clarke stood up and blew a series of perfect smoke rings. 'There's little point in staying in the city. Our task is to acquaint ourselves with as much terrain as possible. I suggest that Captain Parry takes northern Egypt and Libya, leaving the rest of Egypt and the Sudan for you, Captain Jones.'

Parry looked anxious. 'Will we be helped for other areas, sir?'

'Yes, of course. I hope we will be joined by another officer who can cover Transjordan and Palestine,' Clarke hastily added. 'Dummy tracks, parachutists, tanks, railways, latrines, planted letters, agents' gossip and fake divisional radio transmissions will all help the deception that will be part of your very own "film set" on the grand scale. Two and a half million square yards of rabbit fence and a hundred and twenty million square yards of coloured hessian cloth arrives today. The paint should be here tomorrow.'

The two captains looked at each other, exhaled some of Clarke's smoke which now occupied most of the room, cleared their throats and, managing a smile, chirped in unison, 'Thank you, sir.'

Yet Parry looked concerned. 'What colour is the paint, sir?'

49

'It's a sort of Worcester sauce colour, Captain.' Clarke exuded gratitude. 'The NAAFI's been most generous, I'd say.'

Parry had by now turned rather pale. 'I'm allergic to Worcester sauce, sir.'

'Don't worry yourself, Captain. You won't be drinking the stuff, and anyway it's being thinned out a little.'

Parry's Adam's apple bobbed up and down. 'Oh, that's alright, then, sir.'

'The only thing, chaps, is that once the 8,000 tons of Egyptian home-made paint arrives, you are going to build and paint your "desert film production" pretty much on your own.' Clarke looked more serious. 'Lastly, your work here is top secret. The enemy has a habit of appearing in the guise of belly dancers, snake-charmers, small boys and barmen, all hanging on any words that might pass your lips, gentlemen. You will be supported by an intelligence officer, a Lieutenant Steel. Co-operate carefully with him: it might just save all our skins in this nest of spies.'

LONDON

LATE SUMMER

1940

On the walk down the Strand, Jock's otherwise buoyant mood evaporated a little when he sensed that he was being tailed again. There was a suit behind him with little or no face, for the man seemed to rotate his trilby-hatted head one way and another every time Jock tried to pick up a reflection in the glass that window-shopping provided. Jock decided not to cross to the right and over the road to Southampton Street. Instead, he suddenly made a sharp left into Carting Street, where he could obliquely observe pedestrians behind him without being seen. If it was the Embankment stalker, then it was time to confront him in a nearby alley. Yet as he stepped down into the narrow street, literally watching his step in front and behind him, he saw that there was now no one where he had just been walking. Jock inched his way back into the Strand and checked his sartorial elegance and any nearby activity in the window of the Savoy Taylors. There were a few late diners, but no one on their own lurking in the shadows. He crossed over into Southampton Street and then left into Maiden Lane.

Walking into Rules, he spotted Maurice Delahay at a secluded table directly ahead, at the end of the restaurant where he had his pick of entrances and exits. Delahay, Jock's handler, was buying Jock lunch and was sitting beneath two ebony Nubian statues flanking an ornate mantel clock. Jock usually preferred to arrive at least ten minutes early for most appointments, remembering Hamlet's watchword, 'the readiness is all'.

He was ushered towards a chair next to a framed lithograph of the actor Garrick.

'Good to see you again, Steel. Since it has warmed up a bit, I suggest Pimm's.'

When it was a question of judging the character of a particular agent, Maurice Delahay usually made up his own mind within a few moments of their entering a room. As the waiter drew back a chair for the arrival, Delahay gave Jock a big, wide smile that gave away nothing of the import of this meeting. Apart from a characterless diner three tables away, most of the clientele that evening sat on the other side of the long bar.

'This isn't on the department, by the way. I don't want you to get the wrong impression about MI6 excesses,' Delahay said, before adding with another smile, 'Judging from the meeting with Hollings, there's little chance of you having any illusions about that, though. No, this is just something I always do for my new boys. Entrées?'

'The Killearn salmon looked good on my way in.'

Two double Pimm's arrived.

'Ah, a man after my own heart. We are going to get along, Jock. Cheers … May I call you Jock?'

'Of course.'

'It's Maurice to you.'

Jock began to feel that this might be a union between would-be spy and master without any pre-nuptial agreement.

'Like you,' Delahay went on, 'I'm an ex-colonial – Cape Town – and don't stand very much on ceremony.'

Delahay took in Jock's height, stature and bearing, alert eyes, high cheekbones and swarthy looks, and noted that this was a man who would not easily disappear in a crowd. Not exactly ideal, but on the other hand there weren't many crowds in the desert where Jock was bound.

Jock thought about the caveats that his Uncle Herbert had given him about British Intelligence. 'As you say, I'm aware that we have been neglecting aspects of our defence. Only about a year ago, MI6's expenditure was no more than the cost of maintaining a single Royal Naval destroyer …'

'Really?' Delahay chimed in, looking suitably impressed.

'In home waters.'

Smiling, Delahay said, 'Goodness, I'm glad you're not our auditor. Of course, what the enemy underestimates is that we consider passionate fighting men come first, and expensive new machines, second – which brings me on to you, Jock.' A quick glance and another smile helped place the order.

Jock hadn't been idle in the past few days. He had discovered that Hollings was originally from MI5 and had 'scraped' into the echelons of MI6 after calling in some favours. Apparently, Hollings hadn't been with Six for very long and was rumoured to be piloting a grand operation to make a name for himself. In such circumstances, Jock preferred to emulate the wisdom and daring of the ancient hero Theseus, rather than the plight of the unfortunate virgin Iphigenia. He had no intention of being drawn into a hair-brained scheme or sacrificed to help a senior officer justify his rank and position in the service by becoming a martyr so that wind could be put in the sails of misguided top brass and their conflicts.

Entrées arrived swiftly. Jock was glad to be away from Broadway Buildings so that he could air his doubts. 'I want to know from the outset the extent of Hollings's involvement. I have been followed to meetings with him, and he has little idea who it might have been.'

Delahay's eyes widened a little. 'There was no leak on my side.' He tasted his salmon and poured ample quantities of pepper onto it. 'You didn't think much of your induction?' The spymaster looked up and was quiet for a moment. His cornflower-blue eyes were brisk and alert. 'I can have a word with him, if you like?'

'No, I just wanted you to know why I haven't been jumping at the Colonel's suggestions.'

Delahay changed gear easily. 'Do you like venison? From the High Pennines … Are you a hunting man, Jock?'

'I prefer stalking deer to hunting them, but I do both.'

'Oh, yes? Where?'

'Blair Atholl.'

'Black Watch Country.'

The strong smell of the venison wafted over from the plates of a passing waiter and settled the two men's next choice of course. A little paranoia was convincing Jock that the last few months were part of some British voodoo played on him. Was Hollings's opaque manner a ruse to test him out? Or to make him take flight at the very uncertain way his new career was developing? He snapped out of this seemingly indulgent thought; he was being wined and dined, and weren't spies supposed to have a healthy dose of paranoia about them? Wasn't that part of the essential survival kit?

Maurice Delahay was a regular, and indicated to the punctilious maître d' that they were ready for their plates to be cleared. There were niggling doubts in Jock's overactive mind about watchers, who he was convinced were continuing to tail him. Yet he'd probably said enough already to his new masters to set a cat among the pigeons. Jock would have to follow his own leads while he remained in England, although that wouldn't be for much longer if he took on all 'C''s missions. He might even wrong-foot the traitor before he left for Spain.

It would be an incredible coup to expose the Broadway Buildings traitor, let alone achieve anything else. Everything seemed to depend on that. The more he questioned his predicament, the greater became his determination to solve the mystery. He had been brought on board all along to turn up MI6's bad penny, even though safeguarding MI9's notional armies was also important. That explained why he had been given access to 'C' … Yet that meant that the traitor in MI6's midst could be very senior indeed. Access to Majoribanks was the trump card that Jock could play to ensure that he wasn't compromised by a senior official who had slipped through the net of security checks. He regretted that this was not a sealed operation with only 'C' and Delahay involved. He played devil's advocate: perhaps there were two double agents working in tandem … Or maybe a traitor preoccupied with work rivals' business and on the way up the Intelligence greasy pole rather than keeping tabs on him? That seemed as likely. Jock hoped that he apparently fitted the bill for the protection of Egypt's security so well that a double agent might well drop their guard while attempting to stop either of Jock's missions abroad ever coming to fruition.

The main course arrived. Jock was looking across the restaurant deep in thought.

'Don't let the venison go cold.' Delahay spoke with enthusiasm and passion, like a minister at a baptism. It was a 'baptism', wasn't it? Jock would make sure that Delahay would never officiate in any other rites – a funeral, for instance: *his funeral.* He took heart from the fact that, apart from, potentially, child-rearing, nothing between now and the grave would be as elementally important or as pleasurable as protecting civilisation. Jock would have no truck with Last Suppers. He wanted to live. He also wanted to take his venison more slowly, but he was incredibly hungry.

With natural bonhomie, and not a little mettle, Jock raised his glass. 'Here's to an end to Blitzkrieg abroad.'

The delicious smell of the thick red liquid sent his mind reeling again. The taste of so much compressed sun in the grape of the 1933 bottle of Nuit-Saint-Georges slid down to the core of his body. He missed the heat of Australia, where he had spent his youth; he'd be glad of the opportunity to travel to hotter climes again, courtesy of His Majesty the King.

Delahay ordered a ten-year-old Château d'Yquem with the strawberries and spoke quietly again. 'I know about the traitor, Jock, if that's what you have been thinking? I have to.' He paused. 'It's not me, by the way.'

Jock stared at the light behind Delahay's eyes. 'Who is it then?'

'Who knows? I have to be sure what you are thinking, or I'm done for. At this rate, if we are not totally honest, then we'll all be done for. I never thought I'd say that to a recruit, but this is a predicament for British security that I've never encountered before. You might feel at times like a minnow swimming against the tide, but the bigger fish don't even recognise the waters. What we have here is of gargantuan proportions – a veritable intelligence tidal wave.' Delahay confirmed Jock's own table of tasks. 'Internal security is our priority; Clarke's phantom forces safeguarding their military illusion is next; and maintaining Canaris's pro-democracy stance is a political consideration that frankly still isn't a priority for the PM – but it's a three-pronged programme.'

'It doesn't make for very good propaganda, having an enthusiastic group of ex-Nazis suing for peace, does it?'

'Agreed. Of course, that's your pigeon, isn't it? You were responsible for helping to bring Salazar into neutrality at Hanover Square. Lord Lloyd must have been pleased with you.'

'I sweet-talked Salazar's wife, if that's what you mean.'

'Yes, well done.' He coughed and stifled a laugh. 'Not everyone could, from what I've heard.' Delahay savoured a sip of the Sauternes. 'The British Council isn't the only institution that is grateful to you. But it's more than that – Canaris persuaded Franco in Spain to stay out of Hitler's war, and you've helped match that contribution with Portugal's neutrality. Don't forget to mention that to the Admiral, will you?'

'No, sir.'

'Come on, Jock, drop the formality. Cigarette?'

Jock had been won over, yet declined with a wave of two slightly yellowed smoker's fingers; he was on one of his fitness drives. He didn't want to be dependent on anything at the moment – except perhaps Delahay. He was going to have to trust him. He was being given the chance to locate the enemy before anyone else. He wanted to get out of London; it was too dangerous for him for too many reasons. It was Jock they wanted, not Delahay, 'C' or anyone else for that matter. Few soldiers now had time for leisure and introspection, as the letter he had received from Boulogne reflected. Soldiers were more positive and direct. Jock, with his MI6 role, had time to mull over his situation, which was enough to be going on with at the moment.

He'd made his decisions. 'As I suggested to "C", I won't need to think this all over, Maurice. I'm in on all these missions. May I be so bold as to suggest a name for them, if I am, as you suggest, the cornerstone of them all?'

'Of course, I'll put your suggestion forward, Jock; there's a list of names we often use.' Delahay wore his courtesy like an old school tie and displayed his wide white smile again.

'Why don't we call it Operation Phantom?'

Jock's handler swiftly ordered a malt. 'How appropriate. Sounds good to me.'

It was easy to talk with Jock, Delahay thought, as it always was with men of unusual talent – not that he had yet had the chance to observe all the arrows in Jock's quiver. He was also reassured by the new agent's grasp of the tortuous diplomatic game that Whitehall was playing with the 'Good Germans'. It was understandable from a soldier and fledgling spy (most operational ones were fledglings) that a clear picture of what Jock was up against was part of his excellent psychological comprehension. Few of the department had observed Hitler and Goebbels at close quarters, and Delahay knew that Jock had also been introduced to their SS and SD acolytes on numerous occasions. In order for a man to fight well, he had to know as much about his opposition as possible, and the support with which they functioned. As Delahay looked at the eagerness of the man opposite him, he realised that although Jock's virtues were in no doubt – and that made him a reliable operative – the greatest test would be his ability to fully garner the craft of the spy.

Delahay felt there were still some points to cover. 'I'm sure that you've looked over Canaris's file. He'll be more relaxed in his favourite location, but don't be surprised if his Abwehr soldiers are nearby. Though he'll probably be content to be protected by his favourite bodyguard, Mohammed.'

Jock only reassured Delahay on the points of virtue with, 'I want to make it clear, though, that I am eventually returning to soldiering. I want to complete a sniper's course with Bill MacDonald at Bisley.'

'There's just time for you to do that, and it will support your training as MIRAGE. We've had this agent name on our slate for months and at last we've managed to fill it – with you.'

'This will be your code name, we haven't a code number for you yet. Actually, we want you to go back to No. 8 Commando quicker than you think – but just for a brief period. I understand that you will be joining several commando units not far from your family in Argyll. While you're in Scotland, we'd like you to build upon the Bisley course at Inverailort House. It's part of a unique small-arms programme that should be invaluable.' Delahay seemed mischievous. 'Seriously, though, it'll help you match your opposite number, Marz. He attended such a course in Shanghai before the war. Your instructors are meticulous and will have some notes on his strengths and weaknesses in hand guns and silent killing.' He managed a heartfelt smile. 'We've got to give you some advantages.'

The maître d' brought the peat-smoked whisky.

'You will be contacted at Inverailort,' Delahay went on. 'Between you and me, I'm glad that you wish to eventually return to soldiering, Jock. In some ways, the early years of this game are always the easiest. The secrecy hasn't had time to build up with the suppressed hysteria of deciding which of the multiple lives you are reflecting in the wilderness of mirrors.'

SCOTLAND

AUTUMN 1940

I

Dawn crept through the ruins of smoking London. In the half-light of the early morning, Jock picked his way through the shards of glass on the pavements of King's Cross. As he did so, the young officer heard a grave voice from the shell of a building behind him. 'Guvnor, give us a hand, would you?' It was an ambulance driver with helmet akimbo, doing all he could to shift a collapsed wall. 'There's somebody under there, sir.' Burst mains were flooding the street and the water would endanger anyone trapped at ground level.

Memories came back to Jock of his holiday in Germany with his brother David, who had slipped off their tandem bicycle and landed beneath the massive wheel of a farmer's horse-drawn cart. Jock had employed what spectators by the roadside had described as superhuman strength to prevent his brother's demise by lifting up the cart singlehandedly. Now, with much effort, the two men heaved up large sections of brickwork that should have taken the muscle power of twice their number. Bare-skinned legs were just visible.

'I could have sworn I heard a whimper,' the ambulance driver said.

Jock carefully pulled away sections of brick. He revealed a young woman below them. He pushed the rest of the wall away to prevent it falling back. He saw them: a mother and her baby, white as snow. The mother held the infant wrapped around her side, and they lay as if asleep.

At last the driver spoke: 'They're gone'. He looked up with moist brown eyes, which now had darkening rings around them. 'Thank you, sir.'

Jock thought of the funeral that awaited the father, a serviceman no doubt. This senseless violence suffered by these innocents just made him more determined to shorten the war – 1940 was proving to be the nightmare that had been predicted. He seriously questioned whether the London he knew would actually still be here on his return.

Jock boarded the train from the battered and beleaguered city for Scotland. He had booked a berth for two. He unpacked his bag on the bottom bunk, placed a cutlass, still in its sheath – his preferred shaver – on the bed and shed his sports jacket. After a strenuous round of press-ups, which was about all he had room for under the sink of his cosy but modest compartment, he treated himself to a read of *The Times*. It started to drizzle outside. Plenty of recruits dropped out of the training programme that Delahay had outlined for him, and the course was something that he might have dreamt up for himself: Jock versus the elements, which included foul play along with the foul weather.

The reward of a look at the paper was a mixed blessing. The front page of the paper made sobering reading. After the elation following the narrow squeak of the Battle of Britain, England remained an incredibly vulnerable outpost of civilisation. The Channel might have helped delay Hitler's invasion, but it could not stop the Blitz. Admiral Donitz's successful new tactics were tucked away on page four. That week in October, German U-boats had sunk more Allied shipping than ever before: thirty ships from two convoys were destroyed in forty-eight hours. You didn't need to be a mathematician to work out that Britain was losing merchant ships at a faster rate than they could be replaced. Jock did not relish the thought of travelling by sea that autumn as 'wolf-pack' tactics sent aquatic hounds out on a 'radio leash' from the coast of France. Donitz would radio orders as to which targets to attack, at speed, by night, from above not below the waves, evading the naval escort's direction-finding equipment, and often outnumbering the convoy's armed escorts. There were no British long-range aircraft available yet to protect the unarmed merchant vessels. It was now more dangerous to serve as a merchant seaman than in any branch of the regular British Armed Services.

Yet the war on land was also hazardous. Jock knew that his specialist course in the Highlands could also be helpful to the commando role that he wanted after Operation Phantom was completed. He knew that it was going to take more than a four-day course to survive in the desert. He thought ahead, beyond the self-indulgence of career-gazing, to the maintenance of a gathering alliance of civilised powers which had yet to declare themselves in support of Britain. To gain friends, the British needed results. Unless an antidote to superior Axis air forces could be found in the Mediterranean, the lone British fight would be dead in the water. Jock knew he had a mission in Egypt once Marz was out of the frame.

II

There was a knock on the cabin door.

'Tickets, please.'

The train guard? The voice seemed rather strange and high-pitched. Jock checked his cutlass was to hand and very slowly opened the sliding door. Peering in at him was no vocally challenged inspector, but a giggling Madeleine, his new girlfriend from Somerville College, who again repeated her request in as gruff a voice as she could muster, before collapsing with more laughter into Jock's cabin. Madeleine moved with liquid grace. She was still laughing as Jock held her now with a hand on each shoulder, taking in her natural beauty: her high forehead and cheekbones, the radiant dark-blue eyes that beamed back at him and the full lower lip of a guileless smile that now seductively lapsed into mischief.

She was wearing the pearls that he had given her at their last soiree at the George Hotel in Oxford. He slid the door back the whole way before he lifted her into the berth. If his cases hadn't been organised on the lower bunk he might have collapsed onto it with her, but as the train pulled out of London, he knew that he had time on his side. If he couldn't trust Madeleine, it was indeed going to be a very long war. This pang of aware-ness conflicted with a realisation that regarding everyone as a potential liar was probably the best way to survive his new roles in an extended conflict. *Could he really do this with Madeleine?*

'How did you find me?'

'You remember my girlfriend Angelika?' Jock nodded. 'She has a friend at the British Council who made a few enquiries on my behalf.'

Jock hid his feelings, which were a combination of intense pleasure at the proximity of the Oxford beauty – without a chaperone this time – and annoyance that he seemed to have been tracked and trailed. Angelika's source may well have been Cummings, an ex-colleague at the British Council whom Jock had spotted at the Somerville Ball. He was usually ill, but clearly not too indisposed to reveal Jock's private life, which Cummings knew more about than most, and that probably included the Secret Intelligence Service. If two undergraduates studying languages could locate him so easily, what chance had he got with the likes of Marz?

Jock did his best to disguise his frosty enquiry with a gentle but firm, 'Who else knows you are on this train, Madeleine?'

'Only Angelika.'

'Good.' Jock didn't want to cool the start of their reunion. 'By the way, you never told me that Angelika could lip-read.' He laughed. 'It nearly proved embarrassing when we were last all together.'

'But Jock, *I* can lip-read. Didn't you know? That's how Angelika and I first began to know each other. We both had hearing problems when we were young.'

More relaxed now, Jock said, 'You are a lady of mystery, Madeleine. Still, you can't stay on this train, darling.'

'I didn't think "can't" was part of your vocabulary, Jock.'

'No, you're right.'

'Can.' Madeleine grinned.

'Why?'

'This is going all the way up to Glasgow. Buses to Tarbert for me.'

'You have to leave me from there.'

'I know. Daddy lives in Argyll.'

She leant forward to gaze out of the window. Her blue skirt rode up a little on an athlete's thigh, and he could see the curve of her breasts in the camisole top. Jock felt a chest-shifting surge of attraction. The land was still incredibly flat, but this signalled just how far away they were from their Highland destinations, a unique opportunity for both of them to share a long, uninterrupted journey – in more senses than one. He might never see Madeleine again, and he wondered if theirs might be a match that was not only made in heaven, but also entirely restricted to it. He censured himself for such a thought, but the fact was that life was becoming increasingly dangerous, whether you were a civilian or a serviceman. It haunted him that this might be all that they would ever share together.

Jock made her look at him, but Madeleine was serious now. 'Anyway, I have plenty of good cause to be here. He isn't at all well.'

'I'm sorry.'

'Don't be – he drinks too much.'

He could see the hurt in her eyes; she hated being let down. Yet she didn't indulge her sense of loss for a father she hardly knew any more: her blue eyes welled up momentarily, but then Jock basked in a return of her still-sunny smile. Madeleine was the most unselfish person he had ever met. For someone who was barely twenty, Madeleine was everything that she appeared to be: sincere, sensuous, enlightened and generous to a fault.

'I wasn't allowed to take any detours or connections north of Fort William,' she said. 'So I gathered it was an area that was reserved for Lieutenant Steel.' She made a mock salute but fell about with more buoyant laughter, which gradually subsided into a quiet but husky voice. 'It's going to be dangerous work, isn't it?'

'I don't know. Why do you say that, Madeleine? It has to be more riveting than night exercises behind obsolete equipment in Burnham-on-Crouch. If you don't know everything about my life, then my faith is restored in the security of at least part of this small island.'

'I can't restore all of your faith, Jock.'

'Sit down a moment.'

'What's the matter?'

'You're not telling me everything, are you?'

Madeleine stared at him, mouth open, hardly breathing. 'No. No, Jock, I'm not ... I wanted to talk with you but ... you've been so busy.'

'What's happened?'

'I'm no longer studying at Somerville College.'

'Why ever not?'

'I felt so useless there. Should I tell you that Molière's *Tartuffe* fails to touch my sense of humour, but that he is at least very cunning, with a clear eye for human frailty?'

Jock still felt Madeleine was hiding something. 'So, is he a bit like some of the students studying him?'

'You don't really believe that?'

'I'm not sure right now. Tell me why you're here?'

'I do have a confession to make. Please don't be cross.'

'Alright … Fire away.'

Madeleine managed a smile. 'That's the turn of phrase one might expect from the Welsh Guards' Weapons Training Officer.'

'So, what of it?'

'Well, once I knew that you were going abroad, but not with your Guardsmen, I realised that it was unlikely that you were going as a soldier. I asked myself, why would the Weapons Training Officer be left behind?'

'To train the new recruits?'

'But I've checked … There's a new Weapons Training Officer starting in your place, and you are due to travel abroad – where else would an exceptional Guardsman be bound for? To defeat Hitler, you especially would have to be on the front line.'

Jock conceded the little he had been forced to. 'It's you who have some explaining to do, Madeleine. So, I'm a soldier involved in Intelligence. There's nothing strange about that.'

'Don't worry. I'm not a detective who has to know absolutely every single detail.'

Jock returned her smile. 'Perhaps not, though you're making quite a good job of it from where I stand.'

Madeleine blushed a little. 'I suppose so … But I'm not going to pry, except to say that I've decided to apply for the same outfit that I believe you're in, and while I'm waiting, I'm doing something useful with my languages and incomplete degree.'

'Like what, exactly?'

'I've joined a clandestine group in MI5. I realised that you were doing something in Intelligence because of your imminent posting abroad. I was able to check that you were not listed with the rest of your commando unit on any of the troop ships due to sail at the end of the year. That means something, doesn't it, Jock?'

Jock remonstrated, but it was no use.

'Don't tell me it doesn't mean anything,' Madeleine said. 'What's been interesting for me is that I've already discovered things in my group that are disconcerting and may actually have a bearing on what you yourself are being tasked to work on. The only thing is that I'm a junior there, and probably the only person I know who would not dismiss what I've already discovered – *is you.*'

'Go on.'

'So, I'm making tea for the personal assistant of one of the divisions there. He kept a file on his desk in the adjacent office – a "Most Secret" file of agents operating within foreign embassies that reflected the Service's preoccupation with the leakage of information to the Nazis. The next day, I noticed it was still on his desk, and it struck me as odd. Was he lazy? Careless? The detailed dossier, along with the secret history of MI5, was prepared for internal consumption only, and was hugely sensitive. The personal assistant can't have missed the red lettering at the top that says "Destroy immediately after use". Even I know that files of that nature are a priority for a careful but swift viewing before filing or destroying.'

Jock listened with some incredulity and nodded for Madeleine to continue.

'At the point of discovering all this, I realised that I had a duty … to snoop myself.' Ignoring Jock's concerned look, she went on. 'I realise a destroyed file would avoid identifying and potentially compromising so many valued sources. In the file were the names of the British officials in Madrid who were responsible for gathering and disseminating secret intelligence by the British on the Iberian Peninsula that was consistent with the anti-fascist personnel's mission of keeping Spain neutral and under the control of Sir Samuel Hoare, the British Ambassador. Apart from feeling distinctly cynical about the outfit I'd recently joined, I kept thinking about you. This personal assistant is not following any elementary office codes. I started thinking … If he's not doing that, what else is he up to?'

'I understand that,' Jock said, looking out of the small carriage window. He turned to Madeleine. 'Also, what is he actually doing? What principles or codes is he following?'

'And for whom? He's certainly not working for your old boss, Lord Lloyd. I knew how proud you were to personally support the British Council initiative to keep Portugal neutral. Having achieved all that, here was this assistant jeopardising the other half of the Iberian Peninsula, and all those brave agents in the process.'

Jock was concerned. 'It could be inefficiency, but I have my doubts about that. If he is suspect, then it's his word against yours. You're up against the old-boy network, Madeleine. The way things work at present is that any declaration of your concern would leave you in an unenviable position of vulnerability, given what you have told me – and in spite of it. My advice is to delay your transfer to anywhere else for the moment and make a note of anything untoward – but don't do that at work, and don't keep it in your home.'

Madeleine whispered, 'This could affect everything … Us?'

Jock caressed her forehead and spoke quietly. 'Yes, my darling, it could.'

They said nothing for a while. Then Jock took her hand in his and continued: 'But I am deeply grateful to you for finding me, keeping what seems to me be another ghastly secret of this grotesque war, and for being brave enough to consider staying on in the job. That's a true friend …' Jock turned to her and was very serious. 'But … let me tell you now … that it is entirely up to you, Madeleine, whether you wish to stay on in your clandestine group. What you have just told me has been extraordinarily helpful to me already. I won't be giving this information out to anyone without talking to you first. If you wish, I won't involve you if we agree to divulge this, and in that case it would not be before your transfer to another organisation. If I've missed something in how we deal with your account, I'm sure you'll tell me. If you ever need to talk about it again, let's ideally talk alone, or preferably use a phone box, because if you're working in an office with a traitor, someone might just listen in to any telephone conversations – not just from your workplace, but also any made from your home.'

The scale of the new pressures that Madeleine's information presented to the couple began to dawn upon them both.

She sighed. 'Sometimes I actually wish I was studying *Tartuffe.*'

They laughed. Jock had nearly finished his homily and warnings. 'Tell me something about the personal assistant to your boss.'

'He's called Blynde. He's an art-lover. He's rather aloof, rather grand, in a quiet sort of way. He makes a good cup of tea. Probably drinks like a fish.' Madeleine smiled. 'Not a suitor, Jock, so you needn't have that added worry. He doesn't crave the company of women, as far as I can make out. He does have a friend, called Harkiss, but perhaps that's nothing important ...'

'Keep your professional distance. Be careful. If you think it's in the national interest and might strengthen your case, ask him to show you some art, preferably in a public place – outside office time. I can't think of anything else right now. I'm staring at the most beautiful woman I've ever seen in my life ...'

Jock saw that Madeleine looked both worried and excited; he wanted her to rest and sit, but he stood up and desired her close to him. Madeleine stood too, her cheeks flushed, and her eyes watered as she collapsed onto his chest. 'Oh, Jock.'

Her voice was still muffled, as it had been when she first surprised him, but it was maudlin this time, barely containing her own emotion. She sobbed quietly. 'I've been worried sick about you. I know you've written whenever you could, but you've been so remote recently, and I wondered ...'

Jock again felt Madeleine might be holding something back but he couldn't resist her. His chest heaved with an inhalation of the musty Tweed scent he had bought her on their last meeting. He rested his back against the porcelain behind him, and lifted her chin up as she moved with him.

'How remote do you feel now?' he said.

Her face was slightly streaked as glistening cheeks began to wreak havoc with the minimal make-up that she allowed herself; she looked all the more gorgeous for it.

'Not very.'

She bit her lower lip. Jock stood entranced as the pupils in Madeleine's eyes enlarged as her face lit up again with the dawning of another radiant smile – something he had sorely missed during the months of square-bashing and weapons training.

She opened a petite, navy-blue leather handbag, and took out a letter and a small package. Her voice was trembling.

'I want you to read to me.' She moved lithely out of his grasp and handed over an envelope addressed in bold black ink, then sat on the little space at the edge of the bottom bunk. 'It's from your recent letter,' she said, smiling now, her mouth wide open, 'where you wrestle with your love for me, and the fantastic form that our love might take.'

He knew that life had seemed perfectly pleasant for Madeleine when there had been no one to preoccupy her thoughts. What had she said after their first meeting? *You quite tickled my curiosity and I need to see you again.*

Fry's chocolate was proffered to the letter writer.

'That's treasure,' said Jock, taking the confectionery, then fishing a card from his wallet. 'This is a telephone number where you can leave a discreet message for me to contact you in an emergency. Keep it safe.' He took the letter from her. 'You know, you're a much better writer than I am. You should be reading your letters to me.'

'Are you seducing me with your charm and persistence?'

'Not exactly … I just love it when you are yourself, like now. I don't think Angelika always is, much as I'm fond of her. When you are like this, you're magnificent. If you tried to be someone else, you'd no longer be first-rate.'

'You are different to other Oxford men, Jock.'

'Perhaps …' He slipped off the foil from the chocolate, and carefully placed a piece in her open mouth before popping one into his own. 'I just like my women to keep raising *another* bar for me, even if they do spot my weakness – a bribe … How delicious.' He smiled conspiratorially. 'Who's seducing whom?'

Madeleine giggled. 'Somehow you make me feel like a very superior and refined prostitute. Now you can say "can't". I want you to read something from the letters of our mystically entwined lives that we've christened Joy Street: you *can't* refuse me, Jock. I'm travelling a long way to be here with you, and I've just persuaded the guard to point to the sleeping berth of a man fitting your description.'

Jock was genuinely curious. 'How? That's what I'd like to know.'

'I told him that we were eloping to Scotland.'

'My darling minx.' Jock grinned, but then in mock seriousness he paused for theatrical effect (having earned the moment's silence). 'Did you let the guard cut a caper with you?' *Perhaps Madeleine was a better liar than he had to become?* Yet he saw no deception, just a rare opportunity to soak in a physical closeness that flushed through his every fibre like spiritual champagne. 'Give me the letter and find a pew on the end of this top bunk so I can see your eyes properly. At the moment I can only see your cleavage, however splendid it is looking at you as you chuckle away in that delicious blouse of yours.' Jock hoisted her onto the bed. 'Ready?' And he began to read:

We stepped out of our clothes and slid together into the lake.
It was as though we had entered through a secret door in the
bank below the surface, the water touching every part of us,
pouring in at the laughing mouth, swirling softly, full-bodied
down inside, making the chest heave and glow to its depths
with the inspiration of the new element. Movement was
deliciously easy, just a turn of the wrist, a bending of the knee
and you moved as though you would never stop, more graceful
than a bird, more certain, more secure.

We were outlined like a mezzotint, picking out the form of
nature's beauty. And here we wandered about savouring and
blending, relishing in union and harmony, playing always
the melody and senses which we sang in our souls, sliding
close, catching a waft of perfume, elusive, enticing a taste, a
touch, the throb of its rhythm exciting, its full-throated melody
sweeping along to repletion. We entered a tract of deep colour,

*black-red and midnight-blue. There was a wilder music, a
more sensuous touch.*

*Gently, we glided down towards the surface. I loved you very
greatly as I opened the door to Joy Street and stepped out.*

*I lay on my back in the train and stared up into the pool, back
into the glowing velvet water of the lake. And I saw the kindly
eyes, looking towards me, and smiled. In a low, soft voice they
said, 'You have won.'*

'Thank you. You read as well as you write.' Madeleine took the letter carefully from Jock and folded the paper neatly into its envelope, returning it to her handbag. She spoke quietly now. 'I want to stay with you on this trip.'

'I'm glad of that.' Jock smiled. 'Just this journey?' Madeleine held Jock's gaze. 'Can I bring in your luggage?'

'My luggage can wait, thank you, Jock.'

'Can't.' He smiled, 'Didn't you know there's a war on.'

Jock pulled in the luggage, locked the door and drew himself onto the bunk, and Madeleine brought her knees up to her chest to give him some room. She was almost the spitting image of the small pin-up postcard he had kept in his boat club office – similar to an Edward Weston nude of Weston's wife, but with a bit of clothing. The picture showed a female athlete doing up the laces of her pumps before springing onto the tennis court; the artist had not missed any feminine aspect of that physically sculpted form. Jock took her in his arms, holding her very close. As the locomotive steamed its way northwards, and in the roaring silence of their pulses, both knew that this was the beginning of a journey that was made for them and no one else.

After a while, which seemed an eternity to the couple, he knelt on the bed and caressed Madeleine's face and behind her neck. She arched her back and, as she did so, he kissed her throat many times and then all over her shoulders, which he exposed by slowly undoing her blouse. Madeleine breathed short and quick breaths as she closed her eyes. Memories flooded back to Jock of her blue flared skirt, the one she had worn on their second meeting, the day after his sister's wedding. He saw how beautiful she was – not that he hadn't already imagined that beauty. Her black satin camisole seemed tight around her upper body with its slender shoulders and swelling breasts; flat rouleau embroidery accentuated her bosom with its diagonal trim that spanned her bust and neck. Her one-piece undergarment was buttoned up between sun-lapped thighs that belonged to a swimmer rather than a sunbather. Jock squeezed the firm flesh around her hips and made Madeleine wriggle a little.

He slowly undid the three tiny buttons between her legs. After a time, he carefully peeled back her camisole, taking in again the milky white breasts with their rosy tips. It was early afternoon, and the temporary peace in the corridor became exciting, each careful touch and rise of the chest secret within the little twin-bunk world of the train sleeper. The rhythmic shudder of the train accentuated and muffled the gentle rocking as he moved so slowly that only they could hear the exhalations, teeth pressed into smiling lips absorbing the joyous waves of surprise and pleasure in their abandon. When Madeleine did briefly open her eyes, it was not Jock's brow of black hair that obscured her vision, but the dark of the sleeper rumbling its way into a railway tunnel.

They did not speak for a long time. Then in the darkness, Jock whispered, 'Here's the beginning of my next letter to you: I know that I have power over you to create beauty that passes into the bloodstreams of time on the adrenaline of happiness.'

Madeleine knew that she needed to remember that. Earlier, he had asked her to look after London 'while I'm away'. She reflected how poor they had become through the war, in danger of losing their humanity, sentiment and feeling. These last words, minutes and looks must last them months. Breathing hard with exhilaration, sweat and tears, the young lovers lived and slept their Joy Street dream.

He had dreamt for only a few hours, but awoke clear-headed and vital. The pair lay side by side and watched the landscape change from their bunk as the train snaked its way towards the Highlands. Both had rediscovered not only how to heal the hurts in their lives but also the music of their laughter and talk after the endless search for hope among the traitors in war-torn

London. Their ceaseless solitude of the last weeks and the burgeoning bonds between them gave way to a calm and joy in the moment that they had seemed to disregard. Madeleine held onto to her thoughtful, tall and strong man, so able to understand an unuttered word or witticism. Beneath the urbane and military bearing, his passion pulsed. His whole being, with his words both spoken and scribed, had sung out for her love, and Madeleine had mirrored his deep call for a union made in heaven.

The couple's goodbye was long through the couchette window – as long as the sympathetic platform guard could allow. There were no regrets as Jock gazed at Madeleine.

'Darling,' he said, 'you know I love you and I know I could make you so happy that you wouldn't want to die in case the afterlife wasn't as good.'

The train steamed ahead.

Madeleine couldn't speak; her eyes filled up and she ran along the platform as the train accelerated north. She was just parallel with Jock's window, but now the platform was running out. She stopped suddenly, smiling through the steam and tears, gasping for air.

'Don't forget to write.'

III

In spite of the miserable weather reports, Jock arrived at Arisaig, on the western coast of Inverness-shire to find it bathed in glorious autumnal light. He was laden with kit, partly because the intensity of the course required numerous changes of clothing, and he needed plus-fours for stalking expeditions (the laird's deer were not to be shot). There had also been a special request for his Robertson kilt, having been spotted on the front of a recent issue of *The Lady* magazine by the Inverailort Regimental Sergeant Major. The trumpet he carried was for the regular Friday and Saturday night parties in the mess, where he was expected to play his part in the group's band. His reputation for being headhunted by Joe Loss had gone before him, and he had been requested to replicate his achievement at the 100 Club when the jazz master had acknowledged his prowess. Inverailort House's motto was work hard and play hard.

It was now early evening. Jock was supposed to report for duty at Arisaig's Inverailort House for 2 p.m. the following day, but just as he was settling down to spend a cold night in the station waiting room, he noticed an upright man with an intelligent weasel face that often broke into a smile, purchasing a first-class ticket for the evening train going south. Jock knew he recognised the face, but couldn't place it, so he glided into the station phone box and became the watcher, observing the man break into a grin as he offered to carry an old lady's hand luggage onto the platform.

'Thank you, Mr Harkiss,' the guard called after him.

This had to be the same Harkiss that Madeleine had mentioned. He might be harmless, but he might also be strongly linked to Blynde. Beneath that smile's surface perhaps there was an open wound. He might have passed for an actor par excellence; he certainly possessed the exterior and presence of a thespian, only marred by an occasional stammer. Jock thought he would have been comfortable performing in public, but he suspected that theatre in a 'little wooden O' had to be too limiting for this person.

It was essential that Jock remained unobserved by 'Mr Harkiss', who took out a packet of cigarettes as the train was made ready for the journey to England. Jock pretended to dial a number and kept his eyes on Harkiss all the time as he did so. His gut feeling was that Harkiss was trouble – it was unlikely he was working alone. In the light of what Madeleine had divulged to him, Harkiss might be able to enjoy a productive on-and-off stage relationship with a few bit-part players – perhaps Blynde and his fellow double agents, mere foils to his leading man. If anyone tried to get too close to Harkiss, he might well have the option of cutting their lines entirely, and ad-libbing if he felt so inclined. Jock observed that, though barely handsome, the passenger had a rather graceful charm about him that couldn't entirely disguise a sense of social superiority as he tapped out his broadsheet newspaper, preventing much, if any, communication with others on the station – if he had deigned to speak with them. Jock saw an old dear knitting something for the family on the station bench. On the end of the seat, Harkiss was dedicating his attention to *The People*. If he were a Soviet agent, it could be said he was dedicating his life to the people, but that wasn't to say that he had to meet them socially; he was, after all, travelling first class.

Harkiss was also smoking his cigarettes as if they were going out of fashion. If this was indeed the leading traitor that 'C' had outlined to him, he was clearly undeterred by the machinations of his tangled web of deception, mirrored by the recent Nazi–Soviet pact, which he must have considered a 'necessary evil'. Jock thought he would surely be telling himself in the blue haze – which was now making the old lady cough – that he was betraying his country for the most noble of reasons: the prevention of a Nazi–Anglo pact that would spell disaster for the communists. Perhaps Harkiss did not know that the last patrician in these parts to be beheaded for treason was Simon Fraser, 11th Lord Lovat, who was known for his changes of allegiance and was executed in 1747 on Tower Hill for his part in the Jacobite rebellion.

The chain-smoker must have come from Inverailort House. Most people farmed around here; travellers were surely mostly connected with the house, and his unusual name was too much of a coincidence. Perhaps he had visited to show MI6's interest in Arisaig's new commando training, which would develop the vital traits of stamina and resilience required by the new Special Operations Executive. Perhaps Harkiss was the insider, keeping his hand in, knowing how to harness MI6's distrust of foreigners, with an incinerator at the end of the garden that would be a perfect resting place for all the so-called honourable intentions of the Good Germans. How did the sonnet go? 'Roses have thorns, and silver fountains mud ... And loathsome canker lives in sweetest bud.' Jock recalled the next line: 'All men make faults.'

IV

After Harkiss left for London, Jock discovered from the station guard that the loch and castle at Inverailort took their names from the River Ailort, which flowed into the sea. The peaks of Eigg Island were clearly visible as Jock made his way up the long drive to the Cameron estate the following morning. Eigg looked like a dormant beast basking on a huge sandbank; at its southern end, the Sgurr, formed a tall, narrow point.

He arrived at the Commando School's temporary billets in a grim, grey stone house and showed a special pass to the guard, who handed him a printed form of questions. As he passed the rooms to the first floor, Jock noted the stark lights in the ceilings, which were not shaded. He looked through a window on to the gardens below and couldn't help thinking how romantic was the figure that stood a little way from the old hunting lodge. The form stood out in the Lovat Scouts' uniform on the castle lawn with bonnet, battledress, hill-walking boots and stick, with a stalker's telescope in a leather case slung over one shoulder, and holding a shepherd's crook. He acknowledged Jock, who later discovered that this was Lord Fraser of Lovat; he was, unlike his ancestor Simon Fraser, a loyalist, and he had been appointed Fieldcraft instructor for the Arisaig course.

The whole building had been newly furnished for army purposes, and Jock was allocated a large desk upstairs in the front bay window, from where he could see across the lush valley, which was deserted except for large areas dotted with sheep. He found the shores of Lochailort strangely moving, with their wild, bleak beauty of scoured rock and cold blue water, of light-green bracken and shadowed pine. The new recruit looked carefully around his room, which was sparsely furnished. He checked behind the picture of a Hebridean scene over the heavy, gunmetal bed, wiping a thick layer of dust from the top of the frame. Then something made him look up at the high ceiling. Apparently, he was being singled out for a luxurious light fitting, dust-free and new. *A light-green shade to go with the bracken outside.* He picked up the desk chair, stood on it and found what he was after. A tiny microphone protruded out of the inner side of the lampshade; it didn't look too expensive. Jock smiled wistfully to himself as he removed it, and walked downstairs to the latrine, where a few others were testing the urinal. He waited until he was alone. A penknife did the job of unscrewing the towel rail, and he inserted the gadget where it would be difficult to detect, but where it could pick up the echo of human ablutions amid the plumbing.

A whistle blew, and a roll call was taken on the lawn as a sea mist moved inland. Lord Lovat presided over the assembly and forewarned the group of an imminent survival test of several days alone in the surrounding estate.

'There's magnificent salmon and trout fishing here along the river down to the loch. Help yourself, but I'd advise you to use a line' – he smiled at the group – 'not a grenade you might have smuggled in.' He gave one less attentive recruit a cool look. 'You can kill one sheep, but no more. Otherwise, you'll have a bloated belly, with me and an irate farmer to deal with.'

Jock was in the first batch on Day One for the Arisaig assault course. There was no warm-up. A horizontal rope ladder about thirty feet above ground with two thin ropes running parallel a yard above for handholds joined two pines at least fifty foot in height and about the same distance apart. The trees had been cut back for the purpose. There was another walkway fifteen feet above that, which ascended gradually towards a third giant pine; you could only climb up to attempt this with the aid of some natural handholds and sturdy branches. Jock would have offered to go up first on any account, but in fact his name was top of the list. He traversed the lower walkway. The sergeant below shouted up, 'You can do the top one if you want', but Jock had already started moving towards the higher ropes. Climbing the trees reminded him of the poacher who had opened fire on him and his younger brother barely ten years before in the bush outside Sydney. They had been shooting targets in their spinney hideout from a great height when they had to beat a hasty retreat as the intruder's shots pinged around them. Somehow they had managed to swing across to another tree out of the rifleman's sight without losing their lives. The memory of that day was to help him on the training course in a way he could never have anticipated.

Jock knew the course's top tree was not a choice, merely a temptation to forgo the highest trees and descend to the ground prematurely. He enjoyed stretching his arms and legs after the sedentary journey by rail and was comfortably beginning to reach the top when he first heard the fraying twine. The rope walk was ripping like an old shirt, torn in two. In a split second, he grabbed the remaining rope in reach and found himself both descending and swinging furiously past the giant tree. He had little time to see the blur of anguished faces below. He yelled, fell twenty feet and braced himself for the jolt as the detached rope tautened under his weight. Jock, dangling above the cacophony of shocked voices from the ground, gathered his balance, refused a ladder brought to him, and carefully made his way down the remains of the trunk, remembering also what he had learned when shinning down the fascist flagpole at Mosley's headquarters.

76

The Sergeant looked ashen and apologised profusely because he had personally supervised and checked the assembly of ropes. Yet, once the training party had been told that everything would be put right, and that all manoeuvres were to be postponed for the morning, Jock insisted on staying put, resisting the temptation to move out of the spinney to receive first aid on his rope-burned palms. He instinctively felt the Sergeant had been wasting his breath, while a few of the trainees hung back from the others to learn more of the accident with its near-fatal results. When the remains of the rope walk were brought down by a less-than-chirpy corporal, Jock requested that he look over the cord himself.

'I believe I've earned that piece of rope as a souvenir of what might have been a very brief time at Arisaig, Sergeant?'

'Putting it like that, sir, I can hardly refuse you. Go on, take it, Lieutenant Steel'. As an afterthought, he said, 'The rains must have got to a faulty rope.' With an embarrassed smile, he added, 'With His Majesty's apologies, sir. I'll have a new ropewalk ready this afternoon.'

'I'm more than happy to assist, Sergeant.'

'I'm sure that you are, sir. Rest assured, everything will be shipshape for 1.30 p.m.'

'I'll take my lunch in the spinney, if you don't mind, Sergeant. I prefer the outdoors.'

'As you wish, sir.'

Jock watched his group return to the house. If any of them were involved, then they were brilliant actors, because none of them looked in any way shifty to him. He started wondering if he had been included in this batch of trainees because they were unlikely to volunteer to be the first to start each new challenge without watching someone else manage it first. He had the distinct feeling that he was being played on this course in some way, that someone had conspired and contrived that he would indeed be the one to plunge to his death on the ropewalk. The spies were young like himself, and his gut feeling was that somebody much more senior was pulling the strings on the minutiae of the course arrangements.

V

Jock waited for the rest of the trainees to disperse to the dining room, which he successfully avoided. He found what he was looking for with little inspection. He had rather hoped that, at least for a while, one of them might be thinking that he wasn't in the dining room because he had lost his appetite. As he suspected, there had been an attempt to disguise some wear and tear at one end of the rope, but the material was scarred inside the cord, and the use of a razor-sharp blade to ease the snapping of the hessian was unmistakable. The twisted fibres had looked in good enough condition up in the trees, but the weight of man up there for several minutes would help to disguise the inevitable rip. Someone here at Arisaig didn't expect Jock to complete the course in a fit condition – *or, more likely, to finish the training alive.*

Or perhaps that person wasn't here any more. Perhaps they had taken the train to London? Jock couldn't be sure yet, but it occurred to him that Harkiss could easily have been involved in this 'accident'. The incident concentrated Jock's thoughts: Blynde was in MI5 and he couldn't read 'C''s telexes from Germany and bin them there. But Harkiss was connected to Blynde, someone extremely lax about security at MI5, who had access to diplomatic bags and might be feeding secrets to a traitor in MI6 who could destroy peace initiatives from Good Germans, and anyone who assisted such communication. Visitors to Arisaig's courses would have high security clearance. Jock began to feel he was really on to something, especially when it struck him that perhaps Harkiss was his jinx. He recalled that Harkiss could indeed be the same person he had seen at Woburn before he was nearly killed by Mosley's henchman.

Jock was aware that 'circulating sections' between Five and Six were supposed to share the card-indexing of information relating to vetting and other interests of both services. Blynde's MI5 thought it had a monopoly on the Central Registry, while MI6, the smarter and more glamorous service, where Harkiss operated, used a completely separate card index for inter-cepted German Intelligence. Unbeknown to the senior managers of both intelligence services, this blurring of information by their dysfunctional registries would have helped protect the identity of MIRAGE and other British operatives in some respects if only one of the services had been penetrated by a spy, because that agent would not have had access to the files of both intelligence organisations. However, the threat to British security increased if Blynde and Harkiss straddled both services as a team, and if they were able to piece together aspects of the intelligence jigsaw that each one was unable to complete on their own.

Jock ran back to the house, packed away the incriminating evidence in his room, and obtained a sandwich from the kitchen. He grabbed a soft drink from the bar – though he would have preferred something stronger – and avoided conversation. He found a little copse to sit down in where he could also keep an eye on the non-commissioned officers assembling the new tightrope. He doubted any of these men were in any way responsible for the sabotage that morning, and even if they were, a would-be assassin would hardly choose a similar trick on the same section of the training area. However, to be forewarned was to be forearmed – for the moment, it also helped to be the only one here who was fully aware of the presence of a traitor at Arisaig. It might give Jock the chance to catch any accomplices of the saboteur; there would be little chance of that with a public witch-hunt. As it was, he wasn't sure whom he could trust, apart from, ironically, the current Lord Lovat, and Jock wanted to identify the enemy himself.

Jock insisted on going up the Tree Walk first after lunch, and again the Sergeant concurred with an apologetic shrug. When Jock descended without mishap, he recommended the climb to a worthy recruit who wanted to 'set Europe ablaze'. One man – a Royal Artillery Officer – ignored the demonstration, and Jock's rejection of the easy way, although they were expected to observe and egg on their compatriots. When it came to his turn, he proved himself to have little head for heights. Again the Sergeant called out, 'Do the top one if you want'. But this time, the Sergeant's chorus was met with, 'This is the only fucking one I've got to do, isn't it? You can't con me.' The man's lack of persistence, premature descent and subsequent return to his unit confirmed the nature of the course: the first hurdle was a template for every other element of the intensive training that had already shredded some nerves and failed another officer.

VI

After unpacking and handing in the questionnaire on his qualifications, Jock attended the first lecture before tea. This instructor – a laid-back and plain-looking man called Sykes – didn't carry a bishop's crook, but behaved as though he once had. The students noted his quiet manner as he spoke dynamically about the twenty-two points in the body where a lethal blow could be delivered – yet his calm demeanour smacked more of the retired bishop than an expert in silent killing and pistol shooting. Jock observed that the gospel Sykes preached was that in firing affrays, consecutive shots were literally a matter for the quick and the dead.

'Take your choice,' Sykes almost whispered. 'Don't bother with a special stance where you align your sights. The average shooting is over in split seconds, so a bent arm, or possibly with one hand from the level of the hip, won't get you nail-driving marksmanship, but you will survive to tell the tale – especially if you use a "double tap": two shots in quick succession.'

However, on the lawn, at a hundred yards, Jock, with a now-bandaged left hand demonstrated his preference for accuracy with the Colt .45 and hit the head of a six-foot target four times out of five. He made a mental note of the spellbindingly beautiful, bilingual brunette who had achieved a bullseye with every bullet she possessed; it was some consolation to find out later that she was the best shot in SOE.

Then their coach led the group of twelve into a small, makeshift gymnasium with some furnishings in one corner. Jock stood behind the others so that he could observe the members of his group and also watch as Sykes demonstrated a diversity of deadly moves.

'Any weapon is better than none – half a brick, a bottle, or something that will serve as a club … Ethically, it doesn't matter whether you kill the enemy with knuckledusters or your bare hands. The first thing you have to learn in unarmed combat is to grab your opponent by the balls.' Then he stopped and said, 'Oh, sorry, gentlemen, I forgot: officers have testicles.' A chuckle that helped offset some tension in his 'apostles' hummed through the men.

After the hand-to-hand fighting was over, Sykes smiled with approval for the first time. 'I now want you to use the imagination that I have been informed you all have. I want some corkscrew thinking. What if you do have a weapon, perhaps one you're not familiar with – a metal pipe or sword, perhaps?'

He beckoned Jock to come forward, picked up two cutlasses and threw one, handle first, towards him. Sykes then pulled out a knife concealed inside his left trouser pocket.

'Come on, Steel, parry these.'

The two men paced slowly round the room. Jock focussed on his opponent's eyes, but as he circled around he searched for anything that might come to his aid in the form of an unconventional weapon, because he knew that was all that might be left for him; as he believed his posting abroad was imminent, he treasured any combat simulation.

An unplugged lamp stood by the wall nearest him. The light was ornate, but its stand was made of oak; a useful tool, even if it was positioned on the end of the table furthest from him. He kept his sword pointing towards his instructor's chest and lunged for the desk with his partially bandaged left hand open, sliding it and his elbow along the table surface for some balance. Sykes moved towards him, instantly lifting his cutlass for a side stroke, but Jock had, beneath the ornate shade, two feet of wood, which he deftly used to block the attempted uppercut. The fight stopped there, since now Jock had the advantage – he could lunge at his target easily with the length of the cutlass that dwarfed the reach of the older man's much smaller blade.

'Thank you for your corkscrew mind, Steel. There you have it, gentlemen. None of you consider yourselves an expert unless you can carry out every movement instinctively, automatically and imaginatively. I think we all deserve a drink. Please address further questions in the bar.'

The drinks, that evening, were plentiful, but Jock watched what he drank, which was just as well because the inexpensive liquor served two purposes: the much-needed relaxation at the end of the day was also an informal method to assess how soberly would-be agents could behave after a few, or a great many, drinks. Jock was mindful of the adage 'loquacity will always triumph over security'. Now, he noted instructions on how to play a part, to be one person in reality, and quite another in appearance – to live one's cover was unusually hard for some. The garrulous had to learn to be reticent; even the reticent had to be reminded to form each sentence so that they would never reveal to a stranger more than he needed to know.

A man with twinkling brown eyes, enormous feet and a pointed nose got up from the bar and moved to the piano. Jock longed to play the trumpet, yet he decided that evening to take it all in. He'd rather have his eye on the group and wouldn't be able to do that while playing, as the piano was facing the wall. During the day, he had observed a slight male figure with light hair; now, the young man was partly obscured as he leant in towards a colleague, seemingly engrossed in conversation at the bar. Jock had never identified the stooge who had followed him in London and wondered if he was in Scotland, perhaps even on this course. The opportunities to observe this man had been limited, as he was in a different stick of trainees, but Jock had discovered that the youth went under the name of Quinton Panton.

Eventually, Jock accepted a request to play the trumpet, allowing him a bird's-eye view of the room, but by that time the figure at the bar had turned to leave. Jock had to stay put and show what a magnificent set of lungs could do while the pianist, whose name was Billy, took a short breather.

'Bravo,' Sykes chipped in as the applause subsided.

He had a quick word with Jock at the bar and complimented him on both his musical and martial display. Jock remembered his parting words: 'The greatest risk in the field comes not from the enemy counter-intelligence, but from your own side.' He searched the instructor's brown eyes, but Sykes's expression gave nothing away. If he did know anything about Jock's baptism of fire up in Arisaig's pines, he wasn't letting on.

At the end of the evening, Jock made his way to his room. What he didn't know was that the microphone had been planted by a devastating blonde, code-named 'Fifi', who made it her business to wire bedrooms to ascertain what language students talked in while asleep. 'Fifi' was only called in if a student was bright enough to find and silence the microphone.

VII

As Jock turned the lock in his door, he had an uneasy feeling that his room was occupied. He opened the door slowly and quickly put on the light.

He didn't need to go through any of Sykes's disabling routines with any intruder because a voluptuous blonde sat facing him in the room's only leather armchair. Jock hadn't studied Chaucer's 'Wife of Bath' for years, but the woman in front of him seemed to personify the female that the fourteenth-century poet had depicted in his *Canterbury Tales*, at least in the sense that she appeared to be a robust man-eater. The uninvited guest's recently coiffured locks fell about her shoulders, but her nightgown barely hid her enormous and very handsome chest.

'Good evening, Lieutenant Steel.'

'Good evening.' Jock closed the door. Facing the woman as he did so, he said, 'This is a most unexpected pleasure, if I may say so.'

Her deep-blue eyes rolled above a flash of cleavage and bright red lipstick. 'You may, Lieutenant. You may.'

'And whom do I have the pleasure of currently hosting in my billet?'

'Just call me Fifi. Everyone eventually gets to know me by that name.'

'What is it that I can do for you, madam?'

Fifi was purring. 'Why, there's a question, if ever I heard one.'

Jock moved past Fifi and looked surreptitiously through the curtain to the grounds below, noting that everyone else seemed to have gone to bed.

He turned towards her. 'I'm up early tomorrow morning, so it is a pertinent question.'

Fifi was blessed with a strong bone structure, which didn't in any way impair her femininity due to the curves of her body, which became more conspicuous as she shifted in her seat. 'From an impertinent young officer, perhaps?'

Jock smiled. 'Why on earth would you think that?'

'Because you are in possession of His Majesty's government property and I'm here to return it to His Majesty.' She pursed her not inconsiderable lips. 'If you must know.'

Jock looked at the lampshade above them and thought the blonde might at least be after the microphone. He noticed the ornate rings on her fingers that tapped the arm of the chair as she spoke with a London accent.

He said nothing for a while, and realised that everything on this course was a trap of some kind or other, including the attractive, well-proportioned administrator in front of him.

Fifi changed a few gears. 'Oh, I ought to compliment you on finding the equipment, but actually you've caused some … inconvenience.'

Jock smiled. 'Thank you, madam. I couldn't have put it better myself: I don't like being snooped upon, and therefore you may indeed have recordings of the local men's ablutions on the ground floor.'

With more pouting, she said, 'Yes … I did find that rather amusing. However, now I don't know what language you speak in while dreaming, and I'm afraid that's part of my remit.'

Jock cleared his throat. 'You can stay and listen on the sofa, if you wish, but I'm about to go to bed … I snore very loudly.'

'I bet you do … I'll have to bug the room again … But I'll be more discreet next time.'

'Good luck.'

Fifi was enjoying the conversational spat. 'Thank you, Lieutenant Steel. Try not to be so … forceful … if you do find the next one? You squashed part of the mechanism in the one I found in the Gents.'

Jock sensed that it was time for bed. He walked towards the door, turned and gave a little bow. 'My sincere apologies.'

Fifi's broad grin revealed some healthy-looking canine teeth. 'Accepted, Lieutenant.'

'Is that all?'

'Inverailort House does reward initiative, Lieutenant Steel. We offer a few diversions.'

Jock looked Fifi over again. 'I never doubted that.'

'Actually, you are being offered a day off tomorrow. You'll report back on duty at 2230 ready in combat dress to begin a night and day in the wilds, Lieutenant.'

'How thoughtful.'

Fifi winked. 'I thought so.'

'It would be a real reward if I could use one of the Inverailort Castle vehicles – a bit of sightseeing, just for the day?' Fifi was nodding her head, and Jock took this as a good sign. 'With a 0600 start, I could catch all that beautiful Kintyre landscape?'

Fifi nodded and smiled. 'We've just taken stock of four motorbikes. I'll have a word with the Major who scavenged them.' She extended her fingers out and inspected the lacquer of the immaculately painted nails in front of her. She looked up. 'Sign for it.' She smiled again. 'Just don't crash it.'

'How generous.'

'It is, isn't it?'

Jock held the door open. 'It most certainly is.'

Fifi sashayed across the floor towards the landing outside and rolled her eyes once more on exit.

'Goodnight, Lieutenant.'

Jock closed the door quietly and whispered. 'Goodnight, Fifi.'

VIII

LOCH FYNE

Madeleine had used the telephone number that Jock had given her more quickly than he had expected. She had also been busy on the first day of his course. He used the opportunity that Fifi had given him to meet up in person with Madeleine rather than speak on the telephone when the line wasn't always reliable, or monitored by the likes of Fifi. Jock didn't think any of his local hostelries were particularly secure, but he also wanted to be with Madeleine again. She had called to say that she was going back to London earlier than planned, and might not then see Jock again before he went abroad. So, with the time given him he could drive to Argyll, talk for an hour or so and eventually return north to Arisaig to make ready for living in the hills for a few days with the rest of the trainees.

On empty roads, Jock took in the stunning Scottish coast and hills. He met Madeleine off the bus from Tarbert. The fresh air had done her complexion good; he knew she might be upset about their saying goodbye, but she was more nervous than he had expected.

'You look bonny ... Come here ...' He put his arms around her and embraced her. He saw that she still seemed a little apprehensive. He smiled, and cradled her face with his hands. 'And not a little gorgeous.'

They walked hand in hand past the hotel at their rendezvous and stood by the banks of Loch Fyne.

'Didn't you buy your two volumes of Dr Johnson's *Dictionary* near here?' Madeleine asked.

Jock noticed that she wasn't beaming but looked as if she was putting on a brave front about something. Perhaps she was ill-equipped for the war's inevitable splintering of their new friendship? He ignored that for now and did the beaming for both of them. 'You have a first-class brain and memory in that beautiful head of yours. You've remembered the letter celebrating my purchase of a distraction from commando training here while you were grappling with *Tartuffe.*'

Jock kept the sobering events of his 'accident' to himself including his night visitor the previous evening. He listened carefully as Madeleine opened up about her anxieties.

'I need to be here with you for more reasons than I can almost say… you know that on the train up you were quizzing me about my life in London and perhaps I clammed up a bit. I'm not used to this wonderful but intense male attention.'

'You surprise me.'

'No. I'm serious, Jock.'

'I know you are, my darling.'

'You asked me then to find out more about Blynde.'

'Yes, I remember.'

'I have already joined Blynde's social group near Oxford Street.'

'You are a sorceress – how could you have?'

'It was weeks ago.'

Jock eventually spoke. 'Careful, my darling. Don't get too close.'

'I haven't. I told you, there's no danger of that. We've already been to the local gallery together, and I've met some of his friends and acquaintances.'

'With great respect, you're a faster worker than I had fully appreciated. You didn't mention any of this. Tell all.'

Madeleine looked a little hurt but spoke quietly to alleviate Jock's concern. 'There's a three-storey maisonette off Oxford Street. I stayed over

– on the sofa, actually … Blynde was on another one. Don't look at me like that: I was perfectly safe from that quarter … Anyway, I told you that.'

Jock was usually a good listener but he now couldn't stop himself interrupting. 'Why didn't you tell me?'

'Do you honestly think I wanted to spend the whole of our special train journey talking endlessly about people I care a lot less about than you?'

Jock smiled. 'That's a good answer, but why tell me now – what's prompted you?'

'Well, not seeing you again for however long that might be in this godforsaken war is just one good reason for being here. It's hardly the talk I'd choose on my last afternoon with you for however how long? When you suggested I visit some art with him out of hours I naturally felt a bit guilty because I'd already done that. I think he quite likes my company. I don't find conversation difficult and I don't ask him too many questions. I pour drinks without being requested and enjoy meeting new people. I suppose I'm good company. Let me set the scene for you:

Everyone there drinks a great deal, and the place somewhat reeks of garlic and chicken soup. There had been several gatherings over as many weeks, and a party the night before I joined Blynde in his local gallery. I woke up to a recording of a Mozart quartet playing rather loudly; there was a young man gathering up his uniform that had been dangled on the staircase, and he shouted up to the occupant of Blynde's bedroom who remained dead to the world, despite the smell and the music.' Madeleine continued. 'It was a Saturday, and when I awoke I saw Blynde rubbing a few hours' sleep from his eyes. I remember seeing him watch himself in the pink-tinted glass of the many mirrors adorning the walls; he wryly noted that, like his professional lives – art and security – he appeared in all of them, subsumed in a wilderness of reflections, but the one opposite told him he "needed a dry shave and a black coffee" before visiting the Wallace Collection. The art lover, as a courtesy, had been notified that the pictures might be moved to Wales, and would we like to catch them before they went? You can't miss him in a crowd; as we began our short walk to the art collection, I noticed he's only dwarfed by the tall trees in Manchester Square.'

'Blynde was drawn to pictures like "A River Scene" by Vernet; he commented on the "intimate moments of the joys in completed labours juxtaposed with the bereavement of young lovers". It was with Vernet's portrayal of loss that Blynde was most absorbed. He wasn't a show-off, but he did say that his acolytes didn't expect him to sing that artist's praises in the *Spectator* – that "this was his morning off". He stood gazing at Greuze's celebrations of youth, which he enjoyed on his own, for a short while, even though he "far preferred his Poussin". It was sad … I actually felt sorry for him. He said he felt what he wanted to do was teach. I had the feeling that his own youth had vanished along with the wasted lives of so many students that he could have inspired but for the fatal distractions of war.'

Jock knew that the same attachés who were using the diplomatic bag to brief 'C' on Canaris's rendezvous with himself were in danger of having their reports deciphered by Blynde, or perhaps Harkiss.

Jock was worried. 'Don't feel sorry for him, Madeleine. That could be dangerous.'

Jock had requested a list of responsibilities and roles of intelligence mandarins at Broadway Buildings before leaving London so that, as he had told Delahay, 'I have some idea of the chain of command.' He had found out that Harkiss was working temporarily in St Albans and was also supporting the work of the Iberian desk. Any gaps in the information relating to peace initiatives from Germany to Britain through the conduit of neutrals in Spain or Portugal were being gradually pieced together at MI5 by Blynde. If Harkiss was working for the Russians, a move by Harkiss to the Iberian desk would more quickly provide the traitors with knowledge of Jock's rendezvous with Canaris and any future ones that might develop out of the meeting. If Blynde knew he was suspected of treason, he would have to rapidly close in on the identity of MIRAGE and anyone associated with him – Madeleine, for instance.

'Did Blynde say anything about his friends?'

Madeleine continued, 'You're interrupting again. I need to tell you the whole story. He said he had mixed feelings about some of the party hangers-on, saying many were "looking particularly tawdry and jaded these days". I remember that Blynde telephoned some instructions to one of the flatmates to keep an eye on the goings-on in their flat. It belongs to Victor Rothschild. It even has its own bomb shelter in the basement. Some interesting people stay over – a melee of professionals. I overheard Blynde once say it was "where Bacchus reigned and Venus was shunned". I couldn't have described it better myself. I think some of the people there resembled characters out of a Feydeau farce, with its cuckolds, intrigue, slamming doors and abandoned lingerie.'

'You have done well. You've come out of the jaws of hell … unscathed. But why didn't you mention all this before?'

Madeleine looked tearful. 'I felt guilty. Look, this isn't the sort of thing a young woman wants to be rabbiting on about when she is about to wave her soldier off, is it, Jock? It's not the type of thing you want to reveal to someone you're passionate about – telling him how you've been sleeping on some other man's sofa over a couple of weekends.' She sighed. 'I know I'm more of a party girl than you might believe. Let me tell you, it's been a lot more fun than composing essays in a tiny college room with only falling leaves to stare at.'

'Is this meeting a confession of sorts?'

'Like hell it is – stop being a prude, Jock. No, as a matter of fact I'm explaining this now because we both need the full picture.' Madeleine's eyes were welling up again. 'Perhaps you need to allow me to know more than you yourself have said?'

Jock saw Madeleine swallow her doubts and fears, said nothing, and beckoned her to continue.

'I have something for you that could be very important. I took a telephone call at my parents' home yesterday. It was from a young secretary with whom I've become friendly at work. There's only us two girls in that office building so it's a relief to chat when we get the chance. She was complaining that Blynde needed her to cover for him at short notice because he had to go out of London to see family. She was at a loss because it was her day off and she had something special planned.'

'Did she hear Blynde say where he was going?'

'He mentioned St Albans.'

'A meeting place? A time?'

'No exact location. Tomorrow afternoon.'

Jock couldn't hide his concern. 'Did he now?'

'Yes. What does that mean?'

Jock stood still and looked over towards the sea. He turned back to her and spoke softly. 'It means that now is the time for you to leave MI5. Make some excuse that you've some unfinished business at Somerville College. Continue with your application to work elsewhere. It would be helpful if you can change address, disappear for a while. I will leave a short report on how I see the potential leaks in British security for my new boss. I am due to leave England imminently; a delay isn't possible. I can't follow Blynde and keep tabs on this meeting, but I'm convinced what you've told me is, as you say, very important. I want you to think long and hard about what I'm going to suggest. Everything that I've learned since I last saw you makes me suspect that they are indeed hatching a plot: I think Blynde will meet the friend of his you mentioned before – Harkiss. Kit Harkiss is his full name. He's the blue-eyed boy of the office. Harkiss is based at present in St Albans. Harkiss may have had his suspicions about my existence as an unwelcome addition to his outfit – as far as he is concerned – some time ago. Because of the imminence of my own operation, I'd say Blynde is either calling a meeting between them, or perhaps Harkiss is summoning it. Charming, urbane, well connected and knowledgeable. Never puts a foot wrong ... Until now, perhaps.'

'What would you like me to do?'

'I'm not asking you to follow Blynde, but I am asking you to consider eavesdropping on his conversation with Harkiss. The King Harry is an unofficial venue for security folk; I gather that it has become an essential watering-hole for Harkiss and a few of his colleagues who empty out of their offices for a drink by 6 p.m. He is known for calling informal gatherings at the pub so that he cannot be easily overheard – but also because he is an alcoholic. But he won't want an audience there in the bar either. My hunch is that the traitors will meet at The King Harry but earlier, say mid-to late afternoon; it has two bars. You would have to arrive early, and find a position in the pub so that you can observe the place where the two men are likely to talk.'

'How can that work? Surely Blynde will recognise me immediately.'

'You have to ensure that he doesn't see you.'

'How will I do that? Using a disguise?'

'No, although I would be especially thorough about dressing in an entirely different way to what Blynde has seen you wear socially before.'

Madeleine was concerned. 'It doesn't sound like a plan, Jock. Blynde will see me at close quarters. It's too dangerous, as you say.'

'It isn't without its dangers, and it would be foolish to suggest otherwise – but they will be diminished by one significant advantage.'

'What?'

'On the train to Scotland, you mentioned that you can lip-read. So that's exactly what I want you to do tomorrow.'

'I'm still not sure it can work.'

'Don't you see, Madeleine … The two bars in the pub … You don't have to be in the same room as them. You can find a discreet position and watch them from the comfort of the adjoining room. The place is full of glass – you might be able to watch and listen through it.'

'But they could similarly view me.'

'True, but if you make sure that you arrive before Blynde in particular, you will have the advantage of choosing where you can watch them as safely as possible. When you decide to sit, ensure that of the two, if one has to face in your direction, it should be Harkiss rather than Blynde.'

'What about making a few notes?'

'I wouldn't risk it, but you can always dash something down on paper after they've gone, even if it's in a Ladies' toilet – not the pub's, but elsewhere, where you can't be seen. Take a few props – a newspaper that you can dive behind if necessary, some knitting in a bag, a bit of shopping to go with it. Harkiss is likely to arrive first; he works around the corner.'

'How will I recognise him?'

'Here's a recent mugshot of him.' He laughed. 'Ugly mug, if you ask me … If you decide to watch him, commit this to memory and destroy it before you leave for St Albans.'

'You have a nerve, Jock. You've got it all planned out, haven't you?'

'I'd watch them myself if I wasn't so involved with my own plans. I'm concerned about you taking my place, but I know how capable you are. The aim will be to remain unseen by the two of them while you gather the nature of their conversation. However, though you have worked with Blynde, you can prepare a cover story as to why you happen to be in St Albans in The King Harry on that particular day and time. I can help you with that. I also realise that you might well gain the proof that we both might need to explain why you have your suspicions about Blynde, why you have left MI5 and why you want to transfer elsewhere. Harkiss has the sort of face that can easily disappear into a crowd but looks distinguished enough when he smiles – but I think he may not be doing so much of that tomorrow.'

'Why ever not?'

'If this pair of traitors are meeting at short notice rather than posting a letter, or talking at length over the telephone, it almost certainly means that they consider that either they or their masters are in jeopardy and that they regard the conversation as an emergency meeting. You've already given me reason enough for such a meeting with their monitoring of spy rings in Spain – what I know is that the sensitive information I'm privy to will be making them worry a great deal, something that you could look out for, if you decide to go tomorrow.'

'Where are you going, Jock?'

'You know that it's best that you don't ask me too much, and that I tell you as little as possible.'

'You're going to Spain, aren't you?' Madeleine put a hand over her mouth and then wiped away a tear. 'You're not going to North Africa with your pals, are you?'

Jock took Madeleine's hand, imploring her to keep as calm as possible. Someone was walking past them and they had just looked over at the couple.

'You're walking into some kind of snare, Jock – Kipling's "twisted by knaves to make a trap for fools". I know you're no fool, but I want you to come back.' Madeleine regained her composure and grit. 'I've never loved anyone as much as you. And this treachery is now personal for me.' She looked resolute. 'Will the knaves be armed tomorrow?'

Jock could hardly hide some relief at Madeleine rallying back. 'I think Harkiss is the one to watch there. He may well carry a knife, possibly a revolver.' He put his arm around her. 'Would you be happy to take the afternoon train today?' Madeleine nodded in assent.

'If you caught that one you would be able to prepare things in London by midday tomorrow? I believe that you are one of the few beauties I know who can travel light. If you agree, we could motorcycle to Glasgow from Loch Fyne but you'd have to travel just as you are on the back of the bike snuggled up next to me – plus handbag, of course. You can take the train south from there.'

'I can't wait.' She looked at him conspiratorially, the confidence returning. 'I'll phone from the station to explain that I've been called back to work urgently.' Madeleine smiled, 'I have, of course, haven't I? Is there any work more important?'

Jock gave her hand a gentle squeeze.

'No one's going to miss me terribly for a few days at home here.'

Madeleine went quiet, looked down at her lap for a moment, breathed in very slowly and then looked up at Jock, straight in the eye, 'Should I be armed?'

'I don't think we can underestimate these two. They're passing secrets that are endangering innocent lives, and I'm sure they'd have little compunction about killing in order to continue doing just that. Take my Browning pistol. I think we'll take a walk in the woods and do a bit of gun practice. You could fire off a couple of rounds for a rehearsal – not a full one, but we've just time for something useful. That'll leave four rounds – two for each traitor if it is absolutely necessary. It won't draw any unnecessary attention here because we are surrounded by pheasant and sheep. Before I forget – you are going to need another two telephone numbers.' Jock passed her a small card. 'You need to learn them off by heart and only use the second one in red if you are either in danger or can't talk to me on the telephone when you have new information above and beyond what we've already discussed.'

Madeleine carefully put the numbers in her purse as Jock continued.

'Thank you for making the journey up here. We both know how important it is now for our country's security, let alone for us. I think your leave will have to be extended before excusing yourself from the official security work. Could you say that your father is still ill and your mother needs some home help for a bit?' Madeleine nodded. 'That way you could be free to meet up or telephone me before I leave in the next few days. Telephone the first number if you can tomorrow at 1800 hours. If I am not there, or you are still busy monitoring the two men at that time, ring again exactly one hour later. If for some reason we are not able to talk tomorrow, you'll need to leave a message on the second number about anything new and significant.' Jock paused. 'Where will you make those calls?'

'From a phone box.' Madeleine smiled knowingly. 'And preferably not in the vicinity of where I work or stay overnight.'

'Exactly. Before we head south, we are going for a walk by the loch. I am going to show you some target practice, and give you a potted history about the methods of a man called Sykes ...'

IX

LOCHAILORT

The following evening, his muscles still aching from the previous night's exercises that had run long into the morning, Jock managed to remain undetected as he made his way to the Lochailort Inn, on the road to the Isles between Fort William and Mallaig. He didn't want to interrupt the training by requesting an official telephone call in the name of national security when he couldn't be sure who was betraying whom. He'd correctly guessed that there would be an Inverailort House spy in the Lochailort Inn to monitor off-piste trainees, but he needed to be near the Inverailort Nissen huts where he was expected to report later. The nearest and most secure telephone was the one at the Inn. Jock was forced through the sheer logistics of the course to use that telephone; he had found out that it was one of the gillies who was tasked with the job of being the Inverailort House patron of the Inn that evening and noting any would-be commando avoiding that evening's lecture for a few pints of beer. Jock had told him that his wife was expecting twins and that the doctor was privately worried about the pregnancy. In the end, he didn't care whether the wise old gillie believed him or not because he'd crossed his palm with a very expensive bottle of malt whisky. The gillie would look the other way at certain points in the evening while the 'mad Englishman' squeezed in a conversation 'and a beer no dut' before roll call. Jock would have to talk his way out of his dilemma if the plan didn't work; he'd be forced to involve Delahay, which wasn't what he wanted. However, he liked the old gillie and had packed a dark, but now crumpled suit to change into after removing his combats, so that he would not arouse suspicion and make the old boy look a fool if he was somehow caught 'napping'. Jock wouldn't be drinking, just hunched in the lobby over a telephone.

Madeleine had decided she would leave The King Harry before Harkiss and Blynde supped up and went their separate ways. She had found a pub of her own in St Albans – The Boot, not far from the cathedral and the station in case she needed to leave in a hurry. She had asked to use the telephone as it was an emergency, and had been given a small room to herself. The landlord's wife had fussed over her and even brought her a cup of tea.

Jock walked into Lochailort Inn a few minutes before six o'clock without entering the bar and made straight for the telephone – incoming calls only. Jock took out a pocket book and pencil, and waited. The phone rang almost immediately. With much relief, he picked up the phone to hear Madeleine's voice.

'Are you alright?' he asked.

'Yes, yes.'

'It's safe to speak?'

'Yes, quite safe.'

'Good. Keep your eyes peeled until you get back home safe. Where will that be?'

'Angelika's.'

'Good idea. We may not have much time on the phone. If we happen to be cut off for some reason, telephone again and I'll pick it up on the third ring. It's good to hear you. It would also be good to hear anything about what these men said, and even describe their behaviour. What happened?'

'I remembered that Blynde might be closing any gaps on the

information relating to peace initiatives from Germany to Britain and would gradually piece it together at MI5, and that he would in any event be studying information on your identity and whether he thought he was being watched or not. So, I decided to wait in Manchester Square. I planned to tail Blynde and travel up on the same train to St Albans. I knew I would have to take a cab or sprint ahead in order to arrive at The King Harry pub after Harkiss but in advance of Blynde's arrival. I checked which train Blynde was likely to board, but I wanted to be certain that the traitors' rendezvous wasn't altered for any reason. You had already warned me that the two spies might be a bit jumpy, but I wasn't going to miss any chance of acquiring any knowledge that would protect you. You had explained how Blynde and Harkiss would be incensed at the news of further British suspicions that the Soviets were the real menace to Britain's long-term future.'

'That was very brave of you ... Go on.'

'I saw a tall figure leave the Bentinck Street address and turn into Oxford Street. I knew Blynde to be very alert, and I took care not to be seen by him. I had already prepared a piece of litter that I'd placed on the pavement to pick up as he turned towards Oxford Street so I could also observe him, though I didn't give him a chance to look at me. I stood up and he seemed to walk with a heavy heart as he left the mayhem that was becoming his home by the square. I caught him up a bit as he passed a banknote into a youthful-looking taxi man's hand with a "Keep the change". It must have been a fortune to the cabby, but, I reflected, a pittance for Blynde compared to the thirty pieces of silver that he might occasionally collect from his Russian contacts.'

'I hailed a cab, and told the driver I was urgently meeting a medical specialist at the station because of some "women's trouble" and "could he please hurry". This meant I not only followed Blynde to St Pancras, but actually overtook him towards the end of the journey, enabling me to buy a ticket and a newspaper, and have time to watch him enter the station. I was able to walk behind him, and I moved into a seat two carriages behind his. In the cab, I had wrapped a nondescript shawl around my head and I was wearing a grey overcoat to blend in with the colourless city.'

'I managed to somehow race the long-legged Blynde to The King Harry. I walked briskly on the other side of the kerb, and gained some time when he disappeared into a newsagent's to buy some cigarettes. I had some shopping in a bag, and underneath it the pistol. I slowly walked into The King Harry and spotted Harkiss in the Long Bar, apparently nursing a hangover. I bought a drink in the bar next door and hovered while Harkiss sat down opposite one empty chair. His field of vision meant that he could only see me if he craned his neck and shifted in his chair. I opened the *Daily Telegraph*, sitting at an angle of about 90 degrees to Harkiss and the chair opposite him so I could see him over my paper, as well as anyone who chose to sit next to him by a window. Harkiss was downing one of several very large whiskies and was clearly expecting company, as he swiftly turned when the door on his side of the pub pushed open. Blynde seemed to be stooping a little to blend in with the crowd and minimise his aristocratic figure that otherwise might prove conspicuous among the afternoon drinkers.

'Harkiss was facing the entrance to the Long Bar and beckoned Blynde to the chair by the bay window with an outstretched hand that held out a Player's cigarette. He also offered a drink. Blynde managed a limp smile as he collapsed into the armchair. Harkiss didn't bother asking him if he wanted a double, and got up to buy him a gin with some tonic. He was rewarded with a grateful "Thank you". I had been waiting for this moment to raise my newspaper because, true to form, Blynde scoped the clientele and the drinkers on my side of the pub. But then he turned to listen to Harkiss. I was sure he hadn't seen me go into the pub.'

Jock talked even more quietly now. 'Absolutely certain?'

'Yes, you'll see why. Harkiss noticed that his colleague seemed to be wearing London's particular grey pallor. "You lot are doing too much partying." Blynde began to speak; it was slow and I found it fairly easy to follow the gist of it, as I could even hear it above the hubbub of chat in the bars. "I wish that were true," he said as he took in his surroundings and seemed to relax a little. Most of the clients appeared to be drinking seriously, or were 'actors' heavily engaged in impressing their company at the bar. Then Blynde began his story. "We delayed a flight from Madrid this week, and now have unearthed something that Varley has to know…" He paused. "What's the XB traffic from the Abwehr like?"'

Jock interrupted. 'Are you sure he said "XB"?'

'Certain. Asking for what surely was such sensitive MI6 information was the first of several incriminating conversations. I saw that what was left of Harkiss's jovial warmth drained away at this, and he didn't answer the question as the tall man towered over him in his uncomfortable seat, but merely probed, "Why?"'

'Blynde replied, "One of your Catalan friends is in London trying to sell secrets to the highest bidder, and eight Soviet agents are in the capital apparently watching us there for our daily contacts."'

'I saw Harkiss's ice-blue eyes gleam with terror at this, and I saw the anger and then the fear well up in the MI6 officer, who seemed to be fighting hard to control his daily dose of alcohol, saying, "Graham comes in about this time." He spat the next bit as he stubbed his fag end hard into the ashtray, as if for emphasis. "I don't want him mixed up in any of this … I told you not to come here unless …"'

'Blynde replied with something like, "Unless the unthinkable is …?" Blynde seemed to be disguising some pleasure at holding the information, but the pair clearly know each other too well. "In London, a plan far greater than running rings around our Spanish spy network is in its inception." He added emphasis. "Something that could outwit us all." It could be my imagination, but I think Harkiss's eyes betrayed a look only lovers might be privy to: the fear of everything ending.'

'I committed some of the names to memory – XB traffic, Graham, Varley, the Soviet agents and the unthinkable happening – but relished the discomfort of the pair as I followed their conversation. They were definitely up to no good, and I knew that I couldn't afford to miss anything. I still held my paper tightly in case I needed to raise it again at a moment's notice. I thought how the hunter was now forced to exchange roles with the hunted – a rabbit in a spotlight, Harkiss sat stock-still, and waited. The garrulous spy allowed his more reticent friend do the talking but he managed, "I knew that someone new is asking too many questions in the middle of the building. I nearly dealt with him."'

'This time Harkiss wasn't holding court, smiling and liberated, but instead made a hurtful comment to Blynde, whose face he was studying: "How on earth were you ever known as a Pre-Raphaelite beauty at college?"'

'Blynde ignored the comment and sank his gin. "The Catalan has been watched trading information about." He seemed critical when he said, "An Abwehr meeting in Spain … Possibly with someone from the fourth." I couldn't catch what the fourth was, but then he said, "And that can only mean one thing."'

Jock's worst fears about these men were now being rolled out by the person he loved most. While Madeleine spoke, he had never felt quite so sober in his life, deeply concerned as he was about her in particular, but also himself now. Although he had a fix on who was betraying the British, it was only Madeleine's evidence and Jock's support of it against the conspirators' network of friends in both Six and Five. Jock remembered that 'C' had wanted to go in person to meet Canaris, but that the arrangements had to be as inconspicuous as possible, which was one of the reasons 'C' had been recommended a substitute who could also travel on to Africa and support the launch of Clarke's fictitious airborne brigades. It was also now almost certain that the Soviet spies knew that someone from the MI6 London base was planning a high-level meeting with the Abwehr – 'from the fourth' was likely to mean someone at a very senior level, and that surely meant the fourth floor: the Directorate at Broadway House, and 'C' himself. The traitors didn't yet know who exactly was being sent. So far, 'C''s idea of MIRAGE being under their radar had to some extent worked, except that Harkiss and Blynde had cut to the heart of some of England's most secret telexes and messages, and it was only a year into the war.

'Are you still there, Jock?'

'Yes, darling, I'm still here. Are you still able to talk freely?'

'Yes. There is more – it is even more damning.'

Jock looked across at the gillie, who was in the bar facing the coast. He was dutifully looking at the entrance of the Inn, away from where Jock was wiping sweat off his forehead.

Jock turned back to the conversation. 'Carry on.'

'Harkiss seemed completely lost for words at this news of an Abwehr meeting in Spain. Perhaps he'd also caught himself out with his own habit: there wasn't enough cigarette to draw on, so he quickly lit two, pulled on one and left the other smoking slowly in the ashtray.'

Jock had scribbled down much of what Madeleine had said. 'What you have told me could be instrumental in bringing these two to justice – in the right hands … Did the pair say anything else about "the meeting"?'

'Blynde said, "I've paid him off to stop blabbering about the meeting, but you may wish to deal with him in another way." Harkiss still said nothing, but then he quickly took the second cigarette from the ashtray. Blynde seemed relieved. I wondered if it was the cigarette that took the edge off Harkiss's foul mood. I thought Blynde then said something very odd …'

Jock thought it was all odd, but unfortunately all too real. 'What exactly?'

'Blynde said, "This whole problem is now compounded by the fact that Varley is himself being checked, as we are, by Comintern agents …"' Madeleine seemed to whisper now. 'I found this strange and wondered if I'd read and heard it correctly: *they were being targeted by the Russians, but I thought that they were supposed to be helping the Russians?* Harkiss seemed to lose any confidence he once possessed. I hadn't realised he could trip on his words so – he was now beginning to stutter and claw his hands about in frustration at losing his previous fluency. He erupted. "Ob … Obvi … Obviously you w … weren't f … followed?"'

'"Of course not." I squirmed in my seat when Blynde said that, but not without a degree of pleasure at first. Harkiss relaxed a little and went to the Gents. This seemed to be the most dangerous time for me, when Blynde's focus was no longer on Harkiss. Blynde spoke to himself, and I picked up something like, "Perhaps Kit is to spying what Caravaggio is to Art." I thought that Harkiss and Caravaggio would have got on famously, trailblazing their arts and expertise in between orgiastic drinking bouts and lethal fights; yet it made me shudder. The excitement of spying on the two of them unobserved turned into the horrifying spectre of what I was witnessing and what they might do to me if they caught me out.'

'I was scared. I spilled my soda down my lap, which meant one important prop had gone, and I didn't want to go up to the bar, not just because I might miss their conversation, but because I felt like an exposed actor who had forgotten their lines. Both Blynde's and Harkiss's moods were black, and I couldn't help checking the pistol again in my bag, just in case. I looked down at my newspaper until Harkiss returned to his seat. He at last began to mouth some more words as I glanced towards them. Like me, he was fighting back at his not being on the front foot before Blynde, but for different reasons. Harkiss could see how in control his fellow conspirator was, despite the fact Blynde was suffering from nervous exhaustion. With what seemed like uncharacteristic passivity, Harkiss let his MI5 colleague do the talking again and sound out the news for them both.'

Jock affirmed Madeleine's work. 'This ought to be enough to bring them to justice one day. Well done, Madeleine. Please carry on.'

'Blynde didn't talk so softly now, but seemed to enjoy his commanding position. He also seemed peeved and vented some anger towards Harkiss. I sat up as Blynde nodded and said something like, "a proposed … between the Abwehr and the British spells disaster for us all. We will be even more suspicious to Varley … Out of nowhere, there are eight unwittingly conspicuous agents who stand out dressed to the nines in their outrageously obvious Soviet coats and hats, trawling across our metropolis seeking proof that Stalin is totally correct about the 'Main Issue' problem of being fed apparently false information by us. The loquacious Catalan will confirm their worst fears. Do you know that it's because we have either no agents inside Russia and have told Varley as much, or because the Russian leader is angry that we adhere to this claim of a threat of an Anglo-German peace deal that Stalin is now spying on *us*?"'

'Harkiss began to rally. "What else did the Catalan give you for your money?" He took another gulp of whisky – the old Dutch courage.'

'"Not his body, if that's what you mean?" Blynde said.'

'He was trying to thaw things with a wan smile, but Harkiss seemed distant and cold-hearted. "Come on, Julian, this is no time to be flippant."'

'Blynde moved a little, uncomfortably perched on his wooden chair, and said something like, "Sorry, I'm trying to lift my somewhat depleted spirits. What I have so far is that there is going to be a special-ops flight carrying one agent to parachute into Spain in the next week, and someone very important in the Nazi hierarchy will meet them."'

Madeleine's voice crackled with vulnerability. 'I missed a heartbeat. At about this point, I think I recorded much of that and the rest of the conversation nearly verbatim.'

'Did you take notes then – afterwards – without being seen?'

'No. Don't be cross. I pretended to do the crossword if I suspected a glance from them in my direction, taking care to turn to the exact page of the newspaper, but writing down the conversation in the margins. Jock … are you still there?'

'Yes. I'm still here.'

'I wanted to do it … I thought it might help protect you …'

'You've just used up most of your nine lives. Carry on.'

'Harkiss said, "Who is the agent?"'

'"I don't know," said Blynde. "Still only the code name: MIRAGE."'

'"Not my boss, then?"'

'"No recognisable code number is being used for this operative. Perhaps he has only just surfaced?"'

'"It is unlikely." Harkiss seemed less flustered. "I think you'll find that both our outfits have had to use every one of their agents now as the threat to Britain increases daily. I reckon it must be the new man the fourth floor have recently brought in. If it's not him, it's probably someone like him."'

'Blynde paused. He seemed to be hesitating about whether to elaborate further on his discovery. Harkiss was still in a volatile state. "The Catalan mentioned that someone new might be being used to outwit everyone, including ourselves."'

'Harkiss snapped back, "He would say something like that if it pays better, but I suppose we can't rule that out. Let's hope his so-called spy doesn't know anything about us." He shot Blynde another chilling look, drank any remaining fears down with his whisky, and changed tack. "Did you know that I'm taking over the Madrid desk?"'

'"I'd heard a rumour. Pity that wasn't decided before this cropped up."'

'I thought Blynde looked uncomfortable again. Harkiss seemed to be propelled forward by a second wind and laid into him again. "You know it'll mean you'll have to stop walking around London with documents in that briefcase of yours." Blynde tried to look out of the window, as if he was concerned that someone might have overheard them; it was frosted glass above waist level, and I thought he felt trapped. Harkiss gave him another Victorian look. "The trouble with you, Julian, is that you are so dispassionate about the job." Harkiss gazed across the bar momentarily so as to avoid a familiar face. He turned back to Blynde again and said, "Sometimes I think it's just a game to you. Don't you see that everything we've been working for is in jeopardy? German hegemony has never been so assured. The Nazis might seek peace before being beaten by Stalin, and barter from a position of strength. And then we face the prospect of a fascist world, and a very long spell in the Scrubs – if we're lucky.'"

Jock was aghast at how fragile British security had become. 'Damning, is what it is. How did things end?'

'I saw Blynde wince. I hadn't ever seen him like this before. I wondered if he was trying very hard not to show his own deep concerns about their personal and professional positions. "That's why I came here, isn't it?" he said. He checked himself and seemed to speak more softly. "What now?"'

'"There is only one thing left for us, and for Russia. We have to deliver this plan and the names and places – and heads on a plate – to Varley, but also send an independent account copied to Moscow so that their doubts are not fuelled by this fantasy of MI6 which Varley may be unable to convey to Moscow through the current prism of paranoia in which he works."'

'"In which we all work, you mean."'

'"In which we serve," hissed Harkiss.'

Jock heard a door open in the room Madeleine was using and some muffled male voices.

'Darling, I've got to go … Someone else needs the telephone.'

'Bravo, Madeleine.' It was his turn to plead for contact. 'Don't forget to phone or write.'

BEDFORDSHIRE

WINTER 1940

I

Jock remembered the road now – the Hillman Minx, the silent driver, the Biff Boy – and as he held on to the last few words of Delahay's encouragement, thoughts of Charlotte returned with memories of the ride back past the hawthorn hedgerows on the other side of the Great North Road. This time, he was being driven, but he didn't want to talk now; he just wanted to be with his thoughts, returning to the farewell meal where he had first met his handler. What were Delahay's closing words? 'I spend 40 per cent of my time fighting the enemy and 60 per cent battling our friends.'

Yet it was Madeleine whom he thought of most – no longer safely absorbed with essay writing, but all too fully aware of the depth of evil so close to the heart of the capital, and to them both. He wondered what type of Englishman, from the universities or more likely the City or the military, would be deceiving them all on a daily basis.

As the Wolseley jolted on a pothole, Jock felt a double discomfort: if the Nazis were reading transcripts of messages sent to Moscow, then the SD rather than the Abwehr would endanger especially Canaris, but also himself. The greatest threat was a leak about the imminent mission from England, not Germany. Madeleine's report showed that Harkiss and Blynde were close to identifying MIRAGE. The prospect of engaging three enemies in the same location for this mission was not something that he relished – two enemies and the Admiral, who was neither friend nor foe.

As he checked his kit – the compass that screwed into the top button of his coat, a tube of half-used German toothpaste containing 'C''s codes, the pencil housing a map of the Spanish and African coasts, a Minox camera and the service revolver – Jock saw that he was being driven further north along the Great North Road this time. The car travelled for another half-hour in a north-easterly direction, with mostly flat, agricultural land on either side. As the vehicle slowed, he noticed the outline of outhouses by a railway line – more like little sheds obscured by overgrowing hawthorn copses and a light mist. The Wolseley crossed over a Roman road and then a double bridge, its lights illuminating a farm track of heavy but smooth, light-coloured clay. It drove several hundred yards towards a tiny homestead in front of a large old barn surrounded by thorn bushes. Several hundred yards away, he made out the silhouette of the twin Merlin engines of a De Havilland bomber.

Odd. Where was the Boeing Clipper that was to take him to Spain?

Jock thanked the driver and made his way to a cottage not far from the hangar. The airfield was aligned south-west/north-east and he felt the south-westerly winds on his face. The eastern and northern parts were protected by the west-facing slopes of a wide ridge. He was brought up sharp by the sight of Delahay talking to the Squadron Leader, the genial head of local operations. Places were laid along a trestle table in front of the white-washed walls of what had until recently been a simple farmer's dwelling.

'An unexpected pleasure,' said Jock, but he wasn't smiling as he moved towards his controller. 'You must have broken a few speed barriers to arrive before me.'

It wasn't planned that Delahay should be here; some agents might have been glad to see their handler, but not Jock. Not now. It seemed to confirm his doubts about the operation posed by Madeleine's investigation. *What was the hitch?*

'Don't let Maurice have a chance to brag about his racing skills – the RAF brought him over. Hello, I'm Squadron Leader Rawson. We have only just moved in here as a little experiment. Let's have a spot of supper and then we can have a short briefing in our temporary ops room next door.'

Jock was treated to an extremely tasty meal consisting of stew and dumplings. Though not in the same league as the Simpson's hotpot of lamb kidneys he'd already consumed that afternoon, the country kitchen was a most welcome spread; it would help ward off the chill at seeing Delahay. Something was clearly wrong, and yet it appeared that everything was still going ahead. Rawson made his excuses and skipped the cheese and biscuits, heading for the other room, and murmuring something about the ops set-up, although it was obvious to Jock that everything in the cottage had already been carefully prepared.

That was, everything except an additional briefing from Delahay, who made sure that he spoke first.

'Small peseta bills, which won't arouse suspicion, Spanish cigarettes and a lighter.'

Jock was aware that SOE handlers made checks to eliminate English clothing or giveaway items that could compromise an agent's cover identity, but he knew that Delahay hadn't been planning to travel and arrive before him just to give him these items. Rawson could have supplied them by courier, or even the pilot. *Where was the pilot, by the way?*

'I thought I was travelling in a Boeing Clipper?'

Delahay looked serious. 'The latest De Havilland Mosquito has been specially prepared for you. In fact, it was bright yellow until this afternoon.' He was managing a smile now. 'Don't touch the fuselage, because the black paint's drying. We think it will still be the safest way to transport you. It appears to have the capacity to outstrip even a Spitfire at high altitudes.'

Jock knew his runner was holding something back.

'But?'

If he was meant to be satisfied by new aerodynamics, he certainly wasn't going to show it. Jock sensed that Delahay, like his planes, was stalling. He waited for the sales pitch.

'This Mosquito is now the best long-distance, multi-role plane in the world.'

'I hadn't been aware of that.'

Delahay seemed to regain some of his composure now. 'That's because this particular model is a prototype.'

'When was it tested?'

'Four days ago.'

'What's the catch to this?'

Delahay spoke quietly. 'I thought you would still be interested – it's a lot safer than a Boeing or a troop ship, after all.' He paused, clearly embarrassed. 'Alright … the undercarriage can't quite close yet.'

Jock was bemused. 'But that's where I'd be, surely, if I were fool enough to curl up in the foetal position on a premature flight.'

'The Mosquito underbelly is open about 300 millimetres – the de Havilland family is working on it.' Jock again waited for more information, and Delahay continued. 'In fact, they let their own son test-fly on the maiden flight …'

'I can't wait.'

Jock didn't hide his ingratitude, though he knew very well that he might have far greater protection in a superior-designed, high-speed bomber, albeit there would be no room for bombs if he was the passenger. The bulky Boeing 314 Clipper was clearly no longer a match for this operation.

'The tail plane does experience some buffeting, but we are going to use one of our most experienced pilots, who wants this plane fully taken up by the Air Ministry so he can fly them all the time.'

'You told me it was safe to take the Boeing.'

Delahay seemed pensive and concerned. 'It was, until about ten minutes after I waved you off in London. Perhaps you'll understand further when I can tell you now that we have a leak regarding Canaris's presence in Spain and that it will no longer be possible to meet him in Toledo. Only "C", myself and you know about the change of plane and location. You have the pencil containing your map? Exchange it for this one.'

'I haven't said I'll fly in this aeronautical experiment.'

Delahay implored his agent. 'The Boeing Clipper would now be a sitting duck, and no one will be able to offer you another viable way to get to North Africa via Spain.' Jock began to remonstrate. 'Just let me finish, Jock. We haven't much time.'

Delahay handed over an almost exact replica of the pencil. Jock knew Delahay was right about his reaching North Africa; if he had one weakness, it was his obsession to fight behind enemy lines, and that for Jock was the place to be: thousands of miles of coast and sand punctuated by enemy airfields that he was determined to destroy.

'Please pass me your old pencil,' Delahay said. 'Here is a copy of the updated map that you will find in your new one.'

They cleared the table and Jock saw a larger version of his new directions on the wall.

'You're now off to the south-eastern coast, north of Alicante. You'll be closer to where you want to go. You will be dropped west of the old village of Altea. There is a totally secluded beach three hundred metres long.' Delahay anticipated Jock's thinking. 'There is only one beach, two miles east of the village. At the base of the mountain above it, you will find a shepherd called Fernando, who will use the signal that we discussed before. He will take you to Canaris; there will be no one else there, except possibly Fernando's sister, Peluka. Abwehr bodyguards are in the vicinity, but are under strict orders to observe only from their base and allow you to enter the shepherd's house fifty metres above the sea – as long as Canaris leaves first to the eastern tip of the beach on his own, after your meeting ends at 0230. You should be safer with the Abwehr than any unexpected guests we might speculate could be in the area.'

'I see.'

'I know it's not what we discussed, but in a way you are getting what you want too, you know. The pilot will wait until 0230 hours for you by the plateau to the west of Fernando's home, and while you talk to Canaris, the plane can be refuelled so that it can drop you into Suez and be made ready for someone else.'

'I'd like a bit more on the real threat to these peace talks with Canaris. I'd say it's turning up in the first place, if you don't mind me being so blunt, sir? Who is the threat, if it isn't a bunch of some of their best troops?'

Delahay seemed genuinely disappointed. 'There is a chance that our traitors are closing in on our plans. However, this time we've restricted the last-minute change of plan to "C" and SOE's controllers as a precaution.'

'More lack of security than "C" gave us to believe?' Jock was serious for a moment. 'So I'm walking into a heaven-sent opportunity for some fanatic to kill two birds with one stone.' Delahay's forehead furrowed while Jock continued. 'Well, Canaris and I for a start, which would help destroy any hope of peace with Abwehr leaders and my having a chance to peel my skin off until I tell a traitor which of the 60 per cent of your friends you think you are battling with ...'

'Which—'

'Which you haven't shared with me,' Jock interrupted.

Yet he also didn't have to tell Delahay everything. By withholding all details about Blynde and Harkiss, he would possibly protect Madeleine while he was abroad. If he thought that Delahay could move quickly against Harkiss especially, he might have thought it beneficial to divulge everything to his handler. An inquiry into the two men's backgrounds could be leaked and raise the traitor's suspicions of anyone working with them – in Blynde's case, possibly Madeleine herself. Yet he didn't believe the old-boy network that had successfully ring-fenced the two double agents from being detected so far in the war would suddenly fold in a matter of days. His uncle, Herbert Steel, had mentioned on more than one occasion how investigations into treachery were slow at the best of times. Jock needed a confession from a Soviet or Nazi operator connected to the two deceivers that would represent the proof he could present on his return. Requesting Delahay to activate an investigation into the turncoats' authenticity might actually confirm more of the conspirators' worst fears, only intensifying their efforts to cover their own tracks and make more progress identifying MIRAGE and anyone associated with that and the other missions 'C' had activated. Jock estimated that revealing anything that Madeleine or he reported might possibly protect them both in some way. However, holding it back seemed the safer option for now. Sole knowledge was power, and he needed as much as he could muster. With Madeleine's courageous coup in St Albans, Jock believed that he had the advantage over the Soviet spies, because they thought it was only their own people who were currently monitoring them. He'd tell all when he was ready, and put Delahay under some necessary pressure.

His handler seemed defensive. 'Because I don't know who the traitors are, do I?'

'Don't you? Who organised the course at Arisaig?'

Delahay spoke more quietly. 'I organised the course, but others switched the SOE training venue at the last moment.'

'Hmm.' Jock believed his handler for the time being, but it was the moment to say something and offer a lead to Delahay. 'I would have all course members, organisers and visitors checked all over again, if I were you.'

Delahay barely disguised his impatience. 'Jock, I will ascertain their identities. I'd go to Spain myself, if I didn't think they knew all about me. You know that little is known about you except for the highest recommendations from Lord Lloyd and what tests you have been through with us or the Welsh Guards. A dedicated outsider is essential to this operation, and there is nothing on your file on purpose.'

'Do you think the traitor is in MI6 or SOE?'

'It could be either of them,' Delahay admitted, keeping his voice down.

Jock looked gravely at Delahay. 'Or someone with links to both?' He spelled it out to him. 'Come to think of it, if that was the case, it might narrow down who you're looking for. There can't be that many who have access to both organisations at the moment; they're not exactly in bed with each other, are they?'

A feeling like a cold stone in the pit of Jock's stomach developed as he began to fully appreciate that the spies he was working for at MI6 had great reserves of charm, but that this was no guarantee of their wisdom or cleverness – or loyalty, for that matter.

'Perhaps … I understand why you're speculating, but I'm not sure where this is getting us right now. We have a briefing to attend.'

Jock didn't like the response, which was uncharacteristically glib.

'Of course.'

However, he didn't stir. Instead, he stood silent for a moment, scrutinizing his handler. He knew he had Delahay over a barrel in some ways. Without Jock, his handler would be in an intelligence cul-de-sac, in arguably one of British Intelligence's most vulnerable moments of the war.

'But Maurice,' Jock said, 'I expect you to pass on my doubts and the brief detail of our conversation just now … to "C" himself … *in person*.'

There was a difficult silence before Delahay uttered, 'Granted.'

Jock could sense the anger hidden deep below the surface of Delahay's whole being. This was not how Delahay had planned it. That, in the freezing black night, was the one thing that gave Jock most comfort despite the unanswered questions, and Jock's own instinct – a feeling right down to his fingertips. Jock felt some relief at having aimed a few shots across the bows of the traitors; he had fulfilled a key part of his operations by providing Delahay and 'C' with the wherewithal to draw their own conclusions about Harkiss's treachery so that they could 'own' the exposure, particularly of Harkiss in MI6. At the same time, Jock might offer some protection to Madeleine and himself by allowing his seniors to take the credit for fully checking the files on Harkiss, deflecting the heat on to those most responsible in MI6, rather than its assistants. Harkiss was an up-and-coming pillar of the establishment – to such an extent that he could even be eyeing up the top job, given his recent promotion to the Madrid desk. Jock was a new boy by comparison, and in some ways expendable. 'C' had given Jock a poisoned chalice by offering him the chance to identify a traitor. Perhaps 'C' knew all along who it was? Jock understood that the repercussions of making an enemy of someone with Harkiss's standing at Broadway Buildings might actually jeopardise his own career in Intelligence and in the military. Jock could see that it might even lead to a court-martial if Harkiss drew his favours in – *or perhaps he wouldn't even need to do that to take revenge?* In Madeleine's case, it would also be career-limiting. Her auspicious beginning would be over before it began. How on earth would the fount of power receive the news that an apprentice 'Mother' on secretarial duties had successfully investigated Britain's senior intelligence officers and found them guilty of selling secrets to the Russians on her afternoons off – secrets that then could be lifted by the Nazis, who already knew something of the double agents' activities?

Jock defused the tension. 'Alright, let's go and hear the Squadron Leader. I want to go, Maurice. It isn't simply about soldiering in Africa at the moment. The fact is that I'm in this now up to my neck. If I don't go and eliminate this threat, it rather seems it will catch up with all of us first.'

Some of Delahay's frostiness on that icy evening began to thaw too. 'You know, when you first joined The Firm, your nickname was "the

Accountant Spy" because of your rather unhealthy family interest in the service's finances. Yet you aren't especially interested in money for yourself, are you, Lieutenant? I know I'm working with a patriot, second to none.'

Jock said nothing, but was glad to hear the words.

'What's the book that's bulging out of your pocket?' Delahay said. He was still a little taken aback by how inquisitive he was about his new agent – he liked to think he was *his*, anyway.

'*The Art of War*, by Sun Tzu,' Jock said.

'Fascinating. You must tell me about it when you get back.'

'I'll do that, Maurice, but let me whet your appetite. It's all about knowing your enemy before engaging him; knowing his story, knowing what he loves, where his conflicts lie, how he moves, and why.' Jock thought Delahay looked relieved when he saw his staff car arrive, though he still had a briefing to complete. 'I'll arrange for a copy to be sent to the office when I get to Cairo.'

Delahay seemed about to speak, but then stared into Jock's eyes, taking him in as if he had met him for the first time.

'Do that, Jock, yes … I'd like that very much.'

II

Jock and Delahay sat in front of a set of black and green scrambler telephones, below a large map of Spain bearing some red marks, mostly near the coast, which Rawson explained were high-risk areas for flak. The weather forecast, just telephoned through from the Met Office, was fair, with a slight chance of fog at ground level. Rawson indicated the flight path on the map, and showed Jock a photograph taken by RAF Reconnaissance of the plateau above the sea that would make for a tight landing field on the Valencian coast, five miles north-north-east of Alicante. It showed a level strip of land by a tiny bay at the base of a mountain some 800 feet above. It would not take long to adjust to the moonlight for map-reading. Jock took care to memorise the layout, noting the position of where he might expect his contact to be and the other end of the bay, where Canaris would have to travel to join his elite Abwehr bodyguards after the meeting.

Rawson exuded enthusiasm. 'You are travelling in a "Wooden Wonder", which will hopefully be seriously unleashed on the Nazis.'

Jock had followed the fortunes of the brilliantly conceived aircraft that would dent the pride of competitors and enemies alike, because it was now becoming the fastest plane in the world. The wings could withstand the equivalent strength of 700 men, the concentrated firepower on the wings and in the nose was formidable, and he'd heard rumours that planes like it would soon contain a new radar G set that could be pulled out on an approach to coastlines without being jammed by the Nazis. Jock decided that these encouraging characteristics would help him overlook the fact that much of the fuselage was built by a coffin manufacturer to help prevent the construction of all the invaluable parts being bombed in one place by the Germans. To be fair, English coffin-makers were some of the best craftsmen in the world for such a streamlined wooden shell.

Rawson turned from the map. 'You won't be able to physically view the coastline yourself, Lieutenant, because, as you may be aware, you're in the belly of the beast, so you'll be cut off from the skipper and can expect no help from the unarmed and unprotected plane should it be attacked.'

'Unarmed to limit weight and reduce fuel consumption, sir?'

'Yes. If you are wounded, hang on until you are in Altea, where your contact will look out for you. Take your handheld kit of painkillers and expect your quarters to provide little room for movement, as they have been shaped to fit your body. Though,' he added with a smile, 'Maurice assures me you've now lost some weight since a spell of arduous training. Oxygen supply is there with a radio contact with the pilot. We've acquired an extra thick suit, as it will feel somewhat fresh in there; the undercarriage will be partially open.'

If Jock was concerned about that, he didn't show it. 'If planes ditch into the North Sea, the passenger has less than two minutes before exposure kicks in?'

'Correct, Lieutenant, so the Mediterranean won't give you much more grace, I'm afraid, and there's the question of your dependants?'

'I've left an envelope in the office safe. Maurice has responsibility for that, thank you, sir.'

Jock had not discussed any of its contents, but had a nasty feeling Hollings might be highly skilled with a steaming iron as the department's chief 'cut-and-paste' man.

'I think that's just about it, Lieutenant Steel. Any further questions?'

'Who has paid for this mission? Because I know you've few pennies to rub together for operations of this type.'

Delahay squirmed a little in his seat. 'Squadron Leader, our special agent has an unhealthy interest in inter-departmental finance. I'm sure that the Welsh Guards would say it must be that fraction of Scottish blood in you, Steel,' Delahay quipped, trying to hide some embarrassment. 'We can't exactly refuse you, and you're right, we haven't money enough for this sort of work.'

'So?' Jock's curiosity was relentless and, in the circumstances, difficult to quell.

'The monarch, if you really have to know. There's a slush fund for national emergencies, and without putting too fine a point on it – this is one. Even your plane out there has been mostly privately funded from design to construction and testing.'

Jock looked wistful. 'Thanks for the reassurance, gentlemen. Well, with sponsors of this order, I can't very well refuse, can I?'

Delahay seemed relieved. If chocolate was one of Jock's Achilles heels, royalty was the other; he'd chosen to press the right buttons of his agent at the eleventh hour.

Rawson saluted Jock as Delahay produced the padded suit. 'Good luck, Lieutenant.'

The MI6 handler led the young warrior to his plane. When the pair walked onto the tarmac, they saw an anonymous black-suited figure: the pilot was putting the final touches to polishing the Mosquito, and was only just visible. Jock saw that he was in good hands: a polished machine would give the pilot fifteen extra knots and would use less fuel. Despite the last-minute change of plane and location, everyone involved seemed to be getting everything first time. It felt spot on.

He shook Delahay's hand. 'Will it earn me any commission if I enhance the testing of this prototype?'

Delahay looked bemused. 'Sorry, I … wouldn't have thought so.'

Jock smiled to relieve any embarrassment. 'It's alright, Maurice … only joking.'

Despite some testy moments and doubts in the ops room, Jock realised that Maurice seemed to epitomise lonely honour and unassailable privacy, guarded by a pair of considerable shoulders. Jock climbed into the Mosquito. The bomb bay doors hissed and almost closed like clams as the spy handler ducked out of the way to hear the deafening roar of the Merlin engines being run up. With a squeal of brakes, the small plane jockeyed for position. Delahay watched the great sheets of blue flame flare back as the Mosquito pulled into the night sky. Jock was in the lap of the gods. So, possibly, was the future of British Intelligence and military success in North Africa, where a victory was essential if the British were to finish off Mussolini and continue fighting the Nazis alone.

VALENCIA

I

Jock inhaled the peculiar air in the military aircraft; it had that familiar light, oily and tinny smell. As an amateur pilot at Oxford, he had thrilled with the sensation of disassociating himself from the earth, and with it the pressures of taking the university boat to victory against all odds. As the plane flew towards Spain, he did not feel such a sense of liberation in its hold. If his transport was being changed to reputedly the fastest long-distance plane in the world – even with its undercarriage slightly open – there must be a significant threat to his reaching the Mediterranean in one piece. The Russians almost certainly knew he was coming, and they would do all in their power to stop him, but they might not know everything about his vehicle or its capacity to avoid detection at over 22,000 feet. He wasn't going to indulge himself in too many thoughts of this nature, because it was clear even the British didn't know the plane's capabilities either.

His thoughts turned instead to his own role in the chaos that the world's leaders had chosen, and the irony of travelling to Spain, the one place that had been the crucible for so much of the polarisation of their countries. The Italians – now the prime target of African operations – encouraged the Nazis to help Franco massacre the Republicans; the British parliamentarians had used the conflict in Spain as a spectator sport while Liverpool dockworkers and other true Labour supporters had led the defence against the blue-shirted Falangists. The limbo of inaction against fascism in Spain had caused the fragmentation of patriotism among too many British intellectuals.

More ironies had been unfolding, as Franco had been discouraged from entering the war with Germany by Canaris himself. It had been this knowledge that supported claims by a new type of pacifist in London – not the Halifaxes or Mosleys, but those who believed that Canaris was one of the few powerful leaders who fully appreciated the extent of Hitler's threat to the whole of civilisation. Though not popular with the Prime Minister, these intelligence men had espoused the theory that Canaris was actively obstructing Hitler's destruction of Europe, which was becoming a reality with every new day of a war that was now spreading across the globe. Canaris was unusual, in that he appeared to avoid the rut of clinging to the Nazi narrative that the Germans were not responsible for their woes after the First World War. Jock reflected that in the history of feuding, peace was only possible when self-indulgent narratives of disrespect for an old rival were abandoned: only then could gestures of peace begin. This view also had prevailed with 'C', for the time being.

Jock knew his mission would have some bearing on the widening gaps between the sagacity of the MI6 chief who was still fighting Britain's corner and the narrowing views of the propagandists at Westminster who wanted an unconditional surrender of Germany when the time came – not a negotiated peace led by the likes of the Anglo-German Society. Either conclusion to the war seemed remote following a succession of Nazi victories. The Luftwaffe had killed 3,000 people in Birmingham not long after the Coventry raid, and British convoys had been cancelled after the battleship *Admiral Scheer* sank six British ships. There had also been the real possibility of an invasion of Britain, while Hitler enjoyed apparent security in the East after the Nazi–Soviet Pact.

To the cramped passenger in the bay of the Mosquito, these were all very good reasons to deliver material from 'C' to Canaris and not to dismiss genuine peace offers from Germany while simultaneously strongly defending the British Isles. He knew he had to reach North Africa quickly after that: if Egypt fell to the Axis, Alexandria, the Delta, Cairo and the Suez Canal would be lost. The Red Sea and the Arabian oil fields, Persia and India would then collapse like a house of cards, allowing Hitler to link up with the Japanese. Jock knew that German U-boats and airpower held the key to dominating North Africa, and if he was able to pioneer some of his ideas in the desert, he might help turn the tide against the totalitarians in Russia and the Pacific. Churchill was planning new actions in other theatres of war, but this would be dependent on progress against the enemy in the desert. To lose Egypt now would be to hand over a lifeline to the Axis henchmen who would rule each newly won state in their own hideous image, allowing the fascists to control more than half the world.

Thoughts returned swiftly to a more pressing concern: the high altitude that the Mosquito was now being forced to climb to. A somewhat ironic 'You should be getting oxygen now' was just audible: Jock was receiving oxygen, but very little. His microphone must have also slipped out of position on take-off, because as he moved his chin around to locate it, the equipment wasn't anywhere where it could pick up enough sound. Jock realised that the pilot would know something was wrong, but that was not much comfort because both he and the airman were well aware that this mission was a unique opportunity to meet up with the Abwehr chief and continue it must: short of being shot down, the plane was expected to land near Altea that evening.

As he regulated his breathing to harness what air was left in the human capsule, Jock kept hold of his last thoughts. He pored over the dangers of the meeting in southern Spain once the plane had dodged any enemy fire and was able to land him in one functioning piece. Jock knew that Canaris surely had friends in Spain's Falangist stronghold, but few, if any, had much of an idea that the Admiral had been undermining Himmler's recent negotiations with Franco. If Himmler had been successful, every old score between the two Spanish sides would have been settled once and for all, with the Nazi influence prevailing in Madrid, and dominating much more than the press. That was why Jock had worked so hard with Lloyd's initiative with Portugal at the British Council. Republicans, despite being politically poles apart from the Abwehr, could also benefit from keeping lines of communication open with Admiral Canaris.

II

It was the zigzagging of the plane that jerked Jock out of 'auto-pilot'. He quickly realised that the Mosquito must be too low for comfort, as it was drawing unwanted attention from coastal gunfire. Jock thought that the skin of ice had formed rather too easily on the surface of the small glass spyhole beneath him, and noted that it seemed unusually cold for early December, wrapped as he was in the dark, insulated bodysuit. The plane now dropped several thousand feet, and eventually cruised over the Mediterranean. Once the pilot headed in the direction of Alicante, he attracted little interest; the plane was seemingly just another civilian aircraft on its way south. The detour to Altea would take a matter of minutes; fortunately, there was no fog and only a light coating of snow. Jock saw glimpses of a few lamps in parallel that must be the markers on the plateau above the water. As the plane descended, it became clear that the lights were actually small fires. The landing was going to be tight, as the plateau was more mountain path than runway. Some of the flares were now smoking, and it appeared to be what was left of last summer's gorse aflame, punctuating the edge of the track.

Jock's forehead hit the edge of the capsule hard as the Mosquito landed. He was knocked out as he was flung around the metal tube even though the pilot kept as straight a course as possible and was careful to avoid going over the narrow pathway whose seaward edge offered little room for manoeuvre. The other side was dangerously close to his wing, as there was thirty feet of mountain above it. There was no room for error as the aeroplane only just had the space to lurch to a halt with a tight taxi for take-off.

As Jock regained consciousness, he first punched the salty air, and then began strangling the pilot who had been resuscitating him. He drew in large pants of breath as he glared into the airman's face; then he closed his eyes and threw his head back with much relief, muttering an apology to his saviour. He eventually recovered, steadied himself as his feet touched the ground, looked about and registered exactly where they were, relieved they were finally on Spanish soil. Quickly he noted his position some kilometres level with the old town across the bay. The earth felt good beneath his feet as he squeezed the shoulder of the aviator, strapped his revolver around his suit and left his companion to attend to the aeroplane, which had remained virtually unscathed. Jock looked around and found a loose branch to put out the burning bushes as he walked up the slight gradient he had so recently flown over.

III

The light from the moon winked back at him from the waves below. The climb above the bay in Pueblo Mascarat was welcome exercise after the cabin fever and blackout at the end of the previous hours, and it presented him with few obstacles other than the occasional loose rock, which he negotiated with his boots. Jock's breathing was now deep and steady; he enjoyed the sensation of filling his lungs, hungry for the full capacity he had so recently been denied on the journey. Gloved hands meant the gorse became mountain handholds except for the occasional brush that came away in his fingers. The 900-foot climb above the bay would give him the view he needed to verify that the rendezvous was secure as planned. He would reach his viewpoint once he could see seven peaks on his left and six on his right as he faced south overlooking the sea. He preferred the shortest route to the top of his own 'hill', which meant that he chose the most exhilarating and physically demanding direct path up the peak. He reckoned it was a 1 in 3 gradient.

The silhouettes of the mountain tops were just visible in the moonlit sky. He thought he heard a muffled din echo up the side of the mountain, not far from where he had begun the ascent, but realised that the Mosquito might already be refuelling. As he took in the terrain, Jock saw the bolthole that Delahay had mentioned, right at the top of the peak. As he made his way past the gorse and rocks, which he was careful to avoid disturbing, he could see down into the aperture in the peak with room for a tall, well-built man. He doubted that he would need it, as everything so far had gone to plan. He checked his position with the numerous points on either side of him; it was not difficult from this vantage spot to see everything immediately below. There they were: the flashing lamp lights of Fernando, his contact and lifeline to Canaris. It was exactly midnight. Those torch lights would be repeated again in twenty minutes, so Jock did not reply with the pre-arranged signal. He decided instead to move in closer and ascertain escape routes, and whether the Spaniard was alone.

It took more effort to traverse the mountain without making too much noise. He stopped in his tracks when he spotted the Abwehr hideout containing Canaris's commando bodyguard on the other side of the bay. One of the guards was so sure of himself that he didn't attempt to shade the red tip of his cigarette end – either that, or or he was just foolish. Jock then studied the path back from the safe house to the Abwehr troops, which the Admiral would have to cross alone in exactly two and a half hours. Jock didn't have much time, and he scrutinised the pines on that part of the cliff top that was an equal distance from the house as it was to Canaris's men. If he made his way over there, he could set up a safety net and diversion for Canaris if things did not go according to plan. Carrying only a few pounds of his own home-made explosives, he decided to move over to the pines, and be back in time for Fernando's next signal.

He moved as silently as he could up the rocks to the trees, all the time peering into the darkness on the lookout for any movement. Nothing stirred. Wrapping round the lightweight and malleable plastic, he assembled several one-pound bombs, which he then placed around the bases of several tall pines over the rocky pathway below. Jock then attached time pencils on to the small explosives. He tucked one end of the new-issue nylon lines, which he fixed to the time pencils, into his belt so that the nylon would drop unnoticed over the scree and heather as he moved across it. Jock had been told by the army that it was not possible to provide him with an inconspicuous explosive, and MO9 had not yet developed their own bomb and time pencil, so he preferred to carry the material on his person; the chemicals gave him headaches, but he loved his chemistry too much, though he had not mentioned the explosive to Wing Commander Rawson. Either way, he wasn't sure that he'd want to meet the RAF officer again if it was discovered what else the Mosquito had been carrying. It was time to head back; he resisted the pull to soak in the scenery and the mesmeric crash of the waves in the dappled moonlight below.

In case Fernando, Canaris's Spanish houseboy, had been 'replaced', Jock decided to watch for the signal from behind where it was supposed to be flashed. Due north of the Abwehr base was a peak about twenty metres wide and high. Jock decided he would climb it from the north face. He had enough rope – it had made the journey in the Mosquito that much more uncomfortable, but now it came in useful. He scrambled as quietly as he could up the mountain and ascended the peak in silence. He fixed his ropes at the top and descended, but this time to a smaller peak some fifty yards to the west. He laid another three bombs under the rocky parts protruding out of the junior peak, then abseiled down the senior of the two peaks and climbed round. All the time, he ensured that the new-issue lines from the time pencils didn't snag on any rocks as he made his way to the gorse, below which he hid the nylon ends and his bomb bag. All seemed clear. He looked ahead to see the silhouette of a young farmhand fumbling with a torch. There was no movement or sound except for the hushed echo of seawater as it was sucked back over the pebbly beach below.

IV

Jock whispered, '*Hola*', in the roaring silence. It wasn't pre-arranged, but there was recognition in the dark eyes of the young blood who gestured to frisk Jock. Afterwards, Jock offered his hand. Fernando shone the light ahead and let Jock take the narrow, stony path first. Jock could hear the ivory tones of what sounded like one of Bach's famous preludes. He looked back briefly at the outline of his mined pines; he hoped that he wouldn't have to bring them down as a diversion later on.

The cold barely contained the smell of donkey droppings. The lad motioned for Jock to continue past olive groves on either side of the track; they were gnarled and twisted by the years, with fountains of leaves that would soon become mottled by a trove of small but prolific black globes. Jock's sudden hunger grew as the Spaniard pushed open a thick teak door and hung back as Jock was ushered into a softly lit kitchen and dining room, where the master chef had just started to busy himself by pressing pink pieces of meat into red-hot, thick ceramic bowls.

'Medallions of wild boar, Lieutenant – something I love to make for my guests when I am away from Berlin.'

Canaris was wearing white, but it was the apron of a passionate cook rather than the official dress of a naval officer.

The Englishman saluted. 'Thank you, sir.'

'Life is short, suffer what there is to suffer, enjoy what there is to enjoy while you can … Please, have a seat, Lieutenant.'

The guest appreciated how Canaris had started the conversation in English, and also how the senior officer listened carefully to his own fluent German. Few untruths would have ever passed a spymaster so equipped to use his auditory and visual senses simultaneously. The Admiral watched Jock closely as he answered, while passing some delicious morsels with herbs and salad that complemented the aromas from the kitchen. Despite the tensions of his recent arrival, the whole atmosphere was seductive, and Jock relaxed and tasted the medium-rare meat. From his comfortable stool, he took in the brightly painted walls and high-beamed ceiling of the converted barn, its centrepiece being the kitchenette flanked by a bar on one side and a dining area on the other; the view of the starlit coastline made a good backdrop for the Steinway by the balcony windows.

'I have been holidaying in my favourite country, so I have something to celebrate. As you know, Berlin is beginning to feel the effects of England's own bombing campaigns, and the peace and quiet here is especially precious.' Jock began to speak, but Canaris interrupted him. 'Don't apologise for the merciless killing of our civilians, Lieutenant Steel. After all, it is only cause and effect, would you not say?'

The Welsh Guardsman saw the twinkle and spark of a brilliant mind, and in a trice he caught himself with a sudden rash twinge of admiration for the Admiral. He checked himself. This was the same man whose agents had 'sewn up' most of Europe in a year of fighting. Yet Jock had read the reports about him: he had been one of the few leaders who had a calming effect on Hitler. This provided him with access to the Führer when it was so often denied to others, who often had to make do with a subordinate. Canaris allowed those in his company to do the talking; it had enabled the Admiral to win the confidence of the dictator, whose egoism knew no bounds. Jock himself was ready for that.

Jock knew that Canaris had also 'befriended' the ex-chicken farmer,

Himmler, who had been only twenty-eight years old when appointed to head the SS. Canaris knew Himmler's weaknesses, his fears and demons, and let him know it – although not verbally or in writing. The younger cadre of Nazi leaders were co-dependent on their Admiral of the old guard, whom they began to emulate until it became a love-hate relationship. They could not hate the Führer, but they could despise the senior officer whose credentials could only be superficially mirrored by the immaculate Nazi uniforms, honours and medals of the now grown-up Hitler Youth.

So, here was Canaris, the detached party leader. Like his fellow Greek, Xeno, he believed that with two ears he should listen twice as much as use his tongue. Jock had read the secret reports on how the Admiral was the Party's 'Psychiatrist-in-Chief' without many being fully aware of it. The chief's diligence and research skills were rarely matched by the subjects that he chose to observe and study. This was the senior official who had always refused to believe in a German victory. This was the man with friends in Holland who might have been compromised by the Soviet traitors in London, who feared the Anglo-German talks and understanding that had not yet taken place. Until now. Jock could not be so naïve as to not realise that he could be a pawn himself in a dangerous game of subterfuge that 'C' could play out. More significantly, was Jock himself bait for a prize that the Abwehr chief secretly coveted?

The Admiral could almost whistle to his bodyguard if he wanted them present. Jock didn't doubt that he was being watched closely. And yet, this was the German who feared for European Jewry and was known to both aid the Jews, and retard the German technological programmes that he believed would enable the Nazis to lord it over the world. Jock comforted himself with the knowledge that 'C' had overruled a project to kidnap Canaris, for if the Russians were in the war, it was clear that they too could turn on their potential allies, the British. Then there would be only a few sane leaders with authority in Germany who could mediate with England in the event of the Russian alliance ending in disaster – the head of the Abwehr being a likely choice.

'Bloody Mary?'

Jock's ears pricked up with his host's offer. 'Thank you.' He relaxed a little with the cocktail in his hand. 'I enjoyed the Bach. You are an accomplished pianist, Admiral.'

'Deceptively simple, that prelude.' He looked at Jock all the time that he was speaking now. 'I prefer piano music, while my wife favours the violin. I have often thought a violinist is part predator and part poet; in Frau Canaris's case it is mostly poet, and in the case of her violin partner ...'

'Predator?'

'Yes, Lieutenant Steel. You know about my former protégé's preference for the predatory over the poetic?'

'Indeed. He is otherwise known as the "Blond Beast". As Jew-hunter-in-chief, he has little room for poetry.'

'You're well informed.' Canaris chuckled, 'I am sure your files are bulging on the leader of the SD.' His lived-in face shot Jock an unguarded look. 'And on myself, of course.'

The Admiral changed tack slightly, appearing not disappointed – if he ever had been – that he was in talks with a junior officer rather than his opposite number.

'You must be a very brave man, Lieutenant?'

Jock withstood, for the moment, the sting of doubts regarding Canaris and the thought that he might be weaving about him an Abwehr trap. However, there was no malice in the older man's eyes as he spoke.

'I can't think of many men who would voluntarily walk into an Abwehr den – unarmed, I presume?' He gave a swift look at Fernando, who, with eyes on the Admiral, bowed his head. 'You appear to be travelling light, Lieutenant. Alright, Fernando, please say goodnight and get some sleep.'

The boy nodded, tipped his head to Jock and left, as quietly as he came.

'You clearly inspire trust in the young, Lieutenant Steel,' said Canaris, smiling as his gloved hand passed another scorching ceramic bowl and a wooden platter of wild boar onto the horseshoe-shaped table. He beckoned for Jock to sit and eat in the warm by the kitchen, then poured two small glasses of German red wine, though Jock noted that the Admiral didn't touch his.

'How did you know Bloody Mary was one of my favourite drinks, Admiral?'

'Intuition.' There was a knowing smile. 'Alright, you've been carded by us. Let us just say that I have known of your existence a little longer even than you have known of mine. We thought you were spying in 1937, but that was supposition. Like General Rommel, some of your leaders are keen to use relatively new officers for a host of clandestine missions, in and out of uniform. It's not a complete surprise when a new breed of fighter shows up some of the older methods of his senior officers. I'm not averse to granting great initiative to my foot-soldiers myself.'

Canaris took a platter of diced boar. It hissed as he pressed some of the flesh on the ceramic with a knife. He looked up. 'You didn't exactly keep a low profile while you were in Berlin. We really thought we could turn you for a time, but that was just a part of the Anglo-German confusion before the war that I suspect will always exist between our peoples. The closeness that Saxon blood brings, the fantasy of our leader that northern European cousins could get into bed with each other – *militarily, I mean*,' he added hastily with a chortle. 'An unfortunate analogy, I know – in the case of the Führer, who has always been especially confused.' The humour evaporated, and he became still and deadly serious. 'Which brings us to our meeting?'

Jock was somewhat relieved. 'Indeed.'

'We must get to the point, and stop being so English, if you don't mind me saying. You don't mind, do you, Lieutenant? You're half-Australian, I believe. That's one of the reasons I agreed to meet you instead of 'C'.'

'That's the first time I ever considered my childhood heritage an advantage in the British Army.'

'Rather than your Calcutta birthplace, you mean? Of course, if you had stayed there, you would have had all the credentials of the British establishment, but to us you are part insider, part outsider, without the chance to have been smeared by England's own witch-hunters, suspicious of those even mentioning the word "peace". And yet we both know the dangerous parameters of English extremism that also exist.'

'You mean the Halifaxes and the Mosleys?'

'Exactly, Lieutenant. We have our own appeasers, but at least they want to destroy the Führer, as opposed to your appeasers, who had wanted to cosy up to him, I think you would say in England?'

'Spot on, Admiral.'

'We know that your people – they are your people now, after this meeting especially – are thinking the unthinkable, that if all does not go well, they will have to join with us Nazis against the Russians. Yet things have not yet gone that far, and naturally even I would be reluctant to bed Moscow ...' He gave a wan smile. 'Until such a time – and I mean no offence by this – I want "C" to know that by sending you instead of himself, he might have missed the one opportunity of the war – and it's going to be long; tell him that, won't you – of ever meeting me in person. Tell "C" that I won't sacrifice one of my men to save Central Europe. But I will do my utmost to prevent the Führer overrunning the whole of the continent, especially my beloved Spain.'

An internal door closed behind the kitchen. Jock didn't think they would be alone, but braced himself for more company. It must be Peluka, Fernando's sister.

Canaris seemed to have read his mind. 'We have company, Lieutenant Steel. Fernando will be asleep by now, and his sister isn't in Altea tonight.'

Jock quietly put down the drink that he had just picked up. The Admiral was about to speak again, but thought better of it. He looked disconcerted. He reached out to a drawer by the dining area, but sat back and sighed as the muzzle of a Luger pointed out through the door at the two diners. Jock noted the Admiral really was surprised by the additional company.

The intruder was about Jock's height, with a mop of silver hair, though he was still a young man. His face was ruddy, and he flashed blue eyes that would have made any Aryan proud – except that the apparently German-looking man was nothing of the sort. Compassionless possibly, thought Jock, but somewhat manic and unfortunately English, as his accent and broken sentences in German suggested.

'Good evening. A very interesting conversation – if I may say so. I hope that you have enjoyed your meal. A Last Supper, gentlemen? What sort of Communion do we have here? In your case, Steel, I have no doubt that it is consorting with the enemy. The Admiral will be lucky if he resides at His Majesty's pleasure.'

His mock laughter already irritated Jock. 'What are you?'

The unwelcome visitor with wire-rimmed spectacles shrugged his sauce-bottle shoulders and seemed visibly piqued by the provocation. 'What?'

'What indeed?' Jock was determined not to listen to a monologue by the gun-toter, who was obviously milking every last second out of his apparent advantage. 'An amateur, perhaps?'

The silver-haired spy winced. 'Isn't that rich coming from a new boy like you, Mr Steel?'

'Lieutenant Steel,' Jock corrected, noticing now the grubby and dirty fingernails wrapped around the gun.

'Alright, Lieutenant, you are experiencing a short career, whether you realise it or not.' The mouth slobbered at this – *had he been drinking? Dutch courage, perhaps?* 'And any attempt to negotiate with the Germans is being terminated.'

Jock observed that the spy still managed to look unkempt in his Savile Row clothing, an unusual feat of sartorial inelegance. He barely contained his contempt. 'I am under the orders of "C".'

'Of course you are – *old chap*, but not for very much longer, of course. If this mission of yours goes wrong, and' – the languid figure allowed himself a smirk – 'it appears to be going *very* wrong, your gentlemen's peace process will never get off the ground if there's an accident. I'm here to ensure that you are dealt with and both your names are mud … There will be no Anglo-German understanding; Russia will prevail against both England and Germany.'

The pilot … Jock immediately thought of the unarmed airman. Anger welled up inside. *This was a mess … The Mosquito would be better destroyed than fall into either Nazi or Soviet hands …* The agent in front of him was surely some type of Trotskyite sympathiser. The Bloody Mary had worn off and he was brought up sharply.

'A wrong move by you,' the interloper continued, malevolent eyes fixed on Jock, 'could mean a wrong move by the Abwehr guard on the hill there.'

The Admiral said nothing, but Jock noticed that he had his eye on the unlit doorway from the stairs behind the intruder's back. The SIS Madrid desk would have information on the clandestine nature of the meeting which expressly stated that the Admiral was to be alone to simplify matters and not compromise any interested parties, whether German, Spanish or English. Yet this was an Englishman pointing his gun at the two peacemakers … Special Operations Executive had helped to train Jock, but there had been the problem of being closely monitored in Scotland, and Jock had never felt it was secure there … The rumours of a Soviet cell in the organisation were being substantiated by the wild-eyed youth in front of them now.

The heat of the kitchen seemed to enervate the gunman, who began to wipe his brow. The room now seemed very bright. It was 1 a.m. and there was an hour left to complete a rendezvous with the Germans and escape unscathed.

The traitor spoke again. 'We are entirely alone. I've checked upstairs.'

This was surely Quinton Panton, the shifty youth who had the reputation of never taking a shower or bath on the course at Arisaig. Jock had confirmed his name later, after initially receiving no reply from his enquiries at Broadway Buildings. He hoped that the SOE agent's arrogance would wrong-foot him and be of some assistance to Jock and the Admiral, even though their assailant seemed to be holding all the trumps. He had heard enough of the rasping public-school voice that slurred off a pair of full red lips above chin fluff.

'There's something you've overlooked,' Jock chimed in. 'I am on an important mission in Egypt.' Jock needed to keep him talking. 'I am sure I don't need to spell out to you that the Soviets will benefit from the British defence of Egypt, which will help open a second front against the Nazis, so helping the Russians if they enter the war. The plans of your Soviet masters will be compromised if you stand in the way of that. After this …'

'After this? There is no "after this" for you, Lieutenant – nor your new friend either. Once this initiative of "C" has been compromised, dead or alive, you'll both be unemployable. No one will touch you, especially the Admiral, with a bargepole.'

'The plane?' Jock allowed himself a growl now. 'You are not going to allow the Falangists to pass that onto Madrid, surely?'

'Don't worry yourself about that, Lieutenant Steel. A Republican pilot of ours will fly that back to England – after we've run a few checks on it.' Then, as an afterthought to divide the two negotiators, he said, 'A nice piece of kit that. Sorry you've missed out on it, Admiral.'

Canaris didn't move a muscle.

'A Red pilot?' Jock added.

'Yes, call him that if you like. Soviet-trained.'

'They'll debrief him and smell a rat,' Jock snarled.

'No, no, no.' The communist flashed his smile of mischief. 'He's a double agent; it'll all work out. He'll probably get an OBE for returning the latest aeronautic technology.' Gloating at his apparent advantage in arms and knowledge, he added, 'That's what it is, Mr Steel, isn't it?'

'Lieutenant Steel,' Jock corrected again. He realised that the traitor's effort was still a tense show of nervous confidence.

Panton continued. 'Come on now, we don't want the Mosquito passed on to the Nazis, do we? Not while it's outpacing the Messerschmitt.'

Jock noticed that in addition to his commanding position in the room, his opponent was dangerous for a host of reasons, inexperience possibly being one of them. Jock had to be careful, because he was responsible for the Admiral's life as much as his own, though the spymaster seemed much more relaxed than Panton.

Jock exploited what advantages he possessed. 'You think that you care for your Soviet cause, don't you?'

'I am a lot more passionate than the scum running the British government, if that's what you mean?'

Jock felt he could work on this fanatic. 'Passionate ... for what exactly?'

'Passionate in betraying my ... your elders, who have lied to their youth, ignored the dangers of fascism, and condoned the Axis powers for too long. I need hardly remind you, both, that the Soviets were the only government to help the Popular Front here in Spain.' With a fox-terrier expression, he continued. 'I am passionate, and confident that some of us are actually taking action rather than spouting so many words that belong to an effete and lily-livered generation. Small talk on big issues is the only area in which our fathers have excelled.'

Jock stole a glance at Canaris, who sat poker-faced, but it seemed to Jock that the Admiral was suppressing a knowing smile. 'Uncle', as he was affectionately known by his staff in Berlin, was still exuding hope.

Jock needled again. 'Speak for yourself … Your subjective views are based upon a family disposition – the Soviet family – to obsess with trifles.'

The nervous tic in the agent's left eye was becoming more pronounced, and Panton allowed himself a brief rub of his overlong eyelashes with his unoccupied hand.

Jock continued. 'Have you ever considered the naïvety of your lot's position – that you must side either with Stalin or Hitler' – he laughed with derision – 'or in your case, because of the Nazi–Soviet pact, with both?'

Both hands on his pistol now, Panton replied, 'The time for not taking sides passed some time ago, Steel.'

'I'm not arguing anything different. I'm saying that both those leaders are bent on the systematic extermination of their opponents, from what we gather so far. Your people' – Jock dug as deep as he dared now – 'have not the stamina to wait on events, even a little, and judge the third way of Churchill and his kind.'

'A fat lot of good waiting did for you appeasers – I'm sure that the Admiral would agree with me there?'

Nothing from Canaris. Jock was enjoying the conversation all the more because it was diverting his opponent. He moved in for his kill.

'The Nazi–Soviet pact surely makes that kind of talk the hypocrisy it truly is, as both dictators, along with Franco, are heaping up more distant, weightless deaths, to which you are contributing. News of your totalitarian atrocities are filtering across Europe now. Soviet Intelligence isn't as secure as you presume it to be, and you have chosen a leader and mentor who has no heart, moral spine or principle.'

'You are insulting the Admiral,' he smirked. 'Franco is an acquaintance.' Then smugly, he added, 'A very important one, I understand.'

'How little you understand of German politics.' Jock surreptitiously checked with a sideways glance if Canaris wished to speak, but he sensed no perceptible movement from the senior officer. 'The Admiral, I am sure, is his own man. That is the reason he is here, surely? He does not share the black heart of the Führer, but is responsible for guiding Germany as best he can. An unenviable position for a high-ranking officer to find himself in – something you are clearly unable to perceive.'

'Who is your mentor, Steel? Churchill?' He laughed, but Jock knew he was trying not to fidget.

'Indeed – he has integrity, courage, vision, and much more besides.'

'You are hypocrites, you and the Admiral. Why are *you* here? Is this clandestine meeting with your mentor's say-so, Steel?'

'Is that what promotion does to you people – give you a deep insight into hypocrisy? I assume that this job is a promotion of sorts? You have graduated from feeding reports through to Stalin that anyone hawking newspapers might shout down an English street to being ... a messenger boy.'

Panton was sweating again, and Jock pressed on.

'What type of disciple are you when your master attempts justice through the show trials? Perhaps you will be coached one day to admit crimes you had never even heard of because your face no longer fits? Do you honestly think that you can replace fascism with your own false gods? Working for your prince of paranoia makes you a good candidate for suicide under the Soviet system. Had you considered that? We know more about your colleagues than you obviously do. They are disappearing under your adopted people's very noses.' Jock laughed with derision now. 'And here you are, still wielding a hammer and sickle in Altea.'

The double agent said nothing, and Jock didn't wait for a reply.

'I can't understand some of you English – you are English, I take it? I've never fathomed your habit of looking as if you are about to say something, but then exhaling and thinking better of it. Dinner with the Anglo-German Society, and then more of the same with the Masons, politicians and the like must have left you quite tongue-tied. So now you are ... the Man of Action ...'

'I'd offer you a slow handclap, but as you can see, I'm unable to neglect the pistol aimed at your heart, Lieutenant.'

'Yes, I still have one.' Steel gazed back at the traitor. 'How did you manage at all those Cambridge sherry parties? It was Cambridge, wasn't it?'

'Yes, I ran for Cambridge.'

'I say, that was a slip, wasn't it? It won't be very hard to narrow your coterie down. I can't remember you at the Varsity though. After my time, perhaps? I am sure you did run.' Jock slowly spelt Panton's future out. 'And that you'll be running all your life – or running something. Yet it'll never be more than a sideshow in our future world.' Jock continued to needle. 'Faith without intellect is blind fanaticism, and intellect without faith is some form of higher psychosis. Which do you think you have – *Panton?*'

The turncoat at last recovered enough to mumble, 'To ask the hard question is simple.'

Jock rounded on him. 'Ah, we have a poet in our midst, Admiral, and one of Moscow's new aristocrats. Are you a fanatic or psychotic?'

This time, there was no reply. It was clear to Jock that the chafing exchange was indeed exhausting his enemy. Jock wanted answers.

'Who sent you, Panton?' Panton said nothing. 'Don't worry, it won't be too difficult to guess.'

Canaris, who had been sphinx-like throughout the conversation, allowed himself a small aside. 'You've thought of everything, Panton. Though I doubt that you are English – there's a lilt in your voice that smacks of Southern Europe.'

Panton's guard again momentarily wavered. It was more than Canaris's comment that had unnerved the Soviet spy. Jock became aware of an almost imperceptible creak in his own vicinity. The sound wasn't from a floorboard. He thought that he and the Admiral had the makings of a good duo in turning the spy over. Yet, he was wrong – it was to be a trio. It was then that he remembered Countess Solf's conversation with him about the Admiral. He recalled that Canaris was rarely alone out of office hours, that he always kept a servant ... Someone who apparently gave the Admiral's Berlin neighbour, the feared Jew-hunter Heydrich, the willies ... *Of course ... Mohammed ... The spymaster's silent household 'weapon' ... The beams in the ceiling ...*

Before Jock could fully act on this recollection, the Algerian rapidly sailed through the air above them and onto Panton's chest below the beam with such force that it sent the traitor's pistol well out of reach across the floor.

Jock lunged across the smooth stone floor and reached towards the gun until his fingers settled around the trigger. The Admiral moved behind the kitchen-bar and grabbed the knife that had sliced the wild boar earlier. Jock brought the handgun up a few inches and pointed it between the eyes of the bruised and bleeding face of the dishevelled figure that had so recently dominated the room, but was now struggling to breathe.

'You're approaching your terminus, Panton. Let go of Mohammed's neck, or I'll gladly put you out of your misery.'

'I hope you're a good shot, Lieutenant,' Panton spluttered. 'We wouldn't want a Nazi native ruined in front of his master, would we?'

'My shooting's a lot better than your wrestling – let go of him, or I will fire.'

Panton was like a cornered animal now, and Jock saw both the ignorance and fear distort his bitter and angry face. His Soviet masters were capable, but together they had not researched Canaris's dangerous domestic servants. Panton looked like he was going to vomit: his nose streamed blood as he noticed flecks of crimson on the lurid gold and mustard-yellow wall of the barn.

Canaris nodded, and Mohammed started dragging his victim upstairs. The Admiral looked up at the ceiling and pointed. 'Panton did search upstairs, but he couldn't have seen that the roof has an attic's trap door that opens up to the beams above. The wily Mohammed must have slipped into the roof when we were disturbed and found a way out for all of us. Thank you for returning the favour by saving his life, Lieutenant.'

Perhaps Canaris would horse-trade the prisoner fairly and leave him in a condition whereby Cairo could benefit from information he was happy to dispense with. It was certainly in the Admiral's interests to have Panton's friends in London rounded up.

Canaris called towards the stairs, 'Don't be too hard on him, Mohammed. Don't pull his tongue out – yet.'

V

'Another drink? You've earned it, Lieutenant.' Canaris turned towards Jock with a smile, brackets appearing in the lines around the sides of his mouth. 'Don't you think?' The Admiral mixed the cocktail with relish, facing Jock as he did so. 'We share a mutual friend, Lieutenant …'

Jock had just gained some breath back himself. 'Yes, of course.'

'Countess Solf. I am sorry that she was widowed soon after the family returned from Tokyo. At least Count Solf was spared the awful spectre of Adolf Hitler's new path to destruction.'

'However, you have distanced yourself from Countess Solf.'

'You have done your research well, Lieutenant, despite the censorship of the family's letters.'

'I don't forget an old friend.' Jock spoke quietly, half-listening to the grating chair that Panton was being strapped onto in the room above.

'If you are so loyal to Countess Solf, you should be wary of encouraging any disloyalty to the regime by the Solf Circle – for a circle is what it has become, of course.'

Jock realised that there was a chance now to ascertain a second part of his mission in Spain there and then. The first part was being 'nursed' by Mohammed, no doubt.

'The fact is,' Canaris continued as he beckoned for Jock to take his glass, 'I want "C" to know – how do you say – from the mouth of the horse, that I will not, and cannot, be involved in any conspiracy against the Führer if there is the smallest fraction of a chance that it will fail.'

'So helping Countess Solf is out of the question.'

'Precisely. The Circle is ever increasing, and that can't be good for security.' Canaris sipped his wine. 'Let's face it, Lieutenant – you could probably count yourself a member.'

'An honorary member, perhaps,' Jock added. 'It was still in its embryonic stage when I left Berlin as war began.'

'I can only protect those not foolish enough to walk into the traps in which the Gestapo specialise. They have a lot more time since they've stopped all the "queer-bashing" that began with the Night of the Long Knives.'

'You personally have a war on many fronts, Admiral.'

'Yes, and with the calibre of the Fatherland's commander-in-chief, it won't be long before all Germans have military conflict on all fronts as well as in the intelligence war.'

'Another Total War?'

'Exactly,' confirmed the older man. 'In a world that is unlikely to survive without Western Europe. If I may say so, Lieutenant, you seem to have evidence of a burgeoning frontage of your own, which my Algerian is watching for you. The Russians may well become your reluctant allies, and meetings like this will be even harder to arrange. Mohammed has a few questions I want answered about Panton's connections with Major Marz, and what they've been feeding his boss, Heydrich, and then you're welcome to Panton.'

Jock hid his relief. 'The Soviet agent must survive the ordeal upstairs whatever the cost; his incapacity is enormously beneficial for both our needs. I'm expected to return with Panton. He'll be interrogated in London. We won't want to tolerate another leak like that.'

Canaris spoke more softly. 'I'm happy to split our Soviet' – he smiled – 'metaphorically speaking. Please tell "C" that it is my goodwill gesture for the festive season.' Stifling a yawn, he added, 'It does sound as if your people have allowed things to get out of control, rather. Tonight could have been a disaster. That reminds me – it is morning, and will soon be time for me to go.'

'I have brought you a Christmas present from "C".' Jock passed over a tube of German toothpaste, the microfilm with 'C's codes still sealed and wrapped within the white paste.

'Please thank Sir Simon Majoribanks for me, will you? I am grateful for his efforts, and your visit.' Canaris chuckled. 'But if there is a next time, your people must understand that I can cope with being live bait for the Soviets, but only if it is entirely in my gift to arrange.' He smiled wryly. 'This didn't happen tonight, did it, Lieutenant?'

'No, sir. We've both been set up.'

'Yes, but you helped protect my life tonight, and I won't forget that favour. If I can help you using those codes, Lieutenant, I will.' Canaris gave a wan and tired smile. 'The Soviets have lost this round – for now.'

'Thank you … for your cuisine, our conversations, Admiral, but it's time for me to go also.'

Canaris looked at the clock above the door that had so recently been entered and exited by Panton. 'So it is.' The Admiral walked towards Jock. 'I was born in the wrong generation, Lieutenant. You seem to personify the upper hand in this bloody war, and I wish you well.'

The men shook hands. Jock walked to the door that Fernando had led him to less than two hours before and turned.

'It has been a pleasure, Admiral.'

The two men saluted. With that, Canaris called Mohammed, who handed over the dishevelled and handcuffed Panton to Steel, who waited to watch the Admiral and Mohammed cross the mountain track to the outpost on the hill, guided by Abwehr flashlights. They had kept their word and positions; Jock wouldn't need to set off his pyrotechnics. It was almost 0215 hours.

Mohammed had tied up Panton's wrists well. He had clearly frightened the traitor, because Panton had soiled his clothes and smelt even worse than he usually did.

'You will fly at His Majesty's pleasure with me; it looks like your Red pilot is going to miss out on the OBE,' Jock barked as he pushed the Soviet out of the barn door.

'And you've missed out on him. There's no need to hurry back for our Red pilot; he's not a fighter. After refuelling, he props himself up against a bar in the port.'

'You're not much of a fighter either, Panton. Shoot my pilot in the back, did you? I'm sure you'll be able to explain that in later rounds of questioning in London, where they will be very keen to accommodate you.' As Panton rolled his eyes, Jock reminded him of his order of priorities. 'Don't try anything, Panton. You really should have packed some clothes, but you'll find it's well ventilated in the hold.' Jock quickly dismissed any illusion that Panton might have had about being back at boarding school, detained by a senior prefect. 'Remember – I'll be controlling the lever operating the plane door beneath you. For most of the time, you'll be thousands of feet above the sea and, as a precaution, for this particular journey you *won't* be belted in.' He

137

pulled him aside by the shoulder and looked him in the eye. 'It would be a tragedy for you if a pilot with such a burden accidentally lost concentration. Anyway, while your friends in London are compromising the lives of our SOE agents, you can mull that over in the hull.'

It reminded Jock of the odds still against him – perhaps the cold killer Marz, and anyone who replaced him, might make Panton look like an amateur? What was it about the Germans and their allies? They were very good at destroying life, silencing opponents, blaming and maiming, and clearly forensic about restricting the movement of their prisoners. Yet he couldn't allow that thought to haunt him. He had a pilot to bury, Panton to truss into the bomb bay, and a plane to fly.

CAIRO

1941

I

Lieutenant-Colonel Dudley Clarke's MO9 had developed the fictitious Special Air Service battalions, but they required careful preparations to make the enemy believe that what their Axis pilots were viewing from the air was real. So, in late April 1941, Lieutenant James Robertson collected his orders from Air-Vice-Marshal Wigglesworth: one officer and twenty men from the Argyll and Sutherland Highlanders were to leave by special train for Fuka, and create the impression that there was a strong air force, but they made certain that their move was protracted so that informers could witness the proceedings. The group would arrange positions for dummy gliders to be set up at the disused Helwan Aerodrome near Cairo, to create an airborne threat to the desert lines of communication of Rommel's advancing Afrika Korps. Lieutenant Robertson detailed his men to convert a proportion of his gliders to twin-engine bombers, or 'Meccanoes', which they displayed at a forward airfield to increase the apparent strength of the sadly depleted British Desert Air Force. The dummies were displayed on the South Landing Ground, which was not used by any real aircraft. The '750-strong' Glider Battalion, 2nd SAS Battalion, served the fictitious '500-strong' 1st Special Air Service Battalion.

This measure indirectly supported the new role that MIRAGE would play in securing the area from prying eyes. Lieutenant-Colonel Clarke's brigades were being given some factual fleshing-out. All 'parachutists' were to carry a Smith-Wesson automatic carbine and some specially designed hand grenades; distributed among the clusters of the fictitious fifty ten-man teams were Bren guns, anti-tank rifles and mines, demolition stores and two-foot mortars dropped by parachute in special containers. All ranks were trained in demolition work. They were supported at Helwan by eight dual-purpose Hispano-Suiza guns for anti-aircraft fire and defence mounted on light carriages. In this case, the 'transports' were so light that a man could pick them up with one hand. There was a group of very small dummy two-seater Morris armoured cars.

Days later, these 'vehicles' and the 'defence infrastructure' were reconnoitred by a German pilot. Hours after that, sixty bombs were dropped from ten to fifteen German aircraft. No damage was done, and the firing from the one real anti-aircraft gun shot down one enemy plane. The Italian prisoner of war camp was less than half a kilometre away, and there was much cheering before the German pilot met his death. One week later, the RAF flew over Helwan and dropped dummy parachutists three times, and it was not long before Egyptian spectators corroborated the rumours in the POW camp that British airborne troop-training was alive and well in the Cairo area. Clarke was making good progress from under the whorehouse in Kasr el Nil.

Jock had returned the Mosquito in one piece at Heliopolis aerodrome, much to the relief of Wing Commander Reid, who at first wasn't sure whether to congratulate its pilot or put him on a charge. Jock's journey to Egypt had been convoluted. He had had to make an emergency landing at Mersa Metruh in order to refuel and make the Mosquito airworthy again after a flak attack. However, Lieutenant-General O'Connor had by this time prepared the Western Desert Force for Operation Compass in order to push the Italians west. Rather than hang around in Mersa while his plane was being repaired, Jock couldn't resist the chance to be part of the first large Allied military operation of the Western Desert campaign. His cover story as MIRAGE, in case he was captured by the enemy, was that he was supposed to be travelling with the Glenroy troopship but that wouldn't be arriving in Egypt for some time. So, with prisoner in tow but locked up, he was persuaded to help Brigadier Selby set up a brigade of dummy tanks, and support Selby Force's entrapment of Italians from the 4th Blackshirt Division, which later surrendered. Delayed further by waiting for Mosquito parts sent out from England, Jock sent word to MI9 in order to agree his late arrival in Cairo. Instead of 'sitting on his hands', he wrote to Madeleine, he supported troops that eventually took Bardia, Beda Fomm and Benghazi. However, to avoid capture by Rommel's advance a month later, Jock made his way to Sollum and then back to Mersa where an almost brand new Mosquito awaited him.

Jock avoided a long debrief in Cairo by insisting that he was urgently needed to report to Colonel Robert Laycock, who was channelling the misspent youth of the British army into something called Layforce. Panton was incarcerated. First, he took a rickshaw to the Kasr el Nil and knocked loudly on the office door of MI9. A bleary-eyed beauty blew a kiss down a dangerous-looking stairwell above. Jock took in the curves of the woman as he waited for the avuncular 'Come in' from Clarke; he wryly acknowledged the Egyptian tart and turned a squeaky door handle. The sound of the young woman's jewellery clinked on her voluptuous form as she disappeared up the dark staircase.

'Ah, Lieutenant Steel,' said Clarke. 'I understand you have had a busy few months?'

Jock spotted a silver-framed photograph of Major-General Platt behind the smoke rings of his host, which were being puffed out at a rate of knots. Jock acknowledged the non-commissioned officer also present, a sergeant who was so stocky he didn't have to crouch in the low-ceilinged room.

'Thank you, sir. It was busy but productive.'

'Good. Good. Lieutenant Steel, this is Sergeant Morris. He will be assigned special duties if you need any additional support. Sergeant Morris fought in Norway and Dunkirk, and has a wealth of experience that you may wish to call upon.'

Morris saluted and Jock looked at him carefully. The slightly shorter but square-shouldered man was clearly an all-in fighter, and surviving two disastrous campaigns meant that he had had more active experience of modern warfare than most British soldiers.

Jock indicated his appreciation. 'It's very good to have you aboard, Sergeant.'

Morris saluted. 'Thank you, sir.' He turned to Clarke. 'Here is the letter you requested I write for the family, sir, before undertaking any local operation in Cairo.'

'Oh, thank you, Sergeant. Very good. We are now on high alert for a German spy and any of his accomplices who may be masquerading as British soldiers. Please stand by. That'll be all for now, Sergeant Morris.'

Sergeant Morris saluted, turned and quietly left the MI9 office.

Clarke waited until Sergeant Morris had descended the stairs outside. 'Very good man, that.' Then he rubbed his hands, paused and spoke quietly for a moment. 'I am sorry about your pilot.'

'Yes, thank you, sir. The only consolation is that I have brought in the spy who killed him.' Jock paused and spoke again. 'I understand, sir, that you have instructions for me regarding my mission in Egypt?'

'Indeed I have. I suggest one way to explain things would be for you to get back up into the air. I understand you don't suffer from air sickness.'

'No, that's true, but could I discuss the areas I am to cover around the table here?'

The Lieutenant-Colonel put his pipe down for a moment. 'We could discuss it here, but keeping anything in Cairo secret is almost impossible. As you well know, the entire city is crawling with another army. This one is a highly trained bunch of liars and cheats – the locals, I mean.'

'It's just that they are better paid than MI9, sir?'

'Touché, Lieutenant. The pilot who can help us view the logistics of your mission is a fully paid-up member of MI9 … The whores upstairs, however' – a thick black eyebrow rose – 'are not. Excellent cover for our operations, of course, but you could say they are slippery.'

Jock considered that his erudite and eminently mannered chief was exactly the refined gentleman that he had been led to believe he was. It was said that he was one of the few soldiers in his khaki shirt and army shorts that could be mistaken for a senior church prelate.

Clarke reddened a little. 'I'd keep well away from "Bangles" up there; she'll put you in hospital with a dose if she can get the chance. It wouldn't surprise me if those women of the night are actually in the pay of the Nazis as an unsubtle form of germ warfare.'

Jock warmed to Clarke's sense of fun and no-nonsense manner. 'When would you like me to go up in the air, sir?'

'Soon as possible, I'd say.' Clarke picked up the phone. 'We're ready to go if you are.' The senior officer cupped the telephone and whispered to Jock. 'They say twenty minutes. In fact, as you arrived in Egypt, we began what I suppose is the first Order of Battle Deception Plan of the war. It came into being when we found an entry in an Italian soldier's diary in the Sidi Barrani battle. It showed that the Italians were apprehensive about parachute landings behind their lines. There were no airborne troops available to General Wavell, and little prospect of any for a very long time.'

Jock knew the numbers well enough. 'So, as we are numerically inferior to the enemy, we need to find a multitude of ways to exaggerate our strength.'

'Exactly. You should try and transfer to us on a permanent basis, Steel – you've got it precisely.'

'It would be tempting, sir, but I've recently put forward a proposal to Colonel Laycock for a real parachute detachment, led and trained by me in order to create genuine havoc behind enemy lines.'

'Brilliant. I wish you the very best of luck with that. Sounds very exciting.' Clarke tapped his nose and pursed his not inconsiderable lips. 'I'll "keep mum". In fact' – his eyes widened even more at this point – 'your parachute detachment would weave a wonderful fact and put some nice meat on our rather elaborate fiction at MI9.'

'You mean that perhaps I might be helping you after all?'

Clarke drew on his pipe and blew out some smoke. 'Yes, very much so, and in a fundamental sense, Lieutenant. We thought that if we could fool the Axis that we had airborne troops in reserve, it would not only add to our strength, but influence them to dissipate some of their men in protecting lines of communication, rear areas and airfields against possible attack.'

Jock sensed the humility of the man, and realised that in all likelihood, despite the 'we thought', it was the brainchild of the modest genius, Lieutenant-Colonel Clarke.

'Yes, I introduced "A" Beam,' Clarke went on. 'The Italians gradually believed that the "1st Special Air Service Brigade" of one parachute and two glider battalions, had arrived from England as you made your way to Egypt. Rumours that secret training was taking place in the Transjordan Desert were encouraged.'

'That explains the two soldiers in the uniform of the parachutists recently around Cairo – convalescing from active duties, wasn't it?'

'You don't miss much, do you, Lieutenant?'

'They pulled off the act, as far as I observed.'

'Good. We also published photographs of parachutists in training in Cairo's illustrated paper, *Parade* magazine. Documents were planted in Egypt and Palestine, and also on a Japanese consular official travelling to Turkey, which Abwehr agents are likely to have picked up.'

'The Admiral won't be pleased if he finds that out.'

'Oh, Canaris. Well, you have got to make sure that he never does, Steel. That shouldn't be difficult, as you're a friend of his, aren't you?' Jock did his best to smile. 'Only kidding. Look, I'm one of the few people who might be able to work out what you did en route to Egypt when you were supposed to be on the *HMS Glenroy* with No. 8 Commando, but I promise that your secret will go to my grave.'

'Which hopefully won't be for a very long time, sir.' Jock changed the subject. 'That plane must be nearly ready, sir.'

'Let's go, Lieutenant.'

II

Nothing stirred on the stairs now as they made their way out into the bustle of Kasr el Nil and climbed into the staff Humber that took them to the airbase. Soon they were up in the air; Jock relaxed and enjoyed the aerial view of the pyramids. He looked down out of the window of the light and elegant machine. In the sunlight, he saw the reflected bodies of hundreds of similar neat and metallic-looking vehicles; lorry parks, petrol stations, glider bases, a unit that looked like a helicopter pad. Clarke let Jock take in the spectacle, for that was exactly what it was. A metallic mirage, an ordered illusion, a con trick of gargantuan proportions: Jock was viewing the assembled striking power of the Special Air Service Unit K.

'That's your baby, Steel.'

'I'm not being asked to be the Special Air Service Brigade's sole care-taker, surely?'

'In a sense, you are. There is only "K" Force as such, but we want the Germans, especially, to believe that we have an alphabet of detachments dotted around the Middle East – and L to Z, when we have dreamed up some more fiction.'

'Or fact, sir.'

'Go on, Steel.'

'Colonel Laycock has agreed that I will have a parachute detachment under my direct supervision capable of carrying out raids behind enemy lines by the end of May. We'll work in our group of six and use every element of surprise known to man. Our targets will be aerodromes, lines of communications and enemy resource centres, from fuel dumps to lorry parks. Seaborne operations are mostly defunct, as the Navy won't risk ships without adequate air cover, and there isn't much of that, as 90 per cent of the shipping bound for Malta clearly symbolises at the bottom of the sea.'

Clarke's moustache made an almost perceptible tremble. 'Carry on, Lieutenant.'

'My tactical strikes will be meticulously prepared, planned and executed.'

'Raids in daylight, Lieutenant Steel?'

'No, not like the Germans. We will go in mostly at night.'

'On a wide range of objectives, your small raiding parties could really catch on.'

'Like wildfire, I hope, sir.'

Clarke noticed how Steel was not given to rapture while explaining his own 'baby', but instead he exuded a calm certainty about everything he said. 'So this is why you won't go back to Broadway Buildings or transfer to MI9?'

'Yes, sir.'

'Well, in a sense, you will be supporting us magnificently as you suggest, because all those rumours about elite troops being able to shoot up thirty new, stationary Stukas will become a reality, no doubt.' The senior officer sucked at his unlit pipe. 'I like it, Steel. I like it very much indeed.'

'*In deed* is what I will specialise in, sir. I will ensure that my men will make the enemy wish that they had never been born.'

Clarke allowed himself a moment of rapture. 'I can barely wait for it, Steel.'

'However, sir, I'd like to know how one man can keep ...'

'"K" Force down there? You are to keep that lot secret.'

'You are jesting, surely?'

Clarke's eyebrows arched as he smiled. 'You should know that I never jest. No, you have been chosen to keep that aspect of the whole brigade secure from the wandering eyes and hands of the enemy.'

'I thought the whole point was to let the Germans and Italians see our own strength, sir?'

'It is.'

'So?'

'They can see it from a distance – *but they can't touch*. The entire brigade of trucks, planes, stations and even 95 per cent of the men, including the few special aircrew with unusual insignia on their uniforms in the city's bars that you mentioned, is an entire work of fiction.' Jock grinned. 'Most of that lot down there is either made of rubber or painted balsa wood. And you are going to keep that whopping great lie a secret – with your own life, if necessary. Of course,' Clarke continued, 'we and the Germans are both used to throwing our opposite intelligence units off each other's scent with the occasional fake airbase or even port that MI9 has rigged up. It's just that "A" Beam's phantom force is a lot bigger and extends across the desert to Transjordan.'

The plane had landed and taxied to the offices by the modest airstrip. They got out as Clarke bit hard on his pipe.

'But this is your bit, so to speak, the start of a whole land army over there' – he motioned with his briar – 'with its own complete air support. It's an expensive bluff if it is exposed as the brilliant sham it is becoming.' In a conspiratorial whisper, he added, 'I understand that you don't like waste, Lieutenant. I thought that would appeal to you.'

'Word gets around, sir.' Jock smiled back. 'But expense in terms of the men that you can save by planting the idea of superior forces in the enemy's psyche here in Egypt with all those papier-mâché and balsa-wood models on the bases?'

'Yes.' Clarke breathed in deeply again now, becoming more serious. 'You may have read about the troop of army camouflage-magicians in the newspapers at home.'

Jock sensed strain in the intelligent tones of the senior officer.

Clarke continued. 'Fortunately, the newspapers haven't got hold of the latest story, which we are doing our best to close down. One of the conjurors has been found dead in a flat above a nightclub, not so very far from here. His twin brother is devastated. They were both working on the strategic side of the desert dummies, and it looks like your rival in Cairo has caught up with one of them. You can have a look at the body, and I suggest that you also take a look at the murder scene. Fancy a stroll?'

III

Clarke changed into a suit to match Jock's mufti, and they crossed the road from the office; they didn't want to draw attention to the latest murder in Cairo by blazing into a local club in uniform during the morning. Every action in the streets invariably attracted a crowd, whether from snake charmers or carpet salesmen. Jock inhaled the pungent smell of turmeric and clove oil. Not far from the Kasr el Nil was a fashionable bar that was off limits to most officers because of the expensive tariffs for drinks with accompanying bands and belly dancers. It was here that Jock was shown to an attic room above the club.

It was a small studio flat with a tiny kitchenette built into one end and a folding bed that fitted into the wall of a side room that was poky but utilitarian. Jock immediately sensed the strange atmosphere in the place, but there was nobody in the room apart from the two of them. There was no evidence of a struggle. An almost clean ashtray sat on a small, carved wooden table, and there were a few empty spirit bottles and a screwed-up cigarette packet under a basin in the little kitchen. A once-bright red-and-brown astrakhan rug in the centre of the room caught Jock's attention.

Jock spoke first. 'It might have been ideal for Captain Parry. I understand that he was in the habit of working late on the planning of the phantom army that was being gradually "manoeuvred to point towards Tripoli".'

'It would have been, yes, except that this wasn't his studio. This has been rented. We've interviewed the agency involved and apparently the owner, a Mr Nayyar, is conveniently away on business. He's not on any local police files. The property agent apparently never actually met the tenant, a Mr De Souter, who picked up the key after making a deposit on the flat via the Ottoman Bank.'

'The body is in the barracks at Sharia Malika Nazli, sir?'

'Indeed.'

'How do you think Captain Parry died, sir?'

'It's difficult to say exactly. He's been beaten badly on his back so that it's raw between the shoulders. This was the only rented room on the floor, and the others were unoccupied.'

'No one heard his cries of pain, of course.'

'Exactly. The cabaret last night was a perfect cover for this type of crime.'

'What type of crime would you classify it as, sir?'

'Well, it is now on file as a piece of sado-masochism in a twisted crime of passion that went too far.'

'Thank goodness for that.' Jock also wanted as little publicity as possible if he were to track down the murderer – or assassin, more like.

'Yes, that's about the only positive thing to come out of this murder; we have an unusual crime … even for Cairo,' Clarke added. 'The culprit has clearly left some of his tracks. It'll serve our purposes well if the rumours fly around that it was a cruel crime of lust and passion as opposed to the horrific torture of a young intelligence officer.'

'You have the names of all the recent guests and check-in times at the hotels?' Clarke nodded. 'Clubs like the Royal Automobile Association with the recent arrival in Cairo of that shifty-looking Hungarian count is a bit too obviously a snake-pit of insurrection against the British, but it might also be worth checking in case anyone there has been consorting with our killer.'

Jock opened the only window and let some air into the flat; as he did so, he looked up to the roof and around the outside of the building.

Clarke knew he was working with a dedicated patriot. 'You are very well informed, Lieutenant.'

'It looks to me as though the murderer was disturbed and left in a hurry,' Jock added.

'Field Security didn't comment on that, Lieutenant. There was no sign of a struggle or a rushed exit.'

Jock knelt on the floor by the carpet and felt a chill deep inside. He knew that he was staring at the micro-mess of a sadistic killer, not the hall-marks of a jealous lover, as the local papers would no doubt depict the crime.

'Unless I am very much mistaken, sir, if you look at that rug on the floor closely, you'll see that there are small, now dried, dots of blood on the carpet tassels.'

Clarke leant down and looked around. 'Goodness, you appear to be right, Lieutenant.' The Lieutenant-Colonel took a closer look. 'These stains are barely perceptible because of the mat's design and colour, but there is a myriad of red stains at one end of this carpet.'

Jock looked at the bulging green eyes of the dragon depicted in the centre of the material. The studio was still airless, dusty and humid, and the younger man felt he sensed some of the nausea and terror that must have befallen the unfortunate officer.

Jock broke the eerie silence. 'Parry was held on the floor for the dura-tion and subjected to his ordeal right here. It is possible his executioner wanted to remove the body too—'

The Lieutenant-Colonel cut in, now totally absorbed in the murder mystery. 'Why on earth would he want to lug the body of a man who weighed nearly two hundred pounds – even with the distractions of a nightclub to help cloak the removal – from a room that he would probably never return to?'

Jock beckoned Clarke to the window. 'Take a look out of the window and peer up. What can you see, sir?'

'It looks like a makeshift aerial.'

'Exactly, sir. This may well belong to the killer, a murderer who wanted to return here, but without the stench of a rotting body arousing suspicion along the corridor. It is very possible he left this temporary aerial behind and outside the room where he considered it safe to work a powerful transmitter, say housed in a large suitcase, which wouldn't necessarily arouse suspicion, but with which he could walk out of the building, especially if he needed to do so quickly.'

Jock was convinced that he was closing in on one of the spies that infested Cairo, except this one was particularly menacing. One thing that encouraged him was that this operative seemed to be someone who was beginning to make a few mistakes. He knelt down again to take another look at the carpet. His eyeline was parallel with the basin in the kitchen. That's when he noticed the squashed cigarette packet by the bottles under the sink: part of the brand name leapt out at him. The green packet with a red lid was familiar, and he could see a red stripe diagonally across the box with the letters 'Ati' visible. He realised that he'd seen that particular make of smokes somewhere before, carried by someone he knew.

'Did Parry smoke, sir?'

'No, he detested the habit and often didn't socialise because of it.'

Jock went over to the basin and flattened out the cigarette packet, spreading out the word 'Atikah' across it.

'What is it, Lieutenant?'

Jock quickly checked his watch. It was 11.30 a.m. 'When was the Captain pronounced dead, sir?'

'0800 hours this morning, not long after the cleaner was unable to open the door.'

Jock looked out of the studio's one small window towards the Kasr el Nil traffic. 'He could be out by the perimeter of "A" Beam's dummy glider base right now, taking photographs, transmitting data' – he turned to Clarke – 'striking again.'

'You know who he is, Lieutenant?'

Jock was still deep in thought. 'I don't have time to go to the mortuary at Bab-el-Hadid barracks. You haven't told me everything about Parry's ordeal have you, sir?'

'Correct.'

'I believe that there can be very few murderers in Cairo who leave behind the kind of grotesque calling card that looks like a frenzied lashing, as well as other appalling trademarks: there should also be scars on Parry's wrists and ankles.'

The Lieutenant-Colonel stood stock-still. 'Indeed there are, Steel.'

Jock passed over the crumpled cigarette packet. 'This is a second calling card, sir. It might, of course, be a coincidence.' He picked up the ashtray, examining the single butt of a cigarette recently stubbed out, perhaps the last one from that packet. 'There's only one person I know of who specialises in the torture of elite troops, is connected with Intelligence and also smokes this cigarette. Some German soldiers smoke these, but I haven't seen many of those soldiers in Cairo.' He turned to Clarke. 'Not yet, anyway – not ones that aren't locked up. This crime has all the hallmarks of Marz. He never used to smoke anything else, and I seriously doubt that this belongs to Parry, or any friend of his. It's safer to assume that this murder is the work of Enemy No.1 here in Cairo. I believe that Marz has sensitive information about British domestic security, as well as our own security here in the Middle East. He has to be stopped before he can make use of his radio set to warn Heydrich in Berlin about what he might discover here in Egypt and also transmit information on our battle strength to Rommel on the North African coast.'

'I'll get the security surreptitiously upgraded and a staff car at your disposal. What else might you need?'

'An experienced sniper would help, sir. Let him know please, sir, that we are tracking someone who might have a large box or case on them or in their vehicle. I am still only twenty-seven-years old, and I have no intention of shuffling off this mortal coil like the unfortunate Parry.'

'No, exactly. I'll see to it right away, Lieutenant.'

'Thank you, sir.'

IV

Jock's only advantage lay in the fact that he knew something of Marz's movements, and it was just possible that the Nazi agent believed that he would avoid the attention of the British authorities for a few more hours.

Jock hoped that might be so; whether or not it was, he had to move quickly. Sergeant Morris was to follow Jock's vehicle out onto the desert road to Ismailia. Jock sped along the road out to Helwan, which was lined with the ornamental flamboyant trees. The flame trees had just begun to flower, beginning to form a blood-red avenue arched with seeping crimson. As a child in Calcutta, his ayah had told him that the blood of Jesus had been shed over these same tropical blooms – thoughts of sacrifice he decided to swiftly banish. Passing dazzling white buildings and verdant crops, the road soon enough became a dusty track that weaved through barren land. It seemed to heighten the danger. Jock faced the exposure of one of the Allies' first big secrets of the war with an assistant in Morris who was capable, but someone he still barely knew. It was hardly the recipe to embolden him in his latest mission. For Marz would surely be laying his trap, Jock thought as he bumped along the deserted route. The SD's high priest in Cairo would be waiting for him, just as he had for Parry.

It was likely that the Russians had tipped off Heydrich's SD about Jock's journey to Egypt when the two totalitarian states were still sharing information before Hitler invaded Russia. Marz was attempting to terminate MI6's progress in encircling the Broadway traitor by trying to take Jock by force. Perhaps that was it? Then Heydrich's stooges would aim to make him talk and discredit Canaris's Abwehr and its involvement in negotiations with London. That thought didn't lift his spirits, especially after what he had seen on the dragon carpet that morning. Jock wanted to finish this job even at the risk of being captured and the prospect of any quality of life disappearing like a genie into a bottle. He wanted to end this assignment and soldier on in another way, but one of his own making and under his control as much as possible. The thought of never speaking to Hollings also made the prospect of pursuing Marz almost pleasurable.

Then, as he reached the end of the desert track, he noticed the POW camp inland from the new tarmac road, which was steaming in the heat. Another bogus hand-painted sign indicated the route to the new 'installations': depots, training battalions, divisional headquarters and fuel dumps. They appeared to be surrounded by six-foot fences and minded by a few Alsatians and their military custodians. Jock looked into the distance of the mid-afternoon haze. He could just make out the rows of machines that he had recently spied from the air. They were at least a hundred yards from the base's perimeter; glistening in the sunlight, they appeared far from artificial. Jock could see that the place was almost empty. Not far from the aerodrome were some cabins and huts, and further on were a few tired-looking dwellings by a well. Jock could just make out a few huddled locals – bent-over, female figures carrying what looked like bundles of washing. Other than that, there was little movement.

He parked the truck in the shade by one of Helwan's 'offices', picked up his privately purchased Zbrojovka Brno rifle and walked along the line of buildings that gave the aerodrome its realism from the air. The place increasingly began to look and feel like a deserted film set. It seemed as if it would stay that way, because Sergeant Morris had not arrived and there was no way of ascertaining why; Jock smothered the hollow pang of fear and hunger for closure deep in his stomach. He could hear his footsteps in the silence. He moved more quietly towards the well to see if there were any sign of anyone other than the washerwomen quietly talking and singing about their daily chores. It was as if he were being watched or followed around the edge of the base, as if Marz were ubiquitous in an attempt to instil paranoia on a level that even the makers of this fictitious force could barely conceive. Jock turned instinctively to see dust being kicked up along the track a mile behind, and then it ceased, and that meant a vehicle was now on the new asphalt road. Hopefully, he would have Morris's company in minutes.

As the heat shimmered off that surface, he might have barely noticed the billowing dust, but Jock was heartened: he would have back-up, and it looked like he would need it. His gut feeling was that he should become scarce and reconnoitre a little more before Morris joined him; as yet, he could give him few instructions apart from waiting, concealed, and a short distance from his vehicle. Jock edged closer between the well and an outbuilding which gave him a commanding view of the place without being seen from the road. He was alone in this area of the airbase: the two guard dogs and their servicemen had walked on, to the far end of the site, out of earshot, and the earlier gaggle of voices had by now drifted away; nearly all of the locals were now some 500 yards from him. He observed that most of the women had laid out their washing flat to dry on the ground, as was the custom. For a moment, it struck him as odd that, unlike the others, one of them had draped her cotton on the sides of the well, but then he heard the smudged echo of an engine in the distance.

V

The open-topped Bedford truck screeched to a halt, and the driver, wearing three stripes and the type of headdress favoured by the Arabs, pulled out a rifle with telescopic sight and perched it on the bonnet. Jock was bemused, for the man he believed to be Morris was making himself an exposed target not far from the main entrance to the airfield; he was also wearing the dark glasses usually favoured by officers. Jock didn't have to wonder very long: what made him stand alert now was that the soldier was taking aim in the direction of the dummy planes and gliders. There had been no movement out there, but had Jock perhaps missed something? Jock was beginning to regret asking for any assistance: he had wanted to capture the SD operative himself. Something was so urgent out there that the idea of liaising with Jock first was apparently of secondary importance to Morris.

Then the reports of the high-velocity gun rang out. Jock moved into a position where he could see all of the fake airport. He was just in time to watch a figure in the distance fall as more shots were fired in quick succession. One of the dog-handlers hit the tarmac, followed quickly by his colleague nearby. The howling and whining of the dogs echoed ominously through the air as they too slumped to the ground, still attached to their handlers by their leads. Then the howling stopped. The silence was overwhelming.

There were no other personnel around. Clarke had mentioned that it was changeover day for duty staff, but if they were due here, they had not yet arrived.

Jock took out a pair of binoculars and scanned the figure in the vehicle. The man was taller than Morris – it had to be Marz masquerading as Sergeant Morris. Jock looked again at the back of the truck and saw that the tins of water and boxes of supplies were partly obscuring the unmistakable shape of a large case. He was sure his hunch had been right and this was indeed a possible radio. Jock wanted more evidence and information about what the Germans and Russians knew about himself and Madeleine, let alone anyone else: he needed to capture Marz alive if possible. The assassin produced a Leica camera and a pair of wire cutters, ready to drive around the compound of painted balsa-wood 'planes' and obtain all the photographic proof he wanted.

'Jock put the telescopic sight on the Zbrojovka Brno rifle to his right eye, took aim and swiftly put several rounds into the large suitcase at the back of the truck in order to ensure that Marz would at least be delayed in using any radio that the case might contain.

'Marz!' Jock sang out his name and rolled for cover, reloading his Zbrojovka Brno as he did so. The lightweight, bolt-action piece was his favoured weapon, derived from the Mauser, the main infantry rifle of the Wehrmacht; attaching the powerful telescopic sight made the piece effective up to a range of 1,000 yards. Yet when he next looked down the twenty-four-inch barrel to catch a glimpse of the Nazi, he saw nothing. He had, however, achieved another of his immediate objectives: distracting the German from photographing anything.

But now his only trump card of surprise vanished with the echo of Marz's powerful voice in the blistering heat. The compound gates were locked, but Marz had left little trace of his movements. Both men knew they would achieve far more if they captured the other alive. Jock moved rapidly between each hut, checking he was in no sightline and diving for shadow whenever he could. His best chance was to move back towards his own truck alongside a line of counterfeit but similar-looking Fords. They were all stationed not far from the vehicle that had undoubtedly been wrested from Morris by Marz, with the possibility of fatal consequences for the Sergeant. Jock might be fortunate enough to verify whether the German had taken his car keys with him, remove them if still in the ignition, and isolate the German completely. Most if not all the other trucks on the base were made of plywood – they were further away, where his own vehicle was parked alongside, and he hoped that Marz in the blistering temperatures might be delayed in establishing the exact location of Jock's getaway vehicle. So, he worked his way back around the 'living spaces', still without hearing or seeing any untoward movement. For an intelligence officer weighing over 220 pounds, Marz was remarkably nimble on his feet. In the beguiling emptiness, all that Jock could hear now was the roar of the sea in the distance.

VI

Without a sound, Jock crawled on his elbows and knees with the Czech weapon. He was twenty yards from the hijacked vehicle when Marz's voice pierced the silence.

'Drop the gun, your hands on your head.'

The voice was omnipresent, but there was still no Marz. That was when he saw him, looking straight ahead at him behind his rifle. The SD officer had never left his vehicle; he had crawled under it, patiently waiting for Jock to give himself away. Jock couldn't roll left or right and fire because there was no cover anywhere. He didn't think Marz wanted to kill him then and there, so reluctantly, and literally gritting his teeth, he did as he was ordered.

At first glance, the man pointing his rifle at Jock's head might possibly have been almost anyone in that headdress and glasses, but moving closer Jock had no doubt it was Marz despite the surgery on his face. The build of the man who had once spent so long in front of a mirror at his local gymnasium still spoke volumes about his well-endowed muscle and fitness; it was strength across the body, but also in its depth. Jock was several stones lighter than the German, who, Jock was well aware, could have killed him with a boot to his head. Jock still had hope: there was a knuckle-duster knife, favoured by his commando colleagues, strapped to his right ankle, hidden from view under his lightweight and baggy trousers. One other consolation was that Jock knew how Marz operated. SOE had recently opened their own file on him and had their own reasons for apprehending the Nazi because of his craving for taking a leading part in the torture of enemies of the Reich, but especially anyone part of the Commando or Intelligence services that purported to be more dangerous than the SS, SD or Abwehr. Jock neatly fitted into the category of all those British opponents. With a prone position in the sand, Jock knew he had some sort of odds in favour of survival; he just wasn't sure of the ratio yet.

Marz was efficient and quick. Handcuffs were swiftly applied to Jock's wrists behind his back and soon Jock was pulled onto his feet and frog-marched towards one of the dwellings. There was still no sign of anyone or anything. There was nothing between him and the wrestler, the acolyte of Heydrich, except the five inches of the blade that he couldn't yet reach, and a car key he kept in his pocket that he had not so far been asked for. It was siesta time, and Jock had the distinct feeling that this afternoon lull was not going to suddenly end, neither with a new duty shift from Cairo nor with a local washing party at the well. It was becoming too hot and late for that. What began to concentrate Jock's mind was that Marz had him to himself for the afternoon.

The manacled figure who was pushed into one of the 'administrative blocks' with walls not much thicker than papier-mâché sweated profusely in the knowledge that the kaleidoscope of phoney images with which the British had wanted the Nazis to be mesmerised and fooled by at Helwan were nearly as numerous as the cock-ups in Jock's multiple missions. It might not be long before the SD man explored inside the perimeter to substantiate the nature of the paper-thin forces at close range and find that the entire base was a spectacle of ersatz. It would then become obvious to his captor that 'K' Force was only one part of a force that didn't exist; the rest of detachments A–J in enemy eyes would then likely collapse like dominoes … It would be Jock's turn to talk, or so Marz intended. The oral evidence was needed by the SD to incriminate Canaris, and Jock knew that Marz, with his speciality in making commandos talk, had a very strong idea of how his prisoners could be made to bleat – even without the threat of ripping their faces with which he also menaced his captives.

Jock was made to halt in the middle of the hut. Marz pressed the nozzle of an automatic rifle into Jock's back and then disengaged. It was possible for a victim to disarm someone who kept the point of their gun wedged between their shoulder blades with a lightning revolving movement, but the Nazi must have known this and didn't leave the rifle long enough on Jock's spine, even though the prisoner would have struggled to push the weapon aside with handcuffs on. Jock reminded himself that Marz had also studied under the same weapon's trainer as himself – but before the war, in Shanghai. Even if Jock managed to use his knife, Marz would not be thrown by any techniques intended to create a surprise lunge at the German.

'Undress – you won't be using clothes again, Lieutenant. You're as good as dead, and you can bargain for the way you die.'

Jock had written to Madeleine the night before in Cairo: '*I have power over you to create beauty that passes into bloodstreams of time on the adrenaline of happiness.*' Now, he drew strength from his muse, banishing fear far over the dazzling horizon which he imagined beyond the windowless, temporary shed that was fast becoming his mausoleum. As he had scribed: '*You chose some of the most difficult tasks to preserve our defences at home. I have chosen the most difficult and dangerous work that is to be done here.*' To ease the pain of capture, thoughts of and plans with Madeleine, as well as ideas on extending his training to fight in the North African deserts, flashed across his mind.

The North African desert he knew had remained a place of mystery and legend even to the Arabs, with their knowledge of oases and artesian wells, and experience of traversing swathes of sand by camel, but Jock had wanted to immerse himself in what he had hoped to make his new home. He had imagined himself sinking momentarily into the sand on long, maybe even eventually legendary walks, where every calculated step in this foreign land became more certain with the image of Madeleine in his mind. Osiris was believed to be the true ruler of the Desert, for no human had completely mastered it. None of the ancient military powers had penetrated there, and the Greeks had thought that no one ever would, because they believed that it was the home of the Gorgon Medusa.

Jock thought that Osiris, as ruler of the dead, was a small compensation in this mostly barren existence because the male god was sometimes called 'the king of the living', but that was because the Ancient Egyptians considered the blessed dead to be 'the living ones'. More of Jock's kind had perished in such places than had travelled freely and survived. Now, stationary, indoors, far from the inland sands, with the possibility of dehydration and hallucination, he was more at risk than he had ever been there in the desert. Here, in this pretend installation, he was doing his most dangerous work, but it was not the type that he had envisaged.

With difficulty, Jock tried to comply with the command to undress. In fluent German, and with equally fluent irony, he continued to barb his opponent.

'I have heard some funny stories about training methods in Berlin, but this beggars belief.'

Marz replied, 'You will be rewarded for your facetiousness, Lieutenant. I want to hear everything you know about Canaris, the Special Air Service Brigade, its weapons and the equipment it uses, and the British order of battle here. If you help me, I may be able to keep you alive a little longer than normal.'

'I didn't think you did "normal"?'

With that, Marz shoved Jock to the floor, ripping Jock's trousers as he did so, quickly pointing the end of the gun into his back again as a warning for him to stay still. Jock knew that this was probably his only chance. Marz had torn off the material around his left leg and was about to work on what remained of the other trouser leg. Handcuffed as he was, Jock knew he had to reach for his knife now. Marz had slung the automatic rifle around his shoulder and produced a hefty-looking whip, which in his hands was almost as dangerous.

'Let me pull the rest off then. Can't you allow me some dignity?'

Jock was still speaking in German, and knew he must challenge his captor firmly in order to gain the initiative. He moved his fingers to pull more of the cloth off his ankle, hoping to get just one split second to grab the knife while Marz had only the whip in his hand.

Marz had a complete view of the situation, and second-guessed the move. The whip cracked. Jock felt the leather strap temporarily wrap around his right hand, which was within inches of the commando knife, pulling it away from his leg; the interrogator couldn't resist showing off his skills with his favourite instrument of torture. Having located the knife with his other hand, Marz grabbed it, and now quickly loosened the grip of the whip before his victim could pull on it and attempt to unbalance the Nazi.

'The instruction in Berlin is a lot better than you imagine, Lieutenant.' With that, the Nazi peeled Jock's shirt off his back in one movement. 'Get up. Kneel. Face the wall.'

While Marz still had the point of the gun pressed against Jock's naked back, he jolted him in a rapid movement by pulling the handcuffs back to his now bare ankles. Jock could hear the sound of something being unwrapped and then snipped with what sounded like a pair of cutters – which had also been brought along, no doubt for cutting the perimeter fence. It dawned on Jock that Marz was about to continue his obsession with using barbed wire as an instrument of torture – a thought confirmed when he felt the unmistakable pain of several sharp points pressed into his shins and around each heel. Marz pushed the twisted points in hard as Jock took in a deep intake of stale, warm air.

Jock could feel the teeth of the wire embed into the skin above his ankles that were now wet with his blood, staining the floor below. They wouldn't remain wet pools for long, because the crimson mess was likely to congeal and harden in the afternoon heat. Methodically, the metal fangs of Marz's implement of torture sank into the flesh on each of Jock's wrists; these wire points were smaller but the blood still oozed from them.

'You can keep your arteries for the moment,' Marz said.

Most of the oxygen left in the airless space seemed to have been sucked out of the room. The temperature of the hut had soared, and sweat drenched the length of Jock's body. The room must have been a temporary storeroom. There were a few forgotten mosquito nets and buckets, and also some lead piping standing upright in one corner beside rabbit-wire and rolls of hessian cloth – a potential weapon, but it was out of reach, even if by a miracle he managed to walk on his knees across the room. As the detainee took this assortment of objects in, he was struck by the fact that Marz was being made to feel at home by His Majesty's government, for there in the corner lay more barbed wire. Marz now moved around to face Jock, who couldn't help but think of Parry; Marz clearly needed another victim within days of his previous kill. Jock imagined the Captain's squalid demise on the grotesque carpet with its morbid dragon spattered with droplets of blood. Yet now he had to focus on his potential for escape if he had any chance whatsoever of survival.

VII

'So, where shall we begin, Lieutenant?'

Jock, at the mercy of an Aryan wrestler-turned-torturer, refused to be subservient. 'It's like bringing coals to Newcastle.'

'What?'

'They must have known you were coming.'

'Why, Lieutenant?'

Jock pointed to the wire at the end of the room. Marz seemed perplexed by the English idiom, but shook it away, intent as he was on launching the next phase of his interrogation.

'I have a few questions for you, Lieutenant. What are you doing here?'

Jock answered by stating the obvious. 'This is a British base. Why shouldn't I be here? You have clearly added masochism to your sadism by leaving a murder trail inside this city, surrounded as you are by your enemy. You're a very long way from home here, Marz.' Jock paused to let the bold statement sink in. 'Surely the question is, what are *you* doing here?'

'This is an unusual airbase, Steel.' Marz waited for a reaction and received none. Thwarted by Jock's stubborn answer, he continued, unravelling his whip as he did so. 'And after I have disposed of you, I will gain all the evidence that Field Marshal Rommel requires before he makes an all-out attack on Tobruk, and on Cairo itself.'

Jock decided to follow his training to the letter; he would say little, and let his rival indulge himself in his apparent supremacy of arms. The tyrant in a seemingly unassailable position of power might just reveal invaluable information.

Jock exerted some pressure of his own. 'You seem to have forgotten something, Marz. There are troops arriving here at any moment, and you may be unlucky to come across the changing duty staff who precede

161

them – they will immediately find that their colleagues are dead on the airstrip outside. They are not going to be very happy about that. They'll want to shoot you on the spot. If they don't shoot you as a spy, then air reconnaissance will pursue you wherever you try to disappear. You haven't got a chance of getting away, even if you attempt to kill me.' Jock's self-belief rose up like a pillar of hope that made him still hold his head up high. 'In fact, if you think about it carefully, I'd say you yourself have a much better chance of staying alive longer in my company.'

'Somehow ... I think not, Lieutenant.'

Marz tried to close the lid on Jock's instinct for survival. Jock ignored the pain of the new barbaric manacles and let more of his training kick in: he slowly counted, though Marz looked like he would put a stop to that at any moment ... *perhaps not just yet.* Jock could feel his hair matting with sweat around the crown of his head. Slung over the intruder's shoulder was a Bren light machine gun. It was lethal at 800 yards and could fire 500 rounds a minute – ideal for hunting in an airbase where nothing landed or took off, and where the slightest movement could catch a bullet. In his khaki, Marz would have passed for a British soldier. Perhaps he had pretended to hitch a lift and disposed of Morris's body along the road, no doubt under cover, or taken a shot at Morris on the coast road. Yet how did he know that the Sergeant had been on his way in the first place? Jock calmed himself as best he could with slow counting. That wasn't working as well as he had hoped, so he started playing Canaris's Bach prelude in his head. He just hoped that when he could eventually escape – no offence to Canaris – the music wouldn't continue playing in a mental meltdown.

Marz spoke more quietly, in a mock gentle voice that Jock thought was no doubt intended to obtain a confession. 'Lieutenant Steel, there is a way that you might live a little longer, but not long enough to be reunited with our ... Senta.' He laughed now. 'That Berlin glamour-girl is very much an ex-girlfriend of yours. I planned to remove you from the scene some time ago with one of my English cousins – a Blackshirt, if you must know. The hell I'll put you through is for him too, not just the Fatherland.'

Jock thought of the Biff Boy who had escaped after surviving the crash outside Woburn, but who surely must have been permanently altered like Marz after his motor racing crash in Germany. What a grotesque pair they made. He shuddered with difficulty in his constrained position.

The German watched Jock reflecting on the incident. 'Yes, Lieutenant … I wanted Senta that much … I thought you two might find each other again – even in wartime. So, you see, this isn't the first time I've wanted you dead. And here you are now … You've walked right into a trap.' He gloated, allowing that thought to sink in. 'She's on my payroll now. How can you still earn a few minutes of life, Steel? Can you guess?'

Jock refused to flinch. 'You're going to tell me anyway.'

A whip lashed out of a concealed hand and landed right across his damp, already reddened face. The whip had opened up the skin of Jock's left eyebrow, which stung again as droplets of sweat dripped down his face; it was crystal clear that Marz had only just begun to draw more British blood.

'Tell you what?' Marz produced another hit on the other side of Jock's face – another cut.

Jock went on the offensive again. 'Didn't you once work in a circus?'

He had found the Nazi's vulnerable spot, as the whip coursed down his back and found one of his own, pulling away as it did so most layers of skin parallel to his spine. Jock couldn't help but tense up, his back arching like a question mark. Marz seized his moment, knowing that if his prey tried to move around too much the wire points would cut away at his arteries.

'When did you meet with Admiral Canaris?'

'Why would I want to do that when I have enough to do fighting your people in the desert?'

'I take no lectures from a junior officer, especially one so foolish as to walk into the jaws of an Abwehr nest in the heart of Spain. Clearly, you have your own masochistic demons to deal with.' He laughed. 'And not just because you keep the company of the Abwehr. I thought you loved life, Lieutenant?'

'I thought you loved Senta.'

Marz shot him a mirthless smile and looked straight through him. Jock now noticed a small scar on the torturer's cheekbone, older than the amateurish surgical work on the forehead – no doubt a relic of sorts from the duelling days with swords that had been popular just before the war when 'blood and honour' became part of the Aryan mantra. Hopefully, Jock thought, Marz would believe that he was in the uniform – before it had been torn from him – of a soldier enlisted to counter spies in the desert. As his tortured mind and body wrestled with his own fate and that of 'A' Beam and the Good Germans, Jock looked again at the whip. He noticed that there was a leather grip around the German's wrist so that the force of each switch could be more effectively executed, and also so that there was no risk that Marz's hand would loosen its hold of the strap and, as some-times occurs in conflict, be turned against the oppressor by the oppressed.

Somehow, Jock saw another glimmer of hope, in the very weapon that had been used to murder Parry and turn elite servicemen into little more than broken rag dolls.

VIII

'I want a cigarette,' said Jock. 'Can I at least have a smoke?'

'Not that trick, Lieutenant? What on earth do you take me for?'

Jock had gained some composure; he had counted to over four hundred before he recalled the Bach, but now he was trying to count with it still playing in his head, and counting to the rhythm gave him an absorp-tion and deeper detachment to help excise the pain and any influence that Marz wanted to increase over his mental state. Jock was also still bleeding profusely. With every minute that went by, he would become weaker.

He stared defiantly at Marz. 'I am a British officer – you have my rank and number. You will give me my due in a way that you never did … for Captain Wintour. You've made a very big mistake, Major.'

That was all it took. Marz swivelled and cracked the leather hard, again wrapping it temporarily around his victim's face. Jock had held back his knowledge of Marz's heinous crimes on the road to Dunkirk to provoke the sadist, and had prayed for such a move, preferring this to the dangerous-looking hands that had not yet attempted to rip open his mouth; perhaps Marz was waiting for other opportunities to maim if he was unable to force a confession by beatings? It was Jock's turn to strike back in the only way he knew; it seemed to be the last remaining act of defiance that the Lieutenant could make that might make a difference to his horrifying ordeal. It was now or never.

Jock used all his remaining strength. He waited for the lash of the whip to crack around his face. It came ... cutting open the edge of his mouth as it did so. Jock's teeth, however, were unaffected, and he clenched them around the leather of the torture instrument with lightning speed, biting swiftly into its hide. Marz looked genuinely bemused and began laughing again. He tried to retrieve the whip by pulling on it, but this unwittingly allowed Jock to sink his teeth deeper into it. With every neck muscle that he possessed, Jock used the only leverage on Marz that he had – with a violent jerk of his head, he pulled the Nazi forward, and towards the side of the room. That was where the piping rested against the wall.

Marz was very heavy and had seemed stable, but he had been startled. Jock, knowing with every cell in his body the importance of surprise, had succeeded in catching the German off balance. In the confined space, Marz could not bring all his muscle power into play to counter the lunge of his own body. The Major, tied by his wrist to his favourite weapon, careered into the piping on the wall, headfirst. Jock watched in amazement as Marz crashed to the ground. The Bren gun was trapped beneath the Nazi's now-limp body; it would be impossible for Jock to get at it. Marz lay dazed, utterly in shock. The side of his large head had hit the top of the first metal conduit.

The type of room he'd chosen for his chamber of horrors had led to his downfall. When he tried to break the fall with his hand, Marz found that it simply went through the thin material of the lightweight wall. The impact of his body mass was absorbed by his temple; most people might well have died from such a collapse. Jock estimated that Marz's face had hit the metal rods above his cheekbone, and he remembered that his medical brother, David, had once warned him of the dangers of such an accident, where the parietal bone was often unable to prevent a blow from damaging the brain. In more ways than one, the bogus cell was no stronghold any more, and half of Marz's body had gone through the flimsy wall. Although alive still, the German was rendered unconscious.

Jock's only gambit had paid off for the moment, but he knew that Marz was not to be trusted in any position or condition. What then happened was oblivious to the Nazi, but Jock, in an excited state, became confused at the sound that he now heard. The door of what was left of the hut creaked open.

A huddled, black-garbed Arab entered the room. With his back to the sound, and with peripheral vision only, Jock could just make out the sight of a washerwoman. He could barely believe his eyes. The difference between this local and the crones that he'd seen before was that this form had a bundle of washing held close to her stomach. There was a familiar smell that had wafted into the room with its owner, but Jock couldn't make out where he had smelt the aroma before. His sideways glance glimpsed the protrusion of something else that was even more welcome: the barrel of a Browning pistol, pointing directly at Marz.

In a growling but high-pitched voice, the unexpected visitor broke the silence, a pair of bright eyes narrowed below rather dark arched eyebrows.

'Move and I shoot.'

Marz seemed to lazily open an eye; he looked as though he might have been woken from a siesta. Then, half-conscious, he couldn't stop his mouth from gaping wide open, salivating and moving involuntarily as it did so.

Jock realised that Marz was still concussed, and he didn't translate the screamed English into German. Nevertheless, the washerwoman then barked at the unfortunate German, 'Stay on the floor, but face down. Now! You are a prisoner of British Military Headquarters, Cairo. You are not dressed in any recognisable uniform and will be treated as a spy until further notice.'

If Marz had heard this, he gave no indication that he had registered it.

The outlandish figure spoke again: 'One false move from you, Major, and it may be your last.'

Marz was still slumped on the wooden platform which, thicker than the walls, doubled for the building's floor. Jock still wasn't sure about the Egyptian who was so fluent in English. In some ways, it didn't matter very much who it was, except that he wished it was Morris with a flair for a costume change. Even in his own state of stinging suffering, Jock was almost as taken aback by the events of the last few minutes as Marz, except in the Guardsman's case, his hope had not been extinguished, having prayed for a way out of what was now a dungeon close to collapse.

He began to laugh out loud.

'Who the devil …?'

His armed saviour pulled back a shawl to expose the complete pair of eyebrows belonging to what appeared to be the gaze of an overgrown choirboy in drag. Looking at the disguise of a 'washerwoman' with a double-take, the rescued soldier hedged his bets.

'I don't know how to thank you, sir.'

'Don't worry, Steel,' chirped Clarke. 'I'll think of something, and you can start by translating.'

Jock now took great pleasure in translating for Clarke. Marz seemed to be grunting, and was obviously in a lot of pain, but nothing compared to the ordeal that he had just put Jock through.

Clarke's contempt for the crumpled SD officer seethed through the small mouth that, in the camouflage of the locale, would have passed for the sensuous lips of a woman. He must have quickly shaved off his treasured moustache in order to make his concealment complete.

'Throw the keys to the handcuffs across the floor to me,' he said to Marz. 'Slowly, Major, slowly. I really would like to clean this barrel by firing it into you, so don't give me a chance, will you?'

Marz heard Jock's German translation and began to recover slightly as he fumbled clumsily for two keys, which he slid across the rough planks towards the intelligence chief. Clarke undid Jock's bonds, taking especial care with the barbed wire still embedded in his body after the struggle.

Seeing the mess that had been inflicted on Jock's wrists, he spat out, 'You bastard! Stay on the ground and put your hands out in front of you! We are going to have more role reversal, Major.' Clarke allowed himself a tense smile, his nerves holding steady because the two Englishmen considered themselves still in danger. 'I see you have been especially careless with His Majesty's personnel and property, and the Lieutenant's uniform. You are going to undress, Major, and Lieutenant Steel here will now have to put on your clothes.'

'I think we can safely say, sir, that the enemy has been scotched.'

That seemed to alleviate some of Clarke's anger. There was no emotion, no response from the vanquished. Jock's description was entirely apt for a host of reasons, one of them being the fact that the German was still suffering from impaired vision, and seemed unable to perform the relatively simple task of undressing. In fact, the damage to his head meant that he was unable to gauge exactly where he should undo his belt, in what place he could unbutton his damp shirt, and how to undo his laces.

The Lieutenant-Colonel was vigilant. 'He's still dangerous … He might try to kill himself, or more likely escape. If you try anything, Marz, we will shoot you as a spy. You won't get too far in that birthday suit, Major.' Clarke spat out his contempt. 'Do they teach that phrase in Berlin?'

Jock continued to translate the senior officer's taunts, but Marz was incapable of stringing any syllables together. The two allowed themselves a chuckle, as much as to relieve the tension in that claustrophobic hell. Yet neither would be able to fully relax until Marz was clamped in irons and taking his turn to answer questions in the basement of the high-security prison not far from 'Grey Pillars' in HQ Cairo.

Clarke looked almost offended. 'How did you know it was me, Lieutenant?'

'The smoke, sir.'

'What smoke?' The innocence and enthusiasm of the cherubic 'chorister' in the dishevelled shawl had reappeared.

'You reeked of your favourite pipe tobacco, sir.'

Clarke seemed relieved at this, and pulled out his pipe. Biting on it, he looked obliquely at the Lieutenant, who was changing into Marz's voluminous trousers.

'Ah, the disguise worked. That's alright then.' He allowed himself another smile. 'Actually, Steel, I tried to let you know that help was at hand, but it must have been absolutely rotten in here in every sense.'

Jock suddenly twigged. 'The washing on the well … Of course – no Arab would have left it to dry there. I spotted your handiwork without identifying its author, but I should have realised it was a signal of sorts.'

The Lieutenant-Colonel was ever resourceful at the grisliest of times, thought Jock – a very good man in a tight corner.

All the time, Clarke kept his eyes fixed on Marz, and Jock noted how, just as he had a penchant for disguise, the senior officer was also able to switch from relieving the tension for himself to winding it up for the SD agent.

'Give this to him in your excellent German, Lieutenant,' he said. Then he screamed at Marz, 'Just one false move from you, and I'll shoot you limb by limb until you start yelping for your mother!'

Jock's fluent German did the trick. Marz understood, and winced while he undressed. In another role-reversal, Jock gingerly pushed the other clothes towards him, and Marz painfully finished dressing. Then Jock quickly and carefully wrote a few lines on a scrap of paper and passed them to the older man, who still had his pistol trained on Marz's head, even though the German would have struggled to move very far in his condition.

'I would be grateful if you would ensure that Major Marz reads this message before his interrogation, sir.'

Clarke read the note: '*Major Marz, you are unlikely to survive this conflict, but when your country is defeated, the weight of your cowardly deeds of torturing prisoners of war will mean that even if you do somehow make it through the war, it is extremely unlikely that you will play any part in the bloodless revolution that will become the transformation of Europe. We will insult you, not by wasting our breath or speaking your name, but by pursuing a life of fulfilment and happiness. No one will remember you. Some who might have done so are already dying in raids on Berlin and on the Russian front. You and your Fatherland have failed.*'

'I will, of course, provide a good translation if Marz fails to understand anything.'

'I am sure that you will, Lieutenant Steel. Can I tempt you to join MI9?'

'Thank you, sir, but no. I'm off to join my commando battalion.'

'Not in that outfit you're not, Lieutenant. I'll see that a new uniform is sent around for you at Shepheard's.'

'Thank you, sir.'

Jock saluted and hoped very much that he would indeed return to soldiering.

MERSA MATRUH, EGYPT

SUMMER 1941

I

Jock glanced back and took his fill of the pure white buildings of Mersa Matruh set against the sparkling blue liquid of the Mediterranean, and braced himself for the dry, thin desert crust that was mostly clay and surface gravel. He left behind the ridges leading to Mersa, the dusty, sage-green scrubs, and began to cover a hundred yards of sterile, moonlike landscape. He was careful to stretch out a uniform pace, and transferred a stone from one pocket to another every hundred yards, ensuring that he didn't lose track of the distances achieved. By trial and error, Jock used himself as a guinea pig rehearsing each staggered programme of marches on his own so that he would not put the lives of his men at unnecessary risk in training. He turned his art into a science by testing his own pacing after varied distances with a range of loads, during the day and at night, when he planned his operations, and on different surfaces, appreciating the greater effort required on gravel as opposed to sand. His parachutists would need to be able to determine distance and time, and whether their rations would support the type of march they all envisaged. He wanted it to be the cornerstone of the first modern, elite selection course. He had been building on his pioneering walks in the desert since late spring when he and so many Layforce commandos had been pulled from pillar to post with no incentive but a few 'Great War' training sessions.

General Arthur had expressed little surprise that some men had rebelled by burning down part of a service cinema in the capital. Jock hadn't left the intelligence services to go backwards by standing still, and fought against the disillusion that ambitious soldiers of all ranks were experiencing with the commandos' current inactivity. He developed new tactics for a novel war, checking water consumption in his very first forays into desert training as one of 'B' Company's leading subalterns in the area. Ready to immerse himself in soldiering again, his individual preparations, from explosives to long-distance marching, gave him the right to request his own parachute troop. He walked down Tomolbat Street and into HQ Cairo, the belle époque-style apartment block called 'Grey Pillars'. It was like an adapted department store for a bureaucracy that controlled two continents. Jock passed endless doors stencilled with army abbreviations and eventually found Colonel Robert Laycock's office in a converted bedroom. Jock asked for forty men and received half a dozen, yet he contented himself with the knowledge that by transforming small-skilled groups into elite servicemen he could still prove his concept of guerrilla warfare.

Jock started by checking the water flasks of his men on a twenty-mile march, and after observing that the bottles were not empty, the young officer congratulated his soldiers, knowing that without water discipline he would be leading them to an early grave. He smiled at one trooper who was just audible as he grumbled, 'No one's checked the Lieutenant's friggin' water ration'; Jock passed his canteen to the grumbler who now held a bottle that looked almost untouched during a day's desert voyage in 45° C in the shade. The men on that occasion were lost for words. In their downtime, they watched him disappear into the desert. Rescue was out of the question on Jock's solo walks when he was piloting the desert marches, and might be the case in actual operations; he wanted his men to adopt the right psychology, and no one in the army so far had shown him anything that could match it, so it could only come from this type of work.

Jock had at last returned to soldiering, as he had told Delahay he would, but he also wanted independence from the officers in the West End – the 'passengers', he called them: the soldiers whom he compelled to return a salute, however reluctant, by meeting and maintaining their gaze. So, Jock escaped the gin-swillers, the gamblers, the short-range desert group and the barnacles in administration who attempted to destroy a few private armies because they were a bit of extra paperwork, as well as those soldiers who preferred to run the risks of the Berka district. The Berka's round, white signs with a black 'X' denounced Cairo's oldest profession, which was centred on the run-down quarter of Clot-Bey, as 'Out of Bounds to All Ranks'. These seemed, even added to the threat of an encounter with the Military Police and the high risk of contracting venereal disease, not much of a deterrent to the average British soldier.

Yet here in the desert, there would be no approximate approach to fighting the Axis alliance … Not much of an alliance, given the staggering lack of success on the part of the Italians whose newspapers had so recently exclaimed 'Nothing can Save Britain Now'. The seas of desert offered few or none of the distractions of the city. Yet in a world of uncertainties, the white, grey and coloured sands revealed not just the direction of the wind but, like the spectrum of alliances within Cairo and within the enemy facing him, the identities of all Jock's opponents, who, like the sands, were shifting.

So far, Panton had left few traces in the desert. Jock was content to leave the likes of him and Marz behind in a city where his own officer class had too often been passive in their own self-imposed imprisonment in the sweltering fleshpots of Cairo, and the white, shining arsenal of Suez, its French-colonial style unable to hide the poor and seedy place it had become. Many of the English, unsettled by intrusion, and obsessed with class – a national religion – indulged their island nature by keeping ordinary soldiers limited to districts and restricted by curfews. Despite the flies and heat, many found a way to feel at home in the overcrowded city, where tea was still served at 4 p.m. Jock had truly escaped from that place and the uneventful small horizons of English life there.

Jock's feet literally set him apart from it all. The inactivity of unchallenging training by the Army led him to bring the war to the enemy with his own original parachute group, taken from the sole survivors of a battalion that had been decimated before his very eyes by pure indulgence more than anything else. He'd told Madeleine in a letter that '*even the sound of one bullet fired in anger might have saved us from decadence … the sight of one dead man would have filled every faint heart with zeal … but here we still are: breathless virgins, forever toppling on the brink of death or glory and forever repulsed.'* Jock had nothing but contempt for the orders that had tricked him into leaving his long journal to Madeleine and possessions in the Ottoman Bank, Alexandria, on the pretext that they must take no surplus kit into 'action'. He only had time for shorter letters now, and he wondered if they would be enough to satisfy a young belle with the hope of an engagement, despite the thousands of miles dividing them. Jock was waiting for news: the address he had advised Madeleine to establish and whether she had been able to lie low, or whether her transfer to a different security service had transpired.

The Russians were now supposed to be Britain's new allies. That wouldn't stop Field Security interrogating Panton. Jock was also comforted by the fact that Marz was going nowhere fast. Jock suspected that was just as well, for his own cards had been marked some time ago by Panton's associates in London. As long as Jock was at large, the Soviet traitors would never be at ease, whether Russia allied itself to Britain or not. Jock realised that any leaks about even a proposal of peace between Britain and Germany would substantiate the fears of traitors like Panton. At present, Jock's military career was shielding him from Moscow's henchmen in London, and soldiering in Africa seemed much more pleasurable than spying. Yet he knew that Marz and Panton were not indispensable. There would be someone lining up to replace them, and he would have to be on his guard against ubiquitous enemies.

II

Jock returned to his tent and signed off his letter to Madeleine. Was he her Ulysses, her brave adventurer – or her pen pal? That was what the separation was turning them into. He signed off with '*Ulysses*' when he felt bravest, yearning for the '*soft white arms of his Penelope*', the name she used when '*you matter a great deal, Jock*', which didn't seem to be enough of the time, but he would have to change that. She had first made the references to the mythical lovers when Jock had started his journal to her after he had gained the support of the Layforce and Commando leader himself without any top brass networking or favours from any other military services, Intelligence or otherwise. He had achieved it by dint of his reputation as an up-and-coming professional soldier with plenty of ideas and the unswerving determination to follow them through. He thought back to those times when he had felt compelled to pioneer something, *anything*, as long as it contained the element of surprise and struck at the superior numbers of troops assembling along the North African coastline.

Jock had intercepted a shipment of fifty silk parachutes bound for the Second Indian Airborne early in May. He had befriended a quartermaster at the depot in Abbasiya and received a telephone call from him at Layforce's 'B' Battalion base, Middle Eastern Forces. With his band of cutthroats, as he called them, he filled a truck with thousands of pounds worth of silk at £80 per chute. As he said to the helpful Army store man, 'A lot of kit goes missing in the Army, but these will have a good home, certainly not turned into stockings.' *True, except for a couple of pairs that found their way to one particular pen pal.* The Second Indian Airborne were still waiting for the chutes months later, but would have realised that much of the British shipping at the time was lost in transit with little air protection. Jock remembered assuring his men about using their chutes on their first 'daylight raid', and not to worry, because 'the Army keep a record of everything, except what's useful'.

That was the time when Jock had been asked by the six-foot-six Scots Guardsman, Lieutenant David MacDonald, if he could join Jock's parachute detachment. He remembered how the Scot had surprised the parachutists by his wish to go on extra exercises – strenuous training hadn't been something that MacDonald was known for. Jock had met MacDonald in joint commando practice raids and knew that he wasn't enjoying soldiering.

The stooping MacDonald was keen. 'You've really hit upon something, Jock. No parachuting role is being envisaged for any troops in the Middle East, and, as you say, somebody has to do "something".'

Jock, though still wary of his fellow officer, saw MacDonald's desperation to break into a fighting role and be 'blooded' somehow after months of languishing on and off in Alexandria Hospital. Yet Jock had appreciated his enthusiasm and responded to it.

'We were told by Admiral Sir Roger Keyes back in December that we were embarking on "an enterprise that would stir the world" – some enterprise.'

MacDonald concurred. 'I agree, Jock. The training arrangements are poor.'

'I think Colonel Laycock is a worried man, David; he's not receiving all the help he deserves. We have been asked to rehearse raids at Mersa on our own beaches. Yet you've seen how the men are being instructed? Anybody would think we were training to attack the Pas-de-Calais on a dark night.'

The Scot was animated. 'You're right.'

Jock saw a malingerer transmogrify then and there into a wounded animal that wanted the enemy's blood. MacDonald ignored the streams of sweat caused either by his medication or alcohol the night before and continued.

'In England, our training was almost totally devoted to adopting formations on beach landings suitable to Northern Europe with everybody lying down as soon as a burst of live rounds is heard.'

'It's bloody ridiculous,' Jock concurred. 'Commandos are sitting ducks in the Western Desert on a Mediterranean night, when commanders should know that any blind Arab selling eggs on the coast would be able to detect us kilometres away. Way-finding back to the beaches after these abortive practices is inadequate, and with those noisy ships arriving on and leaving the coastline, you might as well be firing Very lights before landing to warn the enemy of our attacks. Do you feel "stirred" by the old-fashioned training?'

MacDonald shook his head and listened attentively.

Jock continued. 'Underwhelmed, more like. So, here's my solution.'

'Parachuting?'

'Yes, you've heard, David. The parachutists are to take the war to the enemy, slipping into their bases invisibly and quietly.' Jock added, 'But hundreds of miles behind enemy lines. Now, that might stir the world. Haven't the top brass seen any of the film of the *Fallschirmjäger* in their successful parachute attacks on Crete?'

'Apparently not.'

175

Jock looked out to the starry night sky. 'Eventually, I want the men to stagger their jumps at different heights so we all land simultaneously.' He turned to MacDonald. 'Look, we're going up in that old post plane at Fuka tomorrow. Would you like to join us?'

MacDonald's eyes lit up. Jock didn't want to upset his plans with a soldier whom he couldn't yet fully trust, but he thought it churlish to deny a willing graduate a chance to experience the new learning.

'I thought you'd never ask.'

The two very different soldiers shook hands. Without fully realising it, each had found their match in more ways than one.

III

'Watch out for your exit – the Valentia plane hasn't been designed for jumping out at 800 feet,' Jock warned. 'You'll be knocked around a bit for a few seconds by the air turbulence. Then you can deploy your canopy.'

'I'll be careful,' MacDonald assured the young warrior.

Jock saw the smile of an enthusiastic young boy. MacDonald had been thought a rather cynical and disillusioned young man, but this was no longer the case, it seemed.

'Also, there is a dispatcher, but he hasn't arrived yet. 'I'll go out first, then Davis, followed by you and Gorry. First, though, I'd like to try some dummy jumps into the sand. Are the ankles alright after the spell in hospital?'

'Good enough.'

'Private Gorry, bring over the Ford and I'll demonstrate a backward roll at fifteen miles an hour for Lieutenant MacDonald here.'

'Right away, sir,' Gorry said.

MacDonald immediately took in the great respect in which the officer was held by his small troop. He watched as Gorry drove past to get some speed up in order to allow Jock to drop out of the back of the van, something that the 'cutthroats' were clearly well practised in. The Scot watched as Jock made a perfect landing from a forward roll; the one backwards seemed as good, if not better. Then it was MacDonald's turn. The impact on the ground seemed much greater than jumping off a fifteen-foot wall, which any good parachute school could have provided if there had been any in the Middle East then. Ringway in Manchester had not yet sent out their training manual, and the RAF wasn't ready with its planned training school in Palestine. Jock made do without them. He showed his men a series of further rolls up to thirty-five miles per hour.

The Valentia had never been used for parachuting, and the static lines had to be attached to the legs of the aircraft seats. Jock demonstrated a perfect jump and landing out of the plane. The weight of a man's body much lighter than MacDonald's would normally pull the rip cord so that the parachute would open automatically, but the design of the plane meant that there was a small chance of a parachute snagging. From the ground, Jock watched the giant of a man jump out and begin what he expected to be a sound landing. The Scot anticipated that he would be only buffeted by the slipstream for a few seconds before a gentle falling sensation, but Jock watched in horror as MacDonald's canopy caught on the end of the plane; he saw that MacDonald was held by his silk, flapping on the tail-plane, in momentary suspension. Then MacDonald started travelling faster through the air than Davis, who had jumped before him.

Jock shouted for a medic and he watched the Scot hunch up his elongated bulk and close his eyes. The parachutist's spine took the brunt of the fall. Jock checked the spindly form that had collapsed like a rag doll in front of him; the Scots Guardsman's sight was gone, but he was still breathing. Jock checked MacDonald's pulse and put his jacket around him.

His mind raced ahead. Now there was a different 'headache' for the parachutists: reports of this accident might jeopardise the group's reputation with HQ. While Jock's new ideas on surprising the enemy were held in limbo, Rommel was regaining much of the coastline that the Germans had lost the previous year. As he went into his makeshift mess, Jock thought an answer to these questions might be forthcoming in the shape of a small brown envelope sent from HQ Cairo. It was a request for a meeting with the Layforce commander.

IV

After sending MacDonald back to Alexandria Hospital, Jock arrived at 'Grey Pillars' to find Colonel Robert Laycock's news hard to accept. Colonel Bob, as he was known affectionately by his men, stood a few inches shorter than Jock. Big blue eyes were set wide apart below a straight, broad forehead, all above a mightily built body. Jock had enormous confidence in him, even though he felt he was deceived by a few of his officers.

'Thank you for coming over to 'Grey Pillars' at short notice. Please sit down, Lieutenant.' Colonel Laycock looked genuinely crestfallen. 'Jock, the top brass is having second thoughts again about night attacks behind enemy lines. There have been a few disastrous raids by others recently, and they don't want even the risk of that happening at this time.'

'With respect, sir, this isn't a large, cumbersome raiding party that will be obvious to the enemy. It amounts to six men – they will be an almost invisible force who can get in and get out, destroying valuable enemy planes in minutes.'

The Colonel put on a brave face at his superiors' timidity. He paused and looked at Jock. 'There is, however, something for an intrepid commander, an innovator with your expertise.'

'What might that be, sir?'

'Nazi motorised divisions are digging in at Tobruk, and the garrison needs someone of your calibre to snatch prisoners and generally put the wind up the enemy. The brigadiers out there want a daring raider, and I told them you fit the bill.'

Colonel Bob had been overruled, but he knew that Jock's meticulously prepared raids on enemy airfields for his band of cutthroats would have eliminated the chance of failure. His senior officer was as furious as Jock.

Laycock ushered Jock, who had remained standing, into a chair. 'I am very sorry, Jock. These excellently planned attacks on Axis aerodromes would, I am sure, have been a resounding success. However, there's always Tobruk.' He looked up towards Jock. 'Also, on another matter, I've been asked to make this office available to you this afternoon. The phone should ring from London any time soon.' Colonel Laycock anticipated Jock's curiosity, and, looking out onto the sunlit lawns outside, whispered, 'I don't believe there is a connection between the call and the procrastination of some of our pen-pushers here. Anyway, I have a meeting to attend to, but I do so hope everything is alright at home and that all will work out for you, Lieutenant.' Colonel Bob saluted. 'We will miss you while you're in Tobruk, Lieutenant Steel; a privilege working with you in Egypt.'

It wasn't long before Jock was left alone to take his telephone call.

'Hollings here.'

Hollings – two disappointments in one afternoon. Hollings was interfering; he spoke about the change of strategy after the invasion of Crete and the redundant role of the commandos in Egypt, and how Jock would soon be better off based in London.

To make matters worse, Hollings dropped his bombshell. 'Panton escaped his Cairo captors before he was properly incarcerated.'

'Why on earth was he allowed to escape, sir?' Hollings said nothing. 'Why has it taken several weeks for anyone to tell me?'

'It only happened a week ago. Since your departure for special operations, we weren't exactly sure where to find you.'

Jock was incredulous. 'You think, however, that Panton would find me?'

'Something like that, yes, Steel, and if you're going to Tobruk, that is more likely, isn't it?'

Jock felt that he could discern enough smugness in the Brigadier's plum voice to detect the senior officer's pleasure at checkmating Jock's attempt at independence as a soldier.

Hollings continued. 'I also think that this rather puts your hat back into the intelligence ring? Unless, of course, you'd rather forgo this chance in order to have a shot at the Hun as a desert raiser? There isn't much else on offer for you soldiers at present, is there?' Jock said nothing. 'Alright, go to Tobruk, but watch your back, and see what you can find out. Panton wants to talk with you first, and almost certainly kill you afterwards.'

Jock regretted his wishful thinking. 'Surely with Hitler's invasion of Russia, there won't be any official intelligence-sharing between Germany and Russia. Aren't the Pantons of this world now less important?'

'Unfortunately for you, the likes of Panton remain highly significant. He appears to be still very worried you'll sniff out his handlers in London. From where we are, it doesn't look as if he'll stop until he finds you.' There was a pause. 'Don't forget the next war. Good luck, Lieutenant.'

Hollings rang off.

'Such a cheery soul,' Jock whispered to himself.

He had also been informed by Field Security in Cairo that Marz had refused to talk, and London had requested he be flown there to be interrogated again and shot if he couldn't be turned to spy for Britain. The old spy was correct about one thing: if Marz was no longer talking and giving up information about Nazi monitoring of Soviet transcripts of the messages from traitors in London, Jock was one of the few live agents who might guess at the scale of Panton's involvement in the Soviet exploitation of British Intelligence. Jock didn't himself know as much as he would have liked to without discussing Madeleine's report with Delahay or 'C', but somebody, apart from Panton, believed he did. 'C' might have identified Blynde and Harkiss as traitors, but even if he activated an investigation into their activities and it didn't move at a snail's pace, Panton was still on the loose, and possibly still guided by the likes of Blynde and Harkiss in London.

As far as Jock's longevity was concerned, he might as well have been privy to all there was to know about the host of double agents at home, because it seemed that his pursuers didn't want to take any chances with the extent of his knowledge, however paltry he himself might consider it, removed as he was from life in London. Agents, Soviet or otherwise, had one main role: to use any method to prevent their opponents knowing any of their country's secrets. Jock saw that his awareness of traitors in the heart of London's security was still a big enough secret to make his life not worth living. Few could ever get to Canaris, who had seemed almost untouchable, until the slippery Panton witnessed the meeting in Altea. Moscow might be fighting the fascists, but they might too believe that their double agents in London were in danger of being exposed by a frustrated soldier in a military vacuum. Controllers were likely to consider that Jock was accessible in a way that Canaris was not, and that unlike the Admiral with his Abwehr bodyguard, Jock was a human operative who eventually could be tracked, interrogated and broken. Jock didn't fool himself that the Russians wouldn't spend very long trying to turn him into another viper spy to add to the MI6 nest. Hollings had been right about a few things: raiding Tobruk would be with one eye over his shoulder, but it was also an offer he couldn't refuse. The only glimmer of light in any sort of war effort for Jock lay in that, and in the opaque rays of Intelligence reflecting off a paranoid prism of spies.

CAIRO

LATE SUMMER
1941

Lance Corporal Webster spent a peaceful night in the barracks of the Field Security Police, where he received parachute badges on both arms and was given Royal Artillery badges and buttons. Webster was also issued with a special certificate to be kept in his pocket at all times in order to avoid getting in trouble with the Military Police through wearing badges of another regiment. He was to take the part of Lance Bombardier Smith, Royal Artillery, of the First Special Air Service Battalion, Clarke's fictitious parachute detachment, and he was to keep this act up during a week's stay in Cairo. Webster had memorised his legend, information that had been created for him, and his 'movements' over the past two months.

The role of the Bombardier was to recuperate after his period of 'intense active service', and attract enough attention to give credibility to the rumour that No. 11 Commando had been transformed into an elite battalion that would inflict heavy losses on the Germans and Italians. As he walked out of the cinema after watching *The Great Dictator*, Lance Bombardier Smith made his way to the Services Club for a dance later that evening. Charlie Chaplin's humour hadn't been lost on him, and although he had to be discreet and wary, this temporary role was in some senses light relief after months serving with the battle-weary Tank Corps.

Panton watched Smith go out of the cinema exit and checked that he was unobserved. He stepped out of the shadows with Smith's back to him.

The film had been an interesting diversion for him, too, after a busy afternoon tailing his target. The Bombardier's new counterfeit uniform would be a perfect fit for him. Panton was almost exactly the same height as the soldier, just a little slimmer. He had watched the Lance Bombardier pull out only one transport warrant for all his various journeys, and noted too that his brushes with the Military Police were always dealt with discreetly with a small flourish of paperwork from his chest pocket. The uniform and the two pieces of paperwork carried by Webster made him very vulnerable to a desperate assassin like Panton.

What made things still more dangerous was that the Soviet spy enjoyed conundrums and had already deduced that there had never been to his knowledge a First, Second or Third Special Air Service Battalion. But it was obvious from the way the Military Police responded to the Bombardier that Webster was involved in something very special indeed – an intelligence role, at least. Panton had little doubt that Steel was involved somewhere in all this, and the Soviet was convinced that he might be killing two birds with one stone by targeting this particular soldier.

Panton was armed and also carrying cheese wire in the heel of his right boot. Ironically, the very fact that Webster was an actor in disguise would only help another imposter like Panton take on his role, because those in authority would be giving some leeway to the amateur actor playing the Bombardier. Though Panton did not yet know the soldier was maintaining an act, he had realised that there were few other members of the battalion; this would help Panton if he could steal and don such a uniform, because it meant he was unlikely to keep bumping into other battalion servicemen, or be forced to regurgitate a 'legend' or story about how he got involved with the unit. In the Bombardier's uniform, Panton understood that he could hide behind the hush-hush outfit if he didn't want every Tom, Dick and Harry approaching him or asking questions.

The Soviet imposter had also taken the trouble to contact Harkiss through Batukin, Panton's case officer, in London, and discover where the most active of the Welsh Guards in the Middle East were now serving. The information had taken a while to get through the diplomatic channels, but it was no surprise to Panton that Jock was headed for the sharpest fighting outside of a tank: the No Man's Land around Tobruk.

Panton waited for the Service Club dance to end. Webster wasn't too much the worse for wear, unlike so many other underemployed soldiers that summer. All of the revellers were military, so the predator had to keep in the half-light. As the Bombardier took a blind alley up towards the cabaret on Sharia Enad el Dine, his assailant struck silently with a blade through his heart. It was over in seconds as Panton's free hand closed over the bombardier's last anguished exhalation.

TOBRUK

LATE SUMMER 1941

I

Jock arrived at the outskirts of the Tobruk garrison. The evening sun brought out the deep blues in the harbour and he saw that the water was darkly stained with oil. The harbour was a graveyard of wrecks, listing hulks and sunken ships, their twisted propellers and rudders lying exposed at odd angles above the azure slicks. On land, one enemy barracks was still strewn with the detritus of war: oil bottles, old food cans, cigar boxes, cases and uniforms covered in sand. How huge was Mussolini's imperial dream? Here, at least, the British and Australians had ensured that it lay in tatters.

It was the Afrika Korps that Jock turned his attention to now, in order to deny the enemy fuel and military hardware. Jock soon found that he was tasked with leading the majority of the most dangerous night raids in Tobruk. He had briefed his men about the pitfalls of any of them working with him for one main reason. He wasn't prepared to say any more than that there was a bounty on his head, as far as the enemy was concerned; he wanted them to be discreet. The men didn't press him, yet they believed him because everything he did as a leader made that image of Jock as a thorn in the enemy's side credible. Within months, Hitler would be putting a price on them too as Jock's parachute force gained notoriety.

The previous few days had been deceptive. They had rested up in the sun beside a beautiful little inlet that caught the occasional sea breeze – it was nicknamed 'Rest and Be Thankful Bay'. No sooner had they arrived and settled down than they were asked to move to the terrible bleak and barren place called Palistrino, with the enemy barely a thousand yards away, hammering the mortar and machine guns. Spandau Sammy, as the Germans were nicknamed, caught a number of good blokes from the 23rd Australians who just didn't get their heads down below the torrent of bullets. The desert wind had whipped up fine, powdered dust into billowing clouds of swirling brown-yellow grime and sand. There was no shade, almost no water, and the tea was so sandy there was little choice between skimming the dust off the surface or stirring it in, in the hope that it would descend to the bottom.

Jock had been tasked with capturing a prisoner. He remembered all too well how systematically he had checked and considered everything about his raid in advance, noting it concisely in a breast-pocket diary. Every fact had been sifted forensically: the Axis's armaments, phases of the moon, the weather, the chance of concurrent operations, and, most importantly, all elements of surprise. The men, a group of six, filtered gradually into No Man's Land, passed a derelict tank burned-out long ago, and into the black night lit up only by the opaque disc of the moon hanging above.

II

The mercurial Panton had been selected by his handler in London partly because of his linguistic abilities. He was comfortable wearing an Italian uniform and could carry that act off just as well as impersonating a British bombardier or German soldier. Growing up in the Tyrol had left him a polyglot. In Tobruk, he had continued to wear Webster's fictitious Artillery 1st SAS uniform. It hadn't been difficult to guess that Webster was an artillery parachutist from a battalion consisting of very few bombardiers. Panton would have plenty to discuss with Jock because the SOE traitor scented what he knew Marz had been close to establishing – that battalions like Webster's were as artificial as the badges Webster had worn and that Panton was wearing now. Moscow would value a realistic appreciation from Panton of Britain's forces in Egypt; co-operation with the British against Hitler had been partly on the understanding that British soldiery were strong enough to support Stalin on a second front against the Nazis. Holding North Africa would be key to helping the Russian armies. Irrespective of Stalin's new arrangement with Churchill, it was important for Panton to give his Soviet masters every opportunity to gain the upper hand in the new alliance. Few Russian patriots were in any doubt that this was simply a convenient military agreement against Hitler; it barely healed the last generation's wound of the West's anti-communism. It was mainly Panton's duty to find out what Jock knew about his Soviet comrades in London, embedded as they were in the MI5 and MI6 control centres. Yet if he established the potential weakness of the British position in Africa with the possibility of their phoney detachments and battalions, it would surely crown his success in the eyes of his Soviet controllers.

Jock knew that Panton was an entirely different case to Marz. He was so different that it began to be a significant concern to him. If Jock had seen the report that Varley had shared with Harkiss, he might have been even more worried. Panton had shown his dedication to Moscow by helping Blynde within months of war commencing in 1939, when 'Jules' had been withdrawn from the Intelligence course at Minley because his communism had come to light. Panton had come to the rescue, and with mutual friends arranged for the Deputy Director of Military Intelligence to intervene. Blynde had then been accepted and was posted to Military Intelligence, returning from France after Dunkirk. Despite this display of dedication to the cause, an internal report on Panton had still expressed misgivings about his personality traits.

However, before he started to become too relaxed in his elite outfit, he would either have to locate Jock soon or find another British disguise. The opportunity to move as freely as he had been doing would now be short-lived, as Webster's paperwork included a warrant from 1st SAS Brigade HQ: in two days' time Webster was to travel in RAF transport via Jerusalem to Amman, where he was due to meet 'A' Force's Brigade-Major at the King David Hotel. Panton was now heading in the opposite direction, and Bombardier Webster would definitely be missed, even if his body hadn't already been dredged from the Nile.

Panton had already travelled with ease west along the coast road. The

Nile had been in flood, and the dry fields beside the road had become brown lakes, with *fellahin* gathered together as the Nile had risen and disgorged its silt. Cadging a lift hadn't been difficult at first, but almost everyone he met yearned to have news of improved developments in the British Army's prospects. Soldiers wanted to believe there were new schemes for secret detachments bringing the war to the enemy. Panton noted the signs of General Auchinleck's build-up of supplies, ammunition and petrol dumps. The Eighth Army was moving gradually further west in order to break the stalemate at the front. The loss of Crete and the rumours about the threat of the *Fallschirmjäger*, the German parachutists, meant that the bombardier reporting for a clandestine course in Tobruk was again to be welcomed rather than inspected too closely by British servicemen.

The cultivation diminished in colour and variety, simplifying into infinite beige, and the dunes rose as he went north. Most of the ruined hardware was Italian; burnt remains of corpses lay scattered over the sands. The only sound across the otherwise silent battlefield was Panton's vehicle grumbling through its low gears. Eventually, he passed through the town of Sollum, climbing the meandering path that ascended the Halfaya Pass. Looking out over Sollum Bay, with its dazzling wealth of ever-blue skies, seemed a welcome break, but looming and glowering clouds were closing in from behind him. As he spied Tobruk, the desert rose up into the sky with a storm that now reduced his visibility almost completely. Panton became confused as debris flew and clattered onto his door; a wrecked vehicle appeared out of nowhere, its charred passenger appearing momentarily like a ghoul from a macabre ghost train ride. Yet, for now, fortune seemed to favour the traitor. The storm raged as he arrived at the city, and the Australian guards with shrugging shoulders seemed unconcerned by his failure to produce an adequate pass.

Panton had recently benefited from a little help from Harkiss, who had settled into his new role on the Madrid desk, and with his links to Cairo had identified the most dangerous part of the Allied defence of Tobruk, where the active German Motor Battalion had complete superiority in terms of patrols, sniper fire and observation. That was where a small detachment of Jock's 'B' Battalion was likely to be found.

III

Palistrino was the toughest sector of the Tobruk perimeter. About three miles west of the fort, the detachment had prevented the enemy advancing east and west or moving through the desert to the south, and Jock's military mission was proceeding well – until Sergeant Quilley, a Canadian with Irish blood, caught his foot on a tripwire. Quilley dropped to the ground before the mine splintered at chest height, and though most of the group were blown off their feet, Jock felt the full force of the landmine's murderous blast only feet away from him. It wasn't a question of saving breath, since it had been knocked out of him. Every bone in Jock's body rattled; every nerve was shattered. All of the men lay motionless; Jock didn't need to explore all his body. He might be pockmarked with desert sores, but he knew that his circulation was in excellent condition; he was almost certainly the fittest man lying flat, but the cut on the edge of his mouth was bloody. He articulated an order clearly enough for the men to report back alphabetically. Jock quickly took control, despite having to lisp a few orders: in order to return safely, they would be spending the time until sunrise exploring the mine basins and 'teats' – the deadly bomb pins protruding out – as if this were the most delicate piece of foreplay in the book. The humour stayed with them, even with the announcement that hundreds of steel balls – 'no pun intended there,' he later recalled saying – 'jumped up and dispersed liberally at chest height'.

'As high as that,' Quilley quipped, but then he in particular needed to let off something more; Jock encouraged steam on this occasion.

He controlled the humour too.

'Don't forget the tripwires,' he stage-whispered.

After grovelling in the dirt on their stomachs in one of the most agonising journeys of their lifetimes, the wit was rewarded. Jock realised in the first signs of golden light that the minefield had only recently been laid, and in the last part of their return, the telltale smooth lines around the mines were as exposed as the tracks of the minelayers. The sandstorms had not yet covered this area up, and Jock liked to think that nature was protecting them: the desert winds had been held back to preserve the mine markings with the early sunlight to guide their way back safely.

They were inching back over the treacherous earth towards friendly lines during four of the longest hours of their lives; the desire to take the turn to lead the group was huge because following behind was worse, tortured by the fear that the man in front, however good a buddy, might not entirely and properly check every millimetre of soil.

Having dispelled some of the tension and made some progress, pangs of anxiety had now been replaced by those of hunger. After several hours of painstaking work, what Jock could do with now was a spell in Stone's Chop House off Piccadilly, another of his old haunts; a place he had once taken Madeleine. Women and food had a way of seeping into his rather weary consciousness ... You could purchase a bottle of Margaux there for five shillings, and the steak and kidney pie was less than half that ... Then, something, deep in his rumbling guts, from somewhere, started to worry him. It wasn't just his belly; it was the rest of him that mattered even more. He looked around in the half-light. There was the tank they had passed earlier on, clearly visible now and within one hundred feet. Out of the blue, a thought struck him like lightning – *was it a concealed listening post?*

At that moment, a hail of bullets was fired into the ground around the back of the men in their prone positions. It had to be Panton. He was trying to get lucky with a hit on one of the many small, plate-sized exploding devices. With their three pins pointing out just under the surface of the ground, there was a reasonable chance that Panton could detonate enough of the S-mines to kill them all. A mine went off in the distance; bursts of gunfire slowed. Visibility was poor, but the troop still had to keep their heads down on the ground. Jock heard Panton's high-pitched shout – more of a scream. The direction from where his voice had erupted was still not obvious to anyone but Jock, who had been doing his turn mine-sweeping in front.

It seemed that the traitor had them pinned down exactly where he wanted them.

'Throw your weapons to the side! I only want Lieutenant Steel. Take your choice with a death-walk, Steel. Do the right thing and save the skins of your men while you can. This is your fight, not theirs, and you owe it to them.'

Divide and rule was Panton's real communist mantra, thought Jock.

It was true that the men had to remain flat; they were still not out of the imminent danger of the mines millimetres away. They were confused as well because they were still not sure where the screaming had hailed from. Was Panton prepared to risk Jock being blown apart? Perhaps he thought that Jock could emerge out of that acre of S-mines alive, and the raid leader needed to because he wanted to talk to Panton. Yet he wasn't going to risk allowing this field to become another corner of England with a new cemetery dedicated to his men.

He whispered, 'Stay put for now.'

Quilley nodded his head; he couldn't believe how quickly Jock had spotted the enemy in the poor visibility. Jock swung his Zbrojovka Brno to one side and fired at the tank. This had the desired effect of helping to diminish further the rain of lead that had started falling around the soldiers. Jock didn't want to kill Panton yet, and took the risk of shooting away his cover, reloading furiously to maintain the shots needed to destroy the little protection left to the traitor.

Jock moved cautiously away from his men, still checking the surface of the sand as his group stayed put as commanded. He moved gingerly to one side of them so that any shooting on his part would draw away fire from the literally grounded and almost paralysed force. Panton was right about one thing: this was Jock's battle and it seemed that it was better fought on his own. Jock knew SOE would send someone else if Panton kept escaping.

He boomed out, 'We're coming for you, Panton!', all the while stealthily moving forward. He was covering ground more quickly than he would have liked, fully aware that a wrong move could set off the S-mine's 400 steel balls like a swarm of angry buzzing bees. All the time, Jock was gauging what sort of weapons Panton had at his disposal. So far, he was encouraged that all his opponent could offer was gunfire. He pulled the pin out of his grenade and threw the explosive into the air with the sort of power that Mr Bradman had shown him with a ball on the cricket pitch in Sydney as a boy. It sailed through the early-morning air and landed comfortably near the redundant tank.

It was close enough to worry Panton. Jock smiled with conviction. The Soviet Panton was clearly no soldier: Jock didn't even need to use his weapon because the agent turned and fled. It was little consolation. Jock knew the best place for Panton was inside a straightjacket in a high-security jail. Panton was dangerous because he was again on the loose and still obsessed with his pursuit of Jock and therefore also a potential threat to the new Special Forces unit – let alone Military Intelligence. The turncoat might have undergone SOE training, but the minefield episode showed he could be out of his depth in his fanaticism. Jock would need to exploit that weakness, but for now he would still be looking over his shoulder.

IV

A tall, gangling figure with a stoop formed a conspicuous profile against the camouflaged gunboat lying low in the harbour at Tobruk from which he alighted. The vessel was now posing as another harmless wreck and helped to cover the seaward flank of the Western Desert Force. Much smaller than the ugly 'insect'-class gunboats, unpromisingly left over from the First World War, it was a lightly armed 'fly' class. It was called a 'small Chinese gunboat', but low in the water, travelling at fourteen knots and armed with one three-inch and two six-inch guns, the craft was deceptively innocuous. The hunched officer's worn khaki uniform was damp with dark patches of sweat between the shoulder blades and under his arms, attracting hot, powdery dust blown by the prevailing khamsin wind; there were three pips on each shoulder.

Clutching a screwed-up piece of paper, he enquired about the whereabouts of his colleague at the dock. The light was beginning to fade as he was driven away in a staff car, around a beautiful bay and past date palms, fig trees and several freshwater wells. It was, MacDonald thought, like something out of *Beau Geste*. And then he saw the visible ravages of war in what must once have been a prosperous little valley. The ground was strewn with smashed-up cars and lorries; Italian equipment stuck out of the sand like a forgotten cemetery. Two golden eagles soared over their home in the wadi. The peace, immense calm and grandeur of the wild nature all around was deceptive as bursts of gunfire crashed and rolled down the wadi and echoed up the sides of the canyon. The officer, still clutching his scrap of paper, walked around the makeshift homes of the raiders, which were really little rings of loose stone wall, and continued his quest.

Jock was writing to Madeleine on a small stone table in a bunker he had christened 'Stonehenge'; the desert 'escritoire' remained one of the few things in the hideout left unsullied by the Italian occupation. He had selected it himself after removing the Italian detritus – the result of several weeks of binge-eating if the empty olive, ham and anchovy cans that had once decorated this particular entrance to the Lieutenant's new accommodation were anything to go by. It was a kitchen, no bigger than a fair-sized car, and above ground were five or six chairs sticking out of the desert. The soldier's mess was shared by Amir Khan, an Indian doctor, who had a greater claim on the billet, as he had been based there for weeks. This arrangement was serendipitous because Jock was fighting against desert sores and exhaustion, not having taken any leave or a break for most of the year. The soldier had been told that he required medical attention, something more than just the simple cocktail of chlorinated tea and ascorbic acid tablets that he downed now with a gulp. Jock had paused for this drink, which Daniel the cook – a little imp-like Indian of sixteen or seventeen years, very black with big bat ears – brought to him.

The boy stood mesmerised by the framed photograph of Madeleine on Jock's simple table.

'She is very beautiful, sahib.' He nodded at the picture and smiled. 'I think you will marry her soon.'

'I would love to, Daniel, but I cannot take leave at such a difficult time in this terrible war. I am sure your own mother is very beautiful too, and that your father, like so many of the Indians, is a very brave and highly organised soldier.'

'I have no pictures of them to show you, sahib. I believe that they have left our old home in the Punjab. When this war is over, I will find them.'

'You are brave like your father, and determined and hardworking like your mother – keep believing that they are safe and you will be together one day, Daniel.'

'When will Dr Khan Sahib's medicine work on you, sahib?'

'When I can stop raiding for a while, Daniel.'

The boy spoke quietly. 'Will you ever stop raiding behind enemy lines, sahib?'

'Perhaps, Daniel. There isn't much of it going on anywhere else and someone must do it.' Jock smiled. 'We don't want the Nazis to think we have gone to sleep at night, do we?'

Daniel shook his head with much gravitas. 'No, sahib.' He sensed this was the time to leave his Lieutenant with a chance of snatching some rest. The boy's eyes shone and the light of his gaze was almost supernatural as he lowered his head to leave the dugout.

'Goodnight, sahib.'

'Goodnight, Daniel.'

Jock finished his letter to Madeleine. His life was one of liberation and deliberation, and he would indeed marry Madeleine as soon as he could reach her again. Her correspondence usually arrived some time after he'd sent his own. However, they had helped fuel his unswerving purpose and energy that was envied by all the soldiers with whom he was acquainted. Faith and hope kept him going.

The lovesick scribe was just about to put out his hurricane lamp when he heard Daniel cough loudly and knock on the makeshift entrance to the wasteland hollow.

'Sahib, is a MacDonald Sahib come to see you.'

'What, at this ungodly hour? Oh, show him in, thank you, Daniel.'

MacDonald looked rather worn out; Jock thought that was odd considering that he had been relaxing in a hospital bed for six weeks. Yet he then remembered that there might well be a poker game going on at the Tobruk port, where his vessel must have come in earlier that evening.

'What on earth are you doing here, David?'

'Hello, Jock. You know why I am here. The *Aphis* came into Tobruk under cover of darkness a few hours ago.'

'You've got a thing about knocking people up at night when they're trying to get a bit of kip before raiding the Hun in the early hours of the morning, haven't you?'

'Sorry, Jock. Your lamp was burning.'

'Indeed. This is your third trip in as many weeks.' Jock smiled and turned to him. 'You're almost becoming a part of this sector's family, aren't you?' MacDonald shifted his feet a little, but Jock was genuinely concerned. 'How's the recuperation from the accident going? Don't tell me you are getting bored with those Cairo nurses? Or has the Matron found you out?'

'Alright, Jock, you've made your point. Look, I'm serious. No swanks – why would I risk being blown up in that Chinese gunboat for an all too short visit to you?'

'I know it's damn good at dodging bombs. Made any progress since last time?'

'Just a bit. I've found you the ideal job, which you very nearly persuaded Colonel Laycock to fully grant you when you invited me to join your parachute raiding party.'

'Do you mean that HQ Cairo are going to increase my small detachment from six to the forty that I originally requested?'

'No.' MacDonald smiled. 'They are going to give us sixty men and four other officers.'

'*Us?*'

'This is the start of a brigade, Jock. I have managed to get your planning and parachute proposals as high as Auchinleck now.'

As the Scot smiled his boyish grin, Jock saw how MacDonald's charm and contacts must have helped in 'Grey Pillars'.

'Your work in Tobruk,' MacDonald went on, 'has also shown them what we all knew ages ago, that anything you seem to touch in this Army of the Nile seems to turn to gold.'

Jock looked at the extra pip on MacDonald's shoulder. 'Thank you, David. Congratulations on your promotion. I appreciate what you have just said. Militarily speaking, perhaps you are right, but I don't think that this extends to my own domestic situation and finances in general ...'

'No, sorry they couldn't stretch to two promotions; just me, I'm afraid.' MacDonald was embarrassed and looked away, but added rapturously, 'Actually, getting this far at all is nothing short of a bloody miracle.'

Jock looked at Madeleine's photograph on his makeshift desk. 'I would be in a better position to propose to a rather beautiful young lady.' He turned to his colleague with a detachment that MacDonald found difficult to fathom. 'No matter, David. Premature promotion isn't an ideal situation either.'

If MacDonald had understood the irony, he didn't show it. 'Everyone knows that you want a free hand in the new type of warfare that you've already done so much to innovate: the brass request that you have another chance.' MacDonald continued to sing for his supper. 'Naturally, I'd be a fool not to approach the best offensive crack patrol commander in this Tobruk perimeter, and the only officer who has both pioneered his own parachute detachment and has the ability to carry forward this force's exciting new task.'

'What do you think it is, David?'

'To be fully backed to make your surprise attacks behind enemy lines a reality, and streamline them with Clarke's fictitious armies and Auchinleck's strategy in the Western Desert. In fact, everything that you've always striven for.'

'It's even more than that, David.' MacDonald looked at Jock, who exuded a sense of mission second to none. 'It's about working in a team where you know the men in front of and behind you will hold their ground if necessary in any circumstance; men who will wisecrack rather than scarper in such conditions of conflict.'

'That's the kind of outfit I want to be in.'

Jock finished off the chlorinated tea that Daniel had brought him earlier and turned to MacDonald. 'Then my advice is simply this. Never run; once you start running, you stop thinking. Now remember that, David. I'd need to take four of my exceptional NCOs from Tobruk to kick-start my recruitment and get permission to leave my duties here.'

'I'd expect that.' The Scot looked hopeful. 'Men seem to be less of a problem than equipment, Jock.'

Jock looked at MacDonald a moment and eventually spoke. 'Perhaps. The new brigade would need a suitable plane – you, especially, can't afford to have another training accident.'

MacDonald paused. 'There is no plane as yet, Jock.'

Jock didn't allow himself to be put off by the daily problems of inadequate equipment. 'Where would I have facilities to prepare my first raid?'

'The Bitter Lakes. It affords covert training. The Royal Navy has a base, but it's barely visible from where we are.'

Jock looked up towards the night sky and paused. 'That's at least a hundred miles from Cairo. We'd be out of HQ's clutches, and that's the sort of distance I could use for night marching over several days. We both know there is no fighting role for the commandos here.' Jock nodded to MacDonald and allowed himself a smile. 'There are no vessels returning to England, and though I'm madly in love, you might just have me in a checkmate, David.'

'Did you hesitate because of my malingering days?'

'Of course … Yet if you are, as you say, serious about this military enterprise, I could bring all the special training I've already been testing with my men and make it work in six to eight intensive weeks for more of them, but I would exact some concessions.'

'Such as?'

'I'm not interested in working under anyone else's direct control any more, David. I've seen enough of the top brass's outmoded and sluggish approach to fighting this enemy. Countless chances to disable the Hun slip through their fingers with their overwhelmingly sedative announcements of "imminent action". I have other irons in the fire … I want to be in charge of the camp, all training and day-to-day administration, and I choose the first NCOs.'

'That seems fair.' MacDonald looked almost relieved.

Jock continued. 'I want to be in control of the running of the fledgling SAS, unofficially at least.'

MacDonald wiped the sweat off his forehead and a little awkwardly combed his hair with his fingers.

Jock paused. 'Is that a yes or a no, David?

Hesitating momentarily, MacDonald said, 'Okay, unofficially at least, yes. Fair enough. Look, I must leave you. I'm going back to Cairo on the *Aphis*. I like the old gunboat and I paid for my trip by beating the crew at baccarat.' The Scotsman's grin returned, and he was starting to relax now that he seemed to be winning the Welsh Guardsman over.

'So, while you're living the life of Riley in Cairo, David, I am tasked with creating a camp one hundred miles away. Everything's from scratch there?'

'Yes, you'll be starting from scratch … as you say, and that can include my desert training. Thank you, Jock.'

MacDonald didn't want to do much more talking, or keep Jock awake longer than necessary. He wanted him out of Tobruk as soon as possible before he took a bullet. Even he was beginning to resent how Jock was being borrowed by an embarrassing number of brigadiers who lacked their own raider of his standing. He made his farewells, but bumped into Daniel on the way out. He tipped Daniel, who was only slightly taken aback by the sahib's convoluted exit from Jock's hollow. MacDonald then passed the teenager a scrunched-up piece of file paper. It read: *'Apologies for the Lieutenant's pay, but hope a few days in the Cecil Hotel will help you rest. Please charge room service to me at your leisure. Yours, David.'*

Daniel watched the tall officer turn and leave, his three pips glinting in the moonlight; he saw the emblems of command, but he also knew in his heart which one of the two men was the leader, and which the follower.

MacDonald slipped away into the warm August night and towards what fleshpots still remained in Tobruk. He was bound for the gunboat's journey back to Cairo before dawn. Anyway, he had something to celebrate. The new brigade would indeed be airborne with Jock. There was as yet no equipment, of course. He'd see to that.

Jock retired to bed. He was pleased by MacDonald's concession, which meant not only that he would be almost entirely responsible for, at present, a non-existent camp, but also autonomous in most areas. A dawning of humility in the Scotsman had won the day, though the Scot believed he had Jock cornered with few options open to the ambitious young leader. Jock's desert sores, and his own accompaniment of personal parasites, desert fleas, ticks and lack of sleep meant he was in no position to argue against working more closely with his colleague for a third time that month.

Daniel held the note that the tall officer had given him, then flattened it on Jock's 'escritoire' and folded it carefully. He would give it to his sahib at breakfast the next morning. It had been a long day and he knew that his master would not require the note that evening when he really needed a deep sleep. It could wait until tomorrow. He tucked the message into his breast pocket, where it weighed heavily on his heart. His sahib was being drawn away from Tobruk. Would he ever find another officer to serve like Lieutenant Steel?

V

The next evening, non-commissioned officers Diamonds, Foley, Quilley and Paveney requested Daniel to ask their Lieutenant for a quick word in private. Quilley had returned from a run into Tobruk for rations and had picked up the latest rumours. He seemed to have temporarily lost the wide generous smile that gentle giants can radiate; with his brow knotted, he looked a much older soldier that evening. Not a sight many of his mates would believe, having watched the bear of a man floor the Provost Marshal in Cairo a few months before.

'Excuse me, sir,' said Quilley. 'I and the lads here would very much like a quiet word, sir.'

Jock sensed the soldier's change in tone and gave a warm smile. 'A quiet word with you, Sergeant? I don't know that I've ever heard a quiet word from you, except perhaps in that minefield that we all crawled out of the other night.'

The men smiled; they had all been with Jock that night.

The weary Lieutenant looked back at Quilley. 'What can I do for you, Sergeant?'

The man spoke softly. 'Sir, we know that you're off somewhere up the coast and we want you to take us with you.'

'How might that be?'

'We've heard there's another new detachment being trained by you.'

'Dignified' Diamonds, tall, lean and six foot six, pitched in with his rasping tenor and usual poise, but also looked serious. 'We think, sir … that we'll die in this godforsaken place if you are no longer our officer.'

Jock swiftly responded. 'Come on, Sergeant – what, even after that tour in Tobruk and your expertise in the minefield the other night? You're a lot better than that.'

Diamonds persisted. 'No, honestly, sir, we don't rate our chances. With respect to the other leaders and all that, but the fact is they can't cut the mustard like you can under fire.'

Jock accepted Diamond's compliment. 'Thank you for the vote of confidence, blokes. If only leadership was always like this, eh?'

The men paused momentarily as they listened to the beginning of an air raid over Tobruk harbour; it was a beautiful starlit night.

Jock added to the promise of more dangerous work under his direction with a dampener to go with the welcome but heavy dew. 'You've heard no doubt from our New Zealand neighbours that it is indeed a "do or die" unit?'

'Yes, sir,' they all chorused.

'And you still want to volunteer?'

The men were absorbed by the grubby bandages around Jock's open hands. It was as if he was offering them, not riches, but more hardships that were reflected in his desert-sore palms and fingers. Those same hands had emphasized positions on the desert floor, simulating enemy installations, highlighting the Lieutenant's belief that, 'Just because Tobruk is under siege, doesn't mean we can't go on the offensive.' His corkscrew thinking had bluffed the Axis. They knew he would lead them in the dark, close to the enemy when they least expected a lightning raid.

'Yes, sir,' they chimed again.

Jock looked at them with pride. 'Well, I always knew I'd been fighting with the right men. It would be a privilege and pleasure to continue working with you blokes in roles that will mostly be behind enemy lines. If I can have my way, we won't be cancelling most of our operations at the last moment, because I'll be planning and activating them. MacDonald's understandably dressed things up a bit; he's good like that.' He spoke with a smile. 'But I'd like you to know it's going to be Spartan to start with, so take a good weekend break before we meet up again. I'll send word soon.'

The NCOs, much heartened by the prospect of serving again with their officer, said their thanks and goodnights. As they moved off, the faint squawks and flapping of roosting birds broke the still nightfall. The leprous salesman's pitch from their officer left them with few illusions that they would indeed need to live it up in Cairo while they had the chance. Yet they all wanted one thing that, until Tobruk, had been denied them: action. Where Jock went, the action followed. They each desired a piece of it, and with the 'Meteor', as they now called him, there would be plenty to go around for everyone.

CAIRO

LATE SUMMER
1941

Jock boarded HMS *Hastings* the next day. He took with him two months' experience of intensive crack patrol commanding, especially in Palistrino. The romantic images of his heroic defence of the fort had been overtaken by his troglodyte existence and the daily school of hard knocks. He reflected on why he had thrown in his lot with MacDonald. The top brass had earlier offered to let him have his own parachute detachment, leadership of elite training and responsibility for devising three meticulously planned raids, and then at each turn HQ Cairo had dropped every mission. He was sick of being a hired hand with little sense of identity, and it was time to lead a team he could organise with a true esprit de corps and with a depth of commitment that would more than match the Afrika Korps. He looked at the front page of a Cairo paper to see the headline 'HMS *Vendetta* Sunk'; that was the destroyer he had travelled out on. Perhaps the canny Scot, MacDonald, was wisely travelling light again, his little gunboat barely barnacled, hanging on in the wake of the bigger vessels that drew the German air raids, which were so frequent, you could almost tell the time by them.

Jock took in a deep lungful of the fresh air that was pleasantly dust-free as he walked up the Corniche to the elegant Cecil Hotel. His timing for a weekend of leave, the first in a very long while, couldn't have been better. Alexandrian society was also breathing a sigh of relief, as today there was a local holiday: waiters seemed in a good mood, and were plying their customers with food and drink. Eastern European singers were performing along a route where the sea was never far from sight. He broke with his own regime of denial, which had consisted largely of bully beef and brackish tea, and took a beer at one of the innumerable brasseries, becoming absorbed in a performance by a conjuror – or rather, his female assistant, who could have passed for Cleopatra.

As he watched the beautiful and contorted body take part in the charmer's routine, Jock realised that he too was going to need to be a magician – a military one. There would be little time for company while planning his own training, though one never knew whom one might meet at The Cecil. No, he would be earning every penny as a soldier because Rommel was moving up the coast towards Alexandria, and whatever the Egyptians did, with their pictures of Hitler and the Desert Fox ready to replace those of Churchill and Auchinleck if a German occupation became a reality, they knew in their hearts that a Nazi takeover of Cairo would be insufferable. The leader of the British Military's new private army swigged his last drop of beer, dropped a coin in the bowl of the magician's assistant, and tipped the waiter.

As Jock jested with an entire family of beer drinkers, he turned and faced the Mediterranean which bobbed with little Greek boats full to the gunnels with cheese and spaghetti, and what looked like medical supplies; empty boats belonging to the Alexandrian Volunteer Patrol rolled lazily on the tide. He knew that while tanks full of good men were being 'brewed up' along the North African coast because of their inferior equipment, rather than lack of expertise or courage, British airpower could hardly spare any vehicles for the SAS Brigade that Jock had in mind. Even though the top brass had desperately wanted to create a reality out of the fiction that Clarke's MI9 had woven to fool the enemy into believing there were airborne elite troops all over the desert, Jock winced at the thought that MacDonald and he had only been promised an old post plane that was almost too dangerous to drop out of. It was ironic that the dark-skinned crews of the small incoming boats had more chance of reaching Malta with their illegal hooch or whisky than the British destroyers that were now piling up on one another across the bottom of the sea. It was he who would be in charge of 'MacDonald's Rest

Camp', and it was he who would face the first and most important challenge alone: turning a host of mostly disillusioned commandos into a brigade of totally committed fighting men.

Having cleaned up in style at the Cecil Hotel, Jock left Alexandria, the Greek Levantine city, and took the train to the Islamic city of Cairo. While foreign communities had dominated Alexandria, Egyptian Muslims and literally an army of Englishmen swarmed through the city of the Nile. Tall and muscular, Jock was conspicuous in the crowded streets full of perspiring hordes of private soldiers in thick outfits that were riddled with sweat stains. The soldiers had pink, sunburnt skin: they lacked the deep, penetrating tan of soldiers who had spent months in the desert. Jock's turn to sweat buckets would come again, but alone and in the desert rather than the street bazaar. The place was filling up with old motors piled with over-ripe vegetables, timid flocks of sheep and some goats, all cramped for space in among the small Fiats, motorbikes and pickup trucks. Yet, before making the new SAS Kabrit camp work like clockwork, Jock was determined to live like a prince for a weekend in Shepheard's Hotel, for more than a century a home for the earliest expeditions.

Like a Lawrence of Arabia for a new age, Jock was a man with an unswerving sense of purpose, and in his case, a third mission in the space of a year. Marz would no longer trouble him, yet there was the danger of another agent replacing the SD officer. Jock had also been made aware that there was a leak in the intelligence sent back to Washington. This had originally been set up to keep the Americans in the loop with the British Army's every move – everything from order of battle and forthcoming operations to spare parts and shortages. That certainly put Jock's new brigade equipment into perspective: it wouldn't matter how much kit he received for the SAS if the enemy knew every move they were going to make before they made it. However, he reminded himself that all was not lost, for if the enemy knew that 'L' detachment SAS existed, they might also be persuaded to believe that Clarke's fictitious 'A' to 'K' detachments were real. Jock might be off duty until further notice as an attached member of MI6, but that wouldn't stop him pricking up his ears in the Long Bar at Shepheard's, where patrons were known to be notoriously indiscreet, partly because women were not allowed in there. *Off duty – was he ever going to be that, now that Panton was in Egypt?*

Jock inhaled clouds of burning betel nut, taking pleasure in the beautifully crafted and adorned city. As he walked past the bazaars, he sensed the eyes of hidden females watching through beaded curtains, and behind patterned private gates and windows. The beauty of the place couldn't mask the tension and claustrophobia that he shared there, though, unlike the women, he was free to walk where he wanted. He passed the shaded terrace where copies of *Parade* magazine, with their pin-up of Rita Hayworth on the back, obscured many of the wicker chairs and tables that usually commanded a lofty view of Ibrahim Pasha Street from Shepheard's Moorish Hall within. The intimate setting, with its octagonal tables and antimacassared chairs, suggested a discretion Jock thought illusory, in a city infested with double agents. However, that did not prevent the young officer enjoying the delicious cool of the room in the shadowy light beneath a coloured glass dome.

There was a lull after tea had been served and drunk. He padded to the Long Bar and tipped the Swiss barman, Joe, who was probably one of the best-informed people in Cairo. Jock sipped his Bloody Mary, took in the clientele and listened.

'Any news, Joe?'

The only snippet of gossip that he could glean was indeed scant. Joe laughed. 'Little news, sir, except that the British Ambassador here, Sir Miles, has discovered that his servants have mislaid the only two pairs of swimming trunks he possesses. This oppressive heat, sir, and humidity, and the fact that replacing them would not be immediate, has caused a huge debacle on the lawn of the embassy this afternoon.' Joe rolled his eyes on cue. 'Apparently, Lieutenant, the staff can't lay their hands on an alternative pair of trunks that are ... big enough.'

Jock laughed with Joe, but that was hardly going to assist him in gauging whether his new desert force was being closely watched from the heart of the Coptic centre. He sipped his cocktail again and became absorbed in the frieze above him, which depicted the ancient Egyptian winged goddess Isis. With such a symbol, he could portray both the spiritual and military force of the work he intended to complete with MacDonald; a parachute rather than a scarab beetle between two-tone dark and light-blue feathers representing the Oxbridge leaders would look well. The hard-working beetle that helped fertilise and renew the banks of the Nile would be suitably replaced by the badge and emblem of a genuine special service epitomised by his expanded parachute detachment, which would inject life into breaking the illusion that the Nazis were without military equals. It would encapsulate his new mission to safeguard Africa for success against Rommel.

Joe called over from the bar. 'Excuse me, sir, I nearly forgot. There's a letter for you, Lieutenant.'

Jock had always avoided opening letters from the bank before retiring to bed. In some ways, he wished he had done the same with the dark-edged letter passed to him by Joe. All his MI6 communications were concealed in death notices, an agreed form of messaging. However, the text of this message was in German. The parachute leader was brought down to earth fast as he translated it:

'Panton will follow you to Kabrit.'

Jock was forewarned by Broadway Buildings' intelligence, but it only went so far. He didn't think this was from MI6, despite the envelope. Jock was not privy to the information that Harkiss had seen about the dangerous recipe of characteristics that made up the Soviet fanatic on the loose in the desert. He knew that traitors like Harkiss and Blynde would try and protect their associates by intercepting anything that might help MIRAGE and therefore undermine Panton. However, Jock couldn't help but feel this was information possibly provided by Canaris. The old Admiral said he would return a favour, and it looked like this might be it. Jock needed all the help he could get.

Panton's intelligence operatives seemed to be as thorough as any of those belonging to the Germans, or British. Kabrit was over one hundred miles away and it was supposed to be the secret location of the first real SAS detachment – 'L' detachment.

It was definitely time for a kip before the dawn of Jock's creation of effective Special Forces, which he had worked so hard to achieve, but which was already in jeopardy. As his head hit the pillow, he contented himself with the German maxim: 'Viel Feind, viel Ehr' – 'Many enemies, much honour'.

The saying was more appropriate than perhaps Jock realised. At the same time, unbeknown to Jock, a psychological profile of Panton had been given to Moscow by his handler, Batukin, using his code name 'WAISE', which meant 'orphan'.

> WAISE *makes mistakes occasionally because he is*
> *inexperienced, often acting on his own initiative without*
> *asking us, but the urgency of* WAISE's *lead on MIRAGE*
> *and the danger of possible exposure of our friends in London*
> *mean we are not in the position to slow him for now … He*
> *will come and tell us everything. He told me that he was not*
> *fully prepared for his previous attempt on MIRAGE and that*
> *it won't happen again. When he told me about this, he was in*
> *very low spirits, because he felt tortured by regret that he had*
> *failed to protect our people in London.*

Batukin concluded with an observation:

> WAISE *is a hypochondriac individual and seems to be*
> *a manic depressive with a dependence upon alcohol. He*
> *often thinks that we do not trust him completely. That can*
> *be accounted for by two leading features in his make-up –*
> *internal instability and loneliness. It should be stated that*
> *in the time he has been working for us, he has improved*
> *greatly in the first area. He has frequently tried to persuade*
> *me that we are his saviours. Hence his alertness and worry*
> *that he could bring dismissal from our service. I demonstrated*
> *my trust to him by the fact that I am his friend and do not*
> *consider him a stranger, but our valued comrade.*

KABRIT, EGYPT

I

Jock combed the sand out of his hair as his train pulled up in the pre-dawn glow beside the dirty little platform. Perspiring Cairenes jostled together in the gangway, but the officer extricated himself from them and moved into the stationmaster's office to ring for a car.

Did Jock have his posting order? He did? Well, in that case a car would be sent around as soon as possible.

The administration hut was a short walk from the little station. There was no one in there so he found a neighbouring tent and popped his head inside. A captain looked at his papers and offered him a cigarette, which he accepted.

'So, you are going to join "L" Detachment?' he said.

'Yes, sir.'

'If I'm not mistaken, Lieutenant, you appear to *be* "L" Detachment at the moment.'

Jock smiled. 'Is that so, sir?'

'I believe so, Lieutenant.'

'You've not seen any other officers, sir?' Jock thought of Panton now. 'Or any other personnel?'

'Now you mention it, I haven't. It's down the road there, if you can call it a road.' He laughed. 'About half an hour's drive …' He broke off to swat a fly on his desk. 'The detachment's going to practise parachuting, I believe.

Of course, everything's very hush-hush down there.'

'Really, sir?'

'Indeed. It is John, isn't it?'

'Jock, actually, sir.'

'It's an interesting name for a Welsh Guardsman, if I may say so, Lieutenant, ah, Jock,' he corrected himself.

'Yes, the nickname evolved from "Jock-strap", my rowing crew's pun on my manhood, and it's stuck ever since, sir.'

'Ah, yes, I see.' The Captain blushed a little. 'Oh yes, very good.' He coughed a little on his cigarette. 'I expect they will keep you pretty busy. I can't understand why I never knew you were coming.'

Jock did not mention that, for his part, it would have been strange if the Captain had known of his posting. Very rarely in the army had his official posting been expected by the authorities of the reception area, despite the fact that the whole business took up an inordinate amount of paperwork.

'Anyway, I am sure you will like the unit,' the Captain reflected. 'There will be plenty of exercise; there's swimming, of course, in the Bitter Lake. Apparently, there is this genius of a training officer with an extraordinary scheme to turn a bunch of cutthroats into something that Churchill could only dream of.'

'Is that so, sir?'

Jock didn't have the time or inclination to enlighten the Captain further, but realised that the rumour in Cairo meant that Panton would have plenty of helpers to point the way to 'L' Detachment, the real part of the fictitious SAS force. He reflected that the Captain wouldn't fit easily into the band of 'cutthroats', should he even desire it, which the young Lieutenant doubted. Meanwhile, Jock would need to get his thinking cap on and perfect the systematic methods that he had piloted before and during the successful German invasion of Crete if he were to live up to his reputation.

Jock wanted to shorten the war by destroying Nazi infrastructure, thereby saving the reputation of British raiders in North Africa. Firing live rifle rounds close to his men's heads, navigation by the stars, long-distance marches, water discipline, familiarity with all weapons, including those of the enemy, basic medical care, and even moving planes around the aerodromes his men were to attack behind enemy lines, were all part of the corollary of novel warfare that he was creating in order to invade the soft underbelly of Germany and Italy.

'Driver!' the Captain yelled. He turned back to Jock, smiling. 'See how you get on, and do let me know if you are in difficulties.' He opened the door and looked out towards the white glare of the sand outside. 'Damn the fellow … Where's he got to?' The Captain blinked and screwed up his eyes as he looked outside; he might have been calling for a truant Labrador, but then Jock saw the Lance Corporal pull up by the tent in an Austin Tilly. 'Take Lieutenant Steel to "MacDonald's Rest Camp" – next door to the Navy Camp at Kabrit.'

'Yes, sir.'

'Well, goodbye, Lieutenant.' He held out a lily-white hand. 'I do hope you enjoy yourself.'

Well-meaning enough chap, Jock thought, as he climbed into the Austin, which purred along the road where it was flat, skirting the edge of the Bitter Lake. Shimmering in the haze lay the white shore of Sinai; in the mid-ground were a few barges. Leaving the verdant cultivation behind, hot air swept across the black, meandering snake of the recently asphalted road. Jock also thought it unlikely that the Captain's driver would swap his chauffeur job for the desert marches and parachuting he had in store for the recruits he had to swiftly assemble.

The car swung past the aerodrome and turned towards the canal signalling station.

'It's somewhere over here, sir,' the driver said. 'There we are, sir, HMS Saunders. It'll be next door, I imagine.'

HMS Saunders seemed an organised naval base. Jock saw the notice warning of exceeding more than ten knots an hour. He certainly wouldn't be using this area to forward roll off a truck in order to simulate a forceful parachute landing. The Austin turned off the road just beyond the camp and now bumped uneasily along towards one large tent. The white dust billowed up in a cloud behind them and briefly hovered there, obscuring a simple wooden board, balanced precariously on a sand-bagged entrance to the marquee. As the sand particles drifted away, Jock craned his neck to read the legend 'L Detachment SAS'.

'That looks like the entire Brigade camp, sir, office and all,' the driver remarked with a wave of his hand, and he jumped out and leaned forward to reach Jock's bag and the Zbrojovka Brno, but the officer had already retrieved it. 'Is that all, sir? I'll have to get a move on, or they'll give my breakfast to the Captain's hound.'

Jock was fully aware that the Army simply couldn't function without the Austin's chauffeur, especially an army that had at first been outnumbered by twenty-five to one and was still trying to fight something akin to the First World War.

'Thank you for the lift, Lance Corporal.'

'Goodbye, sir.'

'Goodbye.'

Jock walked around the lecture tent, found the opening and went inside. There was nothing except a large table, little air and considerable heat. So, this was 'L' Detachment. No men as yet, one piece of furniture, one tent and a great deal of sand. Jock closed his eyes and breathed a deep sigh of relief. He was truly content for the moment. This was a great opportunity. He was again not going to be taking orders from indecisive halfwits, but giving purposeful commands – this time to even more pioneers, and importantly, even further away from the interfering clutches of HQ Cairo. His spring experiments with marching and battlecraft had the potential to yield to him the freedom to work as a soldier in the way that he instinctively knew best. He unpacked his one-man tent, drank some water from his pint flask, pocketed some nuts and raisins in a small rucksack with a few oranges, and counted out ten small pebbles, which he put in one of his trouser pockets. He started walking towards the horizon. It was not long after dawn; the temperature was already increasing to 45°C in the shade.

This was where he could reflect on his mission in Egypt, but also on his pain: the nagging splinter in his heart that told him he had been out of contact with Madeleine for too long. Away from the city, he would paralyse his sense of anguish that she might be in as much danger as he was now.

However, the young pioneer had come home.

II

Here, he would decide whether to live or die. As Jock counted his pebbles in tens, marking each set of a hundred paces, he knew that no one would break his fall should he collapse in the punishing heat that pulsed through the red and rugged desert. Yet this was a place of salvation both for him and for the Arabs: to look forward without turning back with fear, but with the freedom to live on the edge of terror in the spaces between the dark and light, and the darkness within. He had warned Madeleine in his last letter, '*I shall not scheme to return to England because it is ordered that I serve in Egypt.*' Jock realised that such news arriving months later in Scotland at her parents' would almost certainly go down like a lead balloon. Jock's presence, but especially his absence, could infuriate her; she missed him terribly and he knew that her lying low and waiting for job interviews was not the distracting pursuit that soldiering was for him.

The sand, with its tiny particles of lime and sandstone, reflected back the rays of the morning sun like burning glass, and the air shimmered up like that above an overheated engine. Jock sought out the route to immediacy, the path to connecting with sands and the brilliant light that had so often been portrayed as the other enemy in the desert. This was the beginning of Jock's path to victory in the Western Desert, victory in love, victory in death, victory over the Hun. He plumbed the depths of his stamina and strength while fathoming the training programmes, the love letters, orders that must originate from the recesses of his lateral-thinking mind. Edward Thomas had referred to 'the keyless chambers of the brain', and his own new ideas, like the poet's, must come from there. One thought hurtled into another, and he sensed another forebear of sorts – this time a Thomas Edward: T.E. Lawrence, the Uncrowned King of Arabia, as the Prince of Mecca had once described him. He, like T.E., would saturate himself in the Arab world. Who else now was able to create a desperately needed new art of war in North Africa?

He hoped that the temporary detention of Quinton Panton had led to the exposure of the Soviet sympathisers and traitors in London because then Madeleine would be safer. Like Lawrence in Aqaba, he would create a feint in the remotest areas to outwit an increasingly confused enemy. So, the bittersweet joy of being the only soldier alive in that desolate place allowed him the familiarity of danger, the risk of one blurred mirage too far, one hallucination too many. He counted his thirtieth mile and delighted in his environment: the lack of anything man-made, no traffic or smells away from fly-blown Cairo. Barely hidden in the sand, he noticed bleached skeletons of camels or perhaps even humans.

Jock could feel the roaring silence. He could feel it on his skin. The purity of the light was mesmerising: every colour submerged into an optical illusion of shining oblivion. He had to choose to breathe again and find his way out of the wilderness. It seemed apposite to return. His eyes glowed with a film of sweat but also with the thought that if Panton wanted him, the Soviet servant would have to risk death just looking for him out here. Jock swabbed his damp forehead, forestalled hunger by chewing some more raisins and turned 180 degrees, contentedly making his return journey. There would be no interruptions by amateurs; no one knew where he was, nobody probably cared, except his gorgeous Madeleine, and he was glad that she remained blissfully ignorant of his complete lack of vehicle, medical or radio support. He would master being on the terrifying edge of Life, and under the edge of the Axis sword that threatened to steal his and Madeleine's life and future. He would win this war with his own body and brain, with the forces of nature, from a paltry water bottle to a handful of pebbles, and a keen interest in the position of the stars; with science and technology, with his nerve and sinew.

Hours later, unlike fellow Arab travellers, there was no homecoming at his camp. However, wiping the sweat from his forehead, he noticed something: not a fire, but a truck's headlamps and dust kicking up in the distance. He was on the border of the Kabrit camp. Perhaps this was more equipment for the new 'L' Detachment? If it was a homecoming of sorts, it was to be vacuous.

It wasn't long before the familiar Austin pulled up by the lecture tent. In the beam of light, a younger man had also observed dust from his own vantage point, barely able to see the officer who, like the desert phantom he was fast becoming, was partly masked in clouds of sand issuing from his steps.

The Lance Corporal looked apologetic as Jock approached.

'Sorry to have to disturb the training, sir, but you have an urgent long-distance call from the War Office in London. The Colonel said that he would telephone again in half an hour's time.'

'I see. Thank you, Lance Corporal. We had better go then.'

Back past the canal and aerodrome, they retraced their tracks towards the new coastal road, and as they did so, Jock realised that if he was not careful, the events of the last few days would amount to nothing more than yet another of the false starts that so many of the commando units had suffered for almost twelve months. Hollings hadn't managed to get hold of him after he had left Tobruk, and arrangements had now been made for Jock to waive any leave and turn a crew of ruffians into something resembling an elite force.

The Captain at Kabrit once more offered Jock a seat in the cramped office, which seemed a life away from the desert walk with its hallucinations, undulations and ocean of sand. The officer excused himself, and quickly produced a cup of sand-less tea. The sweat that was still dripping off Jock's back stained the canvas on the only chair.

Jock waited an hour in vain. The telephone didn't ring. He had been experiencing the rapture after the disordered operations of the peripheral nerves during deep exhaustion; he felt the natural anaesthetic of satisfaction at completing the ordeal that had come with the stretching of his mind and body to its limits. Yet it didn't quite manage to dull the feeling of discomfort that had not ebbed away; in his guts, he knew that Hollings was trying to get inside his head. Hollings was trying to bring him back to London.

III

A group of non-commissioned officers gathered around their new quarters, which mostly consisted of tents. Members of the 'Tobruk Four', whom Jock had led in raiding experience and who were now the powerhouse of the new SAS brigade, were testing Corporal Leonard. 'Lennie' – five foot nine, with jet-black hair combed with Brylcreem, wiry, alert, one of life's survivors – was holding forth about the new detachment and its training. Reg Paveney, a fine boxer with legs like tree trunks and a chest that Lennie could only dream about, smiled at Jim 'Dignified' Diamonds, who personified the art of patience as he took in the Corporal's tirade. As he did so, a fleet of tired-looking Bedford vans pulled into view by Jock's tent. The paint had worn away on the vehicle's axles, possibly stripped off by sandstorm blasts.

'Well, Jim,' said Reg, 'there is the Lieutenant's new secret weapon.'

'Elaborate for the incredulous, Reg, otherwise you'll be next for the Corporal's verbal barrage.'

Reg pointed to the vehicles and with a strong Fenland accent elaborated: 'That there is the means to our becoming the desert's most elite parachuting force.'

Lennie waded into the fray in his high-pitched cockney. 'What on earth do you mean by that?'

'Wash your ears out!'

Lennie howled back. 'Can you bloody speak English, please?'

'We are rehearsing the jumps in those trucks.' Reg spoke with an irony that Lennie was unable to fully comprehend.

Corporal Leonard was totally absorbed in the rusting vans with his mouth wide open. 'You are bloody joking.'

'Do we look like we're joking, Corporal?' Diamonds looked back at Paveney in mock seriousness with raised eyebrows.

'Why do we need trucks when we could probably simulate a proper jump from a twelve-foot wall?' Lennie whined.

'How many twelve-foot walls have you seen out here? Yours is not to reason why, yours is to do or die,' chirped Paveney.

'I thought it was to dare not die?'

'Touché, Corporal, but the fact remains that *you* were the smart Alec who laid down the gauntlet to the Lieutenant in the first place.'

'How do you mean?'

'Well, you remember the first day, when some of the men complained about digging the foundations for the first base camp and Lieutenant Steel jumped onto the lecture table and called us all *yellow*!?'

'Yes, so?'

'So, you bloody chimed in that we'd all do everything asked of us as long as the Lieutenant did the same – but did it first.'

'And?'

Paveney looked incredulously at Lennie. 'Well, you seem to have forgotten that he's a bloody "Meteor", a top athlete and totally bloody fearless – and where he goes, Lennie, you're going to go, because you sealed that deal the night we thought we might lynch the Lieutenant.'

'Well, I'm not jumping out of a truck at ten miles an hour.'

Diamonds straightened his back and rasped with a sideways shake of the head, 'I dare say you won't be, Corporal.'

After Paveney's barb, this apparent crumb of concession from the more experienced soldier made Lennie start to feel a bit better about himself.

'There you go then, Sergeant,' he said.

Yet the illusion of an easy life was about to be punctured.

'There you go at more like twenty miles per hour,' chirped Diamonds.

'You are bloody joking.'

'No, we're not, Corporal. Actually, Lieutenant Steel will probably warm us up at twenty miles per hour – that's forward rolls off the vehicle.'

Lennie was still not entirely certain he was not being bluffed so, egged on by Paveney, Diamonds added, 'Backward rolls may start at fifteen miles per hour.' Lennie's mouth fell open again. 'And of course we'd go up incrementally,' Diamonds said, with more feigned earnestness. 'In five-mile-an-hour slots.'

The two sergeants exploited the Corporal's discomfort for as long as they could. Lennie was beginning to wonder if his worst fear would be realised – that the training, as Corporal Rose had earlier said, 'was more frightening than running into a Nazi patrol'.

Diamonds scratched his head and asked Lennie with mock seriousness exactly what he was pondering. He did his best not to release the suppressed laughter that kept threatening to turn his voice into a husky giggle.

'What do you think will be our top speed?'

Lennie's eyes began to moisten. He struggled to speak. 'Thirty?'

'That would be a reasonable estimate, but it is more than likely he'll personally experiment with nearer forty miles an hour than thirty.' Diamonds added, 'Don't worry, mate, we'll all be spinning through the air at the same speeds.'

'That's not much of a consolation.'

Paveney responded, 'You should try being six foot four then, Corporal.'

At five foot nine inches, Lennie was considerably more aerodynamic than either of the sergeants who dwarfed him, and with that realisation he stopped whingeing.

IV

Jock had demonstrated the forward and backward rolls and at a range of speeds off the back of the lorries. The men eventually remonstrated, especially after even the Lieutenant had sprained a wrist. He cancelled the backward rolls, but the forward rolls continued despite other injuries. Yet, even with the healthy peer-group criticism that was part of the ethos that Jock engendered, everyone knew that they needed to harden up fast because HQ Cairo might want them on a 'party' to prove themselves before Jock and MacDonald were ready. The Scot had impressed upon Jock that the situation was bleak with regard to equipment and that the petty jealousies of the deskbound were starting to kick in as word spread of a secret army that ran itself in an unconventional way without due reference to the administrators, or without respect for the sensibilities of the sedentary army's sense of protocol. For the moment, 'L' Detachment had to be content with cast-offs, hand-me-downs and substandard equipment. Jock, never one to be daunted by the cynics and bearers of woe, decided that the men must be as self-reliant as possible, using the bare minimum of kit. If it was to be denied them, they would turn it to their advantage. Yet there was one thing they desperately needed: custom-built explosives.

The men had joked that Jock was getting his own back on the 'whingeing Poms' who were still grumbling about wrist injuries by conducting experiments on explosives during any brief rest times. Colonel

Merriman had sent for an ordnance officer to go to Kabrit to discuss Jock's request to give the SAS Brigade 'teeth' with the explosives it needed to become more than just an observation corps with the occasional firefight. The ability of the parachutists to move about the Western Desert on foot and return alive was only a beginning for the brigade. Jock knew that the independence they had been given would need to be paid for in results. The key to victory was inextricably linked to cutting off Rommel's lifeline: fuel was being transported to his bases, but the British still could not boast that they possessed any air superiority. In such conditions, Auchinleck held back Operation Crusader, aimed at overpowering the Panzer Army. Jock's brigade needed to support Churchill's strategy to counter the sinking of aircraft carriers such as *Ark Royal*. Once achieved, it might then be possible to release airpower for the new Russian ally.

As Jock was planning to solve this puzzle with regard to explosives, the *Maritza* and *Procida* were being prepared to leave Italian ports as air-fuel cargo to support Rommel's supply lines. Churchill had written that their destruction was of 'decisive importance'. Each of Jock's and MacDonald's men had to destroy what a group of ten commandos could achieve. The SAS were manoeuvrable and self-reliant, but the litmus test of the fledgling unit was whether they could blow up enough Axis vehicles and installations that were assisting the Desert Fox's logistics.

The Ordnance Major arrived one afternoon during break-time in the brigade's daily routine. Jock put the finishing touches to a letter to Madeleine as the staff car pulled up, indulging in a fantasy to help alleviate the relentless demands made upon him. One of his paragraphs was haunting him:

> *'Come on, hand in hand out of the gate, quickly down the lane, scramble through the hedge into a June field where we can walk slowly through the thick grass. Slowly, slowly, pacing side by side with the excitement of your skin on mine as we walk ... We seem to be fencing with each other but are really striking at the cold heart of the third walker in the depth of the field ...'*

The war had spawned phantoms that unsettled him, and he was aware of the ghostly presence of the viper in his 'June field', the figure in his mind that was also a menace to a love affair that should be made in heaven, if there wasn't so much hellish war to drive through first. In snippets of letters written days after Jock last saw Madeleine (he had still received little word from her), between the lines, stood circling males, sparring for the attentions of Madeleine, who had occasionally in her last letters seemed unconvinced about the idea of marriage made in heaven. Yet, having never met these men, he gave them various names in order to help him laugh at his unenviable predicament of being alone in the desert while they drew her to Cambridge, on and by the Cam; they mirrored the invisible threats in Broadway Buildings at MI6.

Madeleine's ghouls and pursuers doubled in his mind as the Soviet passengers in the Special Operations Executive: the Pantons of this world, the men who had tailed him in London, the smiling chameleon that he believed to have been Harkiss in the Bentley at Woburn. They were all part of the enemy's claws that threatened to rip out England's heart. The Nazis and communists no longer possessed a heart themselves, and they wouldn't allow others to beat with a true pulse. Were Madeleine's suitors in England – 'Taxi-man', 'Cam-man', 'Con-man', 'Gift-man', Charles, Mike, or Don – trying to take her away from him? As well, there was the possibility of traitors like Panton undermining the chance of peace that everyone seemed to forget, or despised, because they were too pumped up with propaganda. Perhaps once, Charlotte – 'Corncurls' – could have been 'the third walker' in his own 'June field', but that was a year ago now. With few temptations in the desert, it was Madeleine's turn to challenge 'the cold heart of the third walker', the ghost of her fears, the tempter, the actor. Jock knew that the Mess at Esher this Christmas would be full of what Madeleine called *'the well-fed and rich young men at an oyster party … charmingly dishonest, delightfully insincere, in their blue cloth and shiny buttons.'*

He had a love affair too with England, for all its flaws, and he wasn't about to let it slip into the abyss, destroyed by the Nazis and Soviets, and their extremist friends. As a boy, Jock's first love affair had been with explosives. He smiled at the transitions he had made in investing in his passions, from bombs to women, to an island … and now back to explosives again. The challenge was to connect his obsessions. He'd never been put off by the dangers, even as a young lad in short trousers with the gift of an entire chemistry set that most schools would have envied. The day his brother, David, nearly killed him on the back porch had inspired him to continue experimenting rather than give it all up. Most children get back on their bicycle when they fall off; Jock took the same approach to explosives. He discovered some of his habitual reserve, humour and iron resolve. David had his own 'gun': a .303 brass cartridge case clipped down to a hunk of wood. Jock had set out to demonstrate that it was dangerous, and rammed it with what he thought to be gunpowder – but David omitted to mention that he had mixed his own potassium chlorate, which was unstable, instead of the saltpetre that his brother Jock had expected.

'Pack it hard, Jock,' Owen, his pal next to him, had chanted.

David was on the other side of the creek, working a home-made cannon, absorbed in the construction, oblivious to the boys a mere twenty feet over the water. David was trying not to get distracted by a spider the size of his hand ogling at him from a nearby piece of timber that was partly submerged. Jock remembered the whole childhood scene that seemed to have changed his life:

'It's nearly readeeee…' Jock didn't need to say any more. He was thrown to the ground as the veranda shook with the force of the explosion. Owen saw Dodgson, the family cat, leap farther and higher than he'd ever seen before. The boy knew that Jock was badly hit as somewhere the blood started running down the sloping wooden floor. Then Owen, looking down at Jock, thought his friend had lost more blood on the way down but he'd been hit too; he ignored the neat horizontal cuts on his own bare legs and bent down to scream for Mrs Steel.

Owen started yelping, crying for help. Jock had shut his eyes and was breathing fast, short breaths; he felt pangs of pain and shocks of shooting warmth running through his arm, the end of which he clutched with his left hand. Everything went slow; occasionally he looked up at the cloudless sky, and deep down he knew that this could have been his very last cloudless day. His right thigh was sore and he knew that it must be with bits of metal and wood. The thing had blown up in his hand, bits embedded in him. His little finger was hanging off his right hand. He turned his head a few inches very slowly so he could see through the veranda towards the nearest edge of the creek; David was alright, but there was shrapnel in his brother's legs too. Once bandaged up by Dr Harbisson, all Jock could think about was getting better quickly so he could get back to some more chemistry.

The memories faded as he stepped out of his tent into the bright day to greet the Ordnance Major.

'Good afternoon, sir.'

'Good to meet you, Lieutenant Steel. It's a pleasure to meet the author of a concept that promises so much wanton destruction.'

'Thank you, sir.' Jock looked at the bullish-faced officer, who seemed affable enough, but not a great danger to the Germans – or even the Italians, for that matter.

'I have brought our smallest and most regular explosive with me; I can have plenty of these allocated for your first raid.'

'Our task, sir, is to destroy trucks, ammunition, equipment and fuel on the ground. We require explosives that will not only detonate and destroy the targets, but set them alight instantly.'

The Major proffered his answer to the brigade's challenge to find a bomb light enough for Jock's parachutists to carry in large numbers around desert.

'The technology available is an explosive device with its own fuse, and a separate incendiary, with a separate fuse timed to ignite after the first bomb, lighting up the fuel released by the first explosion's damage to, say, a fuel tank.'

Jock looked at the cumbersome bomb. 'May I?'

He picked it up and winced. The explosive must have weighed in at five pounds, and he realised that the choleric-faced Major lacked any depth of curiosity about how to disarm an enemy aerodrome, though it was part of his remit. There was one significant threat to the British and that was still the Nazi's air superiority. The Long Range Desert Group had recently shown the capability of small, armed groups travelling freely in the interior of Libya, revealing that the great Libyan Desert was not a secure flank for either side in the war. Destroying enemy planes in significant numbers would put considerable pressure on the Italians to divert valuable troops to guard installations in the defence of distant outposts that were vulnerable to the likes of Jock. Yet, if Jock's men would find it difficult to blow up aeroplanes by carrying five-pound bombs to their targets, everyone else would discover it to be nigh-on impossible.

The senior officer sat down and swatted a fly off a table so that he could show off his equipment and share his ideas.

'You cannot get a bomb lighter than that, Lieutenant – not for the sort of mission you have in mind. The gelignite, thermite and other ingredients can be used like this to either explode or ignite, but *they can't do both*. This problem has already defeated scientists on numerous occasions.'

Middle Eastern Headquarters had offered their nominal support to the SAS, but in fact had probably told the 'expert' that he was wasting his time. Countless scientific problems had managed to defeat numerous scientists because of the infallibility of the medieval popes. The top brass seemed to be acting with the same infallibility, but Jock thought better of mentioning that and just stated the facts.

'An exploded hole in a plane's wing or tank won't necessarily set fire to the vehicle. Damage can be easily made good by the enemy, and the threat of Axis air forces will continue, sir.'

'I agree with that, Lieutenant.'

'Of course, sir,' Jock replied and saluted.

The Major returned the salute, wearily picked up his heavy bomb and fly-whisk and drove off, unencumbered by awareness.

Jock turned to his Tobruk veterans.

'Sergeant Diamonds, get hold of a couple of plane wings this afternoon, will you? It doesn't matter what type exactly because I'm going to blow them up and simultaneously set them on fire – otherwise it's going to be a very long war. It's going to be the difference between having a self-defence force or an army worth its name.'

V

Like the professional scrounger that he had now become, Jock dismissed the intransigence of the Ordnance Major with his five-pound bomb, and obtained more of the new plastic explosive. He had been told by his quartermaster that some of the new charge materials that had recently arrived in Cairo had 'gone missing'; there had been a 'hoo-ha' about it, but no one, including the store, had any idea where it was. The Egyptian workers employed by His Majesty's government had been blamed for mishandling stores on the port; some pay had been docked in lieu. Jock started playing with his new military toy while Sergeant Diamonds returned with a suitable plane wing and a couple of big oil drums.

'A pound of this explosive should do it, along with a primer, some Cordtex and detonators. We'll meet up this afternoon at 1400 and see how much damage we can do to this Savoya wing. Thank you for the scrap, Sergeant.'

'A pleasure, sir,' whispered Diamonds. A hot desert wind had begun to whip up and clouds of swirling brackish-coloured dust permeated lungs in the excessive heat where shade was at a premium. Throats weren't just parched, but stung by flying sand.

Jock pressed on. 'We could postpone this work outside, but that would mean a step back from the enemy, instead of what I hope will be a huge leap forward.'

'I'm sure you'll come up with your own Seven League boots, sir.'

The Lieutenant laughed. 'Let's hope so, Sergeant.'

Jock knew that without a miracle, or at least some results, his and MacDonald's brigade would be stopped in its tracks. Five-pound bombs would mean an early grave for any soldier brave or stupid enough to carry them. Jock used an old ration bag as a carrying container and painted the modest-sized bomb with a liberal coating of tar. He stuck his new creation on the Savoya's wing, where it would be little more than three foot away from its fuel container; he had created a dummy out of diesel, which he knew would assist the desired explosion even more than petrol. The bomb would need to penetrate an aeroplane's metal petrol tank, which was at least a quarter-inch thick.

Jock lit a standard fuse and watched the home-made device crackle and burst into the wing with a deafening thud. A hole the size of a fist appeared in the body, but the fuel beneath just leaked, the explosion over;

there was nothing to spark a flame. The wing could be used again, and on this occasion needed to be. Jock picked up another pound of plastic and thermite to both burn and blow up; he sat in his canvas chair kneading the material in his hands and pondered the problem. If there was a God, it was now He should show it.

Jock had to make this material stay alight and work its way along the wing to heat and spark the inflammable liquid, not just momentarily, but grandly announcing itself with a loud report like a noisy but almost ineffectual chemical genie. What would make the whole 'firework' last and prevent it from being just another 'now you see it, now you don't' display by one of the Army's troupes of conjurors? Something that would dampen down the explosion without actually putting this work of force and fire out … Something that would prevent the chemicals from simply blowing up within seconds and make them take longer to do all their work …

Sergeant Diamonds was reassembling the wing for another dose of medicine. Jock threw the plastic ball of ingredients between each hand like a baseball player, kneading it again in between catches. Diamonds watched Jock deep in thought, but nearly dropped the end of the wing when his officer bellowed out the word, 'Oil!'

Of course! Oil! Sergeant Diamonds had barely finished positioning the experimental wing when the shouting figure ran to a nearby truck and brought out a can of engine oil as if it were a vintage wine, except that Jock dispensed a liberal helping onto his hands. 'Dignified' Diamonds watched him manipulate some thermite and the other elements together with the speed of a schoolboy tearing open a box of chocolates, eyes lighting up with an insatiable appetite for satisfaction.

Swiftly, Jock then tarred the mixture and secured the new bomb onto the wing.

'The oil is going to gobble up some of the air in the explosion and slow it down; it has to.'

Several men had poured out of their tents and begun to realise what was afoot, watching as a fuse was lit. 'BOOM!' followed by a 'WHOOMFF!' indicated a new sound – the bang of the explosive producing another hole was now assisted by the burning of the new material that now licked along the plane wing.

'THIS IS IT!' cried Jock. 'THIS IS IT! OIL! IT'S OIL! The lightweight explosive and incendiary – literally rolled into one!' Jock shook 'Dignified' Diamonds with his filthy hands. 'You know what this means, Sergeant?' Jock turned to the crowd of soldiers that had gathered about. 'This changes everything! Jerry hasn't got a chance now; the SAS is fully operational. Their airfields are at our mercy. Some of them aren't even guarded, and their planes are ours for the taking. Just like this bomb, we have all the elements to succeed. I think a bit of celebration is in order.'

JALO, LIBYA

AUTUMN 1941

I

Panton, with help from London, wanted one more crack at finding Jock. He had enough of an idea of the raider's whereabouts, following his trail from Tobruk to Cairo, where he arranged a lift along the coast road with a member of the Royal Automobile Club, who was happy to assist the young 'journalist' for a small fee. Panton had needed to leave Cairo because Field Security had indeed brought up Webster's body from the rising Nile and had confirmation that his assailant might be using his disguise and papers – even if only for a few days, it could increase the damage that had already been done. There could be no publicity or alerts about the Soviet agent, as this would compromise the security of the phantom forces that had mushroomed over the year, and developments like the real, fledgling SAS, which was about to give greater credibility to all the rumours that had been carefully laid to build the smokescreen of Clarke's fictitious armies.

Only a zealot would have pursued Jock. For the raid leader had already moved again from Kabrit after a big first attack on the enemy was staged in a thirty-mile-an-hour hurricane. Nearly all Jock's troop of ten men had survived from the third of the original sixty who had taken part but not been killed or captured. Jock's marches and elaborate training programme had proved that his men on their first SAS mission could navigate back over fifty miles with almost no natural cover, without support and in some of the worst weather. In better conditions, the force would have great opportunity to damage the enemy, avoid enemy aircraft and fight another day. Yet critics of Jock's and MacDonald's SAS force might seize on the significant number who were killed or captured on their first raid; this might fold up the desert force if it returned to Cairo without a series of successful strikes.

Jock and MacDonald then chose to move away from HQ Cairo but still with the chance of striking the enemy where they least expected it: Jalo was west of the Great Sand Sea. There were hundreds and hundreds of miles of uncertainty in the form of shifting ochre, yellow, grey and white fine sands, and days without water. There were some rocky valleys offering a little shelter and even date palms at the end of such an arduous journey, yet even the location of these oases was uncertain because of the changes in weather and shifting dunes. No one was expected to survive there for long. No civilian aircraft could fly over the area without drawing the attention of battling air forces along the coast. No one from HQ Cairo or anywhere else could possibly attempt to shelve the SAS before it successfully blew up enough airfields to prove its worth and validity because no one would know where to look – no one, except perhaps Panton.

Panton's information was that Jock's next attack would be near El Agheila, south-west of Benghazi. Panton again posed as a journalist. He also brought with him several national uniforms, including a South African Long Range Desert Group jacket and an Italian outfit, hidden in a flat, inconspicuous compartment of his case, along with a camera, a tripod, knives, ammunition, pistols and spare film. Most of these would have been acceptable in a civilian car during wartime and would not arouse the suspicion of his driver, who had organised fuel, petrol and water dump pickups, a primus stove, rolls of canvas with wooden cleats to help the vehicle out of soft sand, food and plenty of cigarettes. Armed with his blade, Panton also still carried a cheese wire in his personal armoury, easily accessible in the heel of his right boot.

The passenger assisted with navigation, but spent much of his time assessing the locations where Jock would leave his fortified base camp. Panton's one advantage over Jock was that he already knew that the planes in that area were going to fly westwards from their coastal bases to avoid attacks similar to those Jock's parachute detachment had inflicted a fortnight earlier. He knew that Jock was hungry to damage the enemy's war effort, and there would be few targets to destroy in the region. He now began to narrow down the likeliest possible targets that Jock might aim for in order to track his quarry down.

II

Meanwhile, Jock, binoculars fixed on the coast road, noted the type, number and flow of vehicles moving east and west. His main focal point was the largely unguarded airfield a few miles away. Yet, with horror, he watched the entire groundforce take off towards Tripoli. The complete operation would have to be cancelled, but at least he had valuable information to give to the RAF and HQ Cairo. It wasn't enough for him, and he thought quickly, looking around at his men, the vehicles and the equipment at their disposal.

Some of the men were still cursing the fact that he had brought with them a captured Italian lorry, a Lancia. It had a tendency to stick into the sand and break down more frequently than the other vehicles. Much to their chagrin, they had dug it out more times than they could mention, and considered it redundant to the operation. Jock had nearly agreed with them. Until now. The gripes about the vehicle alerted him to some astute military improvisation. It had always been his intention to use the Lancia to deceive the enemy behind their lines, especially when Axis troops were over one hundred miles from Tobruk and well within the apparent safety of their own occupied territories. Mersa Brega was a staging post for vehicles and senior Axis officers thirty miles north-east of El Agheila, not far away.

He broke the exciting news to the men. 'We are definitely not going back to Jalo empty-handed.' He then looked at the Lancia. The men looked at the Lancia, and then back at Jock, and waited. Jock spoke with much deliberation. 'I will drive that Lancia along the coast road for about an hour. You follow behind in the unmarked trucks. We'll wave to enemy vehicles, smoke on the rooftops if it's too cramped inside, and I'll park alongside one of the Axis camp's own Lancias. We'll use these bombs of mine to blow up the staging post and destroy their vehicles. There are over a hundred enemy there, but they like their comforts and most will probably be by the bar in the camp compound. VIP servicemen are also there and we should take the odd prisoner. Anyone care to join me?'

'Sir, that Lancia's been the bane of my life,' Paveney said. 'I've crankshafted her so often that there has to be a good reason for it.' He added, 'I'm all in.'

Diamonds nodded in agreement, and the other men were keen. Jock knew the basic layout of the camp at Mersa Brega. He had done his homework and read through the numerous confessions of prisoners, which all helped to piece together these particular enemy facilities along this stretch of the coast road. The men concentrated on his drawings of the base in the sand; the pebbled surfaces around the target made a perfect medium for the entrance to the lorry park, its HQ, and the exit and entrances he targeted. Jock didn't just want to give his men a 'party' and destroy enemy vehicles; he wanted to show them that anything was now possible in the desert.

'Kit check: Breda, Thompson machine guns, small arms, ammunition, fuel, maps, desalinators, medicine box, water – check?'

'All there, sir,' Paveney countered.

The men were ready. 'We've still got some light. Excellent – let's get going.'

Jock led the party, and their other vehicle was followed by the Long Range Desert Group as dozens of German and Italian convoys passed them in the hot late afternoon. They were all travelling in relative comfort on new, well-made Italian roads. The parachutists' light-khaki clothes were indistinguishable from those of the Axis troops heading south of them towards Benghazi, past El Agheila, from where they had recently departed. Drivers on the other side of the road, wearing similar khaki-coloured outfits, waved to the small groups of British soldiers, completely unaware of their identity; Jock encouraged his men to wave back cheerily to complete the deception. If only Clarke had been there to enjoy the audacity of the deception, Jock thought. The Breda machine gun was primed and in the back of the truck following Jock's own vehicle. They were still in daylight.

The hearts of the men pounded as they approached the entrance barrier. Some of them could hardly believe the way the guard stood to attention for them as Jock saluted: they didn't have to smash through it or need Jock to say anything other than '*Danke*'. The Italian guard obviously knew his place with his German allies and acknowledged the raiders in the Lancia with a nod of his head. Over two dozen enemy trucks were parked around the rest house, mostly fuel tankers. Jock asked his driver to park so that the British detachment could have enough space to turn and face the gatehouse entrance they had just driven through with such ease – a rapid getaway would be essential. The men watched as Jock found a space next to another Lancia lorry. There was music, shouting and laughter coming from the main building, and a radio crackled out 'Lili Marlene'. The drivers stayed put in the Italian transport and the three unmarked British vehicles, engines running, while the rest of the men got out and quickly set the time pencils for ten minutes on Jock's bombs, which they placed on the enemy petrol tanks. Jock in the vanguard and Quilley in the rear of the party were each tasked with capturing a prisoner – any unfortunate Italian who strayed near their path as they went about their business. So far so good – no one had taken a blind bit of notice in the base-camp office. A corpulent driver, however, stepped out of one of the Italian trucks in front of Jock after Quilley, still at the back of the British line, had surreptitiously captured an inmate wandering around the camp, securing him into his own motor at the back of the fleet.

The Italian driver walked towards Jock. At that point, Diamonds, who had his hand on the Breda, found to his disgust that the cool evening air had congealed the oil and the weapon wasn't working. With only small arms at the ready, the SAS men froze along with the Breda as the driver reached for his pocket. Yet all he produced was a packet of cigarettes.

'Got a light?' Jock said nothing, but already had a hand ready and flicked open his lighter. 'Thanks.'

With the other hand by his pistol, Jock looked directly at the Italian and replied in fluent German. 'I suppose you have guessed that we are English?'

'*Inglesi*?' The driver theatrically threw back his head and laughed. 'You Germans have such a wonderful sense of humour.' Puffing on his habit, he began to turn to walk towards the road house.

Jock held his ground and continued in German. 'This isn't a joke;

you'll be a lot safer in there.' He nodded towards the Lancia, pointing the pistol. 'Get in, now!'

The well-fed soldier was bewildered, indignant but also meek, and did exactly as he was told. Perhaps he believed that his war was over.

The men, kitbags of bombs over their shoulders, operated on their own, splitting the Axis vehicles between them. It was agreed that Jock's one-pound bombs should be set for ten minutes. There was no room for error. Using rule of thumb, the men snapped off time pencils that were now less than an inch in length. Every bomb was the size of a tennis ball and Quilley, the tallest of the group, had pre-packed his in old socks: he was tall enough to sling them easily and exactly where he wanted to on the canvas tops of the highest three-ton vehicles, where the enemy would not discover them until too late. Others squashed the malleable plastic explosive underneath the vehicles by the petrol tanks. What the men didn't do was place them in the same positions on the lorries; they wanted to confuse and slow down the enemy even if they managed to get near enough to deactivate the explosives on any of the Lancias in time.

Most of the small team were about to finish when Paveney ran out of time pencils, so he squashed Jock's plastic explosive into anything that wasn't too conspicuous. He loaded a handful into the exhausts of several trucks, stuffed some in the saddle of a motorbike and used up his supply quickly since the clock was ticking away: eight minutes had gone by. Like the other men, he wanted to cause absolute havoc. If any plastic failed to go off with exploding petrol from other detonated vehicles, Paveney knew that the unstable mixture might suddenly explode days later, causing mayhem all over again. The Axis had wanted war and this was now their comeuppance.

Disconcerted faces were pressed against the windows of the building opposite as the men returned to their vehicles, darting between their targets as they did so. Jock's prisoner had broken down and was crying. He was an Italian soldier being kidnapped over two hundred miles inside his own lines; the shock was too much. Confused Germans and Italians began firing revolvers at the group from the camp hut, but Jock's Lancia had already begun to accelerate out of the gates. It was a textbook raid. Paveney dived into the largest vehicle protecting the rear of their short convoy. The small British force split up into groups again, partly to mine the telegraph poles and the road a few miles out of the enemy camp. They drove towards the coastal path that would enable them to drive south towards Jalo.

Behind Jock's vehicle, at the back of the fleet of cars, Quilley's group was also celebrating. As Quilley's vehicle left the new tarmac coast road for the desert floor, his men all bumped together in the back of the truck, cheek by jowl around the Breda machine gun and the new member of the vehicle. A drop of rum was being passed around, even to their Italian soldier, who had given himself up so easily. He had stopped looking sheepish, and even managed a grin as he gulped down some of his liquor. They were all smiling now as the prisoner spoke bits of Italian that none of the men could understand. He was a rather effete-looking young man in his newly ironed officer's uniform, with grubby hands and graveyard fingernails. He wouldn't need to be bound and gagged. The unusual youth seemed to smell bad to Quilley; he sported mere fluff on very little chin, and had sauce-bottle shoulders and silver hair waving around a pair of blue eyes. Quilley believed that he had another harmless Italian volunteer for the POW camp in Cairo.

When the Lancia and all the unmarked vehicles returned, the men brewed up some tea while Jock interviewed his prisoner. Quilley had locked up his own man and brought over a brew to Jock as he conversed with his own captive in Italian. It was dark, and the men were able to relax as Axis aeroplanes had been unable to track them through the air. Telephone lines between Mersa Brega and other enemy bases had been completely destroyed, and it would take days to repair them. There had been no pursuit by the enemy on land after their leading vehicle hit the first newly laid mine and they cried off.

'Thank you, Sergeant. Keep an eye on our friend here, will you? He wants to be known as "Sammy". He seems to be a good sort, and perhaps we'll get him to talk after a night's sleep. He knows his war has just ended. He seems to be an ordinary soldier who just wants to go back home in a war he never wanted to fight in the first place.'

'Right you are, sir.'

As he walked over to the other lock-up where Quilley had put his prisoner, Jock reflected that there was often an easy relationship between his men and any prisoners they came by, which was usually how he managed to obtain so much information from them. Marz should have known that when you persecute and torture your enemy they will say anything and almost everything, but it wouldn't necessarily be accurate. Somehow, their detainees knew that the gentle giants who guarded them were at ease because they weren't vindictive or lacking in compassion, but rather benevolent captors who had much better things to do than humiliating captives; they enjoyed their work as soldiers and were confident in their mission in the desert. They just didn't suffer fools gladly.

Jock paused outside the small prison hut. He could smell the prisoner from outside; it wasn't good. Many soldiers evacuated their bowels at various stages of being the reluctant guests of the SAS. This one just smelt bad. Jock unlocked the door, opened it and realised why.

It was Panton.

'Well, well, well, what a surprise,' Jock said. 'Back again to humiliate yourself are we, Panton? Enjoyed your rum in the truck with Sergeant Quilley?' Jock couldn't believe his fortune in chancing upon the traitor in the middle of the Libyan Desert. 'I don't suppose he'll be passing you any more rum after he finds out you pinned him down in that Tobruk minefield for an extra half hour.' Panton said nothing. Jock couldn't help but enjoy the vulnerability of Panton's position. 'Who is going to tell him: you or me?'

Jock quickly stepped outside, locked the door and called over to Quilley. 'A word in your ear.' Jock walked over to the Sergeant, away from the lockups. 'The prisoner you brought in is called Panton.'

'Quick work, if I may say so, sir.'

'You are to be congratulated, Sergeant.'

'Thank you, sir.'

'He is a traitor, and I want you to be responsible for his incarceration. He may not look a threat, but I can assure you that he is a very dangerous fanatic and huge security risk. Please don't discuss that in detail with any of the men except to say that he's poles apart from "Sammy" in that regard. The rum ration that Panton no doubt guzzled back in the truck was his first and last. He is to have no contact with Sammy, or any of the men unless personally selected by you. In effect, Panton is in solitary confinement. If you have to delegate a duty with regard to this, then that soldier must be armed at all times. If you hear Panton talk about anything when he's awake or asleep, keep that knowledge secure until we speak together, but I will be personally in charge of obtaining information from him. Bring a can of water and an old cloth that we won't need to use again, will you? And your gun, of course. We'll both get something to eat later because we are starting immediately. On your return, stand guard outside while I speak to the prisoner.'

'Understood, sir.'

Jock opened the lockup and saw that Panton was clearly exhausted, but he stood still, showing no nerves this time. To Jock, the traitor seemed more sure and arrogant than ever.

'You are going to wash yourself,' Jock called through the door. 'Sergeant, the prisoner will remove his clothes and wash himself outside for a few minutes. Ensure he does so properly, will you? I will call him in when ready.'

Jock could see that Panton had started washing without removing his boots. He knew the man was lazy, but with Panton there was usually a reason for everything he did, and Jock was suspicious.

'Bring me his boots, Sergeant. He is to wash any underwear with what water is left.'

'Yes, sir.'

Jock watched Panton's reaction to the orders all the time, and saw that the spy couldn't entirely hide his discomfort at parting with his footwear.

Jock felt around the inside of Panton's boot with one hand while gripping the heel of it with the other. The leather was almost new, like the traitor's uniform. Unlike HQ Cairo, he wouldn't be letting Panton escape a second time, and he had justified claims on managing the Soviet's detention. No one could stop him anyway. He wondered if Panton had secreted currency for bribes or paperwork underneath the surface of the inner sole and so Jock tried to lift the instep up with his fingernails. It didn't budge. However, as he did so he felt a slight movement of the heel. That struck him as strange because the boots had hardly been worn. He turned it upside down and noticed what looked like hardened mud on the surface of the heel. If anything, he would have expected possibly sand or even fragments of small stones pressed into the leather rather than earth. He scraped away at it and saw the glint of metal and as he picked away at the dirt, saw the top of a screw in the middle of the base.

He used his army tag to loosen it; the heel turned gradually around and, once removed, he found what he was looking for. The weapon was a garrotte, coiled like a shiny miniature serpent in its lair – no doubt intended for his own neck. He pocketed it quickly and then picked up the other boot. Undoing the same false compartment revealed a tightly rolled tube of paper. Jock unrolled it and saw lines of tiny black symbols that he didn't recognise. However, he felt sure that it was a significant find because if it was part of a code, it might be the very one that Panton used to contact London, Moscow or both. He carefully placed the paper in his breast pocket and buttoned it up, then screwed everything back together.

Panton was still wringing out his underwear by the sound of things. Jock sat on the makeshift prison bed and thought about his discovery. He mulled over his success in gathering up a prisoner on most of the operations he ran, the value he placed upon information that had enabled this last raid at Mersa Brega to be so rewarding, and his relishing of shouting 'Cry Havoc!' when raiding behind Tobruk's enemy lines before returning with some frightened Italian, to whom he insisted on showing plenty of compassion because so often they just wanted to give themselves up. Panton was a different matter altogether, but he would be allowed some dignity. He thought he would make Panton wait a little longer though because he was still mulling over the significance of his recent discoveries. He knew that members of his sister-in-law's family had a favourite uncle who read out lines from *Henry V* before their attack on Dunkirk. He had played the king in a school production years before. The treasures of those lines came back to him now, and two in particular: the Duke of Bedford's confirmation to the king's council of Henry V's exposure of treachery before he went to war:

'The king hath note of all that they intend,
By interception which they dream not of.'

Jock realised in this moment that the British, rather than prevaricating about who was or was not a traitor, needed to test out the smallest suggestion of any code on Panton's person. Looking at the fake heels, Jock wanted more than ever to play the Soviets at their own game. Their duplicated messages of British and German information would be compromising him and Madeleine, and if that was true there must be an army of men and women whose operations were being prevented from achieving any success because of lack of security. A team that could intercept or decode Panton's messages could also create new doctored ones, gain a reply and then decipher it. He didn't know what those symbols represented, but he knew that Clarke could find a team that could read them. If they were fortunate, it might be a way to play back enough misinformation to turncoats like Harkiss in order to record the responses from him and his contacts that would be needed to reveal their self-confessed treachery and help MI6 discover the entire Soviet operation in London.

Jock called out, 'Is he dressed, Sergeant?' Panton shuffled towards the lockup's entrance as Jock passed the boots to Quilley. 'Take these, Sergeant, and send Panton in. Lock us in, would you? I want a word with him.'

'Yes, sir.'

Jock was standing, and waved Panton to sit down. 'You will be issued with new shoes in due course. Prisoners aren't allowed boots on SAS camps. There will be a bit of a wait though because the Quartermaster is about 800 miles away and he won't be making any long trips for you. However, to take your mind off that, there is someone special I want to introduce you to.'

Panton looked at the door.

'Don't worry, he's not here yet. Before you have the privilege of his company, let's start from the beginning ...'

Would Jock ever recover from being an amalgam of spy, voyeur and patriot who might rifle through someone's clothing and open letters on the sly ... or a younger version of Hollings, MI6's cut-and-paste man? Soldier or not, Jock had to accept that he was indeed a spy after all.

POSTSCRIPT

Did Admiral Canaris actually meet at any level with members of MI6, which was led by 'C', Sir Stuart Menzies? Much of this novel is based upon true stories, and the possibility of such a meeting taking place was discussed at a high level in MI6; this scene is imagined. With traitors like Kim Philby placing British security and Britain's potential for peacemaking in jeopardy, MI6 was at risk of not being able to negotiate with enemies whose values it did not share. Closing off options to solve global conflict was no more viable then than it is today. Hugh Trevor-Roper, later Lord Dacre, worked for the Radio Security Service monitoring German intercepts and he liaised with senior members of MI6 such as Kim Philby, the notorious double agent, who served the interests of Stalin and the Soviets. Trevor-Roper was suspicious of Philby's loyalty, and also came to some interesting conclusions about the turf war between the Nazi party and the German General Staff. He believed that it was being fought out in the field of secret intelligence and that Canaris was making repeated journeys to Spain and would welcome a meeting with the British and even his opposite number 'C'.

According to Trevor-Roper, the final document on these conclusions was submitted for security clearance to Philby who closed the file without circulating it because he thought it was 'mere speculation'.

However, 'C' saw this report which confirmed what he already knew about Canaris.

It was certainly in the Soviets' interests to ensure that links with Canaris and 'C' were cut. There is some evidence to suggest that Kim Philby was involved in an operation to betray the SOE cause in Holland, which also had links with Canaris.

How reliable are the recollections of Trevor-Roper? It seems that he was one of the few officers to both investigate Philby's divided loyalties and also to stand up for British security and reveal the identity of the MI6 traitor, despite it jeopardising his own wartime work. Later on in the war, he was transferred by Menzies (to salvage his career) when Trevor-Roper risked a court-martial by bringing Philby's dubious management and loyalties to his superior's attention. Philby treacherously worked towards undermining the possibility of Germany and Britain ever reaching an agreement that would threaten his Soviet masters. Trevor-Roper had been reprimanded for alerting Menzies that Philby had blocked another report, this time suggesting a German plot to assassinate Hitler...

AFTERWORD – AFTER 1941

Julian Blynde

Blynde is partly based on Anthony Blunt, one of the Cambridge spies. He worked from inside MI5 and took files out of his workplace to be copied for his Soviet masters; he left MI5 after the war. He was Professor of Art at the University of London, Director of the History of Art at the Courtauld Institute of Art, and Surveyor of the Queen's Pictures. He was outed as a spy in 1979 and publicly disgraced, and wrote that spying for the Soviets had been 'the biggest mistake of my life.' However, soon after his exposure as a double agent, he informed Tar Robinson, the MI5 spymaster, that, 'It has given me great pleasure to have been able to pass the names of every MI5 officer to the Russians.'

Admiral Canaris, Chief of the Abwehr

There is some evidence that Canaris helped persuade Franco to keep Spain neutral in the war. I interviewed Inga Haag who was an Abwehr secretary and she corroborated reports that Canaris saved hundreds of Jews from Nazi persecution. He posed as co-operative when at first working with the SD in order to gain Hitler's trust, but eventually Hitler dismissed Canaris and abolished the *Abwehr* in February 1944.

Canaris was arrested on 23 July 1944 and was accused of being the 'spiritual instigator' of the July Plot's attempted assassination of Hitler. His close association with many of the plotters and certain documents written by him led to the gradual assumption of his guilt. Recently, Canaris has even been dismissed by some historians as merely incompetent. However, it seems he was much more complex a character than some writers would have us believe. Canaris also helped shield men in the Abwehr like Johnny Jebson who was privy to significant secrets in the planning of D-Day. Jebson refused to talk while being interrogated by the Gestapo. Canaris was executed on 9 April 1945 after being found guilty of treason by an SS summary court at Flossenbürg concentration camp.

Brigadier Dudley Clarke, CBE, CB, Legion of Merit

Brigadier Clarke evolved Deception, almost from scratch, as a vital part of Allied strategy. General Archibald Wavell, the commander who would later gave Clarke free rein in Middle Eastern deception operations recognised Clarke's original, unorthodox outlook on soldiering. Clarke's success in North Africa was such that the enemy overestimated Allied strength there by a quarter of a million men. This helped prove a model for other theatres of war, culminating in the success of such significant achievements as D-Day. Clarke's efficiency, ingenuity and impish sense of humour was instrumental in helping the British achieve numerous and significant victories. After the war, some who wrote about the conflict were restricted in what they could put down on paper. Many of Clarke's talents and schemes were not fully reported for many years and, in some senses few appreciated that he had probably achieved more than any other officer in uniform during World War Two to shorten the war.

Hugh Gaitskell

Hugh Gaitskell taught Jock Lewes at Oxford and witnessed first-hand the political suppression of the social democratic workers movement in Austria by the conservative Dollfuss government in February 1934. This event made a lasting impression, making him profoundly hostile to conservatism but also making him reject as futile the Marxian outlook of many European social democrats. This placed him in the socialist revisionist camp. In May 1940, Gaitskell worked with another of Jock Lewes's tutors, Hugh Dalton, as a senior civil servant for the Ministry of Economic Warfare, giving him experience of government. The shock of Gaitskell's death in 1963 was comparable to that of the sudden death of John Smith in May 1994, when he too seemed to be on the threshold of 10 Downing Street. Gaitskell's death left an opening for Harold Wilson in the party leadership; Wilson narrowly won the next general election for Labour twenty-one months later.

Kit Harkiss

Harkiss is partly based upon Harold Adrian Russell 'Kim' Philby. Philby helped to develop the Cambridge spy ring. He held some of the most senior posts in MI6 and on an almost daily basis took secret files out of MI6 to have them photographed for the Soviets and returned the next day. One of the most remarkable things about Philby's story was how he was able to avoid detection for so long, despite suspicions being raised about the leaking of secrets and the unmasking of elements of the Cambridge spy ring, with whom Philby was connected. After he successfully defected to Russia, in a final piece of advice to Stasi spies, he told them how he did it: 'And all I had to do really was keep my nerve. So my advice to you is to tell all your agents that they are never to confess.' Philby, with the help of men like Blunt, put the lives of many British service personnel and their allies in jeopardy with fatal consequences.

David MacDonald

David MacDonald is partly based upon Colonel David Stirling DSO, OBE, co-founder of the SAS. Jock Lewes introduced his own concepts on creating an elite force capable of fighting behind enemy lines to Stirling – not the other way around as numerous books on the SAS have attempted to argue. In late 1942, Stirling explained that Jock Lewes was the real creator of the SAS to Jock's father, Arthur Lewes. In 1984, Stirling publicly stated that the SAS was due to several co-founders, including Jock Lewes. With the exception of one memoir in 1945, the intervening forty or so years between Stirling's letter to Arthur Lewes and Stirling's public statement, showed that the history of the SAS went through some distorted reconstruction which belied the true origins of the Regiment. It has taken twenty-five years to begin to change that. Jock Lewes and David Stirling complemented each other well and worked successfully together. Both shunned gratuitous violence so that Jock Lewes would even punch and knock out Italian troops with no stomach for a fight rather than unnecessarily take away a life. Both Lewes and Stirling were more interested in destroying enemy planes, machinery and infrastructure; they were ahead of their time in a host of ways. While Jock was in Tobruk after the top brass shelved his parachute detachment, Stirling, who had been injured in Jock's parachute training, realised that among his contacts with the top brass he stood a chance of bringing back Jock's detachment but with sixty instead of six men. That August, in a celebrated and audacious effort, Stirling, who was still using crutches climbed into HQ Cairo, making it through to Major General Ritchie's office. From then on, Stirling looked after the protection of the unit in Cairo while Jock proceeded in Kabrit with what he had already begun evolving from March 1941. Jock Lewes created the first comprehensive written records of the SAS from a leader's viewpoint – and often on the hoof – in his notebook, journals and letters. In them he writes a great truth: 'Together we have fashioned this unit. David has established it without, and I think I may say I have established it within.'

Madeleine McLean

Madeleine is partly based upon the life of Miriam Barford, a beautiful and talented linguist who accepted Jock Lewes's offer of marriage in her letter sent to him in late 1941. Miriam married a Captain Richard Wise two years later, and their son, Michael Wise, published Jock and Miriam's love letters in *Joy Street: A Wartime Romance in Letters 1940–1942* (published by Little Brown in 1995). Miriam was at least as accomplished a writer as Jock Lewes, and their letters tell of a relationship strained by the demands of long separation, but strengthened by a love they both hoped would last forever. After gaining her degree from Somerville College, Oxford, in 1942, Miriam became a Lance Corporal in a British Army Intelligence unit.

Gunther Marz

Gunther Marz is based on a member of the Sicherheitsdienst (SD) who specialised in torturing members of Allied Special Forces. M.R.D.Foot, who was awarded the French Croix de Guerre for his work with the SAS in Britanny in the 1940s, was sent to prevent further such torture taking place. Foot got close to the SD officer and was captured but fortunately his interrogator was not the villain in question. Unfortunately, the actual villain, who is partly based on a torturer called Bonner, represented a particular brand of Nazi sadist where any method of torture was considered and used on Allied service men and women.

Jock Steel

Jock Steel is partly based upon the very distinguished Lieutenant Jock Lewes of the Welsh Guards. He, like the protagonist of *A Spy After All*, removed the Blackshirt flag from Oswald Mosley's fascist headquarters in Oxford. He regarded extremists as 'nitwits' and as a young member of the fledgling British Council made an important contribution towards persuading Salazar to stay neutral. Jock Lewes notched up a significant number of personal achievements in the 1930s that help explain his success in creating the main ideas and training upon which the SAS was later based. He had learned to lead and manage men with great skill well before war broke out. As President of the Oxford University Boat Club in 1937, he had honed a happy crew who were consistently developing in the months before the Boat Race. So much so, that Jock insisted that his great friend, David Winser, take his place in the crew to make the boat go faster. Cambridge, which had beaten Oxford on average by at least four lengths every year for the past thirteen Boat Races, lost to Oxford by three lengths that year. Jock also had made a significant number of friends with Germans who were later persecuted by the Nazis; he observed the menace, mindset and danger that Hitler's servicemen posed to Europe and this helped prepare him to make the training of the SAS tougher than the military preparations made even by his opponents. When Jock went to North Africa, he did everything in his power to shorten the war so that he could return and marry his lover, Miriam Barford. From March 1941, Jock Lewes was evolving his unique methods and was later given permission to create his own parachute detachment in May 1941. The blueprint for elite forces was only possible because he experimented on himself in this period with Lewes Marches and desert discipline that made daring raids productive behind enemy lines. Without Jock Lewes's practical application of his skills and vision to make an elite force a reality in mid-1941, David Stirling, his SAS co-founder, would not have been able to appreciate that his proposal for a unit ten times bigger was possible later that year when he gained Auchinleck's backing. Inventing the Lewes Bomb, along with Jock's key SAS concepts, enabled the SAS to be successful before the end of the year when the Brigade showed they could destroy significant numbers of enemy planes. Jock Lewes was killed during a low-level attack by a Messerschmitt 110 fighter. In 1942, the then Major David Stirling, Jock's SAS co-founder, explained in detail to Jock's father, Arthur Lewes, why in his view, 'Jock could far more genuinely be called the founder of the SAS than I.'

To fully appreciate the role and significance of the Regiment today, especially during a time of global tensions and conflicts, it is necessary to also understand its true origins. That can only enhance the value placed upon the existence of a developing SAS to whom many continue to owe their lives. Out of the ashes of imminent defeat that faced Britain in the early 1940s, a phoenix had risen up that Hitler didn't understand and therefore feared: the development of the Special Air Service.

It is valuable to remember the unity and concepts of its first men, and leaders, Lieutenants Jock Lewes and David Stirling. Jock Lewes's design of the first SAS badge and wings, is a clue to the vision and conviction of SAS men that we all can draw from. Based upon the wings of the Egyptian goddess, Isis, the timeless divinity of rebirth, the elite force was forged to protect its members symbolised now by the parachute rather than the Egyptian scarab within its guarding wings. The wider significance was that the SAS represented the security and protection of humanity from evil and sacrilege, represented then by Hitler's subverting of an ancient cross of peace into a swastika. Today, Islamic State (ISIS) have misappropriated the goddess for their name but they have subverted it to glorify the death of themselves and 'unbelievers' in the pursuit of the Caliphate and making their version of Islam an imperial power. In order to provide security against the bloodlust of a similar force in 1941, it meant that the SAS needed a clear vision of the most effective measures against an enemy whose leadership instigated the most barbaric deeds seen in the modern world to that date.

Familiar with concepts of military strategy by ancient writers such as Sun Tzu, Jock Lewes knew that he had to have a strong idea of who he was fighting, and having met members of the elite forces in Germany in the 1930s he could gauge the grotesque spectre of Nazi illusions. He knew that his opposite numbers might be brought to the table to talk but if the Nazi ideology had also to be brought to the edge of extinction to do it, then he was up for that too. The SAS were not trying to contain the enemy in World War Two but destroy every single means by which they perpetrated evil.

David Wintour

David Wintour is partly based upon David Winser, Jock Lewes's great friend at Oxford. He won the Newdigate Prize for English Verse with a piece called *Rain* in 1936. He also wrote several novels, one of them for Longmans; he also published under the pseudonym of 'John Stuart Arey'. He rowed in every Boat Race between 1935 and 1937 and he shot for the Oxford V111 in 1934, defeating Canada's most accomplished marksman. Wartime found him a medical student at the Charing Cross Hospital. Rather than evacuate with other students and patients, he chose to remain in London and help victims of the Blitz. David joined 48 Royal Marines Commando as their Medical Officer and landed with them on D-Day. He was awarded the MC for gallant work within days of the fighting near St. Aubin-sur-Mer on Juno beach. All troop leaders were killed and of the five hundred men, fewer than half were available for duty the following day. That November, David Winser was killed in action in an amphibious landing against the island of Walcheren, which commanded the approaches to the vital port of Antwerp. In the sandhills there, he was trying to help a wounded soldier after they had landed in a raid on 1st November 1944. He was buried there with the wounded soldier and his orderly at the Bergen-op-Zoom War Cemetery (Grave 6.B.3).

ACKNOWLEDGEMENTS

I am indebted to many people who have provided guidance, encouragement and hospitality during the writing of this book. I am very grateful to a host of people who kindly supported my research into the life of Jock Lewes and his role in creating the blueprint for the SAS. This involved many of his veteran colleagues who kindly answered a host of questions. Many are credited in my biography of Jock Lewes: *Jock Lewes Co-founder of the SAS*, published by Pen & Sword Books Ltd, 2000. The names are incomplete, since some of those who were most helpful to me have asked, for professional reasons, to remain anonymous: I am very grateful to them.

I am indebted to my good friend Mrs Ann Hadfield MBE for her great support of my writing. I am also grateful to Esmé Barrett, her children, my cousins, Andrew Kazimirski and Margot Kazimirska, and my cousin, Martha Wailes, for their encouragement. Dr Joanna Jaaniste, my sister and godmother, has always encouraged my writing – so too has Andrew O'Shaughnessy, Vice President of Monticello and Professor of History at the University of Virginia.

It is a privilege and pleasure to have *A Spy After All* produced by Whitefox; my thanks to George Edgeller, John Bond and Annabel Wright for their unfailing patience and efficiency. I owe a particular debt to Ian Critchley for his superb engagement with the text, his suggestions and saving me from numerous howlers. I am also indebted to Mike Jones for his commitment and great help as an editor and Stuart Polson for the evocative cover of this book. I am particularly grateful to Nigel West for looking over my galleys, and I much appreciate the support and advice of Rebecca Carter, Literary Agent at Janklow & Nesbit UK, and to others who viewed the first drafts of the novel, in particular: Dr Stephen Sullivan, Stephen Carroll, and Helen Orssich of Bare Films. Many thanks also are due to Christina Lewes for looking over much of the text as a family editor, and to Dr Jeremy Saunders for commenting on several chapters. I am grateful to Dan Snow who allowed the true Jock Lewes to be revealed in 'Dan Snow's History Hits'. My thanks go also to Eamon Hardy, Matthew Whiteman and Katie Rider and all the team at the BBC who helped open up much of Jock Lewes's story in *SAS: Rogue Warriors* presented by Ben Macintyre for BBC2. Ben Macintyre's work has brought much life to the history of espionage and continues to be an inspiration to anyone interested in the subject. Colin Skevington and Sian Davies at Moon Watcher Media have supported the development of the Jock Lewes story with very helpful web design and advice. Discussions with Dr Christopher Macy on his new research of the SAS has been invaluable. The team at Pen and Sword Books Ltd continue to help develop the appreciation of the significance of Lieutenant Jock Lewes: Charlie Simpson, Katie Eaton, Lori Jones, Jonathan Wright and Jon Wilkinson have been most helpful. The Imperial War Museum and their staff, notably Kay Gladstone and Fiona Kelly have supported me over questions relating to World War Two sources for many years. Chris Terrill and Uppercut Films, and Gil Boyd BEM have encouraged further research into Lieutenant Jock Lewes. Richard Garrett, Director of Bedford School Association and Clara Policella have been very helpful as have Robin Grant and John Sharman of the Bedford School Old Boys' Association. My thanks also go to Jonathan Egan and my colleagues at Bedford School. I am also grateful to Laura Morris Literary Agency; Lorna Almonds Windmill, Duncan McAra Literary Agency; Anneliese O'Malley at Little Brown Book Group; Ben Fitch; Jeff Heenan and the Welsh Guards Association; Marcus Scriven. I am much obliged to all publishers for leave to cite works they published which also includes *Poems* by W H Auden, *SOE: From SOE: 1940–1946* by M. R. D. Foot published by Arrow. Reproduced by permission of The Random House Group Ltd © 1990, *Hitler's Spy Chief: The Wilhelm Canaris Mystery* by Richard M Bassett, published by Cassell, *Stalin's Englishman: The Lives of Guy Burgess* by Andrew Lownie, published by Hodder and Stoughton. The letter from Boulogne is part of the letters and papers of Jock Lewes but so far it remains anonymous, and despite efforts to ascertain the attribution of the piece, the Imperial War Museum had no record of it in their archives at the time of publication. The author and the publisher are grateful to the above for use of copyright material. Every effort has been made to trace the copyright holders of material quoted in the text. The publisher would welcome the opportunity to rectify any omissions brought to their attention. I am also grateful to Michael Moynihan; Miranda Doggett; Wendy and Mike Mansell; Paul Aston; Nigel Aston; Jacqui Hagan and the staff at OVL; Antonio Frano and the staff at Bedford Library, and Matthew and Sara Bennett at OPN for their help to me.

I would particularly like to thank my aunt, Mrs Esmé Barrett, for her example of keeping the greatest secrets. Esmé is 101 years old at the time of writing and modestly recalls that she enjoyed working in a minor capacity at the MI6 base, Broadway Buildings, 'for instance, opening the building up in the morning and placing the correct telexes on the appropriate desks.' Esmé was known in her office as a sophisticated, efficient and stunning dark-haired beauty. She was also godmother to the same boy whose god-father was Donald Maclean, one of the Cambridge spies. Now that we know that Kim Philby was circulating around offices in order to copy classified secrets, Esmé's 'opening up the building' and distributing the latest secret information throughout the numerous floors of MI6 certainly posed some enormous risks to maintaining her job there; the chance of Esmé being seen observing anything untoward perpetrated by a man like Philby meant that she and her colleagues were vulnerable inside their own offices, let alone elsewhere. In fact, memoirs by the masters of MI9, introducing their signed memoirs to Esmé, 'Broadway Babe', give clues to her support of MI9, the counterpart to Dudley Clarke's own Deception operation in Cairo. MI9's range of responsibilities became worldwide and from MI6, Esmé helped leaders of MI9 such as Lieutenant Colonel Jimmy Langley MBE, MC, support Allied escape and evasion, thus making the Axis powers' attempt to control the world much more difficult. Esmé not only served in MI6 but later supported her husband, Lieutenant Janusz Kazimirski, with Poland's representation at Supreme Allied Headquarters in Washington DC.

The whole of the Lewes family deserves praise for supporting another tale of wartime derring-do. Christina and David have always been involved; and to Anna, all my love.